MOST OF
ALL YOU

ALSO BY MIA SHERIDAN

Archer's Voice

MOST OF ALL YOU

A LOVE STORY

MIA SHERIDAN

FOREVER

New York Boston

Copyright © 2017 by Mia Sheridan
Cover design by Elizabeth Turner
Cover copyright © 2017 by Hachette Book Group, Inc.

Forever
Hachette Book Group
1290 Avenue of the Americas
New York, NY 10104
forever-romance.com
twitter.com/foreverromance

First Edition: October 2017

Forever is an imprint of Grand Central Publishing. The Forever name and logo are trademarks of Hachette Book Group, Inc.

The publisher is not responsible for websites (or their content) that are not owned by the publisher.

The Hachette Speakers Bureau provides a wide range of authors for speaking events. To find out more, go to www.hachettespeakersbureau.com or call (866) 376-6591.

Library of Congress Cataloging-in-Publication Data is available upon request.

ISBN 978-1-5387-2734-8 (trade paperback edition)
ISBN 978-1-5387-2732-4 (ebook edition)

Printed in the United States of America

LSC-C

Printing 5, 2022

This book is dedicated to Danita,
who has her own angel Gabriel.

And to those everywhere who have
been given up on.

MOST OF
ALL YOU

PROLOGUE

ELLIE

I didn't want to go. "Please, Mama, can we go tomorrow?"

My mama didn't answer for a minute, pushing her blonde hair away from her face and wiping at the sweat that dotted her forehead and upper lip. Her cheeks were bright red with fever again, and her green eyes looked dull and shiny at the same time, like the surface of the puddles in the parking lot at our apartment complex after it rained. "We have to go, Ellie. I feel well enough today, and I don't know if I will tomorrow."

Mama didn't look like she felt well. She looked worse than I'd seen her in weeks. Even worse than the day she'd found the paper stuck to our door and cried and then got back into bed for three days. It scared me how sick she looked, and I didn't know what to do.

I used to knock on Mrs. Hollyfield's door and ask for help

when she still lived in our building. She would come over with chicken soup and sometimes a box of Popsicles, and she'd talk to my mama in a quiet, soothing voice while I watched cartoons. I always felt better after Mrs. Hollyfield left, and it seemed like Mama did, too. But Mrs. Hollyfield didn't live at our apartment complex anymore. Something called a blood clot had happened to Mrs. Hollyfield, and they took her away on a white stretcher.

After that, some younger people who I'd never seen before came and cleaned her apartment out. When I heard them arguing about who was going to pay her funeral costs, I knew she was dead. My mama cried and cried and kept saying, "What am I gonna do now? Oh, Lord God, what am I gonna do now?" But I didn't cry, even though I wanted to, because once, when my mama was at the doctor's, Mrs. Hollyfield told me that when you die, you fly away to heaven just like a bird. She said that heaven is the most glorious place any person could ever imagine, with gold-paved streets and flowers in colors that didn't even exist here on earth. So I tried to be happy for Mrs. Hollyfield even though I was going to miss her hugs, her laughter, the red Popsicles that were my favorite, and the way she made my mama smile.

"Pick up your feet, Ellie. I can't drag you." I walked quicker, trying to keep up with Mama. She was walking fast, and I almost had to run to stay at her side. "We're getting close to your daddy's house."

I swallowed heavily, a dizzy feeling in my head. I wasn't sure if I wanted to meet my daddy or not, but I was curious. I wondered what he looked like—if he was handsome like the soap opera actors Mama watched. She seemed to like them a whole lot, so I knew that was the sort of man she would have picked to be my daddy. I pictured him in a suit with thick, wavy hair and big straight teeth. I hoped he would think *I* was pretty despite my ragged clothes. I hoped he would like me even though he'd left us before I was even born.

We got to a small house with peeling paint and a shutter that was hanging crooked, and when my mama stopped in front of it, she squeezed my hand. "Lord, please give me strength. I have no choice, I have no choice," my mama murmured before she turned and kneeled down in front of me. "Here we are, baby." Her eyes were watery, her lips were shaking, and I was alarmed at how sick she looked. But she smiled so sweetly and looked right in my eyes. "Ellie, sweetness, you know I love you, right?"

"Yes, Mama."

She nodded. "I didn't do a lot of good in this world, baby. But one thing I did perfectly was *you*. You're such a good, smart girl, Ellie. You don't forget that, okay? No matter what, you don't forget that."

"Okay, Mama," I whispered. I felt even more scared, and I didn't know why. My mama stood and then adjusted my sweater with the missing buttons and unraveling hem. She frowned at my shoes, her eyes staying on the hole in my toe for a few more seconds before she straightened up, taking my hand and leading me toward the door of the ugly little house.

Mama knocked, and I heard a man shouting on the other side of the door. He sounded angry, and his voice scared me. I pressed myself into my mama's side. She put her arm around me and we waited. Mama felt so hot, and now her whole body was shaking. She leaned into me, and I worried we both might topple over. I knew she needed a doctor, but she'd stopped going to the doctor months ago even though she didn't seem to be getting any better. Weren't doctors supposed to make you better?

After a minute, the door opened, and a tall man stood in

front of us with a cigarette hanging out of his mouth. My mama gasped. I peeked up at him, and he stared down at my mama and me. "Yeah?"

My mama ran her hand over my hair. "Hi, Brad."

The man was quiet as he sucked on his cigarette, and then his eyes widened and he finally said, "Cynthia?"

I felt my mama relax, and I looked up at her. She had a big smile on her face. The one she used when she was trying to convince Mrs. Gadero to let us pay our rent late. I took another peek at Brad, *my daddy*. He was tall like the soap opera actors, but that was the only thing they had in common. His hair was long and sorta greasy looking, and his teeth were yellow and crooked. But we had the same blue eyes and the same color hair—golden brown, my mama called it.

"Well, I'll be damned. What are you doing here?"

"May we come in?"

We went into the house, and I looked around at the old furniture, no better than the furniture Mama and I had at home. I heard my mama take a deep breath. "Is there somewhere we can talk?"

Brad squinted his eyes and looked back and forth between my mama and me before he said, "Sure, come on in the bedroom."

"El, you sit on the couch, sweetness. I'll be right back," my mama said, seeming to weave slightly before she caught herself. The red spots on her cheeks were even brighter.

I sat down and stared at the TV in front of me. There was a football game on but the sound was muted, so I could hear my mama and daddy talking from down the hall.

"She's yours, Brad."

"What the fuck do you mean she's *mine*? You told me you got an abortion."

"Well, I…I didn't. I couldn't. I knew you didn't want her, but I couldn't get rid of my baby."

I heard my daddy swear, and a big lump formed in my throat. My daddy hadn't wanted me. At all. He hadn't even known my mama kept me until just now. He hadn't even known I was alive. My mama hadn't told me different, but in my mind, I kept hoping there was a good reason my daddy had left. I kept hoping that when he saw me, he'd take me in his arms and tell me everything was going to be okay, and that he was proud to have me for a daughter. *Like my mama says to me all the time.* And then he'd find a doctor who could make my mama better.

"She's a really good girl, Brad. You see how beautiful she is. And she's smart, too. She's real sweet and well behaved—"

"What do you want, Cynthia? Money? I don't got no money. I got nothin' for you."

"I don't want money. I need you to take her. I'm…I'm dying, Brad." Her voice lowered so I almost couldn't hear it. "I have stage four cancer. I have such little time—weeks, maybe just days. We've been evicted from our apartment. I thought a neighbor would take Ellie…but she's gone, and I don't have anyone else. You're all Ellie has in this world now." My heart tightened inside my chest, and as the room spun around me, a tear ran down my cheek. *No, Mama, no.* I didn't want to hear this. I didn't want this to be true. I didn't want my mama to fly to heaven like a bird. *I want her to stay here. With me.*

"Well, I'm sorry to hear that but take her? Goddamn, I didn't want her seven years ago, and I don't want her now." I grimaced, picking at the skin around my fingernail, feeling small and ugly just like the scrawny cat Mama never let me feed.

"Please, Brad, I—" I heard shuffling and the squeak of a bed as if my mama had sat down. She asked for a glass of water, and my daddy came out of the room looking mad. He shot me an angry look, and I sunk down into the couch. I thought I heard a door open and close at the back of the house, but I wasn't sure, and then my daddy came out of what must be the kitchen with a glass of water in his hand and went back down the hall.

I heard him swear. I heard him calling my mama's name, and then he came rushing out to the living room and threw the water at the wall, the glass shattering. I screamed and curled into a ball.

"Well, isn't that a fine thing? That slut just up and left. Snuck out the back door. *Bitch.*"

I blinked, my heart racing. *Mama? No, Mama, don't leave me here! Please don't leave me here!*

I jumped up and ran down the hall where I found a back door, throwing it open and rushing out into the alley behind the house. There was no one in sight.

My mama was gone.

She hadn't even said goodbye.

She hadn't even said goodbye.

She'd left me here.

I fell to my knees on the ground and sobbed.

Mama, Mama, Mama.

Brad picked me up, and the harsh sting of a slap across my face made me gag on my own tears. "Shut up, kid. Your mama's gone." He dragged me back inside, where he threw me on the couch again. I clenched my eyes shut, fear racing through my body like the little needle pricks I felt when I'd been sitting on my foot for too long. When I opened my eyes, Brad was staring at me. The look on his face scared me even more. He made a disgusted sound in his throat and then turned away and left for what felt like hours. I stayed curled up on the couch, rocking myself slowly, as the day turned to night.

Mama never leaves me for this long. I'm always a good girl and do what I'm told, but she never stays away so long. I don't like the smells here. I don't like the sound of the dripping water. I don't like this scratchy couch. I'm scared. I'm scared. Mama, please come back and get me.

When Brad finally returned, flicking on the lights and causing me to squint into the sudden brightness, he looked even more mad than before he'd left. He sat down and lit a cigarette and sucked in a puff of it before blowing the smoke out, causing my eyes to water. "What am I gonna do with you, kid? Just what the fuck am I gonna do?"

I looked away, tried to swallow back the sob that wanted to escape.

Mrs. Hollyfield told me that hearts are meant to beat all the time to keep us alive. Mrs. Hollyfield said that when your heart stops beating and you go to heaven, you don't feel pain anymore. Mrs. Hollyfield's heart had stopped beating. *My mama's heart is going to stop beating, too.* My heart was still beating, even though it felt like it was crumbling in my chest. I didn't want to hurt anymore. I wanted my heart to stop beating so I could fly to heaven and be with Mrs. Hollyfield. *And Mama.*

I told my heart to stop beating.

I told it not to hurt anymore.

I told my heart I wouldn't *let* it hurt anymore.

Ever.

CHAPTER ONE

Come with me, I'll help you. It looks like you need a friend.

Racer, the Knight of Sparrows

CRYSTAL

Present Day

He didn't belong here. Why that thought came immediately to my mind the moment I laid eyes on him, I couldn't be sure. But it did. It wasn't the way he looked—I'd seen handsome, clean-cut, seemingly wholesome boys here before. Get a few drops of alcohol in them, or a few whiffs of the pack mentality wafting thickly in the air, and they'd be acting just like the other drunken fools eager to part with their money and any common decency they might possess. And it wasn't that he was out of place because he looked scared. I'd seen that before, too—eyes darting around, nervous and excited by the surroundings. No, the man sitting alone at a table near the back of the room, nursing a Miller Lite, didn't look scared, merely curious. His head turned slowly as he took in the room at large, and I couldn't help that my gaze followed his, wondering at his assessment.

My own curiosity confused and disturbed me. It was so unlike me to wonder about any of the men who came here, and I couldn't find an explanation. I closed my eyes, pushing the thoughts away as the loud music filled my head. When my performance ended, the applause exploded and I plastered a smile on my face.

Anthony walked behind the crowd, making sure no one took liberties, pulling the ones who did away from me as they protested. Five minutes later, as I turned to leave, my eyes met those of the man in the back, still sitting at the same table, watching me. I straightened my spine, something about his face niggling at my mind. I knew I hadn't seen him here before. Did I know him? Is *that* what kept drawing my attention?

Once I was backstage, I pulled the cash out of my underwear, uncrumpling the bills until I could fold it all into a thick wad.

"Nice job, honey," Cherry said as she drew closer to me, headed toward the stage.

"Thanks." I smiled, squeezing her arm gently as we passed each other.

I unlocked my locker in the hall and stuffed the tip money into my purse before heading to the dressing room I shared with two other girls. They were off tonight, so for once I had the too-crowded space to myself. I sunk down in the chair in front of the small vanity table littered with cases, tubes, and compacts of makeup, jars of cold cream, and bottles of lotion and perfume. In the quiet of the room, the sounds of the men in the audience who'd just watched me dance filled my head—the whoops, hollers, and the catcalls that described in lurid detail what they wanted to do to me. I could still smell the scents of the beer-laden breath, heavy cologne, and body odor that had overwhelmed me as I'd bent and shimmied toward all those masculine shouts and reaching hands.

For a moment I fantasized using my arm to swipe everything on the surface in front of me to the floor and watch as it shattered and spilled, mixing together in a mess of gloppy, powdery color, and scent. Shaking my head, I stared at myself in the mirror, overcome by a sudden urge to grab a towel and begin scrubbing and smearing the makeup caked on my face. *God, what's wrong with me?* A lump filled my throat and I stood too quickly, the chair I'd been sitting in tipping backward and clattering to the floor.

"Crystal?"

I turned at the sound of Anthony's voice, and whatever was on my face caused him to frown. "You all right, girl?"

I nodded, a jerky up-and-down motion of my head. "Yeah, yeah, I'm fine. Just thirsty." I walked toward the water cooler, picking up a Dixie cup, filling and draining it quickly before looking back at Anthony. "What's up?"

"You got two private dance requests."

I filled the Dixie cup again and took a sip. "Okay."

"Little extra money's never bad, yeah?" One side of his lips tipped up.

"Never bad," I murmured.

Anthony remained unmoving, his lips a straight line again as he studied me solemnly. "I could tell 'em you're sick."

I am. I am sick. Sick of this. Sick of life. I shook my head, attempting to shake off the morose thoughts that had pricked my brain. "No, just give me a minute and I'll be out."

Anthony inclined his head and shut the door behind him. I took a deep breath and moved back to the vanity, bending toward it and using my finger to fix the places where my makeup had smeared. I stood straight and offered the mirror a smirk. "Showtime," I whispered before turning, opening the door, and walking down the hall, where a skinny guy with shaggy, dark blond hair and a long face waited. He jerked as I approached, pulling himself ramrod straight, his large Adam's apple bobbing in his throat. Bile rose in mine. I gave him a sultry smile. "Hiya, sugar. You ready for me?"

* * *

It was getting close to closing time when I performed my last dance and made my way back to the dressing room again, stretching my neck from side to side and sighing with both relief and fatigue. When we girls weren't dancing, whether onstage or behind closed doors, we served drinks. The manager, Rodney, liked our presence out on the floor—liked that bending over tables to deliver drinks and brushing past the men we were serving excited and encouraged them to keep spending money. Dealing with an obnoxious group of them, made bold by the stares of their friends, was nauseating. Tedious. But it also roused their *generosity* when I was onstage, so I did what I had to do. A subtle wink around the table and each idiot thought my next dance was just for him.

I changed quickly into my uniform—tiny white shorts, a black-and-white-striped shirt that tied between my boobs, and red stiletto heels—and opened the door to do a few last rounds of the bar floor. I startled, as did the man standing outside, leaning against the opposite hallway wall. *What the hell?* Where was Anthony? My eyes darted down the empty hall, no Anthony in sight. The man—he was the one I'd wondered about earlier—stood tall and ran a hand through his brown hair, looking momentarily unsure.

"You're not supposed to be back here," I said, crossing my

arms over my breasts, unsure why I was attempting to cover what he'd probably been gawking at earlier.

"I'm sorry. I wasn't sure of the protocol."

I raised a brow. "Protocol?"

He shook his head slightly. "The, ah, procedure for meeting with you."

I cocked my head to the side. Okay, this guy was potentially crazy. "The *procedure* is that you have to go through Anthony. Big black guy? Mean looking? Snaps men in half if they mess with one of his girls." My eyes darted down the hallway again.

"Ah. Yeah, he's breaking up a fight outside."

I glanced back to him. "Uh-huh. And so you made your move?" I took one step back into the room, ready to barricade myself inside if he tried anything.

He blinked and paused for a second before reaching into his coat pocket. Bringing his hand out, he tossed something my way. Instinct made me reach out and catch it. A set of keys. I looked at him, creasing my brow in confusion.

"If I do anything to make you nervous, you can gouge my eyes out with one of those."

"Gouge your eyes out? Yeah, I'd really rather not."

"I won't give you reason to. I don't mean you any harm."

Anthony appeared at the end of the hallway, shaking his hand as if he'd injured it. "Yo, you're not supposed to be back here." *Oh, thank God.*

"I know. I'm sorry. I didn't know the rules."

"Ignorance is no excuse, my man. Gotta eighty-six your ass. You okay, Crys?" I nodded.

"I only want ten minutes," the man said quickly, raising his hands. I wasn't sure if he was doing an *I'm unarmed* gesture or whether his ten fingers went in tandem with the promise of limited time.

"Sorry, my lap-dance card is full for the night, sugar."

"I don't want a lap dance. I just want to talk."

Ah, one of *those*. I almost rolled my eyes. But something inside made me pause. I couldn't say what it was. He was handsome, sure. Pretty, even, with that thick brown hair curling up at his collar and classic masculine bone structure. But I'd known a few handsome men in my time. Each one had a mean streak three miles wide. Handsome got you a big fat nowhere in the end. In fact, sometimes worse off. In my experience, the handsome ones thought they were God's gift to womankind, and that it was their moral duty to spread themselves far and wide.

No, it was something other than that. It was his eyes. His eyes held some sort of innocence I hadn't seen before. Gentleness I certainly wasn't used to. His expression was hopeful, but not desperate, and I didn't detect lust in his eyes. He looked...sincere. Maybe he really did just want to talk. "It's okay, Anthony."

Anthony lowered the hand that had been about to clamp down on the man's arm and stepped back. "You sure?"

"Yeah." I looked at the man. "Ten minutes." I held the keys up, one stuck through my fingers. "And don't make me use these. I don't want to but if you force the issue, you'll exit this room blind, sugar."

"Gabriel," he said, a small smile lighting his face. "My name is Gabriel." Like the angel? No wonder I'd thought he didn't belong here.

"All right." I stood aside, and he moved past me into the room. I nodded once at Anthony and then pushed the door so it still stood halfway open. I knew Anthony would stay close by.

"So what brings a nice guy like you to this den of sin, sugar?"

"Gabriel. And you're Crystal?"

"Around here I am."

He looked at me steadily, and it was disconcerting. After a moment he nodded as if he understood something I didn't. "I see."

At his words, his knowing look, a small burst of flustered anger ricocheted through my belly like the ball in a pinball machine. I smiled suggestively and took a seat on the small, dirty gold settee, reclining, and then crossing my legs. I used my hands to play idly with the knotted material between my breasts. I watched his eyes follow my movement and flare slightly before he looked away. Ah, there it was—lust. Just like every other man. *Familiar.* I took a breath, satisfaction and calm moving through me. "So what is it you want to talk about?"

He cleared his throat and put his hands in his pockets, tilting his head slightly so his hair fell across his forehead. His posture, the way he squinted slightly as he looked at me, triggered my memory, and I suddenly realized how I knew him. *Lost boy.* The words moved through my mind as if someone had scribbled them there. His name was Gabriel Dalton, and he'd gone missing when he was a kid. It was a big-time national news story when he escaped his kidnapper and came home. I was only a preteen at the time, but I'd still heard about it here and there. Of course, right about the time Gabriel had come home, my world was—yet again—falling apart.

The last time I saw his picture on the news had been a while ago, but I knew for certain who he was now. "You shouldn't be in a place like this. If someone recognizes you, I imagine they'll be real eager to take your picture."

He froze for a portion of a second before relaxing again. He took a seat in the metal chair across from where I sat and looked at me expectantly, like one of the men waiting for a lap dance. Only…different somehow. I wished I could pinpoint what it was that looked so wrong about him sitting there. Maybe it was that he looked *nice*. And I couldn't ever remember thinking that about anyone who walked through the door of this club. He blew a breath out slowly and ran a hand through his hair, moving it off his forehead. "I guess it's good you recognized me. Might make this a little easier." He seemed to be talking more to himself and so I didn't respond. He looked straight at me. "I probably should have thought this out a little more instead of just showing up." He rubbed his palms on his thighs as if his hands were sweating.

"Are you going to get to what you want, or am I supposed to guess?"

He shook his head. "No, no, I'm sorry. I don't want to waste your time." He paused again. "The thing is, Crys—" He cleared his throat. "The thing is, because of my history, which it sounds like you know a little bit about, I, uh, find it difficult to tolerate…closeness." Two pink spots appeared on his cheekbones. Was he *blushing*? God, I didn't even know men *could* blush. As if my opinion of him mattered somehow. Something small and warm moved through me, something I had little idea how to identify.

"Closeness?" I frowned, uncomfortable with the softness in my tone.

He pressed his lips together, the color in his cheeks increasing. "I find it difficult to get physically close to people. Or rather, I find it emotionally distressing. Uh…" He laughed softly, an embarrassed sound. "God, this didn't sound so pitiful in my head." He looked somewhere behind me. "Or maybe it did. Maybe it's just worse hearing it out loud."

"What is it I can do for you exactly, sugar?" My voice still sounded soft. Helplessly, my heart squeezed, and I felt a shiver of compassion run through me for the way Gabriel was struggling in front of me. The unfamiliar emotion unbalanced me, and I drew myself up straighter.

"Gabriel," he corrected.

"Okay, what is it I can do for you, *Gabe*?" He didn't smile with his mouth, but his eyes squinted slightly as if he was. But then the lines around his eyes smoothed out, and I wondered if that had been a *sort of* smile, or just my imagination.

"You can help me practice being touched by a woman. Getting comfortable with someone in my personal space."

I blinked at him as he looked down at his hands in his lap. "You want *me* to help you with that?"

His gaze met mine and I saw that gentleness there again—hope—and something about that expression aimed right at me made me feel good and…needed. For the bare glimmer of a moment, it made me feel as if he saw *more* in me than just the piece of ass all the other men who came to this club viewed me as.

"I'll pay you, obviously. It would be an after-hours job, nothing more. You wouldn't even have to take your clothes off."

You wouldn't even have to take your clothes off.

His words brought me up cold, snapping me back to reality, reminding me that he saw me *exactly* as other men did, in fact exactly as I *was*. With my defenses firmly back in place, I stood, picking up the keys next to me on the settee, tossing them his way. He caught them with one hand. "Listen, as much as I hate to turn down a paying gig, I'm no therapist, okay? You want to learn how to touch someone, get a girlfriend. You're a good-looking guy. I'm sure there are plenty of sweet, wholesome girls who wouldn't mind you practicing on them for free."

He stood, too. "I've insulted you."

I laughed. "Sugar, I can't be insulted."

"Everyone can be insulted." Regret laced his tone. He put his hands in his pockets and tilted his head in that way of his, his hair falling over his forehead again. My fingers twitched to smooth it away from his eyes. *What is wrong with me?*

I felt my skin prickling with unease. Everything about Gabriel made me feel uneasy. I needed him to leave. "You don't know me, Gabe. Thanks for the job offer, but I'm going to decline. I do wish you luck with your little problem. Ten minutes is up."

He sighed, not moving. "I really am sorry. God, this didn't go the way I meant it to."

"I'm sure it didn't." I held the door open.

Outside, Anthony was sitting in a chair, wrapping a bandage around his injured hand. "Things kosher?"

I nodded jerkily as Gabriel moved past me. He stopped when he crossed the threshold and turned back to me. "I really am sorry," he said.

I crossed my arms over my chest, my eyes meeting his. Standing this close, I could see that his eyes were hazel with striations of copper. His lashes were thick and lush, curled up slightly—lashes any girl would kill for.

I took a small step back, putting even more distance between us, and blew out a breath. "It's fine. Really. Good luck again."

He started to turn away but then looked back. "Can I just ask one more question?"

I moved from one leg to the other. "Sure."

"What were you thinking when you looked at me from the stage? When our eyes met."

I frowned slightly, about to deny I'd been thinking anything at all but deciding it didn't matter at that point. I'd never see him again. "I was thinking you didn't belong here." And I'd been right.

He paused, his expression enigmatic as his eyes moved over my face. "Huh. Funny," he finally murmured. "I was thinking the very same thing about you."

I laughed, a short huff of sound. "Well, you were wrong there. This is the one place I *do* belong, sugar."

"Gabriel." His lips tipped up slightly, his eyes lingering on me for a heartbeat too long, before he turned and walked away.

CHAPTER TWO

Focus on the good things, even when they're simple. Then bury them deep so only you know where they are.

Shadow, the Baron of Wishbone

GABRIEL

I'd fucked that up royally. *You can help me practice being touched by a woman.* For the love of Christ. No wonder she'd told me to leave. I'd sounded like some sort of psychopath. I shifted into park, turned my truck off, and waited in my driveway for a minute. What the hell had I been thinking? Not only had I messed things up, and presented myself as completely pathetic, I'd insulted her.

Crystal.

What was her real name? I wondered who she was, wondered why my heart had begun to beat insistently against my chest—as if trying to get my attention—when she'd stepped onto that stage, that distant, removed look on her beautiful face. *As if she were made of stone.* And yet her body moved so fluidly, so gracefully. She fascinated me. I hadn't gone there for anything more than to find a woman who might be willing to take on a small side job far less "hands on"—*so to speak*—than what was procured in the back rooms of a place like the Platinum Pearl. But *she* had intrigued me, caught my attention, and hadn't let go. Something about her…called to me. Something that had nothing at all to do with her skimpy outfit or overt sexuality. Something that had nothing to do with the reason I was there in the first place. I let out a small, humorless chuckle that turned into a groan as I raked my hands through my hair.

I couldn't deny I was attracted to her, but even I wasn't stupid or inexperienced enough to think developing a crush on a stripper would be a good idea.

In retrospect, it had been a bad plan from the start. And I realized that the moment I'd voiced my reason for being there to her and watched the expression on her face change from wary to surprised to…hurt. Yes, it was hurt that flashed across her features before her face had gone hard again. If eyes were windows to the soul, I'd witnessed the CLOSED sign being flipped over within the speed of a single blink. *How long had it taken her to master that?*

I'd told her she wouldn't have to take her clothes off, as if she should be thankful for the opportunity not to be demoralized. And yet, isn't that really what my whole plan *did*? Use her? I hadn't thought much of the nameless *her* when I'd come up with the idea—I'd only thought of myself. God, I'd acted like an asshole. It was a terrible idea. An *embarrassing* idea. Made even worse by the fact that she'd recalled my story, probably remembered my full name.

I hadn't anticipated that. Most people who hadn't seen me somewhat regularly in the past twelve years didn't recognize me. I'd stayed out of the spotlight, hadn't granted any interviews, had grown up. I hadn't worried too much about people in a town

miles and miles away—that I hadn't visited since I was a kid—
knowing who I was. But she had. I wondered if it was part of the
reason she'd rejected my request...

I shook my head in an attempt to shake myself free of my own
thoughts and got out of my truck, closing the door as quietly as
possible. I stood for a moment under the pale moonlight, inhaling
a slow breath and closing my eyes as I blew it out. My night had
crashed and burned in one regard, but I took a moment to soak in
the thankfulness I felt for the sweet freshness of the night air, the
breath filling my lungs, and the wide-open expanse all around me.

My house was dark except for the shifting glow of the TV in
the living room. No doubt my brother was passed out in the re-
cliner, as he was most nights. I'd move past him into the hallway,
and he'd never even know how late I'd been out. I didn't feel like
answering any questions. *Especially not tonight.*

"Where've you been?"

I huffed out a surprised breath, dropping my keys in the basket by the door. "Just having a few drinks in town."

"In town?" He looked surprised. And why wouldn't he? He
knew I avoided town.

"Havenfield."

Dominic took a swig from the beer in his hand and scratched
his bare belly. "Ah, the town forty-five minutes away." He
paused. "I would have gone with you."

"I felt like being alone."

One brow rose slowly as he took another swig. "You meet up
with a woman, big bro?" His voice was teasing, but also slightly
hopeful, which made me feel pathetic all over again. Behind him
a woman moaned loudly, and my eyes went to the porn playing
on the TV. He followed my gaze and then turned back toward
me, grinning.

"Can you watch that in your room?"

"Why? You weren't home."

"Because I sit on that furniture, too, and now I'll be second-guessing that."

He nodded, shooting me another unrepentant grin. "Yeah, probably not a good idea."

"Nice, Dominic," I muttered before heading for my room.

"Hey, Gabe, you left this in the living room."

I turned around, freezing when I saw the large envelope he was holding, the one with the University of Vermont emblem on the front, the one addressed to me. I moved quickly, grabbing it from him.

"I didn't leave this in the living room. It was in my room by the computer." I glared at him.

He shrugged and I let out an angry grunt as I turned again, walking toward my room.

"It was a nice letter she wrote you. You gonna do it?" he asked.

I paused in my doorway, not turning my head. "I don't know. I haven't decided."

"Could be good."

"Could be."

"She's hot. I looked her up," he said. "Of course, it was easy. I see you did, too—found it right in the search history. See you've gone back to her bio a couple of times. Is she who you've been on the phone with lately?"

Jesus. "Try minding your own business once in a while." I closed my door behind me to the sound of Dominic's chuckle.

"You are my business, Gabriel Dalton," I heard him yell.

Clenching my jaw, I stood on the other side of the door, reining in my annoyance at my nosy younger brother. I loved Dominic, but I hated constantly feeling crowded by him.

I looked down at the envelope in my hands, the letter from Chloe Bryant peeking from the top where Dominic had obviously pulled it out. I threw it down on my desk and went to the window, opening it wide. I needed the night air flowing in, the sound of swaying trees and a croaking bullfrog nearby. *Peace. Calm.*

I lay down on my bed, bringing the vision of Chloe's picture to my mind—the bio photo that had been published along with an article she had written and suggested I read as part of her online résumé. Chloe, with the brown curls and big green eyes. Chloe, with her open, guileless smile.

Several months before, Chloe had contacted me about the possibility of doing an interview for her senior thesis project about the long-term effects to children that had been abducted and subsequently either escaped or been set free by their captor. There weren't many such cases in the United States, but I was one of them, and it just so happened I was in the same state as Chloe.

Chloe's manner, her friendly, open personality, had appealed to me. And something about doing an interview for a graduate student's thesis, rather than a talk show or magazine, made me feel far more comfortable. I wasn't going to be sensationalized, used for ratings, made to be public fodder. Again.

We'd e-mailed back and forth, traded some basic information; I even thought maybe she'd flirted a little over the phone, though my experience with flirting was woefully sparse. My attraction to Chloe had filled me with a newfound hope. She was pretty and smart, and I was going to have to spend a fair bit of time with her if I said yes to her request. I'd allowed my thoughts to go to a place where, if there *was* an attraction between us, I'd be able to *act* on that attraction.

I thought about Chloe for a moment longer, considering whether I was going to say yes to doing her interview. Once again, I attempted to work through the pros and cons, to get a handle on the nervousness that skated just under a thin pane of excitement, of possibility. But instead of dwelling on hopeful maybes, on the candid expression of a beautiful girl I'd never met, the face of another girl kept invading my thoughts. A girl who, from what I could tell, was the exact opposite of Chloe Bryant. Crystal, with the long, honey-colored hair and the lonely, wary eyes. Crystal, with her guarded, reluctant smile.

Crystal, the girl I'd never see again.

Something about my thoughts unsettled me and I sat up, running a hand through my hair, feeling strangely bereft. Maybe what I really needed to do was *force* myself to step out of my comfort zone. I'd hidden in the shadows for too long, spent too many years enjoying nothing other than the predictable nature of my day-to-day existence: work, home, occasional trips into town where I interacted with few. I took comfort in the expected, found safe companionship in the books I read, and still found joy in my own freedom, but I also couldn't deny that I led a lonely sort of life.

I stood at the open window again, contemplating if I could begin to expand the walls I'd erected around myself. If I *should*. They were of my own making and yet, even so, hadn't I constructed a personal prison? Was it time that I do something to change that?

Before I could talk myself out of it, I took a seat in front of my computer, logged in to my e-mail, and pulled up the last message from Chloe. I typed a short response:

Chloe, my answer is yes. Any dates work for me. Just let me know your travel plans. I'm looking forward to meeting you. Gabriel.

And then I hit send before I could change my mind.

CHAPTER THREE

Some people are mean to their bones. If you can't beat 'em, you just have to survive 'em. Play the hand you've been dealt until you get a better one.

Gambit, the Duke of Thieves

CRYSTAL

My car gave a last wheezing stutter before it jerked to a stop and died on the side of the road where I'd managed to steer it at the last minute. I let out an angry yell, banging my palms against the steering wheel. "No, no, no," I chanted, sitting back in my seat as defeat settled in the pit of my stomach. "God, give me a break." I banged my head lightly against the headrest, my shoulders sagging.

The glare of the sun was strong as I squinted out the open window; nothing in sight but rocks and trees. I was at least three miles from Glendale, the small town where I lived, and there wasn't so much as a gas station between here and there. I pulled my phone out of my purse and dialed the local garage and asked for Ricky. When I was told he wasn't there, I sighed, hanging up.

He was the only one who would have given me a free tow. I dialed Kayla's number next, and it went straight to voice mail.

"Hey, Kay, it's me. My stupid car just died on the side of the road. If you get this and you're not working, call me."

Tossing my phone back in my purse, I rolled my windows up and got out. I stood for a moment considering the five bags of groceries in the backseat and finally blew out a breath, abandoning them as I started walking. I'd get to town and catch a ride back with someone. At least the nonperishables might be salvageable. Goddammit, I'd just spent every cent of last night's tips on those groceries.

The sun was hot on my back, and I felt sweat gathering between my shoulder blades after only a few minutes. In an attempt to make walking easier, I hitched my jean skirt higher on my thighs. My heeled sandals weren't exactly ideal for a three-mile hike. I bent down and took them off, but the asphalt beneath my feet was so hot it burned. *Shit.* Looked like the blister I'd likely get from putting them back on would be the lesser of two evils. I could only hope.

A few cars drove by, but in a town with a population of less than six hundred, I wasn't expecting this road to be highly traveled.

I'd walked about a mile when I heard the loud roar of a truck engine and turned, moving closer to the dead grass at the side of the road and glancing back at the white truck coming my way. It slowed as it went past me and then pulled to the shoulder of the road, idling. I slowed my pace, nervous flutters beginning to move in my belly when Tommy Hull leaned out the window, squinting back at me.

"Hey, girl, you need a ride?"

I released a breath and sped up, pulling open his passenger

side door and climbing in. I hadn't seen Tommy in a while, but he'd been a regular at the Platinum Pearl before he'd married some townie several months before. "Thanks, Tommy, that'd be great. It sure is hot out there." The air-conditioning in his truck felt wonderful and I sighed, leaning back against the seat.

He pulled onto the road and glanced over at me, his eyes moving down my bare thighs, lingering. "Sure is." He started to swerve slightly to the side of the road and looked up, correcting the direction of the truck before glancing at me again. "That your car back there?"

"Yeah." I let out a humorless laugh. "Piece of junk." His eyes seemed to be stuck on my thighs again so I pulled my skirt down slightly, the movement getting his attention. He lifted his gaze and smirked at me.

"You're lookin' real nice today, girl. You wanna go somewhere?"

I shook my head, resisting the urge to cringe. "No, thank you anyway, Tommy." I suddenly remembered the groceries I'd left in the backseat of my car, but decided not to ask Tommy to take me back to get them. I just wanted to get home. Fuck the groceries. Fuck my car and my life. I just wanted to get in bed and turn on some mindless talk show and forget about everything.

"Aw, come on." He put his hand on my thigh and rubbed it lightly. "Damn you're soft. Forgot how soft you are, baby. Miss those lap dances you used to give me." He removed his hand to put it back on the wheel as he turned off the highway onto a dirt road.

"Tommy—"

"I think you owe me a little something for getting you off the side of the road, don't you? Coulda just left you there, walking your ass back to town in the hot sun. Still could." And there it was. My shoulders drooped at the cold jeering in his tone. The scenery around us, the inside of his truck, and my hands sitting in my lap seemed to take on a flat quality, as if none of this was real. I wished it wasn't.

I looked at Tommy blankly, a familiar sense of futility settling over me. What did it matter anyway if I let him grope me in his truck? Here, alone on the side of the road, I didn't even have the thin veneer of safety the Platinum Pearl offered. And judging by the mean look in Tommy's eyes, I knew it'd take more effort to dissuade him.

Evidently the fact that he was married didn't mean much to Tommy. What a lucky girl she was.

I forced my lips to lift into something that felt like a smile. "If that's what you want, sugar." It was impossible to inject any-thing other than fatigue and detachment into my voice. *Not that he would care.*

He stopped the truck, grinning triumphantly at me. "That's my girl." He was on me before I could even blink, his hands everywhere, his mouth fastened to mine, his tongue probing as if digging for lost treasure. I hardened myself, my mind mov-ing elsewhere until his taste, tobacco and something salty he'd recently eaten, was bearable, seemingly innocuous. I tilted my head back against the glass of the window, gazing up at the sky, and noticed a blackbird soaring in the distance. I watched it un-til it was nothing more than a small black speck, watched it until it disappeared into nothing at all.

Tommy thrust against me, panting, his hand desperately pulling at my panties as he licked up my jaw. "Aw, Jesus you get me worked up, baby. You're so fuckin' gorgeous. Aw, fuck." His zipper was down and he was attempting to take his belt off with one hand, still grinding against me in a frenzy, when he let out a loud gasp that ended in a groan, stilling as I felt warm wetness against my bare hip. "Fuck!" he swore, pulling away instantly.

I sat up quickly, jerked out of my daze, pulling my skirt down, wiping at the sour smell of his saliva on my jaw.

He zipped up his pants, sitting back in his seat and running his fingers through his blond hair. "Goddammit! How the fuck am I supposed to go home like this? What do you think my wife's gonna say?" He pointed down at the large wet spot on the front of his jeans.

I stared at it for a moment, and hilarity moved up my throat. *Nice job, sharp shooter.* My chest rose and fell rapidly with the effort not to laugh, some vague sense of hysteria mixed with the laughter that was bubbling in my chest, begging for escape. When Tommy attempted to wipe at the spot with the edge of his shirt and only ended up making it bigger, I couldn't hold back anymore. A burst of laughter exploded from my mouth and I clutched my stomach, doubling over. I laughed so hard tears poured down my cheeks.

I looked up just in time to see the rage etched across Tommy's face, but not in time to dodge the smack that whipped my head back against the window. That killed my laughter. I brought my hand up to my face, my laughter turning into small bursts of wheezing breath.

"Not laughing now, are ya, you cheap slut? Get the fuck out of my truck." He reached around me and opened the door, and since I was leaning against it, I fell out, tumbling backward, hitting the ground so hard the breath was knocked from my lungs. My purse landed in a patch of dead grass to my left, and the door of the truck slammed above me. Trying my best to draw breath, I crawled backward through the dirt as the truck roared to life, turned around, and headed back toward the main road.

I sat there for a minute, sucking in oxygen, all the laughter dead on my lips. Eventually, I pulled myself up, groaning slightly at the ache in my bruised backside, and rubbing carefully where Tommy had hit me. I walked toward the highway. At least I was a little closer to home than I'd been before. That was something.

* * *

Forty-five minutes later, sweating profusely, and limping from the blisters formed on my aching feet, I let myself into my apartment. Dropping my purse on the floor, I began removing my clothes, leaving them in a trail as I headed to the shower. I stood under the cool water, attempting to let the last hour and a half wash off my body and follow the soapy water down the drain. *I just want to feel clean.* When I emerged, I felt a little bit better, cooler at least. I opened my apartment window, though there wasn't much of a breeze, and turned on the floor fan, grabbing my phone from my purse and flopping down on my bed.

No calls. Kayla must be working. I thought about my car, currently on the side of the road with the groceries in the backseat, and a lump formed in my throat. I needed that car—needed it to get to work. Needed it to survive. *Needed* it so that I didn't have to accept rides from men who were likely to take liberties with my body on the side of the road. A sick feeling washed through me when I thought of Tommy again, but I pushed the recent memory away as best as I could.

Thinking about it all exhausted me until I almost decided just to curl up right where I was and sleep the day away.

What am I gonna do now? Oh, Lord...

I jerked to a sitting position and dialed the garage again and asked for Ricky, who'd always been decent to me when my car broke down, even letting me make payments if I wasn't able to cover the whole bill at once.

Whoever answered obviously laid the phone on the counter. I heard him call Ricky's name, then pictured Ricky sliding out from beneath a car, a wrench in his hand, grease smeared on his face. When he barked a "Ricky here" into the phone, I put a smile in my voice and told him how I needed his help.

"Aw, listen, babe, I can tow it for you and let you know what's wrong with it, but you know you still owe me the money for fixing the alternator. I can't do any more work for you until you're settled up here. The old man will have my hide if I do."

My hope plummeted. I didn't even have the money for a tow, much less to settle up and then fix whatever was wrong this time—something expensive no doubt. "All right, Ricky. I appreciate the tow. It's really generous. Thank you."

"Sure, babe."

I gave him the details about where it was and that I'd be over later to pick up my groceries once I could catch a lift from Kayla. Maybe some of the food was still edible.

I sat there for a minute, a dull feeling of loneliness sitting heavily in my gut. How? How was I going to work this out?

I'll pay you, obviously. It would be an after-hours job, nothing more.

Gabriel Dalton's words wove through my mind, and I picked up my phone again, tapping it lightly against my chin for a minute before typing his name into the browser. There was no lack of information. I clicked on a link near the top, bringing up a news story from twelve years before.

The Morlea Police Department held a press confer-
ence on Thursday, June 29, to give more details about
the Gabriel Dalton case. Nine-year-old Gabriel, the little
boy abducted near his home in 1998 while playing in
an empty lot with his eight-year-old brother, Dominic,
caught the attention of Vermonters along with the na-
tion. Gabriel was missing until a week ago, when he
appeared on a woman's doorstep, bloody, identifying
himself as Gabriel Dalton and asking for help. Through
the investigation, police discovered that Gabriel had
been held in the basement of the house next door
to the woman who called 911, and that he had been
there for the past six years. Gabriel had escaped by
stabbing his abductor, identified as Gary Lee Dewey,
with a sharpened piece of rock. Gary Lee Dewey was
deceased when police arrived. Gabriel Dalton, now fifteen, was reunited with his brother, and they are both
currently in the care of their father's business partner at
Dalton Morgan Quarry. Gabriel and Dominic's parents,
Jason and Melissa Dalton, passed away in a car accident in 2003.

Just a year before their son came home. *God.*

I looked up a few more articles, finding similar information.
My eyes lingered on the nine-year-old face of Gabriel Dalton, the
sweet, all-American smile, those same innocent eyes that I'd seen
from the stage. There were only a couple of pictures of Gabriel
at fifteen. In the first one, he was long-haired, wide-eyed, and
looked distressed by the flash of the camera. In the second, he
was standing in the pose that had triggered my memory: hands
in pockets, head tilted, his hair falling over his forehead as he

squinted slightly at the camera. It was the one all the news sta-
tions had used for months on end as they reported on his story.

Biting my lip, I set the phone down, leaning back on my pillows, wondering what hell Gabriel had endured during those six
years locked in the basement with a child predator.

You can help me practice being touched by a woman.

I swallowed down a lump, not wanting to think about why he
was so averse to being touched. Figuring I already knew.

I hadn't wanted any part of Gabriel's self-imposed therapy,
but now, sitting here, I couldn't even remember why I'd said no.
Clearly, I was a willing body, and by the sound of things, that
was really all he required. He needed me, and I needed the extra money. He could have asked any of the dancers last night,
but he'd chosen me, and then I turned him down as if I were too
good for the job, but in reality, I wasn't.

I could help Gabriel become comfortable with someone in his
space, someone touching him, and he could give me the money I
needed to get my car running again. Win-win. How hard could it
be? Yet why did a peculiar sense of anxiety run down my spine?
I squashed it, pulling my towel more tightly around myself, and
picked up my phone again, doing a search on Dalton Morgan
Quarry. It was in the nearby town of Morlea, and although I didn't
know if Gabriel worked there or not, I decided to take a chance,
dialing the number. If I couldn't find him this way, I'd give it up
and move on to plan B, whatever that might be. My heart beat
more quickly as I waited for someone to answer.

"Dalton Morgan Quarry."

I hesitated, feeling nervous, unsure.

"Hello?"

"Uh," I finally got out. "Uh, yes, um, may I speak with
Gabriel? Gabriel Dalton?"

There was a short pause. "Sure." It sounded like the man—*young* man, I thought—was smiling. "May I tell him who's calling?" Yes, there was definitely a smile in his voice.

I cleared my throat. "Crystal. Um, just Crystal."

There was another short pause before the man finally said, "Oh." He sounded disappointed. *What was that about?*

I frowned, opening my mouth to say something, when he beat me to it. "Sure thing. Hold on." Music came on the line and I stood up, holding my towel up with one hand and my phone with the other while I paced in front of my bed. After what seemed like a good five minutes, another voice came on the line.

"Hello?"

It sounded like Gabriel's voice—at least from what I remembered—and I quit pacing. "Hi, Gabriel? Um, this is Crystal. You might not remember me but—"

"Of course I remember you. Hi." I heard footsteps and a door close as if he'd gone into another room.

"Hi," I said, feeling sudden relief, my voice coming out sort of quick and breathy.

"God, I'm glad—"

"I was calling—"

We both spoke at the same time and then both stopped, his chuckle coming through the line. I smiled despite my nerves.

"You first," he said softly.

"Oh, okay. Well, I, uh, I rethought what we talked about, and I hope you don't mind me looking you up, but I was calling to say that if you're still in need of a, uh... if you're still in need of... me, I'd be happy to help."

There was a pause and I started pacing again, waiting for him to speak. "Actually, no, and I owe you an apology for even asking. I hadn't really thought out the idea. I'm sorry about that. Sorry if I made you feel...you know, not good."

"Not good," I murmured, sinking down onto my bed, my hand still gripping the towel to keep it from slipping.

I heard a small, embarrassed-sounding chuckle that ended in a sigh. "Yeah, not good." What else was there to feel *except* "not good"? That seemed to be life's default mode—at least for me.

I snapped back to the present. "There's no need to apologize. I feel just fine. And, well, I understand if you've come up with a different idea, but if not, I'm available." I waited for him to speak, but when he didn't immediately, I rushed to fill the silence. "You can practice on me. I mean, if you still want to."

There was silence from the other end of the line again, and this time I waited it out. Finally, Gabriel spoke and his voice was even quieter. "How would this work exactly?"

I laughed shortly. "You're going to have to let me know that. I figure you can come to the club like last night. I'll make sure Anthony knows you've followed procedure."

I heard his breath release in what I hoped was a smile, and then he was silent for another moment. "You sure about this? You feel okay with it?"

"Yes."

"Okay, then." He still sounded hesitant. "When do you work next?"

"Tomorrow night."

"Okay, I'll be there tomorrow night. And if you change your mind—"

"I won't change my mind. See you then, Gabe."

"No more 'sugar'?" There was a smile in his voice and I smiled, too.

"Whatever you want me to call you, sugar, that's what I'll call you."

"Gabe's fine. Gabe's good."

"See you tomorrow night, sugar."

Another chuckle. "See you then."

I hung up and let out a breath, feeling slightly more energized. Okay, I'd figured out my situation. A little extra money—we'd have to talk specifics tomorrow night—but I'd need to at least double my lap-dance rate to make this worth my time. Feeling slightly better, I dropped my towel and pulled on some clean clothes. When I looked in the mirror, I was surprised to see a small smile on my face I hadn't even realized was there. I blinked, watching the smile slip. There was a large red mark on my cheek where Tommy had backhanded me, and a small welt on my cheekbone that must have been caused by his wedding ring. I picked up my hairbrush, using it roughly on my wet hair, pulling it through the knots until the harsh tugs on my scalp made me wince.

CHAPTER FOUR

You can find hope in the strangest of places, in the darkest of corners. Clutch it close, my darling. It's yours and no one else's.

Lemon Fair, the Queen of Meringue

GABRIEL

The Platinum Pearl was bustling. I took a seat at the same table I'd sat at two nights before and ordered a beer from the cocktail waitress. "Do you know when Crystal's performing?" I asked. The dark-haired server who brought my Miller Lite leaned over farther than necessary to set my beer on the table. She appeared confused when I held eye contact instead of looking down at her breasts thrust in my face, staying in the bent position a beat longer before standing up straight.

"I think she's up next."

My heart thumped faster as I turned to the stage, waiting for the next song to start. I had been shocked when she called saying she'd changed her mind. Shocked and slightly bewildered. I wondered what had changed her mind. Wondered what had compelled her to look me up and call me. I'd almost told her to forget it entirely since I'd decided the whole idea was terrible. But once I heard her voice over the phone, I hadn't been able to bring myself to turn her down. The truth was, I was both scared and excited, and it was an exhilarating feeling—one I hadn't experienced before. I wanted...more. And I thought that was probably a positive thing for me, to *want* at all. But what about her? I kept coming back to that.

The lights flashed and then dimmed and the music started, a steady bass rhythm that had my blood pumping in time to the music. I frowned as I looked around. There was a bachelor party sitting near the stage, and they were practically falling out of their chairs they were so drunk.

When the lights came back on, Crystal was sitting in a chair wearing a tiny silver bikini with fringe hanging from the edges of the top and the bottom and a pair of tall silver boots. I was so intent on her that the cheers that went up around the room startled me. I took a sip of my beer and watched as she began to dance.

Her long hair moved around her beautiful, slender body as she performed, catching the light, a color I didn't recall ever seeing before—sort of a combination of blonde, red, and brown. It made me think of light shining through a bottle of honey. And there was so much of it. I wondered what it'd feel like to run my fingers through it. Her body moved to the beat, her eyes closed, that cold, distant expression in place, seemingly as immovable as armor.

Crystal. No, not crystal. Crystal was perfectly clear, transparent. A person could see right through crystal as if it were glass. Not the girl up there. Not crystal—nothing even close.

What's your name? Your real name? God, I want to know.

"I'd fuck that pussy like a jackhammer!" one drunk bachelor-party goer yelled out to the delight of his friends, who guffawed and held up their drinks in cheers to him. His lewd statement jolted me from my thoughts. He stood and started drilling his groin against the chair in imitation of the sex act he'd just described.

This whole scene opened up some void inside that made me feel angry and sad at the same time. I stood up, throwing a tip down on the table, and headed to the back to wait. I rounded the corner to the hallway where I'd waited for Crystal the first time, and saw that the bouncer, Anthony, was sitting on a stool. "What can I do for you?" he asked in his deep baritone.

"I'm here to see Crystal after she's finished dancing."

"You Gabe?"

"Yeah," I said, surprised. I hadn't expected that she would have given my name to Anthony.

"I'll show you back."

I followed Anthony to a different room than the one where I'd talked to Crystal the first time. It was dim and had purple velvet fabric hanging from all four walls. There was a black leather couch against one wall, a few scattered velvet ottomans, a sound system in the corner, and a large-screen TV hanging on the opposite wall from the couch.

"Go 'head and take a seat," Anthony said. "Crystal will be in after her performance."

"Right," I said, moving deeper into the room.

I heard the click of the door closing behind me and let out a breath. I sat down on the edge of the couch, fighting anxiety. *Shadowy. Locked door. Soundless.* This room felt like a cave, or a dank basement. My eyes landed on the door, and I reminded myself that I could leave anytime I wanted to. This wasn't the same. Not at all.

I wondered, though, if this was Crystal's version of a dank, locked basement.

I wasn't exactly sure why I questioned it, but the thought sat there like a rock, the weight of it pushing on my conscience.

A few minutes later, I was startled from my thoughts when the door swung open and Crystal stepped inside. I started to stand, but she gestured for me to remain sitting and so I did. She had put on a long sweatshirt that came to the middle of her thighs and fell off her shoulders, but was still wearing the silver boots. I smiled at the outfit. She sat down on the couch, turning toward me. My insides twisted. God, she was beautiful. Too beautiful for this room. Too beautiful for this *place*.

She'd put her hair up in a huge, messy pile on top of her head. It looked darker in this light, more brown than gold. Her almond-shaped eyes were heavily made up in black eyeliner and ridiculously long, obviously false eyelashes. "I wasn't sure you'd come." She smiled, the one that didn't meet her eyes.

I massaged the back of my neck, feeling strange, shy, out of my element, and…guilt ridden. "I'm not sure I should have."

Her face fell slightly, and I rushed on. "I'm just…I guess I'm having a pang of conscience."

Her gaze moved over my face for a moment in that measuring way of hers before she raised an eyebrow, standing and walking seductively toward the sound system before turning back to me. "Well, my goodness, that sounds painful. It's not contagious, is it?" She put a hand on her hip and smiled sweetly at me.

I laughed, a burst of warm humor mixed with a bit of surprise filling my chest. It felt good. "No, I don't think so."

"Well, good." She put on some music, turning the volume down low, and walked back toward me, sitting on the couch again. "How about we try out one session, and if it doesn't work for you, if it makes you feel…*not good*, we'll call it quits, no harm done." She gave me a small, teasing smile, and it felt like bird wings had begun flapping between my ribs.

One session. She really was thinking of this as therapy. I supposed that was accurate enough. I sucked my bottom lip into my mouth, still not sure, but not wanting to leave, not really.

I liked her. I liked the way she looked at me, the way she teased, the flash of keen intelligence behind her eyes, her quick wit, the way she seemed so hard, and yet was somehow soft at the same time. I did, I liked her. *Oh, Gabriel, you idiot.*

"We should agree on a fee first."

"You just name the price," I said. "I'm fine with whatever you think is fair."

"Fair," she murmured. "Well, the club takes the cost of a lap dance while we're in here, so in order to make any money for myself, I would have to double that. So fifty." Uncertainty passed briefly over her expression, as if she was nervous she might have asked for too much.

"Fifty dollars?" I repeated, trying not to wince at the knowledge of how little she got paid to do what she did. *The club takes the cost of a lap dance.* Jesus.

"If that's too much, I could do forty-five," she said in a rush of words, a tinge of desperation in her tone. Ah. That explained it. She *needed* the money, small amount though it was. That's why she had decided to do this.

That pang was back again—even sharper this time—causing a stabbing sensation in my gut. I shifted in my seat. "When I was a teenager, I used to go to this psychologist in Middlebury who charged a hundred and fifty a session. I wouldn't pay you any less."

Her eyes widened very slightly before that unaffected look

came over her face again. "Oh, okay. Well, great. Should we start with kissing?"

I blinked and then chuckled softly. It turned into a grimace, and I rubbed at the back of my neck again, embarrassed. "I might not have been totally clear about the extent of my discomfort with having people in my personal space. If I was ready for kissing, I wouldn't be here."

She frowned slightly, tilting her head as she measured me again. She nodded, that bare hint of softness coming into her eyes, but no judgment. I released a breath, grateful for that small mercy.

"I can teach you what I do when someone gets close to me. I remove myself completely, and it makes it bearable." She bit her lip, her brow furrowing as if considering something. "I think I can teach you how to do that."

My body stilled as I stared at her. Her words caused my heart to ache. *Oh God.* "That's not what I want, though. I know how to remove myself. I know how to do that. I want to stay present. That's what I need you to help me with. *Staying.*"

Her cheeks flushed, and she stared at me for a moment before looking away. "Oh." She picked at a fingernail, her brow creasing before her eyes met mine again. There was something in her expression I was having trouble reading. Was it fear?

She shifted, wrapping her arms around her waist and unwrapping them just as quickly, clasping her hands in her lap. She smiled, that big one that was all mouth and cheek muscles, but no eyes. "Well. Let's just get started, then. Can I...?" She used her finger to indicate moving closer to me on the couch. Her gaze met mine and held for a moment as I nodded, anxiety coursing through my blood.

She scooted closer to me as my heart rate accelerated. I felt my body flush uncomfortably, my skin prickling as she again slid closer, our thighs almost touching. There was a red mark on her cheekbone that her makeup didn't cover from this close. I wanted to ask her about it, but I couldn't form the words. The adrenaline pumping through my body at her nearness made me feel dizzy, made me want to bolt, to flee. I was desperate for space, and though I knew it was irrational, I couldn't help wanting to back away, to put myself at arm's distance so I felt *safe*. I sucked in oxygen, her eyes still holding mine.

"I'm going to touch your hand," she whispered. "Is that okay?" Her eyes were wide, and her lips were parted as her chest rose and fell with each quickened breath. I saw it—her nervousness, her uncertainty, but the care she was taking in spite of it—and for one sweet moment, a breeze of calm moved through me.

I let out a strange sound that was half word…half exhale. She hesitated, but kept eye contact. "Gabriel," she murmured. I felt the warmth of her breath as she spoke my name. I smelled her perfume, something fresh and delicate that reminded me of spring rain and newly cut grass, something that seemed to conflict with the heaviness of her makeup, the boldness of her skimpy clothing. *Who are you, Crystal? Really?*

A pulse beat steadily at the base of her throat, and for a wild moment I wondered what it would feel like to place my lips there, to run my tongue over it. Would she let me? More importantly, would she want it?

Her hand touched mine, smooth, tentative, and I tensed at the skin-on-skin contact. *Run!* My thigh muscles contracted in preparation of flight, but I held myself still by sheer will, clenching my eyes shut. Words and phrases and sounds were whipping through my mind, assaulting me, taking me out of the present, back *there*.

Good boy.

Just relax.

You like that, don't you?

No!

I gripped Crystal's hand tightly, and she let out a small groan of distress. My eyes flew open and I let go of her, standing quickly. I was sweating, my heart beating so harshly, I swore she could hear it from where she still sat. There was both relief and disappointment in putting distance between us. I expected the relief, but the disappointment was something new.

"I'm sorry," I said when I could speak. "I'm sorry."

"Don't be sorry. Do you want to try again?" Her words were said quickly, but her voice was soft.

I shook my head. "No. Not...not tonight. That was enough." I let out an embarrassed chuckle. "You sure you're up for this?"

She was still sitting in the same position as she had been when I stood, her hand lying limply on the couch where I'd been. Her head was tilted and her cheeks were flushed, too, though I couldn't say why. She looked slightly confused as she bit at her lip. But then she smiled that practiced smile again and stood up, though she still didn't answer my question.

She wrapped her arms around her waist again, and this time, left them there as she looked at me.

She's as scared as I am. The thought caused me to frown. I wasn't sure where it'd come from or why I'd had it at all. *She doesn't know what to think about this.*

For a second we looked at each other awkwardly. "Oh, uh." I reached into my pocket, taking out my wallet and counting out the cash and handing it to her. She took it with a small smile and stuck it in her bra.

"I don't work tomorrow but I work the night after that if you—"

"That'd be great."

She nodded. "Same time?"

"Yeah. Same time."

"Okay, Crys—" I paused. "Can I call you by your real name? You know, now that we're on more intimate terms. Having held hands and all."

She laughed. "I told you, sugar. Around here, that is my real name."

I frowned in disappointment. "Okay. See you soon, then."

She opened the door and I walked through it, putting my hands in my pockets, glancing back once before I turned out of the hallway. She was still standing against the open door, looking slightly troubled, and watching me as I left.

CHAPTER FIVE

Take my hand and follow me to the daffodil fields. The sweet perfume makes us invisible, you know. We'll hide together, you and I. I won't ever leave you alone.

Lady Eloise of the Daffodil Fields

GABRIEL

I pulled up in front of the post office and stepped out into the summer heat. It'd been unusually hot for Vermont in the last couple of weeks, and I was looking forward to the cooling rain that was supposed to come later this week.

The post office was cool and silent, mostly empty on a week-day at ten a.m. I breathed in the familiar scent of old paper. Bridgett Hamill was at the counter filing her nails. When I stepped forward, she glanced up at me, her eyes widening slightly as she dropped the file and pushed it quickly into the open drawer in front of her.

"Can I help you?"

"Hi, Bridgett."

She snapped her gum, her eyes darting around. "Hello."

I smiled thinly, embarrassed by her blatant standoffishness. We'd gone to school together. I'd helped her up once in second grade after a bully knocked her books out of her hands and she'd cried. But that had been *before*. I supposed when she remembered it, *if* she remembered it, that's what she thought, too.

I paused as she stared at me, finally looking down to the packages I'd placed on the edge of the counter. I pushed the two boxes forward, the one on top toppling off and almost falling to the floor. "Shit." I caught the package, placing it next to the other one. "I'd like to mail these."

"Sure thing." She went about weighing and stamping them and then rang up my postage, flashing me a thin-lipped smile. A couple of people were in line behind me, and after I thanked Bridgett stiffly, I nodded at them. The first woman in line—I was pretty sure her name was Penny—had a little boy with her, and she pulled him against her side, running her hand over his hair as I passed. She shot me a smile that had that same hint of sorrow I was used to.

A rush of warm air hit me as I pushed open the glass door, and before it shut behind me, I heard Penny whisper loudly to Bridgett, "Did you hear about—" The door clicked shut before I could hear the rest of whatever gossip she'd been about to relay.

I got into my truck and cranked up the air-conditioning, sitting there for a few minutes, leaned back on the seat, letting my discomfort fade. I knew why some of the people in town treated me the way they did, understood the vast array of reactions I still received. I should be used to it by now. I *was* used to it. But I hated feeling like the town creep show.

I pulled out of my spot and almost decided not to do the other errand I'd come into town to do, but at the last minute, I turned right toward the hardware store anyway. If I wanted to live a normal life, I had to force myself to start stepping out of the comfort zone I'd created. Plus, Sal's was one of the few places in town where I didn't feel like a bug under a microscope. A bug who was either liable to do something strange and unexpected at any moment, or a bug who still elicited constant sympathy and was a reminder of any mother's worst fear.

I pulled into the parking lot behind the store and walked around to the front, the bell chiming over the door when I stepped inside the dim, stuffy shop.

"Hey, Gabriel," Sal greeted.

I smiled. "Hey, Sal. How are you?"

"Hot as the dickens. I'd be working shirtless today if my No Shirt permit hadn't been revoked years ago," he joked, patting his large belly.

I laughed. "Time to invest in some central air?"

He sighed. "Gina says so, but I say, my grandfather and my father didn't need it and neither do I. Heat makes a man strong. You should know—working in that quarry all day."

"I mostly work inside, actually, but I won't disagree with you. George is about as strong as they come."

Sal nodded. "So was your dad. Now, hey, I got those gloves in you ordered along with the other things George put on the list." Sal stepped into the back while I waited. I could have bought the gloves online, but I preferred to give my business to Sal, even for smaller orders. Plus it forced me to come into town with some regularity, and that was a good thing. Supposedly.

Sal carried a box from the back and set it down on the counter. "These should last you a while, then."

"Yeah."

"I'll just put this on your account."

"Okay, great. Thanks, Sal," I said, picking up the box. As I turned to go, Sal called my name. I turned, and the look on his face was one of concern.

"Hey, uh, I don't know if you've heard, but a little boy went missing yesterday. Still hasn't been found."

My blood ran cold. "A little boy?" My voice sounded hoarse.

Sal nodded, frowning. "Yeah. Ten-year-old riding his bike to the town pool, and he just disappeared. Name's Wyatt Geller. You know him?"

I swallowed heavily, gripping the box under my arm as I ran a hand through my hair. The shop was closing in around me. "No. Thanks for letting me know, Sal."

Sal nodded. "Yeah. You be well, Gabriel."

"You, too." I stepped outside, squinting against the sudden bright light, and breathed deeply as I walked to my truck. *Just disappeared.* Christ.

I didn't even remember starting my truck or turning out of the hardware store parking lot. Suddenly I was driving down the road, my mind focused on that day, the day in the empty lot near my house. It had been eighteen years, and I could still re-call so vividly the way the air smelled that day—like dust and the hollyhocks that grew along the chain-link fence. I could still remember the way the sky had been so blue, filled with billowy white clouds. Peaceful. It had all been so peaceful. And then it had all been yanked away...stolen. *Just disappeared.*

Without making the conscious choice, I found myself headed for that lot now. Of course, it wasn't empty anymore. There was a small white house with a porch and a picket fence sitting in the spot. I wondered if the people who lived there knew. I won-dered if they ever thought about me, ever sat on their porch on a summer evening, sipping iced tea and wondering what it had been like the day I'd been snatched from my life by the devil himself. Right from that spot. If they did, I bet they'd shake their heads and click their tongues and murmur, "How awful. His poor mother. His poor father. I don't even want to think about it."

And then they wouldn't.

But I didn't have that luxury.

And yet, sitting there in my truck, idling on the calm suburban street, a certain peace flowed through me. I was here. I had survived—that day, and every awful day that came after it for six straight years. And I hadn't only survived, I had thrived in almost every way that was important.

Gary Lee Dewey had stolen so much, but not everything. "You didn't get the best of me," I murmured. "Not even close." Despite his best efforts, I had walked out of that dank basement with my soul intact.

Wyatt Geller.

Lord, please let that little boy be okay.

I drove the very short distance to my childhood home, where I pulled my truck over and sat looking at it from across the street. The new owners had painted the house a pale gray with forest-green shutters. The white picket fence looked the same, and my childhood swing, the one my dad had hung, was still in the tree in the front yard. I felt my lips curve into a small smile, hearing in my mind my mother's voice, my father's laughter, the bark of my childhood dog, Shadow. I closed my eyes and swore I could smell the lemon meringue pie my mother would make on special occasions because it was my favorite. I wanted that again. To have a family of my own, someone to love me, and someone I could love in return.

And as I sat there remembering the happiness I'd once known, the face that flashed through my mind was Crystal's.

Beautiful Crystal, so hard, so wary of the world. Why? *What happened to you, Crystal, to bring you to that velvet-curtained room? That purple-walled prison? Crystal.* The name still felt wrong, even in my thoughts. God, I wanted to know what her name really was. Who *she* really was.

And then what, Gabriel? Then what? Will you sweep her off her feet and live happily ever after?

I ran a hand through my hair, exhaling. She was doing a job, and as far as I knew, it was nothing more. And yet, I'd sensed her own battle in the way she looked at me as she'd moved closer on the couch. If she was struggling with something…Christ, I had so little experience with women. And I had a feeling Crystal was far more complicated than most.

Feeling confused and somewhat defeated by my own thoughts, I pulled away from the curb and headed back to the quarry. When I arrived, I brought the box inside the office and set it on the counter. Dominic was with customers in one of the showrooms, so I gave him a nod. He raised a hand before turning back to the woman in front of him, her finger on her chin, looking between two samples of granite.

I walked back outside and took the path to the edge of the quarry area. George was just stepping out of one of the wheel loader trucks and stood for a minute, talking to the driver. My eyes moved around the gargantuan canyon with water at the bottom. I was struck as I always was by the vastness of it, by the miracle of nature, and the fact that the most beautiful things came straight from the earth. When George spotted me, he waved, removing his hard hat and walking to meet me.

"Hey there. I heard you went into town."

I smiled. "Yup."

"How was it?"

"Not too bad." George regarded me momentarily and then nodded, seemingly satisfied by whatever was on my face.

"Good, I'm glad." I followed as he started walking. "How's the mantel coming along?"

"It's done. I finished it early this morning before I left for town."

"Well, damn! Let me see it."

I laughed, and we walked back up the hill to my workshop. The cool, air-conditioned space made me sigh after the dry heat of the outside air. The large fireplace mantel and surround was against the far wall, covered by a sheet that I removed carefully before I turned toward George. For a moment he just stared at it before moving closer, kneeling down and examining the detail. I watched him as he studied the floral designs and leaves vining up each side of the pale gold marble, his finger following the stem of a rose, a look of reverent admiration on his face.

I had been hired to re-create a fireplace mantel and surround for a couple in Newport, Rhode Island, who had bought a mansion built during the Gilded Age and wanted to bring back as many elements specific to that era as they could. This piece would go in the formal living room.

George stood, shaking his head, tears in his eyes. I smiled softly at his emotion—the same depth of feeling he always displayed at the unveiling of one of my pieces.

"You're a master. It's no wonder you have a waiting list a mile long. Your dad would be so damn proud." His arms dropped to his sides. I knew he wanted to clap me on the back, or maybe squeeze my shoulder like he did with Dominic when he had done something that made George proud, but he knew I didn't like it, had been conditioned not to get too close to me. I always felt both relieved and mildly ashamed by it. "It's exquisite."

"Thanks. I sent them a photo this morning. Sounded like they really liked it."

George smiled. "Really liked it. I'm sure that's an understatement, and you're too modest to say so. But I'm glad they're pleased." He winked at me and I laughed softly. "Got the shipping all set up?"

"Not yet, but I will today."

George nodded. "Great. What's next?"

"I have the balustrades for the terrace in Chicago. Those shouldn't take long, and then I'll be starting on the French project."

"Okay. If you need any help, you know where to find me." He laughed as he walked toward the door. We both knew he couldn't carve to save his life. He turned when he got to the door. "I'm real proud of you, Gabriel."

"Thanks, George." And I *was* thankful. I had lost my own dad for the first time when I was taken. But even at nine, he was the man I knew I wanted to be. I remembered clinging to his love for me, his affection, his calm strength, believing that if I ever got out of that basement, it was the safety of his arms I was yearning for. And then I'd lost him again when I escaped and found out he was dead. The fact that he never got to know I made it was a constant hole in my heart. Yet George, the man who had been my father's best friend and business partner, often reminded me that he would have been proud of me. And it helped. It had helped every day for twelve years.

I took my time covering the piece, cleaning up my studio, and filling out the necessary shipping forms for the mantel. As I was putting some supplies away, I caught sight of the small figures I kept at the back of a high cabinet—the figures that had saved my life once upon a time. The figures that had been my only friends. The sight of them no longer brought a heavy feeling of melancholy but instead a small twinge of happiness. They were another reason—maybe even the main reason—I was standing right where I was.

"Hi, guys," I said, nodding at each of them, chuckling softly at myself self-consciously. "Nice to see you." I told myself for the hundredth time that I should just throw them out. What was the reason I held on to them? They were the last physical reminder of the pain I'd endured for years. And yet I still couldn't bring myself to do it. I wasn't sure why my eyes lingered on the figure on the end—the stone girl with the flower held in her hands. I whispered her name. "*Eloise*. Lady Eloise of the Daffodil Fields."

CHAPTER SIX

Everything is going to be okay. Maybe not today, but eventually. Do you believe?

Racer, the Knight of Sparrows

CRYSTAL

I walked off the stage, limping slightly once I was out of sight. "Damn blister," I muttered. I'd been walking everywhere for the past couple of days, and the blister I'd gotten on the highway the day my car broke down still hadn't had a chance to heal. I supposed my job didn't require many fancy dance moves—the pigs out there were happy enough with a few hip thrusts—but I liked to challenge myself to come up with a new routine every once in a while. Not for *them*, but for me.

I had just put my tip money in my locker when I heard yelling from down the hall and walked toward Rodney's office. The door was standing wide open and Kayla was inside, standing in front of him as he circled her. "It looks to me like you've put on a lot more than ten pounds," he said, his eyes moving up and down her body, his expression one of utter disgust. He reached out and took a handful of her ass, and he must have squeezed because Kayla jumped and let out a little yelp. Her eyes were wide with shame, and her neck was blotchy.

"I've been having a rough time, Rodney," she said. "My old man walked out on me and—"

"And it's no fucking wonder!" He threw his hands up in the air. "Why would he want a lard-ass for a girlfriend?" Kayla grimaced, looking down at her feet.

I crossed my arms. "Do you really think you're the one who should be giving diet advice to anyone?" I looked pointedly at his huge gut.

Rodney smirked at me. "I'm not the one shaking my stretch-marked ass out there for paying customers," he said, a nasty edge to his tone. "So don't give me any of that shit. Neither one of you is worth more than your tits and ass, so keep 'em in shape." He turned back to Kayla. "You've got a month to take off the weight, or you can find yourself another club. If anyone else would even have you. And you, Crystal, stop being such a fucking bitch to the customers. Men want a woman who's warm and inviting—not some ice queen. Now get out."

Kayla headed toward me, dejected, and as I stood in the doorway, I felt sick and filled with impotent rage. *Men want a woman who's warm and inviting—not some ice queen.* But Rodney was wrong—men didn't give a hot damn what I was as long as I let them grope my body to their heart's content. Kayla caught my eye and gave her head a small shake. Whatever was in my expression must have told her I was considering ripping Rodney a new one. *Disgusting asshole.* The thought *was* compelling, but I knew anything I said would only make things worse for Kayla, and for me. I needed this shit job. And so I clamped my lips shut and followed her back to our dressing room. I shut the door and let out a growl, picking up a small wastebasket by the door and chucking it. The plastic made an unsatisfying clink when it hit the wall and clattered to the floor, right side up as if it'd been placed there. All I'd managed to do was relocate it.

"Feel better?" Kayla asked sarcastically, sinking onto the settee.

"Fucking prick," I muttered. "You okay?"

She sighed. "Yeah. He's right anyway. I have gained weight. I can't seem to stay away from junk food since Wayne's been gone. Yesterday I stayed in bed with a bag of Doritos and a box of donuts watching old DVDs until three in the afternoon." She looked down at her clasped hands. "I thought he was the one. I'm so stupid. I thought we were gonna get married, I might be a mom someday." She paused, tears welling in her eyes. "And now I'm just…I'm so damn lonely."

My heart contracted painfully. "Oh, Kayla," I sighed. "You call me if you have a day like that. I'll come over and eat Doritos with you."

"Nah, I don't share my Doritos with anyone."

I laughed and she shot me a wobbly grin. "Hey, if we can still laugh, we must be halfway okay, right?"

Her smile slipped. "Halfway okay. Yeah. Is there anything more?"

The silence stretched between us for a minute, Kayla's face filled with so much defeat it broke my heart. She was one of the only girls here who had been a true friend to me since I'd gotten this job. She was never petty, never superficial or competitive like all the others. I *wanted* to tell her there was more. I wanted to share my own hope with her that life held happiness for girls like us. But I'd given up on hope long ago. I'd discovered early that hope was nothing but a cruel and dangerous business.

"I don't know, Kayla," I answered honestly. "But I'm all right with halfway okay. It's better than completely miserable, or halfway dead. And I've been both." I gave her a small smile, and she offered me a sad one in return. I picked up my brush and started brushing my hair in long strokes.

"Yeah," she said on a sigh. "Rodney might be right, you know. What else do girls like us have but our tits and our asses? And what do we do once those are shot to hell by gravity? Who will want us then?"

No one. No one will.

"And," Kayla went on, "what if we get sick? Who will take care of us? What will we do? Die alone under some overpass?"

What am I gonna do now? Oh, Lord God, what am I gonna do now?

My mama's words. My mama's *experience*. Was that where I was headed, too? A feeling not unlike dread moved down my spine. I dropped the wooden hairbrush and it clattered to the floor. I bent to pick it up, my hands shaking as I snatched it and stood again.

"You okay?" Kayla asked. I glanced at her in the mirror, and her face was wrinkled in concern.

"Yeah," I said, the word rushing out, more breath than sound. "Yeah," I repeated more clearly. I set the brush down and turned to face Kayla.

She sighed again. "I was pregnant once. Did I ever tell you?" I gave her a small shake of my head. She looked down at her hands. "Wayne made me get rid of it." Tears welled up in her eyes. "I didn't want to, but he said he wasn't ready for kids, and he wouldn't stick around if I kept it. So I had an abortion." My belly did a slow flip as if I was going to be sick.

"Oh, Kay, I'm so sorry."

You told me you got an abortion…I didn't want her seven years ago, and I don't want her now.

A tear slipped down her cheek. "It was my own fault. I listened to him. I did what he wanted. I chose him over my own baby. And look where it got me—in the end he left me anyway. I hate myself for what I did, and I'll never forgive myself. My baby would be five years old now."

I sat down next to her on the couch, taking her hands in mine. "You're a good person, Kayla." I didn't know what to say other than that, and so I didn't say more. I just held her hands and squeezed them. She *was* a good person. I wished I could tell her how to forgive herself, but if I knew the answer to that, maybe I'd be a lot better off than I was. I sighed, giving her hands one final squeeze before letting go.

"Let's stop beating ourselves up right now, Kay. This is what Rodney wants us to be doing—going over every way in which we should feel ashamed. Let's not give him this power over us. You lay off the Doritos and call me if you need someone to hang out with, okay? And as far as the gravity stuff, I think we have a little bit of time before it starts stealing our assets." I put my hands on my breasts, plumping them up over my bikini top before winking at her, feigning a nonchalance I didn't feel, trying to cheer her up, even just a little. What I actually felt was breakable, as if I might shatter the moment someone looked at me the wrong way.

Kayla smiled. "Okay. You got an appointment with your boyfriend tonight?"

I raised a brow. "My boyfriend? Hardly. He's just another paying customer."

"Oh, I don't know. I heard a special little something in your voice when you told me about him on the car ride here tonight."

I rolled my eyes, going to the mirror, where I wiped a smudge from beneath my eye. "He pays well." And after tonight, I'd be able to give the garage enough money that they'd start fixing my car.

"Uh-huh. Maybe he'll be the one to sweep you off your feet. Wouldn't you like that? Someone to take care of you?"

"Oh, Kay, life doesn't work that way. And anyway, I take care of myself just fine." I turned to her, feeling a strange ache where my heart lay. The truth was, I found myself thinking of Gabriel Dalton more often than I liked since I'd seen him last. I'd woken to the vision of the gentleness in his eyes, the curve of his lips when he smiled, and then the way he panicked when I'd gotten close. The look on his face as I'd moved toward him had felt like something sharp was pressing against an old bruise deep inside. It had *hurt* seeing him like that. It wasn't that I felt sympathy for him, although that was part of it, but mostly it had hurt *me*, and I couldn't figure out exactly why. It made me feel twitchy and restless. *He* made me feel twitchy and restless.

That's what I need you to help me with. Staying.

I wanted to push those words away. I'd felt embarrassed and exposed when he said them after I'd told him I could help him remove himself mentally from a physical encounter. I'd revealed myself to him, and I hadn't meant to, and now he knew far more about me than I wished him to.

There was a knock on the door, and Anthony stuck his head in. "Gabe's here, Crystal."

"Speak of the devil himself," Kayla said, laughing. *Devil?* No, an angel, just like I'd first thought. And angels didn't belong in hell. What had he said to me? *Funny, I was thinking the very same thing about you.* Why would he think that about me? This *was* where I belonged. And in any case, there was nowhere else to be. *Nowhere.*

I felt like screaming. God, I needed to pull myself out of this... *funk*.

"Thanks, Anthony, I'll be there in a sec." He nodded and shut the door behind him.

Kayla stood. "Well, I've got a dance in fifteen minutes. I gotta go get ready." She hugged me. "Thanks for the talk."

"Anytime," I murmured. Kayla left, shutting the door behind her. I stood there for a few moments, attempting to find my equilibrium, to form that protective shell around myself. Memories of my mother, along with the confusing feelings Gabriel brought up in me, made me feel *raw*, as if I'd turned my skin inside out, and I had the brief, intense desire to cry. *Cry*. The feeling shocked me. When was the last time I'd cried? I really couldn't remember. I wasn't a crier. Why cry when it solved nothing? Why be like *her*? My mother had been a crier. She'd cried all the damn time, and what had it gotten her in the end? Nothing. Absolutely nothing.

I grabbed my sweatshirt and pulled it on over my costume, took a deep, shaky breath, and walked out of my dressing room, toward the lap-dance room. When I opened the door, Gabriel was standing by the couch. He was wearing a T-shirt this time rather than the button-down shirts he wore the first two times he'd been here. In one sweeping gaze, I took in his tanned arms, the contours of his muscles, his broad shoulders—not the efforts of a gym rat, but the slim, defined body of a man who used his muscles as he worked. It surprised me to notice at all. Somewhere along the line, men's bodies had all started looking the same to me. Fat, skinny, well built... what did it matter? They all used them the same way: to inflict pain on others, and to take pleasure for themselves.

Gabriel startled slightly at my abrupt entrance and then

smiled, that warm, open smile that put me on edge. But his smile faded when he saw me. "Hey, is everything all right?"

I realized I was frowning and forced a smile. "Of course."

He brought his hand up and presented a small bouquet of white flowers, holding them out to me. "I brought these for you."

I stared at them for a moment. "You don't have to bring me flowers, sugar. You just have to bring me cash." His smile wilted, and he brought one hand to the back of his neck, massaging it as he grimaced slightly. "I told myself it was a stupid idea. I just passed them as I was walking to my truck and I thought of you."

"You thought of me when you saw flowers?" I scoffed softly. "Well, that's one I haven't heard before."

His cheekbones had taken on a pink tinge. I knew I was embarrassing and hurting him, and something small and mean inside me took satisfaction in it. I tried to hang on to the shallow feeling, but the remorse that rose up instead overwhelmed it, and I turned my face away momentarily so he couldn't see the regret in my eyes. When I turned back, he was setting the flowers down on the arm of the couch. A rejected gift.

"Ready to get started?" My voice sounded empty and sort of hollow.

He paused, his brow creasing. "Sure. But is it okay if we just talk for a little bit?"

I sighed. I was about all talked out. "All right. What do you want to talk about?" I sat down on the couch and he sat down, too, in the same positions we'd started out in the last time.

He smiled, turning toward me and putting his palms on his knees. I studied his hands for a moment, laid out flat like that. I couldn't help thinking how beautiful they were for a man, his fingers long and graceful, his skin smooth and tanned. "How has your day been?"

"Just peachy." I crossed my legs, and his eyes followed the movement. He swallowed, his cheekbones flushing very slightly again. "How about you, sugar? How's your day been going?"

He stared at me for a moment in that assessing way, like he wanted to know all my deepest secrets. Some sort of desperation pooled in my belly. "Not too bad," he finally murmured. "Good now. I'm happy to see you."

I laughed, a shaky sound. "Well, if I'm the best part of your day, it couldn't have been very good, sugar."

His brow creased again and he tilted his head. "Why do you say that?"

I shrugged, examining a fingernail. "Do you want to get started, or not? I hate to waste your therapy time."

"What's wrong? Please tell me."

"Nothing's wrong," I said, but it came out too high-pitched. It sounded wrong and strangely far away. "Please, Gabe, can we just get started? I want to help you."

He studied me again, his expression filled with so much compassion it made me feel raw and vulnerable all over again. Needy. Why did he have to look at me that way? I didn't know how to react to that look. It made me want to run away, hightail it out of this room.

"I want to help you, too," he said softly.

I laughed then, and it sounded cold and bitter, even to my own ears. "But I haven't asked for your help, *Gabe*."

"No, you haven't. But I can be a friend. We could go for coffee and talk. Somewhere other than here."

I shook my head. "You're not my friend. You're a client. And you're paying me." My hands felt shaky, and I pressed them down on the leather couch to the sides of my thighs.

His gaze traveled from my hands to my eyes, and he gave me

a small smile. "Then you can buy *my* coffee. I might even have a slice of pie, too. Your treat." He tilted his head and gazed at me imploringly, so sweetly flirtatious. I stared back, a fluttering between my ribs, knowing somehow that he wasn't even aware of his appeal.

"Coffee? Most men request a threesome. The last time I went out with a guy I met here, he showed up at the restaurant with a friend and they asked if they could take turns doing me in the bathroom. Some sort of fantasy they had going, you know?"

He looked momentarily shocked, and then his expression settled into one of sadness. I had meant to repel and disgust him, not make him feel sad. I looked away.

"I'm not most guys, I guess," he said softly.

No, he definitely wasn't. He couldn't even hold my hand without having a panic attack. Maybe he was the safest man on the planet. So why did he make me feel so *decidedly* unsafe? I picked at my cuticles. When I looked back at him, he was studying me intensely, that same sad look on his face.

"I think you're getting the wrong idea here, Gabe."

He pressed his lips together. "How'd you get that bruise?" he asked, nodding to my cheekbone. I had tried to cover it up with makeup, but it had turned a darker purple in the last couple of days, and apparently he'd spotted it. I put my fingers on it lightly. "Hazard of the job. I hit my cheek on the pole."

He nodded slowly, but didn't look convinced.

"Please can we just get started?"

"All right."

I nodded, one jerky movement of chin to chest, and scooted closer. He stilled and his expression changed slightly, but he didn't move. He held eye contact as I drew nearer, his only reaction to the brush of our thighs a soft intake of breath. My own heart picked up speed, and I felt slightly flushed—the same reaction I'd had to getting closer to him the last time. I didn't like it. I let my mind drift, moving my gaze from his eyes down to his chin, focusing on the very slight cleft, the angle of his jaw, the stubble that was just beginning to grow in. His stubble was dark, with a smattering of gold pieces throughout. If he ever grew a beard, it'd be lighter than his hair...

"Don't leave me," he whispered.

My eyes moved to his mouth just as he finished speaking. "I wasn't going to go anywhere," I murmured, feeling disoriented. Why had he thought that?

"No." He brought his trembling hand up and tipped my chin. "Stay with me here." He stared straight into my eyes. "I need you."

I blinked once, then my eyes locked on his. The force of our connection shocked me, as if he had reached out and touched me in some way I didn't understand, and had certainly never experienced before. His gaze wouldn't release me. He knew I'd gone somewhere else in my mind. *He knew.* That desperate feeling in my belly moved up to my chest, into my throat, and I gasped out loud, finally breaking eye contact.

"What's your name?" he asked quietly. *Stay with me here.* I stood, stumbling away. When I turned, he was standing, too. Panic seized me. He'd asked for my name, but it felt like he was requesting my soul. No, *no.*

He was asking too much, and I had so little to give. I couldn't do this. I couldn't.

"I don't think this is working." I pulled myself straight, attempting to shake off the feeling that had overcome me, the inexplicable desperation coursing through my blood. "I...I don't think I'm the right girl. I'm sorry. I know I accepted the job but—"

He took one step toward me, but no more. "I don't want anyone else except you. You *are* the right girl. Please." He attempted to look in my eyes again, but I avoided eye contact. *I can't...I can't bear it. This, whatever this is. It's too much.* The tension in the room was palpable, the silence awkward and loud. I wanted to put my hands over my ears to block it out. *God, why am I feeling this way?*

I shook my head. "No. I'm sorry. I can't."

"Let's give it one more chance. We can take it more slowly. I—"

No, it *was* too much. *This.* And *him.* And it was worthless because I couldn't help him. He needed someone warm and caring, someone who would nurture him and piece together the broken parts, someone who would look in his eyes and be his calming spirit. I was *not* that girl. I couldn't even begin to piece together all *my* broken parts as I'd lost most of them long ago. I shook my head. "No."

His disappointment felt...*tangible.* I wanted to turn away from it. He sighed and reached into his pocket, drawing out his wallet. He counted out the money and handed it to me. I almost declined—I had hardly earned it, but he must have sensed my reluctance because he pushed it forward. "I insist."

I took it and stuffed it in my bra, forcing a smile, forcing myself to look him in the eye. "I'm sorry this didn't work out. It...it wouldn't be right for me to waste your time or money. There are several other girls here who I can recommend to take my place—"

"No, thank you."

I cleared my throat. "Well, okay. Good luck."

He nodded and stepped past me. I heard the click of the door as he closed it behind him, and something about it brought to mind a cell door shutting.

CHAPTER SEVEN

Don't give up. Everything is possible when you have the right friends.

Shadow, the Baron of Wishbone

GABRIEL

"Fuck," I muttered, tossing the small stone bird aside. I'd just accidentally carved off his beak. I picked up a second piece of marble and sat staring at it for a moment before sighing and reaching for my hammer and chisel. For a few minutes I was able to get lost in the work as I roughed out the shape, but then her face crept back into my mind. I set my tools aside and removed my gloves.

I was too distracted to pay full attention to what I was doing. And stone carving required focus. I grabbed a bottle of water from the mini fridge in my studio and drank half of it.

I...I don't think I'm the right girl.

Why had she felt that? And why couldn't I stop thinking about her? Why couldn't I get that haunted look in her eyes out of my head? It had followed me into my dreams for three nights straight now. *Her panic.* I couldn't shake the feeling that she needed me even more than I needed her. I set the bottle of water down and raked my hands through my hair. *Crystal…Crystal.* I kept coming back to the way our eyes had met that last time, the pure vulnerability in her gaze, the way she'd looked lost and afraid, so desperately lonely. For just a moment, she'd let her walls down, and the tender beauty of it had stunned me. It had felt like the time George had brought me a geode when I was just a kid. On the outside, it'd just looked like a plain old rock, but when he broke it open, it was filled with glittering, purple crystals. I'd been surprised and delighted that such beauty could be contained in something so unexpected.

I kept coming back to that geode whenever I thought about Crystal. In that sense, her name really did fit her. But I also couldn't help wondering if maybe I was just a fool captivated by the first beautiful woman I'd ever touched. Christ, I'd barely even touched her. Her dismissal had hurt me, and in all likelihood, she hadn't given me more than a moment's thought since. And here I was, feeling a cold, sinking sensation when I considered that I'd never see her again. That I'd never have the opportunity to find out more about her.

She doesn't want anything more to do with you, Gabriel.

What had changed, though? The minute we'd connected—and there was no question we had—she pushed me away. *Why?* She had told me she could teach me how to turn off when I felt uncomfortable, so perhaps she'd never learned how to connect. *To stay.* Maybe we were more alike than I'd imagined. Considering where she worked, it was understandable that she set firm boundaries. Boundaries I was trying to push. Maybe I'd been wrong to ask that of anyone, even someone I was paying to do it—but it didn't mean I couldn't be her friend. I massaged the back of my neck as I paced my studio.

Be honest with yourself; you have more than friendly feelings for her.

A stripper. God, what was I *doing?*

What about you, Gabriel? How would people describe you *if they were only going by the few things they knew? If they only met you once, only read the newspaper articles, what would* you *be called?*

Damaged.

Ruined.

Victim.

Sometimes we wore such hurtful, limiting labels in this life, whether they'd been assigned by others or by ourselves. I'd felt damaged and ruined once, but I didn't anymore. I was still a work in progress, but I wasn't a victim. I was a *survivor*.

And Crystal was *more* than just a stripper. More than just a girl who took off her clothes for men. I *knew* she was. I'd seen it in her eyes.

It still didn't mean she wanted anything to do with me.

I was confused and frustrated, and my own thoughts were leading me around in circles, filling me with painful self-doubt. I thought about something my father used to say. *When you can't figure out what to do, Racer, you go with your gut. You might not be right every time, but you'll never regret following your own heart, especially one as pure as yours.* I stopped pacing as a sense of resolve settled over me. I was going to go with my gut. And my gut told me to try again. My gut told me she *needed* me to try again. If I was wrong, I was wrong—but somehow I felt strongly that no one had ever put much effort into *trying* when it came to Crystal. Maybe not even Crystal herself.

I flipped off the lights in my studio, locked up, and walked outside into the warm evening air.

The quarry had shut down for the night, all the workers were gone, and I took a moment to appreciate the stillness surrounding me. A hawk cried out, its caw echoing in the canyon, and the hum of insects rose and fell. A light breeze came up, and I turned my face up into it. God, that felt good after the heat of the last few days. The wind brought with it the smell of pine and earth.

"Hey, dude, you heading home?"

I turned toward Dominic as he approached from the direction of the showroom. "Oh, hey, I thought you'd left by now."

"I had an appointment that went late. An indecisive couple who couldn't agree on anything. Listening to them argue back and forth was like watching table tennis. I need a beer. You up to getting one with me?" He eyed me sideways as we started walking toward our trucks.

"I'm actually already going out."

"I'll come along."

I cleared my throat. "Thanks, Dom, but I'm meeting someone."

We stopped at my truck, and he raised his eyebrows before giving me a slow smile. "Who is she?"

"Just a girl I met recently." Guilt ran through me. I felt like I was deceiving him.

"Well, holy shit. Why didn't you tell me? Aren't brothers supposed to discuss shit like this? I knew you were up to something."

"No." I laughed, opening my truck door. "It's really not anything, but I guess…I guess I'm hoping it can be."

Dominic grinned. "If you need any pointers, you know who to come to."

I raised an eyebrow as I climbed in my truck. He held the door open. "Hey, what about Chloe?"

Chloe. Shit I'd almost forgotten I had an e-mail from her, thanking me for agreeing to the interview, that I still needed to answer. "Chloe is coming here purely on business, Dom. I haven't even met her in person."

"Yeah. I just thought you were hoping—"

"I wasn't hoping anything." Another lie, although I wasn't exactly sure what the truth was anymore.

He put his hands up. "Okay, okay. I can see that your head's been turned elsewhere." He smiled, a sincere one. "Good for you, big bro. Have fun. Don't do anything I wouldn't do."

As if that were even a remote possibility. "Night, Dom." I laughed and closed my truck door and drove out of town, toward the Platinum Pearl, toward Crystal.

*　*　*

I sat through a couple of dances at the Platinum Pearl, but when Crystal didn't come onstage, I asked a waitress if she was working. The girl confirmed she was but that she'd already performed and would be out on the floor soon. I ordered another beer, even though I hadn't finished the first. I also ordered a plate of cheese fries just so the waitress serving my table wouldn't get annoyed.

Fifteen minutes later, my heart leapt when I saw Crystal come through the doors with a tray in her hands. She was wearing the same uniform she'd been wearing the first time I'd talked to her, a tiny pair of "shorts" and a striped top tied between her breasts. I took a moment to watch her without her knowing. Her body moved fluidly even when she was just walking from table to table. She obviously felt comfortable in her own skin, had probably been told often enough she was beautiful. But even from here, I could see she had that same distant look in her eyes, that cynical tilt of her lips.

She bent to put a beer in front of one of the guys at a table in her section, and he ran his hand down the back of her thigh. For just a second, a look of pure disgust moved over her face right before she plastered on a smile and said something that made the guys at the table laugh. *She hates them.* She hates *this.* The thought came sure and swift. God, she probably hated me, too. Another man here to use her in some way or another. The same wave of guilt I'd felt when I first met with her swept through me. I took a long sip of beer, doubting myself all over again for being here. That's when she caught sight of me. She seemed to freeze for a portion of a second, her eyes widening before she turned away, walking through the swinging black doors next to the bar that I assumed was the kitchen entrance. I released a pent-up breath.

A few minutes later, she came back out, heading straight for my table. She set the cheese fries down and smiled at me politely. "Can I get you anything else?"

"Yes." I smiled back, though I still felt uncertain, could feel the blush warming my face. "A cup of coffee. But not just any coffee. Diner coffee. I've never had it before and it's been a lifelong dream to experience it. I was hoping you'd buy me a cup."

She let out a breath. "You and your lifelong dreams."

I grinned. "I've got a few. I bet you do, too."

"*This* is my dream, sugar." She swept her arm around the dim club. "What more could any girl want?" She leaned on the table with one hand, her tray held out to the side with the other. "Stop coming here, Gabriel. This is not the place for you. You don't belong here."

"Neither do you."

"*Stop it.* I'm sorry I couldn't help you. I'm sorry I was the wrong girl. But I don't know why you think I don't belong here, because I do."

"You hate it."

"So what? You're the savior of strippers everywhere who hate their job? I have to make a living, *Gabe*."

I closed my eyes, frustrated with her, but mostly frustrated with myself. I was making a complete mess out of this. "Just coffee, that's all I want." *Just to see you smile.*

"That's not all you want. You want to save me from my intolerable life of pain and misery." She put a hand on her chest in overdone drama. "I'm not a *project*, and I don't want your help."

"I'm not here to fix you. I just want—"

"What *do* you want?"

I let out a sigh, running my hand through my hair. "Just to talk. I like you." *God, could that sound any more lame?* I wanted to grimace at my own feeble attempt to sway her.

She stared at me for a moment, something flickering behind her eyes that I wasn't sure how to read. Whatever it was, she was fighting it. That cynical smirk curved her lips, but there was something shaky about it. "Don't they all?" She stood straight, letting out a tired-sounding exhale. "That's just sexual attraction, Gabe. You'll get over it." She didn't say it meanly, though. Just as if she was sharing a fact she'd learned long ago. Something about it made sadness well up inside me. She started to turn away.

"I'm not giving up on you. I'm coming back."

She shrugged one delicate shoulder. "It's a free country. You do whatever you want. But I suggest you get out of here and go find the right girl."

"What if I still think you're the right girl?"

"Then you're wrong." She turned and walked away.

Fuck!

I spent another twenty minutes nursing my beer, contemplating what she'd said. *Was* I here to fix her? Was that even worse than asking her to help fix *me*?

She didn't return to my table. Her section kept her busy enough, but I knew she was avoiding me, and I wasn't sure I could blame her completely. She went to the back, and when she hadn't emerged ten minutes later, I signed the credit card slip the waitress had brought a few minutes before and started walking away. With a sudden thought, I turned back and used the pen in the bill folder to write my cell phone number on a napkin and then folded it in half and wrote Crystal's name on the front. I almost balled it up—who even knew if she'd get it, and if she did, she'd most likely toss it out. With a sigh, I left it there anyway and turned and walked toward the door.

All the way home, I vowed not to go back again. It was hopeless. *Move on, Gabriel. Let her be, and do what she said. Find someone else.*

* * *

The next day, I helped George in the quarry, directing the machines and trucks that cut and hauled the stone. The physical labor involved in constant hikes from the bottom of the quarry to the top, combined with the nonstop activity, kept me distracted enough that I didn't drive myself crazy with my own thoughts. The crew didn't necessarily need my help, but there was always something to do at the quarry, and I enjoyed the strenuous work at least a couple of times a week. It usually helped inspire creativity the next day— something about putting my body to work and emptying my brain. It was a type of therapy, I supposed. Then again, so was carving.

As I was heading up the hill, George fell in stride beside me.

"Thanks for the help today. Got something on your mind?" He grinned over at me.

George wasn't one to pry, and was a man of few words. I didn't often discuss personal things with him, and he'd never asked me about what I'd experienced in that basement all those years. I knew in my gut he'd talk about it if I brought it up, but I'd never felt the need to, not with him, and I appreciated that he respected that boundary. So when I stopped and turned to him and asked, "George, how do you know when to give up on someone?" he looked mildly surprised.

He paused, looking off behind my shoulder, before turning his wise eyes back to me. "We talking about a female someone?"

I laughed softly. "Maybe."

"Maybe." One side of his lips quirked up in a half smile. "Well, is she giving you any *reason* to be persistent?"

I sighed. "Not so much. But I just, I have this feeling…" My words died. I didn't know how to finish that sentence. This feeling that what? *That she's mine.* The words rose up inside me so strongly I almost stumbled. "This feeling…," I murmured again, feeling both off-balance and somehow energized.

George glanced at me worriedly. "Uh-huh." He paused again, seeming to consider his words. "Well, kid, I guess there's no one answer to that. I think you have to go with your gut."

I smiled. "That's what my dad used to say."

He smiled back. "Yeah, sounds like him." Affection moved over his face at the mention of my dad, his best friend. "I think you should trust yourself, Gabriel. The answers are in here." He tapped a hand over his heart. "Whatever you decide, I have faith it's the right choice." He paused as if he was gathering his next words. "It's not the things you do with love and good intentions that you end up regretting. It's the things you *don't* do that you have to live with. Be honest with yourself about your intentions, Gabriel, and then follow your heart. Regardless of the outcome, you'll never live with regret."

"Thanks, George. I kind of needed that vote of confidence."

"Gabriel, where you're concerned, I'm always confident." He winked and walked away, toward the office.

I went home and took a quick shower, George's words—my *dad's* words—echoing in my head. *Go with your gut.* My *gut* told me to try again with Crystal.

Before I could talk myself out of it, I got in my truck and headed to the Platinum Pearl. I'd told her I wasn't giving up on her. I'd *said* it. Maybe I shouldn't have, but I had. I couldn't make a fool of myself forever. If she never reciprocated the effort, I'd have no choice but to give up eventually, but I was willing to check my pride again to prove to Crystal I hadn't just delivered empty words. I had a feeling Crystal was well acquainted with empty words.

I sat at a different table this time, but one still far back from the stage. All the tables at the front of the room were taken—the men crowded together, anxious to see the dancers up close and personal. A small flicker of jealousy lit inside me at the thought of all the men gaping at Crystal, but I tried my best to extinguish it. I couldn't even get her to have a cup of coffee with me. I had no right to be jealous.

I hoped I had arrived after she'd danced but with enough time to be seated before she came out to serve drinks, and it seemed I had lucked out with my timing. Twenty minutes after I got there, Crystal emerged wearing her waitressing outfit. She stopped in the doorway, an empty tray in her hand. My heart flipped over. A loose braid fell over one shoulder, several pieces of hair already escaping and hanging around her heavily made-up face. She looked both innocent and far, far too knowing at the same time. A complete paradox.

I felt somewhat anonymous as I watched her from the crowded room, sitting in a place she wouldn't necessarily expect. I hadn't meant to set things up so I could watch her without her seeing me, but as it turned out, that's just what I was able to do. She seemed to make it a point not to look at the table I usually sat at, but I watched as she moved into the room, and I saw the moment her eyes darted quickly to that table and then lingered on the guys who were sitting there. Something bleak seemed to come into her eyes, a sort of knowing apathy as if she'd figured I wouldn't be there and it confirmed her low expectations. Or was I reading too much into one fleeting expression?

Trust yourself. Go with your gut.

She turned my way, and when our eyes met, I saw her jerk slightly, so slightly, but I'd seen it. She blinked once and then sauntered my way, stopping in front of my table. I wanted to stand, but I had no reason to do that, so I looked up at her, feeling awkward and shy—knowing that just by being here I was asking her to hurt me, and yet not being able to stop myself. Coming back here—it felt irrational and illogical and foolish and *right*.

"You're back," she noted dully.

I attempted a charming smile, but had a sneaking suspicion it looked more like a self-conscious grimace. "I am."

"I'm still not the right girl."

"I still don't agree."

She sighed, turning her hand over and studying her nails for a moment as if I might very well be the most tedious person she'd ever dealt with. "The other girls have been asking about you, you know. They'd like a chance to get you alone in a room." She swept her arm around. "You have your pick. Seriously."

I frowned. "I made my pick. You."

Her lips formed a thin line. "It didn't work out."

"It *did* work out. That's what you're afraid of. Why?"

Her eyes narrowed. "I needed money to pay for car repairs. I got what I needed and now I'm done. I found it…distasteful."

A spear of hurt ripped a jagged path down my spine, causing me to wince. She watched me, and though her expression remained unaffected, her face paled slightly. "Just go, please," she said, her voice cracking on the last word, right before she whirled away.

I took a deep breath, running my fingers through my hair, feeling sad and foolish. *Crystal.*

I watched her serve a few tables, her smile seeming even more hesitant than usual, her laugh more forced. *You're an idiot, Gabriel. She told you to leave. Go.*

I finished my beer and paid my tab, finally walking back to the hallway where Anthony was sitting on his stool. I was going to give this one final chance and then this was it. He nodded at me.

"Will you tell Crystal I'm here?"

"She didn't give me word she'd see you tonight, man."

"Will you ask her anyway?"

Anthony looked at me and nodded slowly, surprising me with the sympathy that came into his eyes. As if he'd been in situations like this a hundred times with poor saps who came to this club, and fell in love with one of the girls, and were turned away. *Typical*, his look said. Sad, but typical. "Sure thing, buddy," he said, standing and walking leisurely down the hall. I put my hands in my pockets and waited.

When he came back two minutes later, he motioned to me. "Come on back." I startled, shocked. I had been expecting to say thanks to Anthony and walk to my truck. Hope soared in my chest. I followed him to the same purple-curtained room I'd met her in before and smiled at Anthony as he pushed the door open for me, nodding once before closing it again.

I rubbed my hands together, the hope suddenly mixing with nervousness. She was giving me one more chance, and I didn't want to mess it up. I didn't want to squander this opportunity, because this was it. I couldn't come back after this—I was already skating the thin line between *persistent* and *stalker*. It could be argued that I'd already crossed it. *Christ.* I groaned aloud because it was true and the noise broke the silence of the room. There was a light knock on the door, and I frowned slightly because Crystal had never knocked before.

"Come in," I called.

The door opened and a woman with short, spiky, scarlet-colored hair, wearing a black leather teddy of sorts and fishnet stockings walked in. "Hey, handsome." She smiled, bright red lips parting to show white but slightly crooked teeth.

"Hi. Uh, I'm sorry but I was waiting for Crystal."

She walked to the sound system, pressing some buttons before turning. A loud, seductive beat filled the room. "Crystal's not available. She sent me. My name's Rita."

"She sent you?" I asked, my voice barely a whisper over the music. *Why would she do that?* She knew I wouldn't want anyone else—knew I'd be unable to *tolerate* anyone else. Ah, God, that's exactly *why* she'd done it. I told myself it was unreasonable to feel so hurt, and yet I felt it all the same. A sick feeling of betrayal.

"Yup." She moved quickly toward me, pushing me backward onto the couch. I sat down with a startled intake of breath, and before I realized what was happening, she was on top of me, straddling my lap. My head filled with fog, a red, pulsing alarm.

She leaned forward and rubbed her breasts in my face, the cloying sweetness of perfume mixed with the musk of unwashed skin. She smelled...dirty.

He'd smelled dirty.

Can't breathe.

My heart rate jumped erratically, and I turned my face away, cold panic sweeping through me at her unwanted touch. *Run! Fight!*

I pushed at her and she let out a surprised yelp as she fell to the side, landing on the couch next to me awkwardly. I scrambled up, my breath coming out in harsh gasps. "God, I'm sorry, I'm so sorry."

She glared at me. "What's your problem? You don't like girls, or something?"

I ran a hand through my hair, fighting to draw in air. "It's not you, it's not—" I needed to go. I was sweating and shaking and I felt nauseated. "I'm sorry," I repeated, practically running toward the door. I flung it open and stumbled into the hall. Anthony looked up as I approached, his brow furrowing. I looked away. He didn't say anything, just leaned back as I passed him.

As I was heading toward the outside door, Crystal appeared to my right, still in her waitressing uniform, holding a tray of drinks, having obviously come from the bar. She stopped in her tracks, her eyes growing wide as she took me in. The shame in her expression was little comfort to me in that moment. She turned her head and looked at the floor.

I looked away, passing by her, pushing the door open, and bursting out into the parking lot.

Air.

Space.

Freedom..

CHAPTER EIGHT

Well, now you're in a fix, worst of your life. Are you going to make it better? Or make it worse?

Gambit, the Duke of Thieves

CRYSTAL

I hadn't thought it was possible to hate myself any more than I already did. But seeing Gabriel fleeing the Platinum Pearl with a look of horror on his face proved me wrong. I'd done that to him. I'd set him up to face his worst nightmare. After he'd already suffered so greatly. I was cruel and selfish—a worthless bitch. If anyone deserved to be hurt, it was *me*.

It was just...it was just that he wouldn't stop coming back, wouldn't stop badgering me. *Stop trying to justify it to yourself. Just stop.* The real truth was that his unrelenting presence made me hope for things I'd given up on long ago, and the reminder of my own forgotten dreams had hurt in a way nothing had hurt in a very long time. The groping, the leering, being used, the dismissals, none of that hurt like Gabriel Dalton asking me to have coffee with him. *Why?* It was like he was dangling this delicious morsel of food in front of me—but directly out of reach—and I was hungry. God, I was starving. And he'd caused me to dwell on that, and it felt like a slow torture, the final crumbling of the very last intact piece of my heart. I knew that sort of hunger. I'd repressed it for so many years. Now I wanted things I could never, ever have. And I was tired, God, I was so tired of this empty life I led.

I sat at the top of my steps waiting for Kayla to arrive. My car was still in the shop but finally being worked on now that I'd paid my past-due bill. Thankfully, the part needed to fix it this time wasn't too expensive. Still two hundred and fifty dollars I didn't have, but I'd be able to come up with it if I was late with the rent next month. The vision of a notice stuck to a front door moved through my mind, my stomach clenching with the memory.

What am I gonna do now? Oh, Lord God, what am I gonna do now?

Bleakness fell over me as if the memory were a heavy, wet blanket. I attempted to shrug it off, but couldn't manage it. Not today, not with Gabriel's tormented expression sitting in the front of my mind.

My apartment was at the top of a three-story set of outdoor steps. What had once been a single-family home had been separated into three apartments, the set of rickety wooden steps to mine on the back side of the building. I gazed down at the concrete area below, the small parking lot that had once perhaps been a grassy area where children played. There were several small puddles from the rain that had fallen the night before, and another memory came to me. Mrs. Hollyfield holding my hand as I laughed and jumped from one puddle to another, splashing her with dirty water.

I closed my eyes for a moment, trying to block out the

onslaught of emotion. God, why were all these memories, all these *words* suddenly running through my mind? I'd pushed them all away for so long and now, for some inexplicable reason, it was like they'd all shown up at my door at the very same time demanding to be let in, demanding I look at them when I really didn't want to.

Still, the memory of the rain puddles persisted. I swore I could feel the cold water as it leaked through the holes in the bottoms of my secondhand rain boots, sense the distant rush of joy as Mrs. Hollyfield scolded me through her laughter and then pulled me into the comforting softness of her side and kissed the top of my head. I remembered gasping at the rainbows floating at the tops of the puddles as if they were magical, and Mrs. Hollyfield had agreed and told me there was magic everywhere if you were just willing to see it. I'd learned later that those rainbows were really nothing more than dirty oil floating on the surface of the water. And I'd felt deceived. What had seemed magical was really nothing more than grime. There was a metaphor somewhere in there about the direction my life had gone, but I was too weary to try to figure it out.

Sitting there, I felt the sadness that still lived inside me at the long-ago loss of Mrs. Hollyfield. I wondered how different my life might have been if she hadn't died. But she had. Because that's what people did. They died, they left without so much as a goodbye—eventually they all went away. If you got attached, if you hoped for love, it was your own stupid fault and you deserved the consequences.

Kayla's car pulling into the lot snapped me out of my grim thoughts, and I stood, descending the steps.

"Hey there," I said, sliding into the passenger seat of Kayla's junky white Chevy. Her car was in even worse shape than mine, which was a true feat. I rested my elbow on the ledge of the open window as the car sputtered its way out of the parking lot.

"Thank God it's cooler," Kayla said, the cross breeze from the open windows streaming in as the car picked up speed. I just nodded.

After a few minutes of silence, Kayla asked, "You okay?"

"Yeah, I'm fine. I think I just need a break. Thankfully this is my last shift before I have a couple of days off. Just...I don't know, burnt out."

Kayla sighed. "Aren't we all?"

"Yeah, I guess so."

We arrived at the Platinum Pearl and both went to our dressing room to change and get made up. I felt like I was partially numb, merely going through the motions, which wasn't exactly new. But I also felt both shaken somehow and especially tired.

"Hey, Crystal," Rita said, walking into our dressing room a few minutes after Kayla had left. I hated nights like this where the three of us who shared the room were all working. I felt like there was nowhere I could be by myself, even for a minute or two. Some nights those minutes were the difference between keeping a smile plastered to my face and being the bitch Rodney had accused me of being.

"Hey, Rita." I went back to applying powder over the foundation I'd just spread over my face.

"Think my boyfriend will be back tonight to give me another try?" Rita smirked.

Anger flashed through my system, but I kept my expression placid. Plus, the anger wasn't really directed at Rita. It was directed at myself. "Doubt it."

"What's wrong with him anyway? Man that good-looking doesn't like girls? A shame, isn't it?"

"Who said he doesn't like girls?"

"He acted like he was scared to death that I'd even touched him. Started breathing all crazy. I couldn't tell at first if he was scared or turned on." Sick shame moved through me slowly. I pretended concentration, attaching my false eyelashes, leaning toward the mirror and focusing intently on what I was doing. But my hands had started to shake, and I threw the lashes down. Useless. The lash strip lay on the table in front of me, looking like a sad, dead spider.

"I guess he just didn't like you," I tossed at her nonchalantly.

Rita glanced over at me as she pulled on a pair of bikini bottoms. She turned around and inspected her ass in the mirror. I looked away as she began adjusting her G-string. She spanked her firm, unblemished backside and laughed. "Nope. That can't be it." She laughed again. "But I'm willing to give him another chance to work up the nerve to enjoy my assets. Man that fine deserves at least one more. So tall and hard all over. Nice big…hands and feet. Mmm." She winked, and I found myself wanting to literally kick her out of the room.

"Enough, Rita," I said, and my voice sounded overly hostile. Or perhaps it conveyed exactly what I was feeling.

Rita looked at me sharply. "What?" she whined. "You gave him to me."

"I didn't give him to you," I snapped, picking up the lash strip again. "He's not mine to give."

"Hmm," she said, looking at me thoughtfully as I again attempted to apply the lash strip, having more success this time. "You seem upset, Crystal. What's the matter?"

"Nothing's the matter. That man just annoys me. I'm glad he won't be back."

She gave me a fake sounding laugh. "Okay. Whatever you say.

If you don't want him, someone else will scoop him up quickly enough."

Yes. Yes, that was true. And it was what I wanted. And it was what he needed, whether he was too stupid to realize it or not. I felt slightly better as I finished attaching the second lash strip, standing to get dressed.

Rita sat down on the couch and started buckling her heels. "He looks familiar, too," she said. "I think he might have gone to school with my older sister. I think she dated him in middle school."

No, he was locked in a basement when he should have been in middle school. The thought made my throat feel tight, but I nodded to Rita, murmuring a noncommittal response. "Do you see my white heel?" I asked after a moment, looking around. I wanted to get off this topic. I didn't want to talk about Gabriel Dalton anymore. I didn't want to *think* about Gabriel Dalton anymore.

"Yeah, it's over there by the door."

"Thanks." I picked up my shoe and we started talking about the music we were using that night, and five minutes after that, she headed out the door for her first dance. I used the fifteen minutes I had before I performed to try to get my head on straight. I tried to move my thoughts somewhere other than Gabriel, other than the shame I still felt, other than shy smiles and then the final look of shocked betrayal. But it didn't work. It didn't even come close.

* * *

I only had about an hour left before my shift was over when I approached a table of three young, college-aged-looking guys of the variety I supposed most women would find attractive. They obviously worked out and made sure the world noticed with their tight T-shirts, short sleeves rolled up to showcase as much bicep as possible. I threw a round of cocktail napkins on the table. "What can I get you, boys?"

"You," the brown-haired guy with the extremely square jaw said, ogling me. *Go to hell.*

"Same here," the blond with the short beard agreed, staring at my breasts. "I'll have a *large* serving." His eyes were glassy, and he'd obviously already been overserved.

I smirked. "Well now, there's plenty of me to go around, boys. Come back three nights from now and I'll carve out some time for a personal dance just for the both of you." I winked.

The third guy—the one with spiky black hair who was leaning back negligently in his chair—laughed, tipping himself forward. "I'll get in on that action." He shot me what I'm sure he imagined was a charming smile.

"What if we don't want to wait? What if we want you tonight?" the brunet interrupted, reaching out and giving my ass a hard squeeze. I gritted my teeth. *God, this is tiresome.*

"I'm sorry, the club is closing in an hour, sugar, but there's time for another round of drinks. What'll you have?" I glanced around at them, trying to keep the irritation from my voice.

"Guess we'll just have to *take* what we want," the blond said, pulling me onto his lap and palming my breast. "You like that, baby?" he whispered, planting his face against my neck, his beard scratchy, and his moist breath hot against my skin. "I can tell you do."

I let out a surprised squeak and struggled to get up. *Where the hell is Anthony?* The man held me down. I felt his erection under my ass as he thrust upward, grinding it into me. *Grinding. Pulling.*

Reaching. Taking. Like every other man before him. And like all the men to come…except Gabriel Dalton. Why the simple honesty of his smile came to my mind—his *hesitant* touch, the *respectful* tone in his voice—I had no idea. This was the regular game. *I knew the game.* Yet, the contrast between Gabriel and *this* man inspired some sort of immediate, almost irrational rage within me.

I glanced around at the laughing, leering men, the guy whose lap I was sitting on taking every liberty he wanted. Hatred overcame me suddenly and swiftly—loathing that felt limitless and unending—and I raised my hand and slapped his face so hard, his head jerked backward. He let go of me and I leapt to my feet, stumbling away, shocked by my own behavior. I'd never hit anyone in my life. His friends started laughing like fiends, pointing at the man I'd slapped.

"You fucking bitch," he grated between clenched teeth, his hand moving to his cheek.

"What's going on here, gentlemen?" *Anthony.* I spun toward him.

"Where were you?" I asked, an edge of panic obvious in my voice.

"Taking a piss. Sorry, girl." He turned back to the men. "Out," he said. "Don't make me drag you."

The blond-haired guy pointed at me, his eyes glittering with humiliation. "That two-bit whore slapped me!"

"That's it," Anthony said, picking the guy up by the collar of his T-shirt.

"Okay, okay," the brunet said, standing and weaving slightly. "We were leaving anyway. Calm the fuck down."

I spun away from the whole scene, making my way to the back, where I threw my tray down and stood against a counter for a few minutes, catching my breath and attempting to rein in my shaky rage.

"You all right, Crys?" Janet asked, coming up behind me and patting me on the shoulder. "Those guys are real assholes."

I laughed shortly. "Yeah, I am, and yeah, they are."

"Let it slide off your back, babe. Just another night. Same ol', same ol'."

"Yeah. Thanks, Janet." I drew in a deep breath, feeling so exhausted I contemplated sliding down to the floor right there. That pinched feeling around my heart was back, and I just wanted to go home.

"Oh, hey," Janet said, turning back to me. "I almost forgot since I was off yesterday, but this was left for you on one of the tables night before last. I was going to throw it away to save you the trouble, but I remember him and he was real cute." She smiled, winked, and handed me a folded-up napkin.

Smiling weakly at Janet, I took it, and as she walked away, I opened it up to see Gabriel's name and what I assumed was his cell number. An ache shot to my heart, a strange longing filled with an equal amount of remorse, and I balled it up and stuck it in the small pocket in my server's apron where I kept money to provide change.

By the time I went back out onto the floor, the guys who had been harassing me were gone, back home to their girlfriends, no doubt. Janet was right. Same ol', same ol'.

I finished up the last half hour serving a few more drinks to men who were thankfully well behaved. When I was done, I cashed out, hesitating when I pulled the folded-up napkin from my pocket. I balled it up and held it in my fist, intending to throw it away, and went to find Kayla, who had just finished onstage. "You ready?" I grabbed my sweatshirt and pulled it on over my serving outfit. I didn't even want to bother to change clothes tonight. I'd take a long hot shower and attempt to wash away the despair currently sticking to my skin along with the greasy fingerprints of the jerks who had manhandled me.

Kayla was undressing and turned my way. "Yeah. Just give me five. I heard what happened on the floor. You okay?"

"Yeah." I waved my hand through the air as if it'd been nothing. And in reality, it was. That type of thing had happened a hundred times before and would likely happen a hundred times again. "I'm fine. I'll meet you at the front door."

"Okay. I'll grab Anthony on my way there."

I nodded, closing the dressing room door behind me. I grabbed my purse from my locker and headed toward the front. I heard a commotion coming from the floor and glanced in to see Anthony breaking up another fight, this time between two girls. *Jesus Effing Christ.* Would this night never end?

It was policy that security walk us girls to our cars, and under normal circumstances, I'd have waited for Anthony to finish settling the situation he was dealing with. But tonight…deep weariness washed through me, and I turned back toward the front door, pushing out into the summer night air. It smelled like asphalt and rain, and I headed toward Kayla's car. I couldn't be inside the Platinum Pearl for one more ungodly second.

"Hey, bitch."

My heart stuttered and I whirled toward the voice. The man I'd slapped earlier stepped out of the darkness of the trees that grew along the back of the parking lot, his friends behind him, both looking nervous but excited and still drunk. I sucked in a breath, alarm making me feel suddenly weak. I glanced at Kayla's car and then back at the door. Kayla's car was closer, but I didn't have the keys. *Oh, shit.*

"Not so brave now, are you?"

I turned, facing him fully. I squeezed my fists together at my

sides, feeling the small piece of balled-up napkin. As I stood
there looking at the man who'd spoken, it felt like the final piece
of my will dissolved into nothing, evaporating into the night air
of the Platinum Pearl parking lot. I didn't care what he did to
me. God, I just didn't care. I squeezed the napkin in my grip
more tightly. Those kind angel eyes flashed through my mind
again, bringing shame, but also peace. I deserved whatever these
guys were about to dish out. I deserved it. But before I endured
it, I was going to let them know what I really thought of them.
I smiled. It felt serene. At my expression, a flicker of confusion
crossed over the face of the leader of their little group. "You
know what I think of you?"

"I don't give a fuck what you think of me."

"No, I know you don't *care*. I do know that. I just wonder if
you know. If you can even imagine."

He laughed, a taunting sound. "The only thing I care about is
you apologizing to me by sucking my dick."

I just smiled again. It felt unreal, as if I was nothing more than
the two-dimensional caricature of a woman. Numbness trickled
through me like a welcome sedative. It didn't matter. *Nothing*
mattered. They were going to do whatever they were going to
do to me, and there was nothing I could do about it. And if
not them, someone next week, or the week after that. In a back
room somewhere, in a truck pulled off the highway, in a bed, or
in a dark parking lot. They'd never stop taking from me. *Ever.*
"You're vile," I said evenly. "All three of you are revolting. The
only reason I even let you look at me is because you pay me for
the pleasure. You're not even men—you're ugly, repulsive animals, and your very smell makes me want to vomit." I spat on
the ground and then plastered on the same, uncaring smile.

"You bitch," the blond said slowly, a note of disbelief in his voice as if he couldn't fathom someone like me insulting them. "You bitch."

"Intelligent, too," I said. "What a complete package you are. Ugly *and* stupid."

The black-haired guy tipped just a bit, catching himself and laughing softly. "Hey guys, let's just go. This bitch isn't worth it."

For one hopeful second, I thought they'd leave. My shoulders relaxed slightly, and that's when the one with the brown hair let out an angry grunt and moved forward so quickly I didn't have time to react. He grabbed me and shoved his hand over my mouth, dragging me backward. "Fuck this bitch. She's going to get what she deserves," he growled.

What she deserves, what she deserves...

Instinct made me try to bite him, but his palm was flat against my mouth, and I couldn't get a grip. I attempted to kick, but the blond picked up my feet. They walked me quickly behind the nearby Dumpster, and the one holding my upper body forced me to my knees, shoving my face in the blond's crotch. I *could* get a grip with my teeth there, and so I bit down as hard as I could. My mouth was mostly filled with jean fabric, but I must have gotten some skin, too, because he let out a pained squeal right before I was yanked back and a fist smashed into my face. "Goddamn *fuck*!" he yelled. I felt something jab my side, a foot or maybe a knee, and I cried out from the sudden blow, the asphalt coming up to meet me.

"Hey, guys, wait, this...," I heard the guy with black hair say, but his two friends were too far gone—on alcohol and scorched pride—to listen to him. I was rolled over and before my vision had cleared, another punch took me by surprise. The world swam, colors bursting in front of my eyes. Everything seemed to be happening so fast. They were everywhere, holding me down, attacking me. One leaned over me and another held my legs as I tried to kick.

Whoever had been holding my legs let go, and I felt my sweatshirt being yanked up. I took the opportunity to kick out, connecting with someone. He yelled and swore harshly, and a horrible pain exploded in my right leg. I tried to scream, but something made of fabric was being stuffed in my mouth. I gagged, taking another blow, feeling my shorts being worked down my legs. I fought, but there were two of them and they were so much stronger. I didn't know where the third guy was, but he wasn't helping me. For all I knew, he was waiting his turn. The darkness closed in again, and this time, I let it overtake me, floating away, away, away, to where there was no more hurt, no more pain, only peace.

I came to blearily, hearing sirens in the distance, voices close by, yelling, sounding panicked. So many of them. *A chorus*. The stars were so bright above me, and there was only motion and light and a gentle whooshing in my ears.

Suddenly I was being moved. I thought I was traveling but didn't know where and didn't care. There was a loud wailing noise all around me, and I floated away once more.

When I opened my eyes again, I squinted, the lights above far too bright, as if I'd moved closer to the starlight. There were people in white around me, all hazy and indistinct. Then someone was standing over me, holding my hand as we moved, his breathing quick and loud right next to my face. Was I really floating? I shifted my gaze slowly toward whoever was right next to me and saw those angelic eyes. *Gabriel.* My breath hitched. *Those beautiful eyes.* Only now they were filled with something that looked like grief. *Why?* Everything was okay— I was in heaven where the streets were paved with gold. He stroked a hand over my hair. "Oh, sweetheart, I'm so—" He gasped as if the words had gotten stuck in his throat. "You're going to be okay. Just don't move."

The lights sparkled, and the air itself shimmered. There was a golden halo around his head. He was so beautiful. The most beautiful man I'd ever seen. I tried to smile, but my face didn't seem to be working. "I knew you were an angel," I whispered. "I knew you were." I reached my hand up and cupped his cheek, catching a tear on my thumb. "Don't cry, my angel. Don't cry. Not for me." *Never for me.*

Speaking made me feel so tired. I closed my eyes and let the darkness take me again.

CHAPTER NINE

Shh, darling. I know it hurts, but your body knows how to heal.
And so does your heart.

Lemon Fair, the Queen of Meringue

GABRIEL

The hospital waiting room was dim and quiet, empty except
for me. I sat on an uncomfortable vinyl-covered chair, leaned
back against the wall, my gaze directed at the ceiling. The TV
mounted to the wall had a cartoon on, the sound turned so low it
was barely background noise.

I heard a door open somewhere down the hall and brought
my head straight, looking toward the entrance of the waiting
room. I heard the clack of heels on the floor, and a few seconds later, the woman I recognized from the Platinum Pearl, the
woman who I now knew was named Kayla, burst into the room.
Her wide eyes fixed on me. "Sorry it took me so long to get here.
Any news?"

I shook my head. "No, not yet. I think they're still checking
her injuries." My heart contracted again, and I rubbed at my

chest as if that might help. I couldn't get the picture of her beaten face out of my mind as they'd rolled her down the hall to X-ray, the small smile that had curved her bloodied, swollen lips when she saw me. She'd touched my face and I had barely noticed, so sick with grief to see what had been done to her. *She called me her angel.* The horror of seeing her that way was still coursing through my blood—making me feel sick and filled with fury. When Kayla had called me, she said the men who'd attacked Crystal had run off when Anthony came outside, and he'd tried to follow them, but turned back to help Crystal instead. It must have felt like an impossible choice for him. But I was glad he'd done what he did, because what if leaving her there to go after them was the difference between life and death? I blew out a pent-up breath.

"Thank you so much for calling me, Kayla."

She nodded, biting at her lip and getting red lipstick on her teeth. "I wasn't sure it was the right thing to do, but I sat with her while we all waited for the ambulance, and even though Crystal was unconscious, she still had your number balled in her fist." She shook her head sadly. "All through what those men did to her, she never let go. She held on to it. It must mean something, you know? And I thought...well, Crystal doesn't have many friends. If she doesn't want you here, though, she'll tell you. Crystal can be real blunt."

I managed a small chuckle. "Yeah, I've noticed that."

Kayla sunk down into a chair. I'd driven straight to the hospital after receiving Kayla's call and arrived half an hour after they'd brought Crystal in. I didn't have any details of the attack—just what Kayla had told me on the phone. Kayla shook her head, and tears welled in her eyes. "This is awful, just awful," she choked. "Poor Crystal. Oh, poor Crystal."

I glanced at her, wondering if even she, this woman who seemed to be a friend to Crystal, knew her real name. I didn't ask. "Did anyone inside the club know the men who did this?"

She shook her head. "Not their names, but a few girls were able to give enough information for the police to follow up on. And Anthony gave a description of their truck, though he didn't see the license plate." I nodded. Thank God Anthony had come outside when he did.

The doctor who had been with Crystal's gurney when I'd first arrived entered the room, and I stood quickly, my heart stuttering. Kayla stood, too, as the doctor walked toward us. "I'm Dr. Beckstrom."

"Doctor. Gabriel Dalton." His eyes lingered on me for a moment as if he might recognize me, or perhaps just my name, before he simply nodded, turning to Kayla, who introduced herself as well.

"Are either of you family?"

I shook my head. "We're both friends." I wasn't even really that.

"I see. Does she have family on the way?"

I looked over at Kayla and she shook her head. "Crystal doesn't have any family—at least not that she's ever talked about."

The doctor's lips thinned in what appeared to be sympathy. "Crystal…"

"That's what she goes by."

He nodded. "Okay, well, I can give you information about her condition. If you *are* able to contact a family member, you can pass it along to them."

Fear was moving up my throat. I wasn't sure I wanted to hear what he was about to tell us. "Is she okay?" I blurted out.

He turned his eyes to me. "She's not now, but she will be."
I blew out a breath, running my hand through my hair as he
continued. "She has several broken ribs, and her leg is fractured.
We just finished casting it. Those are the most serious injuries.
The good news is, there isn't any internal bleeding, and her facial
wounds won't cause permanent damage. She'll experience pain
for some time, and her walking will be impeded for even longer.
She took quite a beating."

Kayla made a squeaky sound. "Doctor, was she…I mean, her
shorts were removed and…" I winced at that information, sick
dread sliding slowly down my spine to pool heavily in the pit of
my stomach. *Oh God.*

"It doesn't appear that she was sexually assaulted, no. But her
pants being removed indicates they may have simply been interrupted before they got to that." His eyes were full of weary
compassion, the expression of a man used to delivering news that
was hard to hear. I exhaled a sharp breath of relief at the knowledge that she hadn't been violated, at least not in that way. "If
you want to come back and see her, you may. She's sleeping,
though, and that's what she needs to be doing now, so please be
very quiet."

"Yes, we'd like to see her, Doctor, thank you," Kayla said,
glancing at me. I took another deep breath. I couldn't seem to
take in enough oxygen, ever since Kayla's call.

We walked through the quiet halls. I remembered being in a
hospital similar to this one another time, remembered the stares
of the nurses, the whispers, the wide-eyed doctors who examined
me, the questions, so many questions when all I wanted was to
see my parents. I turned my mind away from that immediately.
I didn't need to be thinking about myself right now.

The doctor let us into a dim room, the sound of a heart

monitor beeping steadily. As we moved closer, my heart lurched. She looked better than she had when I saw her being wheeled through the hall, but still so horribly beaten, so terribly broken.

Kayla sniffled softly and ran a finger over the top of Crystal's hand, the only part of her that looked to be mostly untouched by trauma. We stood for a few minutes looking down at her and then I turned, needing to collect myself, wanting to let Crystal sleep, to heal. *How could anyone do this to her?* Three men on one woman? Jesus Christ.

I exited the room quietly, and a moment later, Kayla followed behind me. "I have to get home and sleep a little bit. I'll come by in the morning. Will you be back?" she asked.

"Yeah. I'll be back." Kayla nodded, giving me a sad smile and turning toward the elevators. I watched her walk away and then turned, sitting on the plastic chair outside Crystal's room. She might tell me to leave tomorrow, but on the off chance Crystal woke up before morning came, or before Kayla got back, I didn't want her to be by herself. I knew what it was like to wake up scared, injured, and alone, and I couldn't stomach it happening to someone else—not if I could prevent it.

A shiver of regret ran down my spine when I thought how close I'd come to getting in my truck and driving to the Platinum Pearl. That dream...I couldn't get the dream out of my head. I'd gone to bed early, no intention of going back to Havenfield anytime in the foreseeable future. I'd given it my best shot and I'd failed with Crystal. I'd fallen asleep and dreamed of my parents, the same dream I'd had so long ago, the same dream that had been so vivid and prompted me to follow through with my plan to get out of that basement.

Only this time, instead of just looking at me with encouragement, my mother had handed me a geode, the crystals inside sparkling in the light that shone down, rainbows glittering in the air around her. I'd woken with a start, the only thought in my head to get to Crystal. But I'd lain there unmoving, and the more my mind had cleared, the more ridiculous I felt. *What the hell did I think I would do when I arrived?* Tell her I had to try just one last time despite her clear rejection? One last desperate attempt to change her mind? Because of a *dream*? For the love of Christ. She was going to think I should be committed. And so instead, I'd forced myself to go back to sleep. But God, if I'd just listened to my own intuition instead of my ego…

My mind drifted back to the moment I'd been woken again, this time by the ringing of my phone.

The distant sound of a siren wailed in the background. I blinked the sleep from my eyes and propped myself on my elbow, a frisson of fear moving through me despite my drowsy confusion. "Hello?" When there was only silence, I repeated myself, pressing the phone to my ear.

There was a rustling on the other end and then a tear-drenched voice said, "My name's Kayla. I know you don't know me, but Crystal's been hurt real bad and…I think she needs you."

I think she needs you.

"Would you like a pillow, sir? You could at least lean your head back against it."

I opened my eyes, jolted from the memory of earlier that night by a kindly-looking nurse.

I smiled. "Yes, that would be great."

"Okay. Visiting hours are over, you know, but I don't think any of us will kick you out." She winked. "I'll be right back."

I smiled gratefully at her, and when she'd gone, I brought my phone from my pocket and sent Dom a quick text telling him I'd be home the next day, not to worry, and I'd explain when I got there. I turned my phone off, not waiting for a response. I assumed he was sleeping anyway.

The sound of the television at the nurse's station droned softly in the background, drifting down the hall to where I sat. My ears perked up when I heard the name Wyatt Geller in the deep, monotonous voice of a newscaster, but then my heart dropped when I heard the words *still no news* following his name. I sagged back in the chair. *Christ.* I stuffed my hands in my pockets and stretched my legs out in front of me, leaning back against the hard wall.

Behind me a broken girl lay sleeping, and somewhere out there, a little boy was experiencing what was unimaginable to most. But not to me.

* * *

I woke with a start, the sound of voices and shuffling feet growing louder. I sat up, rubbing my eyes, getting my bearings. It was morning, and the next nursing shift was just arriving. I stood up, stretching my sore muscles. A nurse was just heading into Crystal's room, and I followed along behind her, peeking in. Crystal was still sleeping, her hands in the exact same position they'd been in the night before. She hadn't moved a muscle. I stepped back out, going to the men's room, where I attempted to clean myself up a bit.

When I got back to Crystal's room, the nurse was gone. I took a seat in the chair by Crystal's bed and glanced at the magazines in a rack on the wall but knew I wouldn't be able to concentrate on reading.

The morning light grew brighter in the room, and for a while I simply stared at the increasing glow slanting through the blinds.

Light. Hope.

When I glanced at Crystal, her eyes were blinking open, causing me to draw in a quick breath. I stood, going immediately to her side. She stared up at me, her gaze confused and hazy. I managed a small smile, though looking down into her bruised and swollen face made my heart ache. "Morning," I whispered.

She shook her head slightly as if attempting to wake from a dream she thought she was still in. It was obvious she was a little drugged, bleary. "Where—?"

"You're in the hospital. Do you remember...?"

By the widening of her eyes, I could tell that it was coming back to her. I saw her expression shift through confusion, dawning memory, and finally, fear. She searched my face, blinking rapidly. "You're going to be okay. There are no permanent injuries." The fear in her gaze diminished minutely.

I grabbed the water pitcher from the bedside table and poured her a glass, turning and holding it up in question. She took a shuddery breath and nodded. I brought the straw to her lips, and she took several sips before turning away.

I withdrew the cup and set it on the bedside table. She was staring at me when I turned around, her eyes still wary, but softer now. "You're back," she whispered, her voice breathy and rough at the same time.

I let out an exhale on a small, thankful laugh. "I am."

She searched my face. "I'm still not the right girl."

"I still don't agree."

Her eyes softened even more, the swollen corners tilting slightly as if she might be smiling. My heart turned over in my chest.

"How...?"

"Kayla called me."

She looked confused, though not angry, and I was about to explain, when the door opened suddenly and I looked behind me, seeing the same doctor from last night. I couldn't recall his name now. "Good morning," he said, smiling at me and then at Crystal. "I'm glad to see you're awake." A nurse trailed in after him, smiling and nodding at both of us.

The doctor came to stand at the end of Crystal's bed and pushed a button to raise her head a little more. "I'm going to examine you and see how you're doing this morning, and Alison is going to check your dressings." Crystal glanced at me, and I cleared my throat.

"I'll just wait outside," I said, giving Crystal a small smile before I left, closing the door to her room quietly behind me. Hearing the clacking of heels on the linoleum floor, I looked up and saw Kayla hurrying toward me.

"Is she awake?"

"Yeah, she woke up a little bit ago. The doctor's examining her now."

Kayla nodded, opening the door a crack and peeking in. "Okay if I come in?" I didn't hear a response, but she must have gotten an indication that it was fine to enter because she turned to me and said, "I'll be back out when they're done."

I nodded, taking a seat in the same chair I'd slept in the night before. Turning on my phone, I saw that Dominic had texted me back just an hour ago, telling me to call him as soon as I could. But instead of calling Dom, I stood and wandered down the hall and called George instead. He answered and I heard the sounds of machinery. He was already at the quarry.

"Gabriel?"

"Hey, George."

"Hey, buddy, everything okay?"

I sighed, running my hand through my messy hair, staring out the window at the end of the hall. "Yeah, mostly. I'll tell you about it later tonight. But, George, I'm taking a sick day."

He paused. "Considering this is the first time you've ever taken a sick day, this must be a big deal. You sure everything's okay?" His tone conveyed his worry loud and clear.

"Yeah, it will be. I promise I'll explain."

"Okay. You need anything, you let me know."

"Thanks. Hey, will you call Dom, too? He'll just ask twenty questions, and I'm not really in a position to answer any right now."

"Of course."

"Thanks, I appreciate it."

"No problem, Gabriel. Like I said, call if you need anything at all."

"I will."

We said our goodbyes and hung up. I felt so damn tired, so filled with mixed emotions and pain for Crystal. Jesus. *Jesus.*

I stood at the window for a while longer, staring down at the mostly empty courtyard below. A few medical staff hurried by, either on their way to start a shift, or maybe to answer a call. I turned away, returning to the chair in front of Crystal's room. The door was cracked, and I could hear bits of the conversation inside.

The doctor was telling Crystal the same thing about her leg he'd told us the night before, going into a little more detail about how long she'd have to wear the cast.

"I've had broken bones before," she said. "I know the drill."

The doctor paused. "A leg fracture is particularly disabling for obvious reasons."

"Will I have a permanent limp?"

"There's no reason to believe you'll have a permanent limp, no, but you may limp for several months after the cast is off."

"I...see." I squeezed my eyes shut at the sound of her defeated voice. She was thinking about her job at the Platinum Pearl.

"Honey, don't worry," Kayla jumped in. "Rodney will let you bartend or something for a while."

Crystal didn't answer. I didn't know who Rodney was—her boss presumably—but I wondered if Kayla believed her words, or if she was just saying them to make Crystal feel better. He might let her bartend eventually, I had no idea, but for a while at least, she was unfit for *any* type of work. Frankly, she was unfit to go out in public.

"Do you live with someone?" The doctor's voice.

"No, I live alone."

There was a pause and then, "That could be a problem. You're going to need assistance. Do you have any family that you could stay with temporarily?"

"No," Crystal answered immediately, and her voice sounded even more flat. *Resigned.*

"Aw, honey," Kayla said, "how are you going to climb those stairs to your apartment? Three flights? It'll be impossible. You know I'd offer my place, but since I moved into the room in Marcia's apartment, I don't have any space to share."

"It's okay, Kayla. I'll figure it out."

They spoke for a little bit longer about her injuries and the doctor's examination, and then he told Crystal he'd be back to check on her the next day. If she was still doing as well as she was at the moment, he'd sign her discharge papers.

Once the doctor and nurse had left, I knocked softly on Crystal's door. "Come in," Kayla called. Inside the room, Crystal was still lying in bed, looking more awake and less dazed, and Kayla was sitting in a chair next to the bed.

"I heard the doctor say he was going to discharge you tomorrow." Crystal nodded, turning her head toward the window. The shades had been opened, and the sun was shining brightly.

"We were just talking about how Crystal was going to manage when she leaves the hospital," Kayla said.

Crystal turned her head. "Kayla," she said, a warning in her tone.

"Well, honey, you got all those steps, and for a while you're not even going to be able to get to the bathroom without help and—"

"I'll manage," she gritted out, her eyes widening as if she was trying to send the signal to Kayla to stop talking.

Kayla apparently didn't get the message. "I know you like to be independent, Crys, but there are some things that are just—"

"She'll come home with me," I said. I was surprised by the resolution in my voice considering I hadn't planned to say it. But suddenly I knew beyond a shadow of a doubt that I wanted to care for her. Suddenly I felt it was meant to be this way. I wasn't sure why I felt so strongly about it, I only knew that I did.

"No," she said. "I can't. Kayla shouldn't have called you." She shot Kayla a stern look. "You shouldn't even be here."

"Well, I am and you can. I live in a ranch home. There are no stairs, and I have an extra bedroom. My brother lives with me, but there's more than enough room, and it's only temporary until you're able to live on your own. I'll work from home in case you need assistance during the day. It's really the perfect solution."

"I don't even know you."

"You know me well enough to know I won't harm you."

Her brow furrowed and she looked down, picking at her fingernails.

"I could stop by your apartment and pick up some clothes for you. And I'd visit as much as I can," Kayla said, clearly in favor of the idea.

"I…" Crystal let the words fade away, still looking down, the crease between her brows still present.

"Unless you have a family member somewhere that you can call, I might be your only choice here. Please accept my help. I'm offering it with no strings attached."

Her eyes snapped to mine. "There are always strings."

I shook my head. "Not with me."

She looked out the window. "Fine," she whispered, almost as if to herself. The statement itself seemed to exhaust her. Her shoulders sagged, and she leaned back on the pillow, turning her head my way. "Fine." She closed her eyes and appeared to be instantly asleep, as if agreeing to come with me had exhausted her so much she couldn't stay awake for one more second. The reaction of a woman who had been fighting alone for a long, long time and had finally surrendered.

* * *

"Dom?" I called, closing the front door behind me and dropping my keys in the basket by the door.

Dom came from the direction of the kitchen, a beer in his hand. "Hey, I've been worried. What's going on? Where you been?"

I headed toward the kitchen, and he turned to follow me. "Let me get one of those, too, and I'll tell you," I muttered. I opened the fridge and grabbed a beer, twisting off the cap and taking a long swallow.

"This must be good if Gabriel Dalton is drinking before dinner. Come on, spill it, man."

I took another swallow, setting my beer down and leaning against the island. "I met a girl."

Dominic grinned. "Yeah, so you said. What? You sleeping with her? Is that where you've been all night?"

I frowned, knowing Dominic would expect me to share that kind of information with him. And also knowing I'd *never* make a point to have a conversation with him about sleeping with a woman even if that were the case. "No. I met her at a place called the Platinum Pearl."

Dominic's face screwed up, and he just looked at me for a minute. "The strip club over in Havenfield?"

"Yeah. She works there."

"She works there? What…as a bartender or something? What the hell were you doing in a place like that, Gabe? Jesus, if you wanted to see tits, I have a whole collection on DVD—"

"I didn't go there to see tits, Dom." I took another sip of beer and swallowed before continuing. "I went there to hire a woman to help me practice getting close to someone."

Dominic's face paled, and he closed his eyes for a split second before opening them and grimacing slightly. "Jesus, Gabriel."

I held up my hand, knowing the information probably upset him. I'd never gone into detail about why I hadn't dated. Dom was my brother, not my therapist, and I'd let him believe my shyness and limited desire to socialize was my biggest impediment as far as meeting women went. "I'm not looking for pity. The only reason I'm telling you is because I want you to understand that *I* went there and *I* sought her out."

Dominic sighed, still looking pained. "Okay, whatever. Why does that matter?"

"Because she's coming to live here."

Dominic's eyes went wide. "She's coming to live *here*? What the fuck? Is she some type of scam artist? Jesus! Gabriel, we have to talk about this. You can't just bring some...trashy stripper into our home and expect—"

"She's *not* a trashy stripper," I said through gritted teeth. "She's in pain—and she's completely alone. And I'm asking you to keep an open mind and trust me with this. She was beaten up and she needs help. She needs care, and I'm going to give it to her."

Dom grabbed a handful of hair on the top of his head and turned around, looking as if he was trying to find some calm. But when he turned back, his jaw was tight. "Don't do this."

"It's already done. And I'm sorry you don't like it, but this is my home and I'm allowing her to stay here." I tossed my beer bottle in the trash and walked around the counter, intending on going to my room.

Dominic swore again and followed me. "This is insanity! Listen, I know you don't have any experience with women so you can't see when you're being conned, but trust me when I say, that's exactly what this girl is doing. She's probably a druggie, too. Most of them are, you know."

"You don't even know her," I said, not turning.

"I know enough to know I don't want to live with her. And I know enough to know she's gotten her press-on nails buried in you somehow. I know enough to know you deserve better. Jesus Christ, Gabriel, a fucking *stripper*?"

I turned, facing him in the hallway. I knew what Dominic meant. It was easy for people—perhaps even me—to make assumptions about women who stripped.

Drug user.

Shallow.

Uneducated.

There was no indication she used drugs, she wasn't shallow though she put on a decent act, and although I had no idea what type of formal education Crystal might have, I knew she was far from stupid. I pictured the intelligence in her gaze, thought about how well-spoken she was. It was part of her appeal—one of the things that made her so intriguing. "Crystal *is* a stripper, Dom, but I hope you'll see her as more than that."

"Crystal? The girl who called you at work?" He shook his head, his lips thinning as he let out a harsh exhale through his nose. "Her being a stripper gives me all the information I need. I don't want a piece of garbage moving in here!"

He was judging her without knowing her at all. "God-dammit, Dom. Give me some credit." I clenched my jaw and took a deep breath, attempting to control my frustration. "Listen, if you don't like it, you can move out. I hope you don't. I hope you'll respect my decision on this and keep an open mind."

"I won't fucking let you do this, Gabriel."

"I'm not asking for your permission." I went to my bedroom and closed the door, shutting out my brother's hostile glare.

CHAPTER TEN

Look! The flowers are just blooming. They're beautiful, aren't
they? Do you see them? Look with your heart. Do you?

Lady Eloise of the Daffodil Fields

CRYSTAL

After agreeing to stay with Gabriel, I slept most of the day, so
weary and in so much pain, all I felt capable of doing was shutting down.

When a detective arrived the next morning to question me
about my attackers, I told him what I remembered and gave the
best descriptions I could. I felt numb as I recalled the attack, as if
it might have happened to someone else.

And yet as reality settled in, I couldn't deny the severity of
my condition: My body was battered and helpless, my spirit completely crushed. How had my life arrived here? How had it come
to be that I was so broken and lost, heading home with a man I
barely knew, a man I couldn't begin to understand, a man who
both soothed me with his gentle manner and scared me with his
knowing eyes? And yet as I lay there, I admitted he was also a

man I somehow innately trusted when I trusted no man. Ever. It was all too much. I didn't want to think. I just wanted to sleep.

The doctor examined me at two p.m. and shortly thereafter signed my discharge papers. I didn't have any insurance, and I knew I'd be buried under a mountain of debt I'd never climb my way out from under. If only I'd thought of that before I'd mouthed off to the three animals that did this to me. Who *was* that girl? She seemed both overly brave and ridiculously stupid, and I couldn't connect myself with her. I couldn't remember who she was. I felt like a mere shadow of myself.

Kayla had visited that morning, bringing me an overnight bag with clothes and toiletries from my apartment. She texted me as I was being wheeled from my room that she had to go into work early, but that Gabriel would be there to pick me up.

Gabriel.

Why was he doing this? Why was he taking me in when I'd been so awful to him? I recalled waking up to see his face above me as I'd been wheeled through the hospital hallway, thinking at the time that I was in heaven and he was an angel. But even in the light of day, there was something so...*steady* about him, something sure and solid, despite his self-professed weakness. He was confusing and full of contrasts. Beautiful, steady Gabriel with his shy smile and tentative touch. The man who had hesitantly offered me a hand-picked bouquet of flowers and blushed when I'd refused them, but then confidently told me I was coming home with him. Who *was* he? What did he want with *me?* Perhaps it was a question better left unasked.

And maybe he had changed his mind. Maybe he wouldn't show up at all. And that was fine, too. I'd...what would I do?

You could call your father.

No!

God, no. Never.

Anyway, he might be dead for all I knew.

"Ready?" the nurse asked, turning my wheelchair and pushing me toward the elevator.

"Yes," I murmured.

"Who's meeting you to drive you home?" she asked kindly.

"My...friend. I think."

"Well, we'll just wait by the elevators. Do you want to call and see if they're held up?"

God, I didn't even have his cell phone number anymore. I'd have to call Kayla to get it. And then what would I do? Call and ask him where he was? Force him to tell me that he'd changed his mind? "No."

"Oh. Well, okay." She pushed me to the bank of elevators, and we stood there together, waiting in silence. There was a clock on the wall, and the ticking sounded loud in my head, the minutes potentially counting down to the moment when I'd be forced to acknowledge that I was on my own. And yet, part of me wanted just that. If only I wasn't virtually helpless. The pain pills I'd taken earlier were starting to wear off. I was in need of another dose, and I shifted in discomfort. The clock continued to move, my heart rate seeming to match its steady tick.

"Maybe—" the nurse began to say just as an elevator dinged open, Gabriel stepping out, looking rushed, his hair pushed back from his forehead as if he'd jumped out of the shower, run a hand through it, and driven here.

His face broke into a smile when he saw me. "Sorry I'm late."

"Oh you're not late," the nurse said. "You showed up just in time."

You showed up just in time.

Just in time?

The words echoed in my head for some reason.

"Good," Gabriel said, smiling at me. "Ready?"

I knew I glowered back, but I couldn't muster a smile. I felt broken, humiliated, confused, and helpless. And it didn't help that I knew I was barely tolerable to look at. At the very least, I had always had my looks. Now I had nothing at all. "Yeah."

The nurse stayed with us as we traveled down in the elevator and out the front doors of the hospital, where Gabriel's truck stood waiting in a patient pickup zone. The nurse pushed the passenger seat all the way back to make room for my cast and helped me into the truck as Gabriel returned the wheelchair to an orderly outside. Five minutes later, we were pulling out of the parking lot.

"How are you feeling?" Gabriel asked, shooting me a concerned look.

"About as good as I look," I muttered.

He grimaced slightly. "That bad, huh?"

I couldn't help laughing, although the resulting movement hurt my ribs. "I think you're supposed to lie and tell me I look great."

"If I said you looked good now, you wouldn't believe me later when I really mean it."

I made a noncommittal sound followed by a grimace as I adjusted my body and pain shot down my leg.

"When was the last time you took something for the pain?"

"Too long ago. I'm due for a dose."

Gabriel nodded. "We're only about twenty-five minutes away. Can you wait?"

"Yeah." I sighed and leaned my head back on the seat. I was so tired. "Where do you live anyway?"

"I live a couple of miles from the quarry where I work."

"And what exactly does one do at a quarry?"

"We sell slabs of granite for various uses—countertops, memorials, stairs, all kinds of things. But I'm a stone sculptor. I use a few different materials—marble mostly—to create pieces for customers."

I paused, surprised, and not sure why. He was an artist? Well yes, I could see it now. Quiet, intense, steady. I supposed you'd have to be all those things to chip away at rock all day—not that I really had any earthly idea how one went about creating things from marble or any other type of stone. "Interesting."

I saw him smile slightly from my peripheral vision, but he didn't respond. We completed the rest of the trip in virtual silence. I watched the scenery go by as we left the town of Havenfield and headed toward Morlea where I knew the quarry—and Gabriel's home—was.

We turned off the highway and drove through the small downtown, moving toward the heavily wooded outskirts. The trees were still green and lush, the forests thick with summer growth. But fall would be upon us soon, bringing the changing leaves and cooler weather and…what? What would fall bring for me? What was there to look forward to?

Gabriel turned down a paved back road, and then made another turn onto an unpaved road that ended in a driveway leading to an elegant yet rustic home of both wood and stone. A front porch spanned the entire length of the house, a porch swing swaying gently in the breeze.

I swallowed. It was beautiful, the most beautiful home I'd ever seen. "I guess stone sculptors do well for themselves," I said, not taking my eyes from it.

"I'm glad you like it," Gabriel said, shutting off his truck and getting out, walking quickly to my side. He opened the door and then paused, a look of mild distress coming over his face. *Oh.*

"I can…I can try to get out if you just hold my hand," I said. "Or…"

"No," he said immediately, an insistent edge to his tone. "No. I've got you." He reached up and supported me as I maneuvered myself out of the truck. I felt dizzy with the pain of my broken ribs, and I had to take a moment to get my bearings.

Gabriel's arms slipped around me, holding me up, and though his stance felt stiff, his grip was solid, his expression one of resolve, and the lean strength of him gave me comfort. His hazel gaze caught mine, his eyes wide, his jaw set with focus, and I could see the obvious effort he was exerting in being this close to me. Was he holding his breath? It stabbed at my heart, breaking through my own pain. He'd touched me—supported me—because I needed him to. Offered something so very difficult for him.

He reached behind the seat with his other hand and grabbed the hospital crutches. I took them one at a time, situating them so I could walk the short distance to Gabriel's front door.

He walked slowly beside me and helped me up the two wide steps to his front porch, opening the large wooden door and leading me inside.

I stopped in the foyer, taking a moment to look around. The whole space was wide open, with cathedral ceilings featuring massive, dark wood beams. There was a living room area directly ahead and a floor-to-ceiling stone fireplace separating what looked to be a kitchen at the back of the house. A set of French doors off the dining room area to the right made the whole space light and airy.

I didn't think I'd ever been inside such a beautiful home. My entire apartment could fit in the living/dining room area alone. I tried to admire it, to look around at the particulars, but my body hurt more and more by the second. I just wanted to sag down onto something soft.

"Where's your brother?"

"He's on a fishing trip." There was something odd in his tone, but I didn't attempt to analyze it.

Gabriel led me through the living room to a short hallway on the left and used his foot to nudge open a door. I hobbled behind him, and when he turned, he must have been able to tell by my face that the short journey from the truck to this room had worn me out completely. He guided me quickly to the single bed, made up with what looked to be a handmade quilt, the simple wooden headboard stacked high with pillows, and helped me ease down onto it. I groaned with the movement, my midsection screaming in pain. It didn't feel as if my lungs had enough room to expand.

"Where are your pain meds?"

"They're in my purse," I mumbled, closing my eyes and grimacing again. "I forgot my bag and my purse in the truck." *Shit.*

He left the room, and I took the opportunity to glance around groggily. Other than the bed, there was a blue dresser that looked like it might have been in a kid's room at some point, some sort of superhero sticker on the bottom drawer, a simple wooden bedside table with a reading lamp and a clock on it, and a rocking chair in the corner. There was a door next to the chair that I assumed led to a bathroom.

With the shade on the window closed, the room was cool and comfortable and dim, the ceiling fan whirring softly above the bed, helping to provide a slight breeze. The bedding smelled like fabric softener as if it had very recently been washed. He'd done laundry for me? A small nicety but one I'd never been given by anyone other than my mother, and that was so very long ago. I couldn't figure out how it made me feel—sort of warm and desperate at the same time.

Gabriel came back a few minutes later with a glass of water and the pills in the palm of his hand. He sat down on the edge of the bed, and I took what he handed me and lay back, praying the meds would kick in shortly. I was suddenly miserable again, hurting, anxious, scared, and dependent on someone in a way I'd promised myself I'd *never* be dependent on another person again. In a way my very soul revolted against. "Well, here I am," I mumbled, "under your control just the way you wanted." When there was only silence, I opened my eyes, squinting at Gabriel through my swollen gaze. The look on his face hit me in the gut. *Deep hurt.*

"I'd never try to control you." *Oh God. His voice.* I could hear the pain. I wanted to turn away, but I didn't. He paused, even deeper torment skating over his expression. "Someone did that to me once, and I'd never do it to someone else. I only want to help you. If there's somewhere you'd rather be where you'll be safe and cared for, tell me and I'll drive you there myself. I'll make sure you get there no matter how far away it is. I don't ever want you to feel like I'm trying to take away your will, Crystal. I couldn't live with that."

Crystal. It was the first time he'd called me by that name, and I didn't like it at all. Especially not now when he'd been nice to me, and I, instead of giving him the benefit of the doubt when he'd shown me nothing except kindness and a generosity I didn't deserve, had been cruel to him once again. I clenched my eyes shut, ashamed.

I felt the movement of the mattress as he stood, and I opened my eyes. "Eloise."

He stilled, his hand on the doorknob, unmoving now. He turned to look at me, his expression confused. "What?"

"My name is Eloise."

He continued staring, the confusion clearing and being replaced by...shock. Because I'd finally told him my name?

"Eloise," he whispered, tilting his head, his hair falling across his forehead.

I sighed, closing my eyes again. The pain meds were starting to work and I just wanted to sleep, to drift away. "I know it's old-fashioned, probably not what you expected. I was named after my grandmother. People used to call me Ellie." *A long time ago.* "You can call me Ellie if you want."

There was only silence, and I drifted closer to sleep, finally hearing the click of the door as Gabriel closed it behind him. He'd given me so much, made sacrifices to care for me, and I'd provided nothing in return.

So I'd given him my name.

It was the only thing in the world I had left to offer.

CHAPTER ELEVEN

Do what you can with what you have, even if it's not very much at all.

Racer, the Knight of Sparrows

ELLIE

The next week went by in a blur of sleep, pain, and strange, vivid dreams that caused me to wake gasping and soaked with sweat. I dreamed I was running down a dark alley that kept twisting and turning and growing tighter and tighter until I was forced to slow as I braced my arms on both walls and walked tentatively forward into the black depths. I cried in fear, the walls moving inward even closer, making me feel like they would crush me. I looked over my shoulder but the direction from which I'd come was just as black—seemingly fathomless. I stopped, sinking to the ground and wrapping my arms around my knees as I sobbed in loneliness and terror.

"You're going the wrong way. You must turn back, sweetness. He's waiting for you."

Mama?

"Who's waiting for me, Mama?"

My eyes snapped open, a desperate plea for her to answer on my lips.

"Shh, it's just the fever, Ellie."

Ellie.

My eyes adjusted, the dream dissipating like fog as reality took its place. *Just a dream. Just a dream.* Gabriel was wiping my forehead with a cool, wet cloth. It felt heavenly. *Gabriel.* Just like the angel. My bottom lip cracked, and I realized I must have been smiling.

"Here, drink this," he said, holding the cold rim of a glass against my lips. I raised my head as much as I could and slurped in the ice water. It dribbled down my chin, and Gabriel wiped it away once he'd removed the glass and set it back on the table. "Sleep, love," he said. "You're healing."

Healing, yes. *Sleep, love.* My eyes slipped closed again, and this time, I fell into a deep, dreamless sleep.

I woke again as something pulled tight around my ribs. I looked down blearily and saw male hands on a background of white as if they were a work of art being presented on a perfect canvas. Everything else around me was foggy and faded, and they were the only things I could focus on. *Gabriel's hands.* They were incredibly beautiful, and though I was so tired, I couldn't help but reach out and touch them, to trace the elegant lines of his fingers, to feel the smooth, hard fingernails, to travel back to the golden, scattered hairs on the tops of his tan hands, to run along each vein, each knuckle. They were so still as I explored them, *too* still, and I realized they must not be real. Gabriel wouldn't want me to touch him this way. No, just a *memory* of his hands…just a…My eyes fell closed and I was in darkness once again.

The fever—which Gabriel assured me the doctor had said was normal as long as it didn't get too high—broke, but right after that, I had a bad reaction to one of my medications. When I vomited repeatedly and felt like my ribs were being squeezed in a medieval torture device, I thought I was going to die.

All through it, Gabriel was there, steady, calm, seemingly unruffled, though I felt his body tense each time he got near me. He was forcing himself to assist me, at least physically, and despite my best efforts to remain unaffected, it made me feel an unfamiliar tenderness toward him.

He made me food and delivered it to me in bed, even spooning it into my mouth a couple of times when all I wanted to do was sleep rather than sit up and eat. He kept in contact with my doctor and made pharmacy runs. He woke me up through the night to take the pills that kept me mostly comfortable, but hazy and out of it. When the sickness had passed, he helped me to the shower, though I locked him out of the room once he'd gotten me situated. I struggled with removing my clothes on my own and putting the plastic cast cover I found waiting on the sink over my cast to keep it dry. He must have asked the hospital for some equipment as well because there was a hospital-issued stool with handles in the shower, making me feel like I was ninety. But in reality, I already felt like I was ninety, with or without the medical shower stool. My soul was as weary as that of a ninety-year-old, and now I had a body to match. *Wonderful.*

Near the end of the week, Gabriel knocked on my bedroom door to tell me a police detective was there to see me. A brief tremor of fear shot down my spine, but I picked up my crutches and followed Gabriel to the living room, where the detective was waiting. He was the same man who'd come to the hospital to take my statement.

"Detective Blair," I said hesitantly as I shook his hand.

"Hi, Eloise. You look like you're healing well."

I made a noncommittal sound. I hardly thought I looked much different than I had when he saw me last, and I still felt mostly miserable. But at least I wasn't flat on my back in a hospital bed. That was a small improvement.

"Would you like to sit down?" Gabriel asked, moving toward the couches, his concerned gaze focused on me.

I gave him a wobbly smile and we all took a seat. Detective Blair laced his hands on his lap. "We arrested the three men who assaulted you."

I blinked in surprise, a trickle of numbness moving through me. I glanced at Gabriel, who was holding himself stiffly, still looking at the detective, seeming as shocked by the news as I was.

"How...?" I asked, my voice sounding hoarse. I cleared my throat.

"One of the men turned himself in and then named the other two."

"Oh," I whispered, recalling the hesitance in the black-haired man's eyes, remembering as he tried to stop them, though not with much force. I had to assume he'd been the one to turn himself in.

"I have Officer Sherman here with me, waiting outside, and he'd like to administer a photo lineup. Is that okay?" I nodded, swallowing, feeling suddenly ill.

"Okay, good. Just one second. Mr. Dalton, I'm going to have to ask you to leave the room with me while Ms. Cates looks at the photos."

Gabriel gave me a questioning look, but I just nodded at him and watched as the detective went to the front door, where he let in a uniformed police officer. After a quick greeting, Officer

Sherman took several photo arrays out of a file and laid them before me individually. I took a deep breath and looked down, my eyes moving from one face to the next.

Guess we'll just have to take what we want.

Hey, bitch.

"These three," I breathed, my finger identifying each of them one by one. I felt cold and gripped my icy hands in my lap. I was surprised I'd been able to pick them out so easily. I'd always been good at forgetting the faces of the men I served at the Platinum Pearl. And yet, I could still picture these men clearly. Perhaps it was because the *anger* they'd inspired—an intensity of which I'd never been able to muster up before—had branded their faces in my brain forever. Or maybe it was because the memory had been very literally beaten into me.

Officer Sherman nodded, picking the pictures back up. "Thank you."

After the detective and officer had left, Gabriel helped me back to bed, saying softly, "You're safe." I realized I was shaking slightly and made an effort to smile and nod. I did feel safe at Gabriel's house, but it was a reminder that I wouldn't be there forever.

The next morning, I woke up early, realizing I'd left the shade open the night before. The rising sun was just creeping over the horizon, the room awash in a pale gold hue. I stretched carefully, realizing that, although I was still very sore, it was the first morning I didn't feel awful. I pulled myself gingerly out of bed, grabbed my crutches, and hobbled to use the bathroom.

After I finished, I brushed my teeth and pulled my hair up into a messy bun. The term *messy bun* had always been a style choice before; now it was very much a reality. My hair was a complete rat's nest.

The swelling had gone down on my face, although I still sported several bruises of varying colors. I touched them gingerly, assessing the damage, finally sighing and turning away from the mirror. Not wanting to wake Gabriel, I opened my bedroom door quietly.

As I made my way down the short hallway into the main living area, the rich, delicious smell of coffee hit my nose. I drew in a deep breath. I hadn't had coffee in a week. I hadn't had much of a taste for anything specifically except the reduction of my pain. But now, the smell made my mouth water.

The coffeemaker sat on the counter, half-full. I opened the cabinet directly above it and found mugs there, including a travel cup with a lid. After adding a generous amount of sugar from a dish on the counter, I tightened the lid and took a sip, sighing as the strong sweetness filled my mouth.

Limping out of the kitchen with the cup held carefully in one hand, I caught movement outside the French doors and leaned forward to look through the glass. Gabriel was outside, sitting at a table on a large patio, leaned back in his chair, his fingers laced behind his head, his own cup of coffee in front of him.

I hesitated briefly but then hobbled my way outside. At the sound of the door opening, Gabriel turned, looking momentarily surprised before a smile took over his face. He stood, taking my coffee from me. "Hey, good morning. You're up. How do you feel?"

I set my crutches aside and started lowering myself carefully into the chair next to him. He placed my coffee in front of me and helped guide me into the chair. I sighed when I was finally seated and turned my head to Gabriel. His face was inches from mine, and when our eyes met, his widened, his breath quickening as we locked gazes. I took a big inhale, taking in the familiar scent of him: some subtly manly-smelling soap that brought to mind the woods in winter—cool and piney. I had the sudden thought that I'd forevermore equate that scent with feeling cared for...with the hand that calmed and comforted in the midst of pain.

The idea startled me and left me feeling exposed—though he couldn't read my mind—and I turned my head away from those soulful hazel eyes holding me suspended. The movement seemed to snap Gabriel back to the moment as well, and he returned to his own chair.

I looked out to the horizon, where the sun was glowing as it rose over the trees. My eyes lingered on it for a moment before I answered the question he'd asked a minute ago. "I feel a little bit better this morning," I said, breaking the strange tension that had suddenly developed between us.

He smiled. "Good. You look better."

I let out a short huff before taking a sip of coffee. "Oh yeah, I'm a beauty." I looked at him, and he was watching me with a small smile on his lips. "What are *you* doing up so early?"

"I always get up this early. I do my best work in the morning."

"Your work..."

"I've been working in the garage this week."

"Oh." Right. I'd almost forgotten he worked at all. A rock sculptor, he'd said. "Can I...see what you do later?"

He glanced at me. "Sure, if you'd like."

I nodded, taking a sip of my coffee, sighing from the pleasure of it. It was the first time I'd felt really human since that night in the parking lot. I started to push that memory away, but it made me think of what had happened just before, why I'd been so filled with self-hatred. I'd hurt Gabriel and detested myself for it. I'd provoked those men on purpose and ended up...here. With Gabriel. Ironic. I snorted at the cosmic joke.

"What?" Gabriel asked, looking at me briefly and then staring back out at the rising sun.

I studied his profile for a moment—the strong line of his jaw, the shadow of scruff on it. He hadn't shaved in several days, presumably because he hadn't left the house. I liked it. "Why did you come when Kayla called you? After what I did to you?" He turned his head, and my eyes darted away, but when I glanced back he was only looking at me thoughtfully, no anger in his expression at the mention of how I'd used Rita to set him up.

He opened his mouth to answer and then paused as if weighing the words he was about to say. "I wish I had come sooner. I had a dream about you."

I watched him. He was serious. I huffed out a small sound of amusement. "A dream. So you're some sort of mystic?"

He shot me a grin, his whole face lighting up that way it did. It was beautiful, but it was also slightly painful in the same way light makes you want to squint when it's turned on in a dark room. I looked away, uncomfortable with the way my stomach flipped, uncomfortable because his smile always seemed to startle me slightly deep inside as if my very bones were reacting. What *was* that? It was a wonder the sensation didn't hurt my injured ribs.

"I wouldn't say I'm a mystic, no. But I'd like to think there's some mystery to life. Don't you?"

You're going the wrong way. You must turn back, sweetness.

I sighed, pushing the memory of my own dream away. *Just a dream.* "Mystery? Sure there's mystery to life. It's a mystery how I'm going to pay all my medical bills, it's a mystery how I'm going to keep from being evicted from my apartment

with no job. Life is just full of mysteries, Gabriel. They're everywhere."

He chuckled and I narrowed my eyes at him. I hadn't meant
to make him smile. "It's true, some mysteries are better than others." The amused smile remained on his lips, and it irritated me.
I took a sip of my coffee, glaring out at the horizon as if it, too,
had done me a personal wrong.

Gabriel sighed. "The truth is, I don't know. Maybe the dream
was mystical. Or maybe it was just telling me what I already
knew but didn't have the courage to admit, or would have ra-
tionally talked myself out of somehow in the daylight when
everything can be dismissed more easily. Maybe I simply used it
as an excuse to come when Kayla called me. Or maybe it was
just dumb luck that I even answered my phone. Maybe it wasn't
lucky at all. Maybe this is the worst thing that ever could have
happened to you, being here right now, with me. Is that how you
feel?"

No. The word came immediately to mind, but I didn't say it
out loud. Instead, I massaged my temples. "How I feel is that all
these what-ifs are giving me a headache."

He chuckled softly again, and I continued to massage my temples. "Yes. The great what-ifs. They give me a headache, too."
He looked pleased, as if we'd both arrived at the correct conclu-
sion together.

When he was still quiet after another moment, I dropped my
hands from my head and really looked around. The patio was
made of large flagstones, and the overhead pergola was laden
with vining white roses. There were large pots of colorful trail-
ing flowers and smaller pots of what looked to be herbs placed
in the corners. The furniture was simple and sturdy, featuring
the dining table we were sitting at and a casual lounge area to

the right. It looked out on a large, grassy backyard, enclosed by a wooden split rail fence. Beyond that, a meadow of wildflowers went to the edge of the woods, over which the sun had now fully risen. "It's beautiful out here," I murmured. Maybe the most peaceful place I'd ever been. And I understood now why I'd thought he didn't belong at the Platinum Pearl. *This* is where he belonged. Surrounded by open air and beautiful things.

There was a large tree several yards from the patio, and a bird feeder hung in it, swaying gently in the breeze. A bluebird flew into the birdbath on the ground below it and started playing in the water. I watched for a minute as he danced with unabashed joy and shook his tail feathers, chirping gleefully. I laughed at his antics and his obvious pleasure. When I looked at Gabriel, he was watching me with a small, sweet smile on his lips as if his happiness was coming not from watching the bird, but from watching me. I blinked and he looked away, back out to the yard. The bluebird flew away in a shower of water droplets and happy chatter.

Gabriel leaned back again, putting his hands behind his head, his T-shirt stretching slightly so I glimpsed a line of tanned, bare skin above his jeans. When I realized my eyes were lingering on that spot, I flushed and quickly looked back to his face. He was still looking out to the horizon and hadn't noticed my wayward glance. My shoulders relaxed.

"When I was locked in that basement, there was this small window high up on the wall. It was barred and impossible to get through, and the glass was tinted, but there was this small scratch in the tint, and the window faced east. Every morning this golden light would show up through that tiny scratch, growing brighter and brighter. Just a bare slip of hope—a reminder that even in a place like that, maybe God still saw me. I told myself if I ever got out of there, I'd spend every morning watching the whole sunrise simply because I *could*."

My heart lurched as I thought back to what I'd said to him about controlling me. I had been so insensitive and cruel. *Someone did that to me once, and I'd never do it to someone else.* No. He wouldn't. I swallowed, something tight and painful moving through my chest. Talk of God made me uncomfortable, slightly itchy, and yet, the look of peace, that steady strength on Gabriel's face also filled me with a longing I wasn't sure how to classify. Maybe it was the picture I had in my head of that tiny scratch on the window of his prison and the idea that sometimes that's all hope is—just a thin sliver of distant light. I cleared my throat. "And you did get out," I whispered.

He looked over at me and smiled. "Yes, I did." He took a last sip of coffee and started standing. "Do you want to see my temporary studio, Ellie?"

Ellie.

You're such a good, smart girl, Ellie.

I shivered, a shimmery feeling of warmth dancing through my veins. He'd called me Ellie when he was caring for me during my fever, too. I hadn't even remembered I'd told him my real name. I hadn't thought I ever wanted anyone to call me Ellie again. And yet, I found that my name felt safe on Gabriel's lips. *Safe.* I gave him a small smile. "Yes, I'd love to."

* * *

The garage was large and mostly empty, the floors painted a dark, speckled gray, the wooden doors standing open, letting in the light.

On the right side there was a long built-in wooden work

counter that housed tools and gardening supplies. And set up right next to it was a table holding a large piece of white rock.

I limped toward it, following Gabriel and stopping next to what appeared to be a solid piece of marble. There were small chips all over it, but if it was supposed to be something specific, I couldn't tell what that might be. "What is it?"

Gabriel laughed. "Nothing yet. What it will be is a cherub. It's for the outside of a museum being built in France."

I snapped my eyes to his. "A museum in France? Really? That sounds pretty important."

He just hummed, turning the piece around on the lazy-Susan-type thing it was on. His brow furrowed as he took it in from all sides, seeming suddenly distracted and slightly antsy, his eyes darting to the tools sitting next to what would supposedly be a cherub at some point. "Do you need to get to work?"

He raised his eyes and blinked at me and then shook his head slightly, a smile appearing on his lips. "Sorry. Sometimes when I start on a project, it feels almost as if it's trapped inside waiting to be..." He ran his hand through his hair, looking suddenly embarrassed.

"Set free?" I supplied.

He tilted his head slightly. "Yeah. I guess." He ran his hands over the rock, his fingertips exploring small divots and raised sections. I was struck again by the beauty of his hands, how strong yet gentle they appeared, how long and slender his fingers were, how tanned his skin was against the snowy white marble. It reminded me of the fever dream I'd had where I touched them, exploring their lines, and a small shiver moved through me despite the mild temperature of the garage.

He moved his hands almost lovingly over the stone as if he were reading a type of Braille that didn't spell out letters but perhaps…potential. "You have hands for creating beauty," I murmured. The words had fallen from my lips before I'd considered them. And yet, I realized how true they were.

Gabriel's gaze rose to mine, those warm hazel eyes soft and full of some type of knowing. "I don't create beauty, Eloise, I just reveal what's already there."

I stared at him for a moment, and that connection we seemed to have vibrated with an elusive energy. Is that what he was trying to do with me? Reveal some sort of imagined beauty? Chip away at all the sharp edges and rough spots until I was what he pictured me to be deep down inside? What he *hoped* I was?

I turned away. It was all too overwhelming. I didn't want him to try to see something in me that wasn't there. It was too much pressure, and he was wrong anyway. I was nothing more than what he saw. There was no beauty to be revealed. My sharp edges were there for a reason—I liked them. They protected me, and I'd be damned if anyone was going to try to take them away. "Gabriel—"

The sound of a vehicle approaching the house caused me to turn toward the open garage door. There was a red truck pulling up in front, next to where Gabriel had left his own truck. I looked back to Gabriel questioningly, and he was smiling.

An older man with a head full of salt-and-pepper hair stepped out of the truck and walked toward us.

"Hey, George," Gabriel called, walking to where I was standing.

"Hey," he said, a warm smile on his face. "I'm heading to the

quarry. Thought I'd stop in and see how everything was going."
He turned his smile on me. "And this must be Eloise." He held
out his hand.

I hesitated briefly before taking his large, callused hand in
mine. He squeezed it lightly before letting it go. "Ellie," I murmured. "You can call me Ellie." I wondered what Gabriel had
told this man about me, who he might be. I felt self-conscious in
front of him, standing there in a small pair of cotton shorts and
a T-shirt, my face battered, my hair ratty, leaning on a pair of
crutches.

"Okay then, Ellie. I'm George, and any friend of Gabriel's is
a friend of mine." He glanced at my casted leg. "How are you
feeling? Heard you had a nasty run-in with a group of wild animals."

I let out a half laugh/half huff. Despite myself, I liked this
man already. "You could say that."

"Truth is, Ellie, I'd like to say more than that, but I try to
watch my language in the presence of a lady." He smiled again.
A lady. That was one I hadn't heard before.

George moved his attention to the piece of stone behind us.
"How's she coming along?"

Gabriel grinned. "How do you know it's a she?"

George laughed. "I guess I don't. I guess that's your call."
They moved over to the piece of stone and I remained behind,
watching them as they discussed it for another moment. *George.*
The news article I'd read about Gabriel had mentioned a business partner that had taken Gabriel and his brother in after their
parents died. This must be that man.

"When's Dom back?" George asked. There was a worried
look in his eye that I wondered about, something under the surface of his words.

"I don't know exactly. End of the week maybe. He took off two weeks from work, right?"

"Yeah. I just wasn't sure if he was going to stay gone that whole time."

Gabriel shrugged, his attention still on the piece of rock in front of him.

George sighed. "I better be heading to work myself. "

Gabriel looked up. "Thanks for stopping by. I'll call you to-morrow." George nodded and started to turn away, when Gabriel said, "Oh, hey, have you heard any news in town about that missing boy, Wyatt Geller?"

George frowned. "No, not a word."

A look of deep sadness—almost grief—passed over Gabriel's expression, and he put his hands in his pockets and tilted his head. *That stance.* I'd heard about the missing boy on the news when I was in the hospital. It had barely registered—it was on in the background when a nurse had been taking my blood pressure, but I remembered now. Did thinking about him fill Gabriel with memories of when *he* was the boy in the papers? It must. How could it not?

"I check the local online news every morning," Gabriel said. "I hadn't seen anything, but thought maybe you'd heard something new in town that might not be posted…"

"I wish I had."

"Yeah," Gabriel breathed. "Me, too."

George nodded, his eyes lingering on Gabriel for a moment before he gave me another warm smile. "You be well, Ellie. I'll see you soon."

I nodded. "Okay. Nice meeting you."

George's truck drove away, leaving a trail of dust in its wake as it moved down the road.

"I heard about Wyatt Geller when I was in the hospital."

Gabriel nodded, his body held more rigidly now than it'd been before.

"I'm sure it…brings back memories." I felt awkward, not knowing exactly what to say.

"It does," he said, and then he turned back to his rough-edged, as yet unrevealed, cherub.

CHAPTER TWELVE

Hold on, hold on. The sun shines for you, too.

Shadow, the Baron of Wishbone

GABRIEL

After that morning, it became a ritual. She joined me on the patio, limping to the same chair, her coffee cup in hand as the sun welcomed a brand-new day. I watched her surreptitiously as her eyes focused on the small sliver of golden light growing larger and larger on the horizon. I loved the expression on her face—cautious awe—as if she wasn't sure she should allow herself to fall in love with anything beautiful, even the sunrise.

Sometimes it hurt me to watch her, hurt me to see that she was so lonely inside, so sure that the whole world was a dangerous place for her. I longed to show her that it didn't have to be, but for now, I offered her the sunrise and a safe place to watch it. I prayed that someday soon she would trust that she deserved this beauty.

It scared me a little that I enjoyed our mornings together so much, because I knew they were destined to end. She was healing every day, and soon she'd leave here.

For a week, she'd been completely dependent on me for her every need. So sick, she allowed me to feed her and keep her hydrated. So weak, she couldn't protest when I held her as the food came back up. So soft, I felt I had imagined the hard, resilient woman who needed no one or nothing. And strangely, being *needed* felt almost cathartic.

For twelve years, I'd been treated with kid gloves. No one had *needed* me. But Ellie had, and it had felt…right. *Good.* Despite her steely façade, her soul was tender, kind. Although I figured she'd probably hate it if she knew how vulnerable she'd truly been, if she remembered what she'd allowed me to see while she was delirious with medication and fever.

And then the morning I'd been changing the dressings on her ribs and she'd reached out and traced my hands, my fingers. I'd felt a disjointed sense of distress, but the longer she'd touched me, the more a yearning rose in my soul, so strong it took my breath. It was the first time I'd *enjoyed* another person's touch since I was a little boy. And though I was still slightly scared, I also undeniably longed for more. I wanted to feel her touch again. I wanted her to stay. When she left, I wanted her to want to come back. To me. If only to see the sunrises…

Don't lie to yourself, Gabriel. You're falling in love with her. Maybe you've already fallen.

Was I? Was this what it felt like to fall in love? A sort of agonizing joy? Or was it just that Eloise was going to make it harder than most, and I knew that and still didn't care?

Eloise.

God, I'd felt like I might fall over when she told me her name. What were the odds?

And what was the strange pull that made me feel like we belonged together? Was I a fool? And if the answer was yes, did I care enough to do anything about it? No. Somehow being a fool for Ellie felt like it'd be worth it. Even this tearing inside reminded me that I was alive. Not *only* that, I was living. I was taking chances, following my heart, willing to risk being hurt for a broken girl too scared to stake a claim to anything at all, most especially me.

She is *going to hurt you, Gabriel. You know that, right?*

Yes. Yes, I suppose I did know that. And yet I was still all in.

A few days after George had stopped by, I found one of my mother's favorite decorations in the attic and hung it in Ellie's room in the evening, knowing she kept the shade open so that the first light of dawn would wake her. The next morning, just as a slip of sun began to show above the horizon, instead of going straight to the patio, I went to her room and knocked softly on the door.

"Come in."

I found her standing in the middle of the room, leaning on her crutches, a look of joyful wonder on her face as she looked around at the rainbows scattered on the walls. Her gaze found mine. "How did you do it?" Her voice was breathy and soft.

I smiled, pointing to the crystal hanging from the window. "It's a prism. My mom used to have it hung in our kitchen." I leaned against the doorframe, crossing my arms loosely, completely captivated by her obvious delight. "When you were feverish, you kept mentioning rainbows. I thought...I thought you might like it."

She tilted her head. "What makes them?"

I smiled, slightly surprised that she'd never seen a prism before. I almost said something about refracted light, but decided the uncomplicated answer held more magic. "Just sunlight."

She looked over at me as if she knew I was simplifying the explanation but smiled anyway. "Sunlight," she repeated, a note of wistfulness in her tone. She stared at me for a moment and then looked around again, limping over to the wall, where she leaned her crutches against the bed and used both hands to cup one of the rainbows in her palms. She looked back over her shoulder at me and smiled, bigger and brighter than the rainbow she held in her hands.

Ah, sweet Christ. *Ellie's smile.* I felt like I couldn't catch my breath.

Her smile faded, but her eyes remained soft as she turned and picked up her crutches again. "Thank you."

"You're welcome."

We took our usual spots out on the patio after pouring our coffee, and she let out a comfortable sigh and stretched her casted leg slightly where it rested on another chair. I took that as a good sign that it was healing well and wasn't paining her as much. Her expression looked more peaceful than it had the previous mornings. Her facial injuries were looking better every day, her beauty now more obvious than the abuse she'd received. There was only a yellowish bruise on her right cheekbone and a scab along her jaw where a cut was still healing. And, God, I loved her face without makeup, loved the clean prettiness of it, the delicate grace, the way I could see what was really *her* and not some phony product meant to exaggerate and enhance a face that needed no such thing. Eloise was beautiful in a way that told me she'd always be at her loveliest first thing in the morning, bathed in dawn's soft glow, her eyes vulnerable and still full of dreams. My blood heated at the vision. But I turned my mind from those thoughts…they'd come to no good, not now, not for me and not for her.

"Time for work?" she asked.

I chuckled. "You mean time for you to watch me work?"

Her carefree expression slipped. "I'd be more useful around here if I could."

"I know that, Ellie. I was only teasing you. I don't expect you to do anything more than heal."

She looked uncertain, and I regretted making her feel that way. In actuality, I liked that she kept me company while I worked. Sculpting could be a lonely job, and although it was easy for me to lose myself in my work, while I was doing the labor that didn't require a lot of focus, I loved having her there to talk to. Although so far we'd mostly spent time discussing what I was doing and what tools did what, I hoped that the intimacy of that time would cause Ellie to open up to me a little bit—eventually.

I had brought a lounge chair into the garage, and that's where she sat while I worked, a blanket draped over her legs. She was still weak, and I could tell that her ribs still caused her pain. *Not that she complained.* I tried to make her as comfortable as possible. Even so, she usually only lasted a couple of hours before she was ready to return to bed, where she slept the afternoon away, waking for dinner and maybe a TV show and then back to bed. To be able to sleep so much meant her body was healing.

As I helped her get settled in the lounge chair, I thought about all the things she'd said while she'd had a fever and was on a strong dose of pain medication. She'd called out for her mama a lot, and she'd also talked about someone named Mrs. Holly-field, red Popsicles, and rainbows. I wondered what it all meant. *Eloise.* She was full of so many mysteries, full of so much pain. I heard it in her fear-filled voice as she cried in the night, calling out to people I imagined long gone. People she'd once loved, if the tears that rolled down her cheeks when she dreamed of them were any indication.

I smiled over at her as I began chipping away at the cherub. "I think he's a boy," I said, running my hands over the stone that had taken shape in the last few days.

She tilted her head, obviously knowing immediately whom I was talking about. "Yes, I think so, too. What should we name him?"

I chuckled. "I don't usually name my pieces."

"You don't? Why?"

I shrugged, a tremor of unease running through me. What I'd told her wasn't completely true. I'd named my work once…and never since. But that was different. "Just never thought of it. What would you name him?"

She sucked on her full bottom lip, and a shivery feeling ran down my spine, my muscles tightening. I cleared my throat, trying to lead myself away from dangerous places.

"William."

I smiled. "William? Why William?"

She shrugged one shoulder, looking slightly embarrassed. "I don't know. I just always liked that name."

"William it is. What do you think of your name, Will?" I tilted my head, pretending to listen. "He likes it."

She laughed softly, sending a spear of joy to my heart. "Good."

We chatted easily for a little while as I shaped William's chubby body, smoothing his fat little stomach. I glanced over at her, and she looked peaceful. One arm was propped behind her head, and her cast was peeking out from beneath the blanket; her face was in profile as she looked out the open garage door, the yellow bruise on her cheekbone highlighted by the sun. She looked like a broken goddess, and if I knew how to paint, I'd want to paint her, to capture all her shadows and light. "Did you ever think of modeling?" I asked. "You have the looks for it."

She turned her head toward me and sighed. "I answered an ad once for models before I started stripping." She was quiet for a moment, again looking off into the distance before continuing. "I went to this studio, and the guy told me I needed a portfolio if I was going to work. A few pictures were a thousand dollars, but if I didn't have the cash, there were other ways I could pay for the photos he took." She looked back at me, the meaning of "other ways" clear. I clenched my jaw. *Disgusting asshole.*

"You'd like to think I left, wouldn't you?" Her gaze was direct, challenging. *Oh, Ellie.*

I kept working, my hands moving in a way they'd moved a thousand times, finding the flaws, smoothing them. The ache inside me went clear to my bones.

"I never did get the pictures, though. I demanded them and he told me to sue him." She laughed, a sound mixed with both contempt and a helplessness I understood, though I wished I didn't. "As if," she murmured, wrapping her arms delicately around her cracked ribs. She opened her mouth to say something, almost as if she was about to offer an explanation about why she'd stayed, but then she closed it, her brows furrowing slightly as if she wasn't sure where to go with that thought. She looked away once again.

"I'm sorry that happened to you," I finally said. "There's a special place in hell for people who knowingly take advantage of others more helpless than them."

She sighed. "Yeah, well…I guess hell better be pretty big, then."

"There are far more good people than bad."

"You think so? You of all people?"

"Yeah. I think so."

She stared at me, a number of emotions moving across her

face: disbelief, anger, confusion, and the barest glimmer of…hope. I saw it a moment before she shut it down, her final expression, indifference, the one she decided to keep. She shrugged. "We're all entitled to our opinions, I guess."

My chest felt tight with hurt and frustration, but she was talking, and it was the most I'd gotten from her since I'd met her, so I decided to push my luck. *Let me in, Ellie. Let all that pain inside you out. I won't hurt you, I swear it.* Only I couldn't tell her that because she wouldn't believe me anyway. The best I could do for Ellie was to *show* her. I'd give her rainbows every day if I could only see the smile she'd given me this morning, see that wonder glowing in her eyes for longer than a minute.

Sometimes, like now, I felt like we were on opposite sides of a tightrope, walking toward each other. One misstep and we'd both go tumbling down, down, down.

I glanced at her leg, not really knowing if what I was about to ask was safe ground or not but deciding to take a chance, deciding to risk the fall. "You told the doctor you'd broken bones before. When you were a kid?"

She narrowed her eyes slightly and then sighed, leaning back. "My dad liked to smack me around." Another challenging stare. "When he remembered I was alive anyway. A couple of times, after he'd been drinking, he forgot his own strength." She shrugged as if she'd just told me it was going to rain later.

Fuck.

Another fierce wave of anger hit me. This woman had experienced hell on earth. I had, too, but of a different sort. It suddenly struck me how very similar we were…and how very different.

I chipped away at the cherub, revealing a tiny upturned nose, chubby cheeks. Ellie remained quiet, watching me work, expressions moving over her face, obviously reliving memories inside her head. A bleak sort of despair settled in her eyes. "You can't fix me, you know."

She'd said something similar to me at the Platinum Pearl and I'd questioned my own motives. But looking at her now, I knew that had never been my intent. I wanted her to *heal*, and I hoped I could be a part of that. But no one could fix anyone else. We could only fix ourselves. "No, you're right. I can't fix you." *I can only love you. And I truly want to try.*

She set her chin in that stubborn way of hers before a sort of worn-out resignation seemed to fall over her like a heavy, invisible net. She started to get up. "I'm tired today."

I dropped my tools, pulling off my gloves before going over to help her up, grabbing her crutches so she could stand on her own. "Ellie, I'm sorry if my questions were invasive. I didn't mean—"

She waved me away as if what we'd talked about had been of little consequence to her. "It's nothing. I just…" She rubbed at her temple. "I have a headache."

I stepped back. "Okay," I said quietly. "I'll check on you later."

She nodded, limping away. I let out a groan, walking back to William and bracing my hands on the table. *Fucking hell.*

You'd like to think I left, wouldn't you?

My dad liked to smack me around.

Ah, God.

I felt hollowed out as I put my gloves back on, picked my tools up again, and started to get back to work. When my cell rang, I huffed out a breath, pulling my gloves off and reaching in my pocket for my cell.

"Hello?"

"Gabriel? It's Chloe." Her voice was so light and chipper, I smiled.

"Hey, Chloe. How are you?"

"I'm great. Thanks. I just wanted to call and let you know that I'll be arriving in town on Monday. I'm staying at the Maple Tree Inn. Everything's all booked."

God, the timing of this was not good. Still, I'd committed. She'd responded with such excitement and genuine appreciation to the e-mail I'd sent telling her I agreed to the interview, giving me approximate dates for her arrival. I'd told her I'd make myself available for whatever schedule worked for her. There was no way I could have predicted the situation with Ellie, but there was also no way I could back out on Chloe now. "Oh, okay, great. I've heard really good things about the Maple Tree. A bed-and-breakfast, right?"

"Yes. It looks so charming. I know this is a work trip, but I have to admit, I'm looking forward to the time away in Morlea—it really seems like a beautiful little town."

I ran my fingers through my hair, walking to stand at the open garage door, staring out at the trees and the road. "It definitely is. The whole area is beautiful. I'm looking forward to meeting you."

"Me too, Gabriel. Thanks again for making time for this. I'm so appreciative."

"Of course. Is there anything you need me to prepare—"

"Nope. All I need is you." She laughed softly. "You know what I mean."

I smiled. "I should be able to manage that. Should we come up with a schedule?"

"Yeah, actually, that's why I'm calling. My availability is wide open so if you can e-mail me the times that are best for you, that'd be great."

"Okay, I can do that. I hope you don't mind, but I'm sort of caring for a friend at my home, and it's a little hard for her to get around right now. Would you be okay with meeting here at my house?"

"Oh, of course, that's perfectly fine. Honestly, I'm okay with wherever you feel the most comfortable. And I'd...love to see your home."

"Thanks, Chloe. Okay, I'll e-mail you the times that work best for me starting Monday."

"Awesome. I'll see you then. Thanks again, Gabriel."

We said our goodbyes and I hit the end button, continuing to stare out at the trees for a few more minutes, thinking about Chloe and how much things had changed since I'd agreed to be interviewed by her.

Chloe.

Ellie.

In a way, both of them were responsible for the changes beginning inside me. *Chloe* was the reason I'd allowed myself to dream of possibilities in the first place, of love, of a family like the one I'd had once. I'd had no idea if Chloe was a woman I'd fall in love with once I met her, or if she would be attracted to me. But I had wanted to show up for the situation with her as a whole man, not some scared rabbit that jumped every time someone got in my personal space. And so I'd ended up at the Platinum Pearl. I'd ended up in a room with...Ellie. I let out a sigh. Wasn't there a saying about making plans being the surest way to make God laugh?

Maybe we were all about to find out.

CHAPTER THIRTEEN

Busy hands, sharp mind. Always keep your edge.
Gambit, the Duke of Thieves

ELLIE

I didn't know why I kept giving Gabriel small pieces of myself. And I was even more confused about why he didn't ever seem to look at me any differently. I kept trying to shock him with the reality of who I was. But he just kept coming back with that same placid look on his face, the kindness shining from his eyes as if nothing I said could shake him. What did he want with me? I wasn't trying to pretend I was someone other than myself, like I had with other men, though they'd left all the same. No, Gabriel still cared for me day after day. Why? Why was I still here in this beautiful house, being watched over, being given rainbows, as if I were someone special?

He obviously didn't want me for my body. I had nothing to offer in that respect—at least not right now. And he tensed each time he got near me anyway—although I couldn't help but notice that was lessening by the day. Still, it wasn't that. It was something else. But what? I couldn't understand Gabriel's motives, and I felt lost and confused, almost afraid of him. The fear went deep down into my bones, because I sensed he threatened something vital, only I didn't know what.

I don't create beauty, Eloise, I just reveal what's already there.

After the day I told him about my father, I decided I wouldn't sit with him on the patio anymore. It was too damn early to get up anyway. And yet the next morning when that golden glow lit my room, and a hundred rainbows appeared, I got out of bed. The lure was too great. I told myself it was the pull of coffee and fresh air, and the peace I felt as I watched the dawn turn into day, and yet I knew I wasn't being completely honest with myself. The truth was, the thing that drew me to the patio was Gabriel himself. Gabriel with his handsome face, his eyes still slightly squinty from sleep, his broad shoulders, those beautiful artist's hands, and the strong, gentle air about him.

When I opened the French doors, I expected that he'd look surprised to see me after our exchange the day before, but he didn't. He just smiled and greeted me as he always did, and we drank our coffee together as the trees swayed in the breeze and the morning sky turned soft pink.

We spent the next few days that way, me still watching him for several hours as he worked on William, revealing the cherub's small, sweet face feature by feature. The tap, tap, tapping of his chisel was our background music, while small tendrils of dust danced around him and disappeared into the air. I was fascinated as William emerged, almost breathless with wonder to see him take shape. "How do you know?" I asked as he worked.

"Know what?"

"What he's supposed to look like?"

Gabriel shrugged. "I don't. He tells me as I go." He stopped. "Does that sound weird? What I mean is, I have a general idea of his shape and I use it as an outline, but I don't know what his exact features will look like, for instance." He went back to work as he spoke. "I imagine it's similar for many artists. Writers... painters...you start out with a vague vision, and the details emerge through the process. The more you do it, the more you trust your own hands to lead you in the right direction."

I liked that. I liked the confidence with which he worked, the trust he had in his own talent. And I was jealous. What must it feel like to possess such a gift? To be able to reveal beauty with your own hands? I didn't have any skills at all. Not unless you counted being able to slide down a pole as an accomplishment. I crossed my arms over my tender ribs, a feeling of worthlessness running through me.

"He's got curly hair," Gabriel said, snapping me out of my despondent fog. I watched as Gabriel moved his chisel and hammer to create a smooth wave over William's forehead. Tenderness replaced the depression I'd been moving toward. I felt almost irrationally attached to William, as if watching him come to life made me somehow responsible for him.

I'd watched William emerge from a square block of stone and now he was a fat, precious little man with laughing eyes and a sweet smile. My heart thrummed with love for him. *How stupid! Ridiculous, really. You can't love a statue.* I almost laughed at myself, but I didn't want to make a sound that Gabriel would question. *Yes, not only am I broken and useless, I'm crazy, too. I love that little stone angel you created more than I've loved anything in a long, long time.*

"Ellie, I wanted to let you know about something."

My eyes snapped to Gabriel's at the seriousness in his tone. "Okay."

"Before you came here, I made plans with a graduate student at the University of Vermont to interview me for her thesis paper. She arrives in Morlea tomorrow."

I tilted my head, my brow furrowing in question. "Thesis paper?"

Gabriel nodded. "Yeah, it's about abducted children who subsequently escaped or were rescued."

"Oh." I swallowed. "Well that sounds...hard. Will it be? I mean will it be hard for you?" I shivered to think about what it'd be like to answer in-depth questions about the worst parts of my own life. I always tried not to think about the things that had hurt me.

He stopped working for a moment as if he was taking a few seconds to really consider my question. "I don't think so, no. I don't often talk about what happened to me, but I don't find it distressing anymore, either."

I frowned again, watching him. How in the world had he come to a place where he wasn't distressed by the memory of being locked in a basement for six years and tortured in heinous ways I didn't even want to know about? How had he managed *that*?

His wise, sensitive, beautiful eyes met mine. "It's closeness I struggle with. As you know."

"Oh, yes," I said softly, feeling suddenly...honored that I might be the only woman on earth who did know that. It felt like a...secret, something personal and private that I alone knew about this man. It made me feel warm and trusted. And I remembered, too, how I had abused that trust, how I'd sent Rita in when he was expecting me. Shame rose up within me, heating my cheeks and making me feel suddenly weak with remorse. "Gabriel..."

His hands stilled and he looked over at me with concern. "What is it?"

I picked at my fingernails for a moment, gathering the words I needed to say. The words that were overdue. "I'm sorry." It came out as a hoarse whisper, and I blinked up at him. "For what I did at the club... I'm sorry."

His eyes ran over my face, down to where my hands still fidgeted and back up to my eyes. "I forgive you."

I tilted my head, my hands ceasing in their pick, pick, picking. "Why?" I whispered.

His smile was slight, sort of sad. "Because what you did hurt me... but I think it hurt you, too."

I let out a quick rush of breath, the truth of his words running through me. God, yes, it had. How had he known? Still, it wasn't about me. I'd caused him pain on purpose, and any hurt I felt because of it was well deserved. I shook my head slightly, not able to decide whether I was glad he'd forgiven me or not, wanting to change the subject back to what we'd been talking about. The interview. I cleared my throat. "Well, anyway, it's nice of you to grant that interview. Sounds like a worthy cause. A contribution to... um, education and all."

He stared at me for a few heartbeats before smiling slightly again and looking back to William, his hands moving over the cherub's curls. "I told you about it because I arranged it with her to come here to my house so I'm available if you need me."

"Oh, you really didn't have to—"

"I wanted to. But I also wanted to let you know in advance so you know what's going on."

"Thank you." It was his house, so he didn't owe me that. I knew I was disrupting his life in any number of ways, and yet he was so kind and flexible. Why? It was the one question I kept coming back to and didn't want to ask because I wasn't sure how the answer would affect me. "I should be able to move back home in a couple of days—"

Gabriel stopped working again, tilting his head. "Why would you, Ellie? Why would you want to manage three flights of steps and an empty apartment where no one could help you if you needed it? You're still healing. It's only been two weeks."

"I don't want to be dependent on you," I mumbled.

Gabriel sighed. "Is it really so bad?"

I opened my mouth to say something, when the sound of a vehicle approaching his house dried up the words on my lips. Gabriel put his tools down and removed his gloves slowly. His back suddenly looked stiff, and I wondered if I was imagining it. Whoever it was pulled out of sight of the open garage, and I heard the engine turn off. Gabriel walked outside to meet the person whose footsteps I heard in the gravel.

"Dom," I heard Gabriel say. Gabriel's brother was home.

"Hey, bro."

"How were the fish?"

"Biting. I brought a cooler full back. Fish fry later?"

They both walked into the light of the open door, Gabriel and a man that looked a little bit like him, although not as much as I'd imagined. He was darker haired and not quite as broad. He was good-looking but definitely didn't have Gabriel's stunning brand of handsome. He halted when he saw me, giving me a narrow-eyed look.

Gabriel's jaw looked rigid. "Dominic, this is Ellie." He was gazing at him with a warning look.

Dominic appeared confused for a moment. "I thought you said her name was Crystal."

My eyes darted back and forth between the two of them, trying to figure out what was going on. Gabriel had obviously told his brother about me. Told him I was coming here. Was *that* why he'd been gone?

"Crystal's my stage name," I supplied quietly, half of me hoping Gabriel had told him what I did so I didn't have to, and the other half hoping he didn't know.

His expression was so disdainful, I was tempted to look away, but I didn't. He obviously knew very well what I did. Finally he muttered, "Ellie," his inflection clearly hostile.

I cringed inside to hear my real name in his disapproving voice. I plastered an unaffected smile on my face, the one I'd perfected so long ago. For some reason, it was difficult to muster. It'd only been two weeks, and I was already out of practice. I felt twitchy and self-conscious just like I'd been at the start of every school year when I'd shown up in my old, ugly clothes and too-small shoes, some years with a bruise I'd covered as best I could. My cold detachment had always been my armor, and now I felt as if I'd misplaced it somehow. I wanted it back. *Needed it back.*

"Dominic. It's nice to meet you. I'm sorry for not getting up." I pointed to my cast and gave him a small quirk of my lips.

Dominic grunted, turning to Gabriel. "I'm going to go unpack my gear." He turned and left without another word, walking through the garage door that led into the house.

Gabriel let out a ragged breath and ran his hands through his hair. He looked back at me, obviously weighing what to say.

"He's not happy I'm here," I said so he didn't have to.

He huffed out a small sigh. "Dom's...protective of me. He thinks he's looking out for my welfare."

"He's not happy you're keeping company with a stripper." I hated the wave of shame that enveloped me. Had I *forgotten* that's what I was? How stupid.

Gabriel walked around my lounge chair and took a seat on the edge. *Close. So close.* He took a deep breath and picked up my hands in his. My eyes moved down to where our fingers were laced, my heart skipping a beat. His hands trembled very slightly, but he was relaxed, the look on his face determined. *Oh, Gabriel.*

"Ellie, he doesn't know you. He'll come around."

I snorted. "Once he gets to know my charming personality, you mean?"

He grinned and my stupid heart skipped yet another beat. At this rate I'd go into arrhythmia. "Yes." It was only one word, but he said it with so much conviction.

I startled myself by laughing softly. "You're...God, I don't even know what you are." I laid my head back on the lounge chair. "It's not fair for me to be here if it makes him uncomfortable. This is his home."

He squeezed my hands gently. "This is *my* home. I own it. And I've been thinking lately that maybe my brother and I could use some space anyway."

"Not because of me."

He shook his head. "No, actually, not at all because of you. But if he doesn't welcome one of my guests, then it's just another reason." He let go of my hands and stood up. I felt the loss of his warm body next to mine, his tender grip. He went back to work, focusing on William, but his expression remained tense.

* * *

The next day, Chloe Bryant arrived. I'd gone to bed early the night before, thinking it best to give Dom and Gabriel some time together without me there. I'd been becoming more comfortable in Gabriel's home, but now I felt strange and uneasy again—as if I didn't belong. Technically I didn't and never would. Despite Gabriel's best efforts to make me feel otherwise, frankly, I agreed with Dominic. I wasn't the type of friend Gabriel needed in his life. Me, a stripper who had nothing at all to offer. Me, a girl who had only taken from him, and had no hope of ever offering anything in return. Me.

I'd spent the early morning with Gabriel as usual since apparently Dominic didn't wake until right before he had to be at work. He left while I was showering, and I was happy I wouldn't have to see him until later that evening. Maybe I could just avoid him completely until I was well enough to leave.

I was limping out of my bedroom when the doorbell rang. Gabriel came out of the kitchen, shooting me a quick smile before he went to answer the door. He pulled it open and a young woman was standing there. Her smile was instantaneous.

"Gabriel?"

"Yes, hi, Chloe." When he stepped back to allow her entrance, she practically bounced in, petite and pretty with brown curls and a dimple in one cheek.

"It's so great to meet you in person." Her smile— impossibly—widened even more. "God, this area is gorgeous. And your home…" She looked up and around as Gabriel closed the door. "It's breathtaking."

As she continued to look around, her eyes caught on me where I was standing, practically behind a lamp. "Oh, hi," she said brightly, walking toward me. "I'm so sorry, I didn't see you there."

I limped forward, trying my best not to look like the pitiful creature I actually was.

"Chloe, this is Ellie," Gabriel said from behind her.

As she approached, her smile wilted. "Oh my goodness, were you in an accident? You poor thing. What happened? Are you okay?"

I smiled a small smile. This girl was like a whirlwind. "I'm fine, thank you. An accident, yes." I cleared my throat, hoping she wouldn't ask any more questions.

Her face crumpled into distress. "Oh, that's awful. Let me help you to a chair."

"Oh, I'm okay, really. I've been sitting all morning. I know you and Gabriel have some business to get to. I was just going to make lunch and I'll be out of your way."

Gabriel came up next to Chloe, his smile relaxed. "Are you going to be okay while we talk?"

"Of course, yes." There was another knock at the door and we all turned, Gabriel's brow furrowing slightly.

"I'm not sure who that could be," he muttered. "Excuse me." He pulled the door open and Kayla was standing there. She was wearing a tiny pair of booty shorts, a tight, sheer tank top that clearly showed her black bra beneath, and a pair of hot-pink heels. The polar opposite of the sweet, wholesome girl who had just entered Gabriel's house minutes before wearing a modest yellow sundress and a pair of low-heeled navy sandals.

"Hey, Gabe," she greeted. I limped forward and her eyes turned to me. "Hey, Crystal." She smiled, but as I got closer, I saw she looked haggard, and I could clearly see she'd lost some weight.

"Hi, Kay."

She came in and Gabriel closed the door. "We'll just go in my room so we don't disturb you," I said to Gabriel, taking Kayla's arm. He nodded and I smiled at Chloe. She had a small, confused look on her face, but returned my smile as we passed her.

I led Kayla to my room, hearing Gabriel ask Chloe if she wanted anything to drink before I closed the door behind us.

I propped my crutches against the wall, taking a seat on the bed. Kayla sat at the end, bringing one leg up underneath her. "Sorry I haven't been visiting more. Things have been crazy. We've all been working extra shifts since you've been gone."

"That's okay. You've been a good friend to me, Kayla, and I appreciate it. How is everything?"

She sighed. "Oh, all right. You know, the usual. Blew a tire out on my car and had to get that fixed." The mention of her car reminded me that mine was still in the shop, presumably fixed but unpaid for, unclaimed. I should call Ricky, but I'd shut out my real life since I'd been here. I hadn't wanted to think about it, hadn't wanted to consider the myriad of dilemmas I was going to face when I was well again.

"At least being extra busy has helped me shed a few pounds," Kayla said.

"I noticed. You look good, just make sure you're taking care of yourself, okay?"

She nodded. "I will."

Out in the living room, I heard the peal of Chloe's laughter followed by Gabriel's masculine chuckle. My stomach tightened in discomfort, and I adjusted myself on the bed. Good grief, *was I jealous?* My God, I was. I was jealous at the easy conversation Gabriel and Chloe were obviously having in the other room. I heard him say something, his voice rising and falling with a sort of vibrant enthusiasm I'd never heard. That's because being around me was depressing and morose. I provided nothing more than dull, dreary conversation and awkward confessions. *Good Lord.*

"You all right, honey?" My thoughts must have been reflected on my face because Kayla was looking at me with concern.

I released a loud breath. "Yeah, I'm fine. I just get...you know, pains." I ran a hand across my ribs as if that were the place causing me hurt.

Kayla nodded in sympathy. "I was so relieved to hear about the arrests. They called Rodney and he told us. Some of the girls were worried they might come back."

I shook my head. "No, it was personal."

Kayla tilted her head. "Yeah, I guess. I heard they're out already, though. You worried?"

I met her eyes. As a courtesy, the detective had called to let me know the three men had made bail. I'd received the news with a numb sort of acceptance, the detective reassuring me that it was in their interest to be on their very best behavior. I'd need to testify at the trial once a date was set, but I wasn't going to think about that just now. "Am I worried that they'll try to find me?" I shook my head. "No. I haven't thought about that." I chewed at my lip. "I feel...*safe* here."

She nodded. "I would, too. It's real nice. Nicest house I've ever seen. And there'd be no way for them to find you here. Even if they wanted to. Which would only make things worse for them."

"Yeah." I studied my nails as I heard another ring of laughter from Chloe.

"He's treating you well, Crys?"

"Yeah. Yeah, he treats me really well. Better than I deserve, Kay."

She smiled at me. "Nah, I think he's just what you deserve." I smiled, even knowing how wrong she was.

Kayla stayed for another hour or so. We chatted about what had been going on at the Platinum Pearl, what had been going on in Kayla's life, some gossip about the other girls. I had one ear tuned to her and one ear tuned to the other room, where the hum of Gabriel and Chloe's conversation continued. I wondered what they were talking about, wondered if she'd started interviewing him, or if they were just getting to know each other. From what I could hear, it sounded like they were chatting casually. I was grateful Kayla had arrived when she did. If not for her, I'd surely be standing at the door listening like a stalker.

I picked up my crutches and walked—well, limped—Kayla out of my room, and when we entered the living area, Chloe was standing, too, obviously getting ready to leave. She was smiling brightly, and Gabriel was just finishing a sentence, the expression on his face open and happy. Jealousy overcame me again, but I stuffed it down. *He's not mine.*

Kayla gave them both a small wave as we moved past, and I hugged her goodbye at the door. When I came back in, Chloe was walking toward me. "Ellie, it was so nice to meet you. I'll be back tomorrow so I'll see you then."

"Oh, okay. I'll, um, see you then. Nice to meet you, too."

"Bye, Gabriel." She smiled at him, and it was tender and full of undeniable affection. I looked away, feeling like I was intruding on a personal moment.

"Bye, Chloe. See you tomorrow."

He held the door open for her as she passed through, turning and giving us both a small wave before Gabriel shut the door behind her. We stood awkwardly for a second before Gabriel smiled at me in that sweetly bashful way of his.

"It seemed like it went well?" I asked.

"Yeah, it did." There was happiness in his voice, and it caused a tightening in my chest.

"Good," I said, clearing my throat when the word came out sounding hoarse. "I, uh, I need to take my medication and then I'm going to take a nap."

"Okay. You all right? Your visit with Kayla was good?"

"Yeah, yeah, it was good." I turned and limped toward my room, wanting to be alone, wanting to turn off the emotions running rampant inside of me because I didn't understand them. Gabriel Dalton was way beyond my league, and I would never have anything lasting with someone like him anyway. Sweet, gentle men like Gabriel Dalton ended up with pretty, respectable girls like Chloe Bryant. And girls like me ended up alone.

* * *

I awoke to a quiet house and tears streaming down my cheeks. I looked frantically around the darkened room, trying to get my bearings.

You're going the wrong way. You must turn back, sweetness.

The words echoed in my mind, the memory of my mother's voice causing both grief and joy to crash through me. I hiccupped, bringing myself to a sitting position.

Why did I keep hearing her voice? Why did I keep having that dream? God, it made me feel desperate and lonely.

I pulled myself out of bed and used the bathroom, still hiccupping on the way out. I needed a glass of water. The clock on my bedside table read ten p.m. I opened my door as quietly as possible and listened but didn't hear any sounds coming from the house. Were Dominic and Gabriel sleeping? I'd make a quick trip to the kitchen and then go right back to my room. I'd been successful at avoiding Dominic around the house, and I wanted to keep it that way.

The water from the tap tasted cool and fresh, and after downing a whole glass, my diaphragm relaxed. I put the glass in the dishwasher and started heading toward my room. As I glanced in the living room, something on the mantel caught my attention, and I walked toward it. Next to a plant sat a small marble sparrow. I ran a finger lightly over it, tilting my head as I took in the fine details, the feathery wings, the small eyes that somehow managed to be soulful, the beak open as if it were singing.

I heard a creak from the floor behind me and whirled around. Gabriel was standing there, having just spotted me as well, his eyes wide with surprise.

He was wearing nothing but a pair of boxers.

I swallowed heavily, my mouth going dry as I took in the masculine beauty of his practically naked body. He was…divine. That was the word that immediately came to mind. *Divine. Angelic. Godly.*

My gaze soaked in his strong, broad shoulders, the tight, lean muscles of his chest, the taut ripples of his stomach. As if my eyes were drawn to him like a magnet, they moved down his chest to his muscled thighs, his well-formed calves and then back up to his boxers, where the outline of his male anatomy was just barely visible against the thin material.

My core clenched, wetness pooling between my thighs. I blinked, completely unaccustomed to this kind of reaction when it came to a man's body. I wanted to simultaneously run away and step toward him, to reach out and trail a finger down his chest the way I'd just run a finger over the tiny stone bird.

"My father made that."

"W-what?" God, my voice sounded too breathy, too stunned.

"The sparrow."

He crossed his arms over his chest, obviously self-conscious about his state of undress. He gave a quick nod downward. "Sorry, I didn't know you'd be up."

Again, my eyes moved to his bare chest. There was a sparse

trail of hair under his belly button leading into the waistband of his boxers. My eyes leapt back up to his, and I practically gulped, sure he had heard it when his eyebrows twitched slightly.

I turned my head, my heart beating so loudly in my own ears I was sure he could hear that, too, even from where he stood. "It's only fair, I suppose," I murmured.

"What's that?"

"Now we've both seen each other half-naked."

Gabriel tilted his head, assessing me in some mysterious way. He suddenly turned and walked back toward his room. I stood rooted to the spot, confused, when he returned just as quickly as he'd left, pulling a T-shirt over his head. He walked toward me, coming to stand directly in front of where I stood. His expression was slightly shy, slightly teasing. "I hope...that if we see each other naked again, it won't be a job, or an accident. It will be because we both want it, and because it means something."

What?

Visions swirled through my mind, unbidden: tangled limbs and twisted sheets. Heat filled my veins, blood pumping between my legs. It was too much. It was...out of my control and it scared me. I didn't want to think of Gabriel that way, *couldn't* think of Gabriel that way. In truth, had never thought of *any* man that way. "Mean something?" My voice was a mere whisper.

He nodded, his expression going serious, his eyes filled with sudden gravity. His hand slowly moved up to my hair, and he brushed a piece back from my face. His hand lingered, his knuckle brushing gently down my cheekbone. My breath hitched at the subtle touch. His full lips parted slightly, those angel eyes moving over my features as if he was memorizing me, memorizing the moment. I was spellbound, caught once again in his gaze. No one had ever looked at me the way Gabriel was right then, not in all my life.

"Yes." It was all he said, leaving me to try to comprehend his meaning. But of course getting naked always *meant* something. A bribe, a paycheck, a coercion, a means to an end…only I knew very well Gabriel didn't mean any of those things, and it was impossible to convince myself he could. I already knew better. And I didn't want to think about what getting naked would mean to Gabriel because the very idea filled me with terror and an aching, needy want. But mostly terror.

I turned back to the sparrow, a jerky movement as I pivoted on my crutches. "Y-your father, he was a stone carver, too?"

"Eloise."

I clenched my eyes shut, refusing to turn my face back to his. "He was very good."

Gabriel let out a very small sigh. I didn't know if I had imagined disappointment in it or not. "Yes, he was very good." His hand brushed my bare shoulder as he reached past me to pick up the sparrow. His touch left a blaze of heat on that small patch of skin, and I wanted to rub it away but I didn't. *Couldn't.* I turned back to find him studying the small bird. He had a smile on his lips. "When I was eight, I went away to summer camp. I was nervous to sleep away from my family. There was a tree right outside my bedroom window, and sparrows would perch in it and sing. My dad carved this guy so I could bring one of the sparrows along. So I'd have a little piece of home with me—a little token of comfort."

I watched him as he spoke, a wistful happiness in his expression, and I wondered what it'd be like to have memories that made you feel like that. Memories that brought happiness instead of fear and loneliness and sorrow. And I couldn't help wondering at the depths of Gabriel's despair when he'd finally made it home after all those years of being locked in a dark, lonely basement, only to experience the loss of that happiness all over again. "He sounds like such a good man," I whispered.

His eyes met mine. "Yeah, he was the best." The stark love in his expression when he spoke of his father jolted something inside me, and for a breath of a moment I found myself afraid for him—for his vulnerability and pure heart. Afraid of how the world would hurt him. But that was ludicrous. He'd already been hurt—in the most unfathomable way possible. So how did he retain that gentleness? The shy tenderness? How did he still wear his heart on his sleeve the way he did? And why would he want to? I couldn't begin to understand.

Silence lingered between us, clunky and awkward as if we were both waiting for the other one to speak. Finally, I nodded. "Well, good night, Gabriel." I started to turn.

He took a step forward. "Aren't you hungry? You missed dinner. I could make you something."

I shook my head. "No, thank you. I'm just...extra tired today." I turned. I didn't really feel tired. What I felt was confused and scared, and most of all, deeply worried that I'd begun to fall in love with Gabriel. *Oh, Ellie, you fool. You stupid fool.*

That night I didn't dream about dark corridors that grew gradually smaller. Instead I dreamed about moonlight on bare skin, hands that caressed, a mouth that explored all the secret places of my body, and angel eyes in the dark. I woke heated and panting, a cry of pleasure on my lips, reaching for someone who wasn't there.

CHAPTER FOURTEEN

Don't stop yourself from dreaming. Dreams are what keep our hearts alive.

Lemon Fair, the Queen of Meringue

ELLIE

I slept in the next morning. I'd tossed and turned all night, unable to find sleep after my erotic dreams, and I simply couldn't drag myself out of bed at sunrise. When I finally did limp out of my room after a quick shower, I turned in the direction of the garage, where I could hear Gabriel working. "Good morning."

He looked over his shoulder, his smile immediate. "Good morning."

I walked slowly to the table where William sat, feeling just a little bit uncomfortable, wondering if Gabriel was thinking about what had happened the night before, wondering if it showed on my face that I'd spent the night dreaming about him. Could he tell that I felt extra vulnerable and slightly confused, and that I was so *aware* of him that my cheeks were flushed? And yet underlying the awkwardness, there was a strange sort of excitement that I didn't know how to categorize. Did he know? Gabriel's expression didn't tell me anything, and so my eyes moved to William. "He has ears." I tilted from one side of the statue to the other as I took in the perfect little shells.

Gabriel chuckled. "And eyebrows. I need to go to my studio at the quarry to get a few things to finish him. Do you feel up to coming with me?"

"The quarry. Oh, uh, okay. Sure."

Gabriel smiled. "Let me just grab my keys. It's literally a three-minute drive from here. We can have coffee and breakfast when we get home?"

I nodded and when Gabriel went back inside, I ran a hand over William's rough head, my lips tilting up as I traced a finger over one of his still-new ears. He seemed like a little miracle to me. I still couldn't believe he'd been created as if from nothing at all. And yet here he was. "Sweet little man," I murmured, laughing softly at myself, feeling silly.

I straightened up, pulling my hand back when I heard Gabriel approaching the garage. A few minutes later and we were turning around in the driveway, headed toward the road.

When Gabriel had helped me up into the cab, he didn't seem stiff, which made me remember the first time he'd helped me *out* of the truck two weeks before. I thought about all the small touches, and the way he seemed to feel more confident around me by the day. Maybe I really was providing him some therapy, though it wasn't purposeful. I liked the idea of that; it made me feel a little less useless, a little less…indebted to him.

A couple of minutes later we pulled off the highway into a parking lot with a large sign that read, DALTON MORGAN QUARRY. Gabriel pulled into a spot directly in front of a commercial building. The area was heavily wooded to the right of and behind the shop, to the left there was another smaller building, and beyond that, I could see a glimpse of a large canyon, which must be the quarry.

Gabriel reached up and grabbed my crutches from behind the seat, leaning them against the truck and then taking my hand as I stepped down. The air had turned cooler in the last few weeks as fall swept in, but the sun was warm on my skin as Gabriel led me away from the front door of what looked like a showroom and offices and down a side path. In the distance, I could hear the hum of machinery and the shouts of men working in the quarry. Their voices echoed and carried.

Gabriel pulled a door open on the other side of the shop, and I followed him inside to a wide-open space with several tables around the perimeter of the room. There was a large window on the back wall that had a view of the trees beyond.

I walked slowly around, looking at carved pieces here and there, a few on the tables, some leaning against the walls, and others on a large industrial set of shelves. Some pieces were half-done, and others looked complete. I was speechless as I studied them, swallowing heavily as my eyes were pulled from one to the next. Gabriel was…my God, I hadn't even realized the depth of his talent.

I stopped in front of a flat piece of rock with the face of a boy, eyes closed, emerging from the middle as if he were pushing through the hard barrier, desperate to reveal himself. It looked like a young Gabriel, and I wondered if it was a sort of self-portrait. Something about it made my throat feel clogged. I ran a finger delicately over the boy's cheek and then moved on, looking at a small dog with only one ear, and a rose that looked as if the stem had broken off.

"Most of these are things I did when I was younger…still

learning," Gabriel said from beside me, and I startled slightly, having almost forgotten he was there. I glanced at him, one hip leaning against a table, his hands in his jean pockets as he watched me look at the things he'd created.

"They're beautiful." *Wonderful. Amazing. Impossibly magical.* "You're…" I almost told him he was beautiful, too, but stopped myself, the words left dangling in the air. I felt sure he knew exactly what I'd been about to say. *You're beautiful.* Examining the things that spoke of Gabriel's incredible talent made me feel brittle, vaguely ridiculous. Made me wonder again what this man saw in me and why. He possessed the ability to bring forth *life* from rock, to summon beauty from stone, and I…I took my clothes off for men and let them watch my tits bounce. Gabriel was a brilliant artist and I was a disgusting, talentless joke.

I turned, obviously startling Gabriel, who looked suddenly surprised, moving away from the table and standing to his full height. "Did you get what you need?" My voice sounded cold, and I grimaced inside.

Gabriel tilted his head, looking at me thoughtfully before his lips tilted up in a smile. "Yeah, I've chipped away at William enough. It's time to start smoothing him out now."

"Smoothing him…"

"Yes, eventually he'll look like this." He picked up the dog, and I saw that although he was missing an ear, he was completely smooth whereas William still showed all the rough spots where he'd been chipped and chiseled, the nicks and grooves of his creation.

"Oh, okay. Ready to go?"

"Yeah. Come with me and I'll show you the shop real quick. I'd take you to the quarry, but the walking trail is too steep for crutches. We could take the road and drive, but I'd rather show you when you can stand right at the edge." He smiled. "You get a better idea of how massive it is that way."

Gabriel locked up his shop, picking up a canvas bag he must have left by the door while I was looking around. I followed him back around to the front of the shop. A bell jingled when he pushed the door open and he held it for me as I limped in after him. Classical music played softly through speakers somewhere in the walls, and there was a fountain to my left that had water cascading down a pane of glass, contributing even further to the relaxing atmosphere.

The whole interior was done in stone from the floor to the walls, and tall counters with granite tops held small samples and catalogues. A couple sat in stools at one of the counters, arguing softly about two different samples.

There were doors on the wall to my right that must lead to offices. Just as I had the thought, one of the doors opened, and Dominic walked out wearing khakis and a button-down shirt and tie. His expression, first one of casual ease, morphed into distaste when he saw me. He gave me one short, quick nod. I fidgeted on my crutches, feeling even more ridiculous than I had in Gabriel's studio. Feeling damaged—worthless—I had nothing to combat Dominic's blatant dislike of me.

The phone rang, and Gabriel reached over the counter and grabbed it, nodding at Dominic in greeting. "Dalton Morgan Quarry." He listened for a few seconds as I attempted to look everywhere except at Dominic as Gabriel told whoever was calling that they'd be open until five and it was best to make an appointment.

The bell over the door rang again, and the man I'd met earlier in the week, George, walked in, a kind smile on his face when he saw Gabriel and me.

"Okay, let me write that down..." Gabriel walked around

to the front of the desk and grabbed a pen, then spoke into the phone again as I said hello to George. Gabriel hung up and walked back around the desk.

"I see you're showing Ellie around."

Gabriel smiled and leaned against the counter in that way of his I'd come to know—so casually masculine. "Yup. I needed some supplies to finish up the cherub for the French museum. I should have him mostly done in the next few days."

George chuckled. "Him."

My heart felt heavy at the mention of William being almost completed. Then he'd be shipped away. Gone. *Get a grip, Ellie.* I fidgeted on my crutches again. A look of concern came over Gabriel's face, and he moved to my side. "I think it's been enough of an outing for today."

Dominic made a sound of disgust in his throat and rolled his eyes. I blushed with humiliation, moving away from Gabriel. "I'm fine," I murmured, trying to stand as straight as possible without stressing my rib cage.

George's eyes moved slowly from Dominic to me and back to Dominic, his lips pursing and his forehead furrowing. When he looked back to me again, his forehead smoothed and he smiled before saying, "I gotta get back to the quarry anyway. But I'll see you later at dinner?"

"Dinner?" I asked.

"Yeah," Gabriel interjected. "Chloe is going to make dinner for all of us. Insisted on it, actually. She's sort of…enthusiastic." He chuckled but there was warmth in his eyes.

I looked away and nodded. "Then yes, I'll see you all at dinner." Dominic shot me one last disapproving look before Gabriel led me from the building, helping me up into the truck and driving home.

Home.

No, Ellie. Don't start thinking of Gabriel's home as your own. That would be very, very stupid. Don't do it.

And yet I suspected I already had.

* * *

Chloe and Gabriel spent another several hours together in the living room as I tried to keep myself occupied in my room.

I called the shop about my car and was told it was ready to be picked up. Ricky had heard about me being in the hospital and generously offered to keep it stored there until I could get over to pay for it, which was a relief considering at the moment, I didn't have a dollar to my name. It wasn't as if I'd be able to drive for a while anyway.

I called my landlady and explained my circumstances, and though she seemed annoyed, she agreed to give me an extension on paying my rent. I had another month and then I'd owe her two months' worth. I sighed, having no idea how I'd come up with it, but deciding to cross that bridge when I came to it. I was used to juggling financially—I'd been seemingly doing it all my life.

I still hadn't called Rodney to find out the state of my job, but that could be put off for another day. *He* was well aware of my circumstances. Not that I'd received as much as a get-well card from him. He was probably pissed that I'd inconvenienced business by getting beat up in his parking lot and causing the police and local media to swarm the building. If there was anything men who frequented strip clubs disliked, it was a bright light and a news camera being turned their way.

At the thought of the clients at the Platinum Pearl, anxiety streaked through my body. Sooner rather than later, I'd have to go there and get back to work. I wondered if Kayla was right, though...wondered if Rodney would let me bartend, not just for a little while, but as a job change. If I studied, I could learn how to mix drinks. *Couldn't I?*

Outside my door, the buzz of conversation could be heard. Today they weren't laughing. Today their conversation sounded hushed and intimate. I pictured their heads bent close together as Chloe learned all the deepest secrets in Gabriel's heart, those soulful eyes focused on her pretty face. I got up and turned on the bathroom fan, keeping the door open. I didn't want to hear them. And yet...the envy I felt knowing Chloe was hearing all Gabriel's most private thoughts rather than me caused an ache to settle in my chest.

You could ask him, Ellie. If you were brave enough, you could ask him to share with you, too.

But then he'd want you to share your secrets as well, a small voice whispered.

A little before five, a knock sounded at my door, and I opened it to find Chloe there. Her smile was radiant. "Hi!"

"Hi, Chloe."

"I don't know if Gabriel mentioned that I was going to cook dinner here tonight?"

"Yes, he did. It's very nice of you."

She waved her hand in the air. "I'm happy to. I'd have taken them out, but I want you to be as comfortable as possible and so I thought a home-cooked meal would cover all the bases."

"You're very kind—"

"And I was hoping you'd keep me company? You don't have to help if you don't want to, but I'd love to get to know you a little better. I'll get you set up on a chair if you can't stand for long."

"Oh, um…" *Me? Why would she want to get to know me?*

She looked at me so hopefully. "Please?"

"Okay."

That exuberant grin spread over her face again. "Awesome."

I sat at the island on one of the stools as Chloe unpacked the bag of groceries on the counter that she must have brought with her when she arrived.

Gabriel came in the kitchen and took us in, his eyes lingering on me for a moment before he turned to Chloe. "You sure you're okay doing this? We could just order takeout."

"Gosh, no. I'm so happy you're letting me cook for you. Honestly, Gabriel, after all you're doing for me, a home-cooked meal is the very least I can do. Don't deprive me of showing my gratitude. It wouldn't be nice of you." She shot him a teasing smile.

He chuckled. "All right, then. Thank you." He turned back to me. "You good?" His eyes were soft as he seemed to assess how I was sitting, where my leg was propped, his gaze like a warm ray of sunshine washing over me.

"Yeah, I'm good."

"Okay. I'm going to do a little yard work while you two are in here. I've been neglecting this place, and the weeds are taking over."

"Six o'clock," Chloe called as he left the kitchen.

"I'll be here," he called back.

Chloe turned her smiling face to me, halting in her work. "He's really…God, he's just extraordinary, isn't he?"

Extraordinary. Oh yes, he is that. I nodded. "He is," I murmured.

Chloe cocked her head, studying me. "I have to admit, when I first talked to him on the phone, I couldn't help wondering if he was single." *Oh.* There was a small, strange, sinking feeling inside me. "But now, seeing the way he looks at you…"

My eyes snapped to hers. "Oh, no. He's just…we're only friends, I mean."

If we see each other naked again…

A warm blush moved up my neck at the memory of the words. Chloe shook her head, a smile tipping her lips. "Oh no, Ellie. The way he looks at you is many things, but friendly is not one of them. He has feelings for you. And if that man has feelings for you, you must be someone very special."

Just as quickly as joy had run down my spine at her declaration that Gabriel had feelings for me, so now did insecurity and a sense of defeat. I laughed, a humorless sound. "I'm no one special, I can assure you of that."

Chloe turned, setting a handful of vegetables that she had just gathered from the refrigerator onto the counter. A look of alarm came over her face, and she took my hands in hers across the island, startling me. "Oh, Ellie, I barely know you and I can already tell that's not true." She grinned and squeezed my hands before letting go. I couldn't help the affection that flushed my cheeks at her compliment. Girls had never been kind to me, and I felt strangely shy. She was everything I wasn't; she was friendly and open, quick to smile and easy to laugh. *Pure. Sweet.*

"So what do you do?"

Here we go. I watched as Chloe searched for something in a few cabinets, pulling out a cutting board and placing it on the counter. "I'm a stripper." I stilled as I waited for her reaction.

She halted what she was doing, her eyes widening slightly. "Are you really? God, I've always had this secret fantasy about trying that. It must be liberating to feel so free with your body." She grabbed an onion and started chopping it.

I frowned. "Um, no, actually. I've never thought of it that way.

I don't enjoy it. I just sort of…fell into it, I guess." I sighed. "I won't say it wasn't a choice because we all make choices, right?"

Chloe glanced up at me, pausing only momentarily in her chopping. "I suppose, but 'choice' is such a loaded word, isn't it?"

I turned that over, putting it away to think about later. "I suppose."

"Anyway, if you didn't like stripping, maybe your accident will be one of those things that you look back on later as the catalyst that changed things for the better. You know, the thing that motivated you to take a different path."

You're going the wrong way. You must turn back, sweetness.

I stared at her, thinking about how confident she sounded, how neat and tidy her conclusions were. *If you're not happy, just make a change. No problem. Easy peasy.* Those were the conclusions of someone who had never really struggled, didn't know that it wasn't only fists that broke you and beat you bloody—no, life *itself* could do that just as easily, maybe more so. She didn't understand the soul-deep agony of loss, of being left behind, terrorized, cast out, taken advantage of. She didn't realize that your heart could hurt so badly you just wanted to curl up inside yourself and never come out again. And yet I couldn't resent her for that. I envied her for it.

"It wasn't exactly an accident. Three men assaulted me."

The knife Chloe was using clattered to the granite counter. "Oh, Ellie! That's absolutely awful. Were they arrested?"

I nodded. "Yes."

She looked relieved. "Oh thank goodness." Still she shook her head, a look of compassionate distress on her face. "God, you've had it rough. I'm so sorry."

She picked up the knife and held it out, wielding it as if she intended to use it as a weapon. "I'd like to be left alone in a room with this knife and the so-called men who would attack a woman. I'd carve them up." She swiped the knife through the air, and I felt a momentary twinge of shock before a laugh erupted from my throat. It was so strange to see this sweet, innocent-looking girl wielding a chef's knife as if she were a pretty version of Zorro.

She stopped, the fierce look dissolving into a grin as she laughed with me. I bent forward, gasping for air, my ribs hurting with the hilarity moving through me. "Ouch." I laughed again.

After a few minutes we collected ourselves, and Chloe went back to chopping, a few stray chuckles still bursting forth here and there.

"Is there another cutting board under there?"

"Yes, hold on." Chloe grabbed another cutting board, a knife, and a basket of mushrooms and put them in front of me, and I began slicing.

"So, Gabriel said your paper's about kids who were abducted and then came home?" I asked after a minute.

"Yes, specifically, it's about the long-term psychological effects." She tilted her head. "The majority of my research has been done using case studies, so I was really lucky that Gabriel agreed to be interviewed." She shook her head, laying her knife down, and took the chopped onion in her hands and threw it in the large skillet on the stovetop. She turned back, grabbing a paper towel and wiping her hands. "I have to say, I expected someone...different. Not so well adjusted, so..."

"Solid," I supplied.

Her eyes met mine and she smiled. "Yes. Solid. That's a good word to describe him. There's something so amazingly strong about him. Remarkable, really." We worked in silence for a minute. "I'm fascinated by the reasons one person breaks while another who's experienced a similar trauma survives and thrives. The mind is such a fascinating thing—and there are always so many variables. I could discuss psychology all day long."

"So you want to be a psychologist when you graduate?"

She laughed. "You're probably thinking the same thing my dad says. How will this girl stay quiet long enough to actually listen to anyone talk about their problems?" She grinned as I shook my head.

"No, I wasn't thinking that."

She laughed again. "You wouldn't be wrong if you were. I like to chat. But I actually do love to listen, too." She gave me a kind smile. "So if you ever need a listening ear, I'm available, and would love it if you considered me a friend."

I smiled, continuing the chopping. We chatted easily as Chloe cooked and I took on the few prep errands I could do while seated.

Gabriel had come into the house a little earlier and gone to his room. He entered the kitchen just as Chloe was on her tiptoes reaching for a platter to use for the chicken marsala, which smelled heavenly. Gabriel had obviously just showered—his hair was still slightly wet, and he had changed clothes. He stepped up to Chloe and grabbed the platter easily, smiling as he handed it to her. She gazed up at him with adoration as she laughed softly. "Thanks."

Gabriel looked at me. "You okay?"

I nodded, and when I looked at Chloe she was watching us, a smile on her face.

Gabriel brought the dishes into the dining area, and I laid them out at five places as Chloe finished the dinner preparations. As I was placing the utensils on napkins, the front door opened and Dominic came in, greeting us shortly and saying he was going to go to his room to change. He shot me one last cold stare before turning away. The small happy bubble I'd been in decreased in size, and for a moment I wanted nothing more than to return to my room and stay there for the rest of the night. But I took a deep breath, not willing to ruin the dinner Chloe had worked so hard to prepare, and continued setting the table, limping from place setting to place setting.

The doorbell rang and Gabriel opened the door to George, who came in with a warm greeting and a smile.

We all sat down to eat, and for the first ten minutes of the meal, everyone chatted and complimented Chloe on the delicious food. It was the first family meal I'd ever experienced, and even though I knew I wasn't welcome by Dominic, I soaked in the experience, watching as everyone laughed and enjoyed each other. I stole a glance at Gabriel sitting next to me. He was relaxed in his chair, one arm slung casually over the back of mine, participating easily in the conversation, and when he caught my eye and smiled, I blushed and looked away, feeling as if I'd been caught doing something I shouldn't do.

He has feelings for you. And if that man has feelings for you, you must be someone very special... I'd wondered why he was caring for me, *why* he might like me. Could I accept that maybe he just *did*? Could it be that simple? Did he see things in me I didn't even know were there? Things that made me good and lovable?

You're such a good, smart girl, Ellie. You don't forget that, okay? No matter what, you don't forget that.

The possibility surprised me, beckoned to me, opened up a well of hope within that caused a fluttering, something I'd thought long dead and buried coming to life. It felt as if a lure were dangling before me, something shiny and beautiful, and all I had to do was reach out and grab it.

The conversation droned on around me, the sound of Chloe's light laughter ringing in small bursts. I followed some of it, what they were saying, but mostly I just watched as they interacted, the casual ease with which they all related.

I watched both George and Dominic smile at Chloe, captivated by her charm, and wondered what it'd feel like to be so happy-go-lucky all the time, wondered what it'd feel like to laugh so effortlessly. How good would it feel to be looked at the way the men at the table were looking at Chloe? With smiles and warm gazes. I smiled at her cheerful radiance, too, laughing softly at a story she was telling about a professor she had.

Under the table, I felt Gabriel's hand as he laced his fingers through mine, his touch gentle and solid just like him, and goose bumps broke out on my arm. *Oh*, my heart seemed to sigh. Our hands linked together in a way that made me feel we'd been created together, that every part of his body might contain a place just for me, a place I'd fit like no other. *As if we'd been sculpted with the other in mind.* Silly idea. Fantastical even. Not me at all. And yet I wouldn't dismiss it because the thought itself felt too good. I was flushed with happiness, and a sense of sudden belonging washed through me, dancing in my veins. When was the last time I'd felt as if I belonged anywhere? Long ago...so very long ago.

I looked over at Gabriel, and he was watching me, his eyes soft and his lips tipped up in a sweet smile.

"How's your leg, Ellie?"

Hearing my name snapped me from my thoughts, and I blinked as I moved my gaze from Gabriel to Dominic, who'd asked the question. He tilted his beer back and took a long swallow. Two empty beer bottles were on the table next to the one he set down. I noticed a shine to his eyes, a slight drag to his words. I knew that look. He was drunk, or if not drunk, getting there.

"Better," I said warily. Something mean came into his eyes. I recognized it, had seen it all my life, knew it like the feel of the stripper pole sliding between my hands—familiar yet unwanted. I braced myself for the cruelty I'd come to expect from men like him.

He nodded slowly. "Good. Can't lap dance on only one good leg. Or can you? Maybe some men enjoy that kind of thing. You'd know."

My lungs felt suddenly constricted, and I looked down at my plate, my appetite gone. Around me the conversation died.

"Dominic," Gabriel said. A warning.

"What?" Dominic asked, taking another swallow of beer. "She *is* a stripper, right? I'm sorry, was it a secret? I was only inquiring about her ability to do her job. She'll have to go back to work at some point, right?"

"Dominic, that's enough. You're being inappropriate and you know it," George said.

I knew George was defending me out of kindness, but it embarrassed me, made it more obvious what Dominic was doing. Made me feel as if I *should* be humiliated by his words. Whereas moments ago I'd felt as if I belonged, now I felt separate, apart, my shameful differences highlighted for everyone to discuss. "Really, it's okay, George," I said softly, my gaze not leaving Dominic. "Dominic's right. I can't dance with only one good leg."

I let go of Gabriel's hand, linking my own under the table. Chloe had paused, and when I glanced at her briefly, I noticed her eyes move between all of us. Dismay flickered in her expression, before her lips set in a thin line.

Dominic held his hands up. "Sorry, didn't mean any offense. Forgive me, Ellie, if I embarrassed you."

Our eyes held for another fraction of a second before I looked away, but not before I'd seen the gleam of victory in his eyes. He wasn't sorry. He'd succeeded in what he'd set out to do: make me realize how much I didn't belong here, not in this house and not with Gabriel. I felt absurd and clownish as if he'd read the secret thoughts in my head, knew the hopeful wanderings of my mind, and made it clear how stupid I was to let myself even entertain such things. I'd let down my guard and he'd taken advantage. Why should it be surprising? Only it was because here I felt…safe. *Less alone.*

"I hope everyone saved room for dessert," Chloe said in that breezy singsong way she had, obviously trying to change the subject and the sudden uncomfortable mood. "Ellie and I made something special."

"I didn't realize you had so many talents, Ellie," Dominic said. His smile was immediate, and he posed the remark as if he was trying to make up for embarrassing me a few minutes ago with a compliment. But I sensed the mockery underneath his words as if he knew very well I had no talents and was attempting again to remind me and to ensure everyone in the room saw me just as he did. I shot him a fake half smile, shifting in my seat.

Chloe brought out the brownie sundaes we'd made, and there were compliments all around as everyone ate them. I'd lost my appetite and just wanted dinner to be over, so the second I could, I rose, gathering a few dirty cloth napkins and some napkin rings.

"Ellie, you sit down. You're not doing any work," Chloe said.

"I can manage a few things," I said, picking up my crutches and moving toward the kitchen, not wanting to feel physically incompetent on top of the hollowness Dominic's comments evoked in me. Even if my "help" was pitifully minor.

Gabriel stood. "You women cooked. We men will clean."

"I can't argue with that." Chloe laughed. "Ellie, let's go hang out in the living room."

Gabriel took the things I was holding out of my hands, trying to catch my eye. I looked away, smiling at Chloe. "Okay, let me just use the bathroom and I'll meet you in there."

I turned, just needing a few minutes to myself, needing to rally my mood.

"Ellie—" Gabriel said, but I pretended I didn't hear him, turning in the other direction.

I went to my room and sat down on the bed, taking a deep breath. Why did I feel this way? Only because I had entertained thoughts of…belonging and was brought back down to earth. But that was good. Letting my thoughts wander there had been dangerous. Really, Dominic had done me a favor with the reminder. After a few minutes I headed back out to the living room.

I stopped right outside my door, standing where I had the slip of a view of the kitchen. I leaned against the wall, watching Gabriel as he laughed at something someone said, grabbing a dish from someone's hand and placing it in the dishwasher.

I heard both George's and Chloe's voices. They were obviously all helping clean up. *Not just the men at all.* Those who fit here were cleaning up. And the scene looked perfect, just as it should. Gabriel laughed again, tipping his head back slightly, and I had that same sense again about this being where he belonged—where he was calm and happy and at ease.

My smile faded as Dominic stepped out of the hall bathroom, stopping where I stood. His eyes moved to where I'd been watching Gabriel in the kitchen.

"He didn't always laugh like that."

I stilled, looking back to Gabriel. He'd moved to the right, and I could only see the tiniest sliver of him now.

"When he first came home, he was so…skittish." He paused. "We were overjoyed to have him back, of course, but he wasn't the same. He'd always been this kid who did everything well. School, sports. Everyone loved him, you know. He just had this…something that everyone flocked to—a sort of confidence rare in a grown man, much less in a kid. In the last couple of years, he's started to get that back. And I'll be damned if you take that away from him, Crystal. He's suffered enough—he deserves the best in life. He deserves to have the life *meant* for him and nothing less. Just because he's always had a soft spot for taking in strays doesn't mean I'm going to let you make this permanent. You got me?"

Crystal.

He thought he was insulting me by using the name, but hearing it gave me strength, reminded me that I had a shield.

I shot Dominic my most flirtatious, insincere smile, and he looked momentarily startled before he narrowed his eyes, his gaze shooting to my mouth.

He rubbed his bottom lip with his index finger. "I see what he sees in you, though, I'll give you that. You have the kind of beauty that causes a man to make stupid choices. Causes a man to lose control of himself."

"Is that right, sugar? Sounds like you know something about stupid choices."

His eyes narrowed even more as he looked me up and down. "The difference is, Crystal, I can afford to make them. Gabriel can't." He paused again. "You know *why* he went to that strip club you work at, right?"

I looked away, refusing to answer him, refusing to let him see I was shaking inside. "He wanted Chloe, but he was too damn insecure to make a move. He'd stare at her picture, talk to her on the phone, get all dreamy eyed. He only needed you for practice, Crystal. It was *her* he wanted. Then you went and got yourself beaten up, and Gabriel kicked into rescuer mode."

My heart stuttered in my chest, and I focused on keeping my breathing even, my expression unaffected, not willing to let him know how much his words hurt. How they were like a knife stabbing me in the gut. Because I knew Dominic wasn't lying.

You can help me practice being touched by a woman.

He'd told me the truth himself. Only it wasn't just *a* woman, it was Chloe. Chloe with her pretty face and her vibrant personality. Chloe. *Of course he would want Chloe.*

Not me. He didn't want me, and he never really had. Or if he did, it was only because he still wasn't completely comfortable with a woman, not quite ready to make a move on someone innocent and sweet like Chloe. How perfect: I was live-in practice. Someone to get close to behind closed doors, under tables. He'd grown comfortable with me because I didn't really matter. I'd go back to the Platinum Pearl, and his relationship with Chloe would grow into something more and...

I smiled at Dominic again. "You have nothing to worry about. I'm no one's permanent anything."

He made a sound that was half agreement, half disgust, studying me as if trying to figure something out. He wobbled slightly, catching himself with a hand on the wall next to me, boxing me in. I met his eyes, refusing to look away, refusing to let him see how hurt I was, how unnerved by his closeness. He ran a finger down my cheekbone in the same way Gabriel had done the other night. Only this time it felt cold, hateful. This time I wanted to knock the hand caressing me away rather than turn into it. I lifted my chin.

"So beautiful...makes a man want to do such stupid, stupid things..." And then he moved in so quickly I was caught off guard. His mouth crashed down on mine, and I made a surprised squeak. His tongue darted into my mouth, and he pinned me against the wall, pressing his groin to my stomach. I almost brought a crutch up to beat at him, but the weight of his words crushed me just like his body was doing.

He only needed you for practice...

You can help me practice being touched by a woman.

I went still, letting him kiss me, letting his tongue invade my mouth and his hips grind against me, not caring. Not caring at all. Or at least that's what I told myself. There was a crack in the ceiling and I focused on that...my mind drifting.

Dominic's face was suddenly torn from mine with a wet-sounding pop, and I gasped, brought back to the moment, pressing my back into the wall, trying to rein in my mind from where it had started to wander. I turned my face away, clenching my eyes shut, expecting a blow of some sort.

"What the hell are you *doing?*" Gabriel's voice, filled with anger. I opened my eyes, opening my mouth to respond. *What was I doing? I...I...*

"Jesus, relax." Dominic was stumbling backward and Gabriel was standing still, one hand fisted at his side, one hand just letting go of the back of Dominic's shirt. Dominic stumbled a few more steps, tilting forward. "I was just trying to figure out what makes her so damn appealing."

It took me a second to register that Gabriel had been addressing Dominic, not me.

Gabriel's chest was heaving as if he was having trouble catching his breath. Before I could even pull myself away from the wall where Dominic had had me pressed, Gabriel slammed his fist into Dominic's face.

I heard a feminine scream. Chloe had just rushed into the hallway, George following her. Dominic reeled backward, hitting the wall behind him, his nose spraying blood as he yelled out a curse.

"Get out of my house," Gabriel practically growled.

Dominic looked up at him, an expression of shock and deep hurt passing through his eyes. "Can't you see what she's doing to us?" he yelled.

"It's *you* who's doing this to us," Gabriel shot back.

"Goddammit, Dom," George muttered, pulling Dominic off the wall and practically dragging him toward the kitchen. Dominic followed George willingly, his hands over his bleeding nose.

Chloe looked between Gabriel and me, her face filled with shock and confusion. She seemed to be weighing what to do. After a second, she turned and followed George and Dominic, obviously having decided it was best to leave Gabriel and me alone.

My heart was hammering, a whooshing sound filling my head. *Oh God, how did this happen?* Gabriel turned to me, and an agonized look came over his face. He clenched his eyes shut for a second and then opened them. "Eloise…"

His voice made me react. I pulled myself straight, feeling horrified, the situation crashing down on me. *Oh God, oh God.* "Eloise," Gabriel repeated, and his voice was a hoarse whisper filled with pain. His bloody fist was clenched at his side. *An avenging angel.* My heart pounded more harshly in my chest, and for a moment the ache was so intense I thought I might cry.

I shook my head, just needing to get away, away from his

tormented eyes, away from the shame, away from the heart-wrenching despair coursing through my body at who I was and would always be. "Please," I said, not knowing exactly what I was asking for. Time? Space? Distance? *Help?* All of those?

I turned toward my room and hobbled as quickly as possible to it. I saw Gabriel reach out a hand, but I moved away and it dropped, his head lowering as well. I closed the door behind me, sagging against it, wanting to disappear, wanting just to melt into nothing.

I limped to my bedside table, where I picked up my phone, texting Kayla five words:

Will you pick me up?

CHAPTER FIFTEEN

Let's not think at all. Let's just find strength in each other.
Lady Eloise of the Daffodil Fields

ELLIE

The Platinum Pearl looked dingy and worn in the midmorning light. I got out of the backseat of Kayla's car, where I'd had to sit because her passenger seat was broken and didn't move back far enough to accommodate my cast, and grabbed my crutches. My leg would be encased in plaster for another couple of weeks at least, but I could already feel that it was knitting together well. I hadn't taken any pain pills in two days and only felt a dull ache in my ribs.

"You need any help?" Kayla asked, slamming her car door and coming around to meet me.

"Nope. I'm good. I'm practically an expert with these things now." I held up one crutch before I brought it to the ground, limping to meet her.

As we walked past the Dumpster, I turned my head, not wanting to think about what happened behind it that night that seemed so long ago. It surprised me that it wasn't the beating that brought me the pang of distress, but the memory of Gabriel's sweet face above me in the hospital hallway, how beautiful he'd looked.

Gabriel…

I forced myself to move my thoughts from him. Thinking of Gabriel now would do me no good. After last night, it was glaringly obvious that I needed to get back to my own life, my own job. It was going to take a while to pick up the pieces, but I could no longer hide away from the world at Gabriel's. It wasn't fair to anyone. And certainly I was no longer welcome. No doubt Gabriel was as disgusted with me as I was with myself.

When Kayla picked me up, I'd been surprised to find Gabriel's house empty when I limped outside, yet also relieved. I'd still felt brittle and ashamed, and I didn't want to face anyone. I'd spent a restless night on Kayla's roommate's couch.

Kayla held the door open for me and then gave me a quick goodbye. "You sure you're going to be okay? I'm sorry I can't stay."

I mustered up a smile. "No, I'm good. I can hang out here for a couple of hours until you're able to come back." What I hoped was that I could use the time to study up on mixing drinks, or if Rodney let me, get familiarized with the bar.

"Okay. I'll text you when I'm on my way."

"Thanks, Kay."

I limped into the lobby and made my way to Rodney's office. Just walking through the club put a sour taste in my mouth. I couldn't help but compare this dim, dirty place with Gabriel's beautiful home, which was so full of life and light. Suddenly, being here made my skin crawl in ways it hadn't before. I forced myself to swallow the sensation.

When I knocked lightly on Rodney's office door, I heard a barked, "Yeah?" and pushed it open with one crutch.

Rodney looked up from the paperwork on his desk, an expression of genuine surprise coming over his stodgy face. He leaned back in his chair as I limped in. "Hey, Rodney."

"Crystal." He looked me up and down before I took a seat in the chair in front of his desk. "How are you?"

I laughed a humorless chuckle. "Just great." *Thanks for checking in on me. Your concern was just heartwarming.*

"You look like shit."

"Why thanks, Rodney. As usual, your charm is overwhelming."

"Just telling the truth."

I licked my lips. "Obviously I can't dance yet. But I was hoping I could do some bartending until I'm back in working order again."

"We don't need a bartender."

"But I have to get back to work. I need the money."

"That's not my problem."

I gaped at him. "I was attacked and brutalized by three customers on my way out of here."

"Company policy says you wait for a security escort to walk you to your car. You didn't follow it."

I took a deep breath, telling myself not to get worked up. "I realize I overlooked policy. But you can't be suggesting that this is my fault."

He shrugged. "Might not be your fault, but the fact remains that I don't need a bartender. And even if I did, no one wants a gimp serving their drinks. Buzz. Kill." His eyes moved to my chest. "Even if you do have a decent rack."

I almost laughed at the absurdity of him, but anger overcame me before a laugh could bubble up my throat. "You are truly just an awful human being, aren't you?"

"I'm a businessman, sweetheart. And business doesn't care about your feelings."

I forced myself to remain still, my small, tight smile in place. "There must be something I can do until I'm healed up enough to perform."

Rodney grabbed what looked to be a used toothpick off his cluttered desk and picked at his teeth as he surveyed me. "Shit, you can't even sweep floors in your condition. I don't have anything for you. Take a month or two off and come back when you don't look like the crash-test dummy." He laughed at his own joke. "I'll see if I can find some shifts for you then."

"A month or two…," I sputtered. "You'll *try*?" Fierce anger overcame me. "I've never once called in sick," I yelled. "I've picked up shifts whenever I was asked, taken your abuse, watched you pick your ass and pretended it didn't disgust me, and laughed at your stupid jokes. And you can't find something for me to do here until I'm healed?"

Rodney's face went hard, a tick starting up in his jaw. "Get out."

I stood up, grabbing my crutches. I wanted to hold on to the small amount of rage I'd mustered, but I just felt broken, defeated. I couldn't hold on to anything—it all just slipped right through my fingers. And anyway, what else could I do? Beg Rodney? God, I'd rather die homeless. I turned and limped out of his office.

At the front door I remembered that I hadn't cleaned out my locker and considered going back. But the only things in the locker were things I needed for the job: makeup, a few costume pieces, and several pairs of heels. I left them there, pushing the door open and stepping out into the bright sunlight.

Feeling drained of any energy I had walking into the Platinum Pearl, I sat down on the curb next to the door, pulling out my phone. I stared at it for a minute and then slowly put it away. The truth was I had no one to call. Kayla would come back eventually, but right now she was moving her stuff to another friend's house. The girl she'd been living with had to ask her to move out when her sister showed up in town and needed a place to stay.

God, we were all just half-naked nomads, moving from one temporary situation to another. It was exhausting. And pitiful.

A truck pulled up next to me, blocking out the sun. I squinted up at the driver. *George.* Blowing out a breath, I pulled myself up and made my way to the driver's side window of his truck.

"I didn't expect to see you here, George."

George tilted his head. "No, I don't imagine you expect much at all, do you, Ellie?"

I blew out a breath, smoothing a few pieces of hair back that had escaped my ponytail. I looked off into the distance unseeing, feeling sapped of strength. Sapped of the will to be anything but honest. "No, I guess I don't." *Never have. Never will. Hope is too dangerous.*

"I take it things didn't go well in there."

"No, they didn't."

George was silent for a moment, looking off into the distance before focusing back on me. "Dominic's moved in with me temporarily."

"Okay." I didn't know how I felt about that. Didn't really want to think about Dominic at all at the moment.

He cocked his head to the other side of his truck. "Want a ride?"

"Where to?"

"Home."

My eyes lingered on George for a moment before I nodded slowly.

"Need some help getting in?"

"No, I can manage." I went around the front of George's truck, slid my crutches behind the front seat, and used the small step to help me climb up into the passenger side. He pulled out of the parking lot, and I looked over my shoulder as the Platinum Pearl grew smaller and smaller. Some instinct in my gut told me it was the last time I'd ever be there, and I didn't know if that was a good thing or not. I really had no other employment options and virtually no skills that didn't include my naked body. I leaned my head back on the seat and let George determine exactly what road led home.

We drove in relative silence, and I was glad because I was exhausted. I hadn't slept more than half an hour the night before, and I took the opportunity to rest my eyes as the whir of the truck lulled me half to sleep. I was too drained to think of anything much at all and was grateful for the reprieve from my own desperate thoughts, grateful that the impact of losing my job on top of everything else seemed like nothing more than a distant worry…at the moment anyway. I knew the feeling was temporary, and so I took advantage of the calm it provided while it lasted.

When we pulled up in front of a small ranch house on a quiet residential street in Morlea, I looked over at George, confused. He nodded his head toward the house. "Come on. We're not going in the house. Just the garage and I'll leave it wide open. Dominic's at work."

"What are we doing?"

"Follow me."

I got out of the truck hesitantly, grabbing my crutches and

looking around at the tranquil, tree-lined street. A woman walked by, a small beagle on a leash trotting next to her. She smiled and called out a greeting to George, and he called back a hello.

George opened his garage and walked inside, calling my name. I approached tentatively and saw that it was a clean space, smaller than Gabriel's, but with a similar work counter taking up the entirety of one wall, an old refrigerator humming in the back. In the middle of the space there was a punching bag hanging from the ceiling.

I stepped inside. "George, what are we doing?"

"I'm gonna teach you how to defend yourself."

"From who? Dominic?"

George had been hitting the bag lightly but now dropped his arms, looking at me with an expression that spoke of disappointment, regret maybe. "Dominic's not a bad kid, Ellie, not really, but yeah, him, too." He sighed, looking older than I'd thought him before. "Not all men will take advantage of you just because they have the opportunity, but you gotta learn to spot the ones who might and then stay away. You got mixed up with the wrong crowd, Ellie girl."

I made a scoffing sound in the back of my throat. "Life mixed me up with the wrong crowd."

"I don't doubt it. But life also brought you Gabriel." He eyed me for a minute, and the way he was looking at me made me feel exposed in some way as if he understood more about me than he really had reason to. "Now that you know the difference, stay away from the wrong crowd." He paused. "Even so, every once in a while, someone's gonna surprise you, and not in a good way." *Right. Dominic.* "That's when you gotta know how to deck 'em so they don't get up again."

I raised an eyebrow. "You're going to teach me how to fight?"

"Yup."

"George, what's that going to do?"

"It's going to help you see that you don't have to take it. I think, Ellie girl, that you've been taking it for a long, long time. Am I right?"

"What choice have I had?" I muttered. I didn't know what to make of this man standing in front of me.

"Maybe not many good ones. I'm going to open up the options for you here. Come on." He bent down and picked something up and threw them at me. I caught them against my chest with one hand, looking down. Boxing gloves. The whole situation was ludicrous.

"I'm on crutches."

"Are you able to put a little weight on your leg yet?"

The doctor had said I could start trying and I had, but not much. Mostly just when I needed to balance, like now, I supposed. "A little," I admitted.

George nodded. "Toss the crutches aside for now. The bag will steady you if you need it." He nodded to the gloves. "Go on, put 'em on. The secret to throwing a good punch is putting your chin down so your arm comes out straight. Come on."

I put the gloves on slowly and then limped into the garage, where George stood holding the bag steady. I laid my crutches down and stood, balancing on my good leg and the toes of my casted leg. Cautiously, I tapped the bag. "I suppose you taught Gabriel how to throw a punch." I thought about Dominic's nose spraying blood, the look of incredulity that had passed over his expression, the hurt. I almost grimaced as the moment I'd been trying not to think about came back to me in vivid color.

"Yup. Taught both the boys. Told them you only throw a punch for two reasons: if someone hits you first, or to protect the honor of a woman." *Huh.* I hit the bag a little harder.

"That's it. Give it a good blow, Ellie. Show it who's boss."

I laughed lightly, doing as George said. We spent the next ten minutes with him instructing me as I hit the bag harder and harder, being careful of my ribs, careful not to jostle myself in a way that would set my healing back. As I hit the bag, a feeling of powerful satisfaction surged through me. I felt...strong, or like I could be. Maybe.

George stilled the bag, smiling broadly at me. "All right, then. This is a good start. You come back once a week and we'll make a prizefighter out of you yet."

I laughed again, nodding as I removed the gloves. "Okay, George."

"Good." He studied me for a moment. "Now it seems to me you need a job."

I stiffened. "You have a job for me?"

"It's not real exciting. But you might have noticed we need someone to answer the phone at the quarry showroom. Right now we pick it up when we can, otherwise it goes to voice mail, but that's not working out real great. We had someone working the front desk a few months ago, but she quit to watch her grandchildren full-time. Just haven't gotten around to hiring anyone else. Seems like we'd both be doing each other a favor if you could stand the boredom."

I chewed on my lip. "I don't have any experience answering phones."

"You can learn." *You can learn.*

At his words, nervous flutters started up in my belly. Still, it was nice that someone had faith in me. When was the last time that had happened? I couldn't remember. It felt good. God, it felt good. I nodded. "Okay. Thank you, George."

He smiled as we walked back to his truck. "All right, then. Take another week to heal. You can start next Monday at nine. Sound good?"

"Yeah, sounds good." I climbed up into George's truck and glanced over at him as he started the engine. "George, Dominic works there and—"

"You won't have any problems with Dominic again." George's jaw hardened slightly. He looked over at me pointedly. "Okay?"

I nodded. "Okay." I considered him, his strong profile, deeply tanned skin with white creases where his laugh lines were, making it obvious he smiled big and he smiled often. He had a thick head of gray hair and the brightest blue eyes I'd ever seen. He was a handsome man. A kind man. The sort of man I'd dreamed would open the door of that ugly little house the day my mama and I had knocked. "Why are you being so nice to me?" I asked before I'd thought better of it.

He shot me a quick glance before looking back to the road. "Because I trust Gabriel, and he deserves to be happy."

I tilted my head, considering his answer. Yes, yes he did deserve to be happy. But in George's answer was the implication that my happiness was connected to Gabriel's. I wasn't sure if that was true, and I wasn't even sure I wanted it to be true. It seemed like a type of responsibility I shouldn't be trusted with.

"You don't have to call his home your home if you don't want to. You can leave again. It's your right. But not that way—without a word or a goodbye. He deserves better."

I nodded, looking down at my hands in my lap, picking at my fingernails. "I know."

We drove toward Gabriel's house, my nerves increasing the closer we got. I started fidgeting with the hem of my shirt. How was he going to react to my being back? I hadn't even said goodbye to him, had just disappeared. George was right; Gabriel deserved so much better. Better than me. And yet I was still so deeply hurt about what Dominic had told me about Chloe. He'd been a friend to me in a way no one else ever had. Maybe that's what I needed to focus on—a friendship with Gabriel. He wanted Chloe, and really, how could he not? And she was clearly attracted to him and thought the world of him, as well. So what if I had more intense feelings for Gabriel? I could put those aside and focus on what was best for *him*. I could. I *would*. I kept repeating it to myself as we drove, hoping I'd convince myself by the time we arrived.

CHAPTER SIXTEEN

Be brave even in your words. Even in your thoughts.

Racer, the Knight of Sparrows

GABRIEL

I heard George's truck before I saw it and stepped from the garage, removing my gloves as my heart hammered in my chest. *Oh God, please let her be with him.* I squinted as the truck moved closer, noticing the outline of two heads in the front window. I let out a relieved breath.

The truck stopped and I watched as George hopped out, giving me a slight nod and a smile, gesturing that he'd help Ellie out. She stepped down and glanced at me nervously while getting herself situated on her crutches.

George started walking toward the driver's side, calling out a quick goodbye to both of us.

"Thanks, George," I said, hoping he understood the deep sincerity of my words. He nodded as he climbed inside.

"Hey," I said, turning to Ellie, who was standing on my walkway, that same uncertainty in her eyes as she chewed at her lip, making me want to kiss her and comfort her all at the same time.

"Hey."

I nodded to the front porch swing. "Will you sit with me?"

She glanced behind her. "Yes."

I helped her up the two steps although she was already adept with the crutches, and we sat down on the swing, strangely awkward for a moment. The porch was cast in shade, and the chocolate mint growing on the side of the house scented the air.

I felt like a young kid on my first date with a girl I wasn't sure wanted to be on a date with me. And I felt like a man who had apologies to make and didn't know where to begin. I let out a slow breath. Best to dive right in, I supposed. "Jesus, I'm sorry, Ellie."

She looked at me, turning her body slightly the way mine was so we were mostly facing each other. "You don't have anything to be sorry for."

"After everything, I didn't keep you safe—"

"You hold no responsibility for that." She looked down. "The truth is, I goaded Dominic. I encouraged him to do what he did." Her eyes were full of a pained guilt, and it made my heart pinch, though I couldn't deny a fierce streak of jealousy raced through me, too, hot and uncomfortable. It made me feel edgy, like hitting something again. Or someone, rather. My brother had kissed Ellie before *I'd* kissed her.

"Did you want to kiss him?"

"No."

I pulled my bottom lip between my teeth, watching her for a moment, wondering why she'd let him, thinking she might not even know. "I think maybe we should lay the responsibility mostly at Dominic's doorstep and leave it there. What do you say?"

A slight smile, a small nod. "But I don't want to come between you and your brother. It's not right."

I looked past her, staring off into the trees over her shoulder, the sun high in the sky, remembering the way my guts had twisted when I saw Dominic pressed against Ellie in the hallway, his face angled over hers.

I clenched my eyes closed briefly, attempting to shut out the image still seared on my brain. "What I told you before is the truth. Dominic and I have needed space for a while. We have a complicated relationship, Ellie, and it has nothing to do with you." I had realized for some time, years probably, that in some ways, Dominic considered himself my caretaker. I'd felt...smothered, though I'd never acknowledged how much. He'd been in college locally when I bought the house, and I'd asked if he wanted to move in for a while. A while had turned into years, and we were long overdue for a change.

We needed this space in general. What had happened with Ellie was just the proverbial straw. A very large, exceedingly weighty straw, but a straw nonetheless. I'd kicked Dominic out of my house because of what he'd done to Ellie. But I should have asked him to leave long before that. It would have been better for both of us.

Ellie's wary eyes moved over my face for a minute before she nodded her head. "George gave me a job at the quarry. I...I can go back home now. I can get around much better and my car is fixed..." She frowned slightly, looking away as if there was something troubling her despite her words.

"Stay here." My words sounded so serious, even to my own ears, and her eyes moved back to mine. I shook my head quickly. "It's minutes from the quarry, and I can drive you there and back. How can you drive an hour and a half every day while you're wearing a cast on your right leg?"

She looked down at her leg. "I think I could but…I guess it wouldn't be the safest thing to do."

"No."

We were both quiet for a minute as Ellie picked at her fingernails, a habit I'd noticed she did when she was nervous or unsettled. "Gabriel, Dominic told me why you came to the Platinum Pearl in the first place. About Chloe…"

Ah, God. I sat back, letting out a breath, even angrier now at my brother for his insatiable need to drive Ellie away. His insatiable need to control. I used my toe to push the swing very slightly. "What did he tell you?"

"He said you had dreams about her…that you came to the Platinum Pearl to find someone to help you get ready for *her*. That…that was my role. And now she's here and…"

I made a small sound in the back of my throat that turned into a sigh. "There's a bit of truth in that." She flinched very slightly, and I looked down at my hands for a moment, gathering my thoughts. "When Chloe contacted me, I let my mind wander to…possibilities. But the whole truth, Ellie, is that Chloe made me realize I was ready to try to recover that last part of myself— the part that's been holding me back from seeking relationships. She *was* the catalyst that sent me to the Platinum Pearl that night. The *idea* of her…" I paused, picturing Ellie as she'd looked that night sitting across from me in her gaudy makeup and too-high heels. "And that's where I found you. I didn't expect you, Eloise, but there you were. And it's *you* I fell in love with."

She looked up and blinked rapidly, and the guarded hope in her eyes almost undid me. But it was quickly replaced with uncertainty, maybe even a small measure of panic. "No, Gabriel."

"No what?"

She shook her head. "You shouldn't love me."

I let out a breath. "It's too late. I already do. I'm sorry but I can't take it back."

Her eyes moved over my face as if she was trying to find some untruth in my eyes, some deception in my expression. I caught that same small glimmer of hope before she blinked it away. *Ellie.*

I suspected she had feelings for me, too, though she might not be ready to admit it, even to herself. I'd first thought so the other night when she was looking at the sparrow on the mantel. I'd seen the same yearning in her eyes that I felt, saw the flush on her face when I touched her, the way she leaned into my hand instead of away. And then the night before at dinner, as she'd watched everyone from under her lashes, looking shy and happy and completely defenseless. I'd taken her hand under the table and noticed the goose bumps that formed on her bare arm.

She'd looked at me and smiled that same dazzling smile she'd given me when she held the rainbow in her hands, the one that filled her face and her eyes and seemed to make her shimmer in some indescribable way. I'd lost my breath again and I knew then I was in love with her. And it scared me and energized me and made me weak with want. It made me want to *touch* her, to know her in every way possible, to *love* her in every way possible, and it made me want to be touched and loved by her as well.

Loving her had begun to heal that last part of myself that still felt broken. So I'd wait. I'd wait for Ellie as long as she needed me to.

"I . . ." Whatever she was about to say after that faded away.

I smiled at her. "It's okay. You don't have to say anything until you're ready. But I got a lesson once about never missing the opportunity to tell the people I love how I feel about them. And it's sort of a motto I live by now." I smiled again and she tipped her head, a small smile appearing on her pretty lips. I glanced at her mouth, feeling overwhelmed with the desire to kiss her. But not today. Not the day after my brother had *taken* something from her.

She looked away from me, out toward the road for a minute before looking back. "I'm sorry for leaving without telling you. I just..." Her words faded away and she shook her head. "I'm good at running, I guess."

I inclined my head, trying to catch her eye, to make her smile. "I don't mind chasing you, Ellie. Just let me catch you once in a while."

* * *

For the next week we fell back into the routine we'd had before. We watched the sunrise together, and Ellie chatted with me as I worked on William. With the admission of my feelings for her, there was a certain tension that hadn't been there before, a sort of knowing swirling in the air that neither one of us were addressing. I had told her how I felt, and now I was waiting for her to do the same. *Hoping.* I saw her sitting alone on the patio in the afternoons, her arms propped on her knee, staring off into the trees, and I left her to think the thoughts she needed to think, hoping to God some of them were about me.

At night I lay in my bed and thought about her, unable to help the fantasies that ran rampant through my mind. Wondering how her skin might feel beneath my hands, what her mouth would taste like, how it would feel to join my body with hers. Thoughts of intimacy didn't scare me as much anymore because when I pictured touching someone, I no longer pictured an unknown, nameless, faceless possibility. I was picturing someone specific now, someone I loved. I was picturing Ellie.

Chloe came to the house almost every day, and we chatted easily as we'd done from the start. Even though the topic was extremely personal, Chloe had a way of making me feel comfortable and at ease. She'd make a good therapist someday. She was warm and intuitive, and I found myself hoping we'd keep in touch even after this project was over.

I couldn't deny that I wondered what it would have been like if I hadn't met Ellie, if Chloe had shown up and I'd felt ready to pursue a relationship with her and she had wanted one as well. Chloe was vibrant and pretty and so easy to be around. I liked her, and maybe under very different circumstances, I could even love her. It would be a comfortable sort of love, I guessed. But she'd never set my heart on fire like Ellie. She'd never move me and captivate me and make me feel a thousand different emotions all at once. I knew that like I knew the feel of stone beneath my palms, the same way I understood how to move the chisel to create a round edge instead of something square, how much pressure to apply to chip away, but not to break. *Because Ellie's mine.* Not to possess. But to love.

Maybe it was something I saw in her eyes that reminded me of the pain I'd experienced, too. Maybe it was the same reason I loved *anything* I loved: because it spoke to my heart and my soul. Maybe it was nothing that could be explained and nothing that needed explanation anyway.

My love for Ellie felt like a breath of life inside of me.

And so, in a way, it felt strange to be sharing intimate details of my life with *one* woman when the only woman I ached for was sitting somewhere in another part of the same house.

One day, after Chloe left, I found Ellie sitting on the patio, and she turned to me and smiled. "I've been thinking."

I chuckled. "Thinking's good."

"What's your favorite dessert?"

I frowned slightly, confused by her question. "Uh, lemon meringue pie."

She tilted her head. "Oh."

"Was that the wrong answer?" I teased.

"No." She bit at her lip. "It's probably not that easy to make, though."

"You want to make me dessert?"

"I thought I would, yes. If that's okay. Dinner, too."

"Of course that's okay. If you feel up to it."

She smiled and it was bigger this time. "Would you mind taking a quick trip to the grocery store with me?"

I laughed, hope filling my heart. She was going to cook me dinner and make a pie. Something about the normalcy of that felt so good. "Not at all." I tilted my head, grinning.

We drove to the grocery store in Morlea. I pushed the cart through the aisles while Ellie read ingredients off her phone from a recipe she must have looked up. I tried not to smile continually, but was hard-pressed not to. Watching Ellie walk through a grocery store—even on crutches—made me happy in a way I realized might be slightly excessive. Still, it felt like we were a couple, and I allowed myself to enjoy it. I felt comfortable with her beside me, found myself moving toward the soft brush of her arm rather than away.

As we were checking out, I noticed the looks, people talking, looking at me uncomfortably, the way they always did. I noticed and I saw Ellie noticing, too, although she quietly went about her business, unloading the items from the cart onto the conveyer. She looked embarrassed—for me, I assumed—and it put a sudden damper on the trip. Something about the expression on her face worried me, though I couldn't say exactly why.

My eyes moved to the newspaper stand, where I saw a small article about the Wyatt Geller case. It wasn't even a headline story anymore. That reality settled heavily in my gut. Other than checking the online news every morning, I had been somewhat successful at not letting my mind settle there. I was completely helpless and just had to hope and pray the police would get a break. Dwelling incessantly wouldn't help anyone, least of all me.

Ellie was quiet in the truck on the way back, but once we'd arrived at home, she seemed normal again, and I helped her unpack the groceries before heading back outside to finish the yard work I'd started the day before.

I'd only been working for about an hour or so when I heard the front door bang open and looked up from where I was kneeling in the front flower bed spreading a bag of mulch. I stood slowly, my eyes moving up Ellie, her white shirt stained with something green, to her face, streaked with flour, up to her hair, which was splattered with the same green sauce on her shirt and in complete disarray.

"Ellie? You okay?" I watched her face, figuring there'd been a kitchen disaster, but not sure why she looked so incredibly devastated.

She came hobbling down the steps to stand in front of me and let out a long, shaky breath, using her hand to smooth back a piece of food-drenched hair. Her eyes were filled with such incredibly raw pain, I was rendered speechless. My heart wrenched as I stared at her.

What is going on here?

"When I was twelve, one of my dad's friends came into my room one night while I was sleeping." *Oh no. Ah, Christ.* I continued to stare at her, unwilling and unable to look away from her wide, pained eyes.

She had failed at making dinner, and this was her reaction. *Why?* Why had a simple failure brought such deep pain to the forefront? Was she trying to shock me again with something from her past she believed made her ugly and unlovable? I stood frozen, waiting for her to voice another thing she thought would do the trick and make me feel the same disgust for her she obviously felt for herself. *Tell me, sweet girl. I can handle it.*

She took a deep breath that made her whole body shiver. "We were together." She raised her chin as if bracing for a reaction. I gave her none. *You were raped, Eloise. Why don't you call it that?* A deep tremble seemed to move through her again, her shoulders raising and her eyes clenching shut for a moment. "He would bring me candy and then laugh and say he guessed he was my s-sugar d-daddy."

Sugar.

Sorry, my lap-dance card is full for the night, sugar.

So what brings a nice guy like you to this den of sin, sugar?

Oh God. Oh Christ. It felt like someone was squeezing my guts in a vise. He was old enough to be her father, and she was just a little girl.

She took another heaving breath, and it was everything I could do not to reach for her. But I knew my gesture would stop her words, and right now, she needed to get them out. "My dad caught us one time and I thought...I thought...well, he didn't c-care. He never cared. It went on for a year and then he s-started dating some woman across town a-and stopped coming over to my dad's house. It was wrong, I guess, but when he stopped coming to me, I went to his h-house and begged him not to stay away. I *begged* him." She spat it out as if it were poison. "I thought he loved me and so I begged him not to leave me. He did anyway, of course, but not before one last roll in the hay to remember me by." A sound came up from her throat, not quite a moan, not quite a sob, but something that spoke of deep devastation, a sound I imagined had been lodged inside her for far too long.

It felt as if my body, *my soul*, was radiating pain. She gave me a shocked glance as if she had just come out of some strange fog and then turned abruptly and limped away, faster than I'd ever seen her move, as if the pain in her leg was the least of her concerns in that moment.

Oh Jesus. Now that she couldn't hear me, I groaned out loud from the pain of her confession, the way in which she'd made herself starkly vulnerable in front of me. She'd been used—*abused*—so horribly and hated herself for mistaking it for love. *God, sweet Eloise.* I knew that type of pain, knew what it felt like to be so desperate for love that you'd try to find it anywhere. *Create* it if you had to. But the difference between her and me was that I had never been abused and thrown away by the people who were *supposed* to love me and keep me safe. My heart ached for her. And I realized again what a tender soul she was, how she wanted love so badly she had even tried to find it in the ugliest of places, in the first attention she'd ever received from a man.

Ellie, my Ellie.

A fierce protectiveness gripped me, the need to comfort her so overwhelming, it was a deep, aching need. And suddenly I realized that my desire to love her was bigger, more *powerful*, than my fear. It wasn't *practice* I'd needed. It was love. Filling my heart so full there was no room for anything else.

I put my hands behind my neck and leaned my head back, staring up at the clear autumn sky, praying my love would be enough for both of us.

CHAPTER SEVENTEEN

You were given this pain because you're strong enough to endure it.
Shadow, the Baron of Wishbone

ELLIE

I was shaking so hard I could barely catch my breath. Oh God, what had I done? And why? I couldn't clear my mind. I felt overwhelmed with pain and horror and grief so strong it felt like it was pouring from my very soul.

I'd just wanted to make dinner and dessert for Gabriel. I'd thought I could do what Chloe had done so easily—just make a meal. I'd never really cooked—always made microwavable things, but had thought, *How hard could it be?* A simple meal and a stupid pie. And it had all gone so horribly awry. I'd started on the pie first, and the custard was watery and I couldn't get the meringue to work, and I thought, *Well, at least there's dinner.* But then I'd burned the pasta, which I didn't even know was possible, and the pesto sauce I was mixing in the blender had exploded and hit me in the face like a blow.

I'd cried out, defeat and misery causing such a terrible, terrible lump to rise up in my throat. I couldn't do anything right. I'd *never* do anything right. I was so useless, and Gabriel had told me he loved me but I didn't deserve it. Chloe had made dinner and it'd looked so easy, so doable, but for me it wasn't.

We'd gone to the grocery store, and everyone had looked at me so disdainfully. I'd remembered Dominic's words about how Gabriel should have the life he'd been meant for. Obviously the people in town didn't think I belonged with him, and I'd dismissed it, but then the pie and the dinner and all the terrible choices I'd made in my life, the way I'd never done anything right, not anything, came slamming down on me and—

"Hey." The word was soft, gentle, and I looked behind me, startled out of my own painful, manic thoughts. Gabriel gave me a small, sad smile as he closed the French door to the patio, where I'd run. I turned away, dropping my arms to my sides, unsure of what to do, what to say, knowing he was going to tell me to leave, that he didn't love me anymore. He'd do it nicely, though, because that's who Gabriel was. He'd offer me a ride, tell me not to worry about the dirty kitchen. And it would hurt, oh, it would hurt but—

I felt him come up behind me, his big body right against mine, the heat from him permeating the cold coursing through my veins. I shivered. He pressed his body to mine, and I inhaled a quick, surprised breath as his arms came around me and he pulled me against him, leaning his head forward so his cheek was right at my temple. I stilled at the contact. *Oh. Oh, Gabriel.* He felt so solid, so sure, so confident, and although I was sick with the horror of what I'd confessed, something inside me rejoiced in this victory for him. He was holding me. We were about as close as two people could get, and I sensed no hesitation in his embrace. I closed my eyes with the power of the moment, tears escaping and coursing down my cheeks.

"I ruined dinner," I whispered.

I felt him smile right above my ear. "I saw."

I nodded, a jerky movement of my head against his chest. "The pie, too."

"I saw that, too."

"Oh."

We were both quiet for a moment as my body stopped shaking in the warm cradle of his arms. He continued to hold me as my breath slowed. "I must exhaust you," I said, and I could hear the note of desperation in my tone. I needed to give him an out, but it hurt so badly. He had said he loved me, that he wanted me, but surely he couldn't want *this*. He *shouldn't* want this. *Me*.

"No. But is that the worst of it for today?" I felt him smile again. He was teasing me, and the reality of that both startled and calmed me. He wasn't horrified. *Why?*

"I...for today," I said, turning my head slightly, too embarrassed to meet his eyes. I felt hollow and far, far too tender.

He chuckled softly, and this time I shivered with pleasure, the beautifully masculine sound of his laugh right at my ear, right against my skin.

Gabriel. Just like the angel. My angel. I want him to be my angel. I closed my eyes and pictured his arms as massive wings wrapped around me, protecting me from the world, and the vision brought forth a smile.

The truth was, what I'd told him *was* the worst of it. The thing that shamed me most of all. The thing that lay deep inside like a secret sickness. The thing that, until now, I'd never shared with another living soul.

"I love you, Eloise. That won't change."

I opened my eyes. He was the only thing that was solid in the whole wide world, and I sagged against him, a small strangled sound coming up my throat.

"Why does that scare you so much?"

"Because...because I'm afraid you'll take it away."

"Do I strike you as a man who loves carelessly or recklessly?"

"No." The word was a broken whisper. Gabriel didn't strike me as a man who did *anything* carelessly or recklessly.

"I won't take it away."

He said it with so much resolve, so much surety, as if it wasn't a possibility at all. I wanted to believe. God, I wanted to so much but I didn't know how to do that.

"Can I show you something?" he whispered.

I felt so unbalanced, so flustered and scared. So wrung dry. So unsure why Gabriel still loved me and why he'd started in the first place. "O-okay."

He pulled back and took my hand, picking up my crutches where I'd dropped them on the ground and handing them to me. I followed him past the kitchen, where it looked like there had been a green and yellow paintball war. "Can I just change shirts quickly?"

"Of course."

I ducked into my room and pulled on a clean shirt, using a wet towel in the bathroom to wipe as much goop from my face and hair as I could. When I was done, I rejoined Gabriel where he was waiting in the hall, and we headed out the front door and into his truck. "Where are we going?"

"We're moving rather than cleaning up that kitchen."

I surprised myself by laughing, and Gabriel grinned. We drove in silence for about ten minutes or so. I was still trying to calm my racing heart, trying to come to terms with my emotional meltdown, still feeling a bit of embarrassment and insecurity, but also a sense that something inside had swollen beyond capacity and burst free. I felt a sense of lightness I didn't know how to explain.

Gabriel glanced at me and smiled warmly, reaching for my hand and holding it until we arrived at the turnoff to a small back road. I thought about another back road I'd been down recently—how Tommy Hull had demanded "payment" for a ride and then smacked me. A distant sense of anger gripped me at the memory, and I wished I'd fought him, wished I'd punched him the way George had taught me. Or better yet, wished I hadn't gotten in his truck at all.

Not all men will take advantage of you just because they have the opportunity, but you gotta learn to spot the ones who might and then stay away.

I supposed I had a hard time spotting them at all. Men who took advantage were the familiar. My norm. It was the *good* men who were unfamiliar, foreign. Ironically, the good men were the ones who scared me. Like Gabriel.

Gabriel made a series of turns and pulled his truck over, smiling at me before hopping down and coming around to help me out, too. I looked around as we walked to the front of the truck. The area was heavily wooded, the leaves on the trees so many colors—vibrant gold and scarlet and small bursts of purple.

Up ahead was a dark red covered bridge running over a small creek. As we moved toward the bridge, I inhaled the crisp scent of autumn and running water. "This is what you wanted to show me?"

"Up here. Is your leg okay?"

"Yes, it's fine."

I studied the bridge as we moved toward it. To me, there had

always been something so quaint and old-fashioned about covered bridges, something simple and romantic. But up until now
I hadn't dwelled much on romance. Not until Gabriel.

He led me to the edge of the bridge and walked along the outside, where there was a small ledge just above the shallow running water, shaded by the overhang of the bridge roof. I looked
at him questioningly, and he took off his shoes and started rolling
up his jeans. I watched as he did so, frowning slightly and then
following suit, kicking off my one shoe. He sat down and put his
feet in the water and laughed, grinning up at me with one eye
squinted. Butterflies took flight in my belly, and I sat down next
to him, scooting one hip back so my cast didn't touch the water
and dangling my bare foot in the creek. A small burst of laughter rose in my throat as the cold water swirled around my toes.
"Oh, that's cold." I laughed again. But it felt good, like cool silk
rushing over and along my skin to tickle up my ankle. It made
me feel present and alive.

Gabriel leaned back on the side of the bridge and pointed
down in front of him. Below us lay a valley of wildflowers in
every hue, surrounded by the vibrant changing trees. For a moment the colorful beauty stole my breath. I'd lived in Vermont
my whole life and I'd never spent more than a minute looking
at the beauty of the landscape. Sitting there with Gabriel, I was
stunned—almost overwhelmed—by it.

"There are rainbows everywhere," Gabriel said, tilting his
head and smiling at me.

I laughed softly, glancing at him, feeling suddenly shy by his
closeness, by the way he was looking at me. A breeze stirred a
piece of my hair into my face, and I brushed it back, closing my
eyes and inhaling deeply as the scent of the wildflowers below
found their way to us.

"I want to give you all of this," Gabriel said softly. I opened my eyes and looked at him, at the serious expression on his beautiful face, the way his eyes seemed to see straight into my soul. The way he seemed to know everything about me. And now, I supposed he did. Most of it anyway.

My heartbeat quickened, and I looked away as my cheeks heated at the nearness of him, the love in his expression. I wasn't sure what to do with it yet, as I'd never experienced it. I soaked in the view again, feeling the rush of the water as I moved my foot languidly through it, the feel of the breeze caressing my face and ruffling my hair. "You can't give someone the wind, Gabriel," I said softly, looking back at him, caught in his gaze.

He reached out and cupped my cheek, and my heart stuttered as I instinctively leaned into his palm. Just like on his patio earlier, there didn't seem to be any hesitance in his touch, just loving certainty. His lips tipped up in a sweet smile. "I can try. Let me try, Ellie."

I let out a soft breath as my own lips formed a smile. I knew what he meant. He wanted to give me the peace of this moment, the...poetry of this place, the romance, the scents and the sounds and the serene beauty all around us. He wanted to give me love. And, God, I wanted to take it, I was just so scared to reach out and grab it. Still so fearful it would be taken away. And if it was, I would never be able to go on. I would never recover.

A few leaves fluttered from the trees, twirling lazily in the light breeze, and I felt a gentle falling inside me, too. I wondered how trees knew to let go of the things they no longer needed, and I wondered if I could do that, as well.

"How do you do it?" I asked. "How do you let go of the fear?" He had been hurt before, too. So very, very profoundly. How did he move past that when I couldn't seem to figure it out? Still held so tightly to it.

"The fear?" he asked, his gaze moving over my face.

"The fear of loving."

A look of sad understanding came into his eyes. "Because, Ellie," he said, and his voice was filled with so much resolve it made me blink in surprise, "I *win* every time I'm bold in how I love. I want to say I win a hundred times a day, *a thousand*, by loving the sunrise, and the wind, and the way raindrops sound on my window." He paused, his thumb moving lightly over my cheekbone, caressing my face like I was precious. "And you, most of all, you. I want to look at you and say, one evil man did not stop me from presenting my heart to the girl who claimed it. You get my heart, Eloise. *You*. And, God, I hope you want it. But if you don't, I still won't regret giving it to you. Even then, I won't regret loving you because it means I win."

I felt a leap in my chest and let out a soft gasp. His words, the way he gazed at me so intently, shredded me, ripped me apart and yet put me back together all at the same time. *Oh, Gabriel.*

His thumb continued to move over my cheekbone, his touch so achingly tender that it made me want to weep. He had come to me as a man who panicked every time someone got close to him, and now he was touching me with such certainty, such strength and conviction. God, I was proud of him, but more so, I was deeply honored that he'd chosen me, deeply grateful that he'd learned the worst of who I was and loved me anyway. I was breathless with the sheer wonder of it.

Gabriel's gaze moved to my mouth and lingered. I saw him swallow and knew he was going to kiss me. The butterflies in my belly all started flapping their wings at once as he leaned toward me, looking hesitant, and certain, and more beautiful than any man had ever looked. His lips parted slightly and then they were pressed against mine, warm and soft, and I let out a small moan of pleasure at the meeting of our mouths. He scooted toward me until there was no room between us, and I wrapped my arms around his neck slowly, weaving my fingers into the silky thickness of his hair.

I tilted my head and opened my mouth so he could explore me, and he groaned, shooting a spark of desire between my legs. He took my invitation, brushing his tongue tentatively along mine, and then with more confidence as our tongues danced and tasted.

When he finally broke away, gasping softly, it took me a minute to realize where I was, that's how lost in him I'd been. A smile spread over my face before I'd even opened my eyes, and when I did so, he was gazing back, looking happy and slightly stunned. His lips were still parted, wet and reddened from our kiss, and his cheekbones were tinged pink. His eyes were soft and full of desire, and I thought to myself, *I am this beautiful man's first kiss. His lips have only touched mine.* And I wished it were the same for me; though, in some ways, I wondered if I'd really ever kissed anyone at all because I couldn't remember any of them now. Perhaps it was because this was the first kiss where I'd been fully present—not just my body, but my mind and my heart.

He reached his hand up and used his thumb to wipe away the wetness on my lower lip, and I laughed softly, feeling happier than I'd ever felt in my life, awed by the almost unbearable sweetness of the moment, of him.

We sat there awhile longer, swirling our feet in the water, Gabriel hooking his ankle with mine now and again as I laughed and leaned into him. We watched the trees begin to bare themselves—colorful leaves floating to the ground—and we chatted about nothing of consequence, feeling the peace of the moment, the joy of each other.

Had I *once* dreamed of romance and white knights? As a little girl, had I imagined that someday a handsome prince with his heart in his eyes would take my face in his hands and kiss me? I couldn't remember now, but I wished I could, because I wanted to imagine that that little girl was somewhere inside of me and that this moment was for both of us, and for all the dreams I'd thought were lost. *Lost to someone like me.*

We let our feet dry in the sunshine and then climbed back up to the road. I wondered at how this day had turned from pain and tears and a destroyed dinner to happiness and peace and a walk under a covered bridge. And our first kiss. The most beautiful kiss I'd ever experienced.

CHAPTER EIGHTEEN

We all have a superpower. What's yours?

Gambit, the Duke of Thieves

GABRIEL

We spent every moment of daylight together that weekend, watching the sunrise, taking drives, visiting my favorite spots in the area, driving to a couple of small towns where we walked through quaint downtown areas and ate in small mom-and-pop restaurants.

We bought several types of Vermont maple syrup, and I cooked her pancakes in the morning and we taste tested them all. Droplets of syrup stuck to her lip, and she laughed as I kissed them away, my blood heating as desire rolled hot and heavy through my body.

I reveled in our newfound physical closeness, still slightly nervous at first, but mostly overjoyed by all the sensations she was helping me discover. Not only did my love for her cause me to crave a deeper intimacy, but I'd become accustomed to her touch slowly over the weeks, and that had made all the difference.

Even now, Ellie touched me almost as tentatively as I touched her, and it helped me gain confidence in the very thing that had once made me feel so helpless. There had been no way for me to know it, certainly no way I could have guessed, but it felt as if I had been pulled to Ellie because our pasts—and our hearts— aligned in such a way that we were *meant* to heal each other.

On Sunday, we made a picnic lunch and ate it in a grassy area under a giant beech tree, its leaves gold and orange and red, casting light on Ellie's hair so that it, too, looked gilded. She lay back on the blanket we'd brought, and the dappled sunshine coming through the leaves moved over her face, making my breath catch. She was so beautiful that looking at her made me ache. She looked soft and happy, and her eyes were filled with something I hoped might be love. I leaned over and kissed her and kissed her until I thought I might go crazy. But I knew Ellie needed to be the one to advance things between us. I knew I needed to let her lead us in that direction if it was going to feel right. I wanted to give that to her, and so I rolled away and stared up at the sky coming through the breaks in the leaves and tried to catch my breath, to cool my blood, to will my body to calm.

I wanted so badly to touch her, to feel her breasts in my hands, to run my tongue over her nipples and feel them stiffen, to skim my fingers down the silky skin of her inner thigh. I almost groaned, but managed to hold it back.

The irony of the situation didn't escape me. I'd come to her to help me feel comfortable being close to a woman, and now I was dying with the frustration of holding back...for her. I remembered the talk I'd had with George about trusting my gut, though, and realized that this was what I'd known deep inside: She had needed me just as I'd needed her. And I was willing to do whatever it took to let her know she was precious to me—her body and her heart.

She propped her arms on my chest, smiling into my face as I chuckled. "What?" I asked.

She shrugged slightly, her smile growing. "I don't know. I'm just...happy."

A leaf fluttered down and landed in her hair and I plucked it out, smiling and then meeting her eyes. *Marry me*, I wanted to say. *Stay with me forever.* "Me, too," I whispered instead. We lay there for a few minutes, listening to the birds cry out to one another as they rustled the leaves overhead.

Ellie used one finger to outline a button on my shirt, and that small movement looked somehow erotic, her slender finger moving slowly around the tiny disc. I barely stopped myself from groaning. "When we went into Morlea to the grocery store, people looked at us...strangely. Is that why we've gone to other towns this weekend? So you don't see anyone you know?" She gazed up at me, questions in her eyes, a bit of insecurity as if she wondered whether their stares were because of her.

"It doesn't have anything to do with you, Ellie."

She tilted her head, her finger still moving in circles on the button. "Then...why? Why do they look at you that way?"

I was silent for a minute. "Mostly because I make them uncomfortable, I think." There was confusion in her gaze. "When I first came home, everyone was really happy. I got attention everywhere I went. I was sort of this local hero." I thought back to that time, how everything had been overly bright, how the world had seemed to waver in front of me every time I stepped out of the house, as if none of it were real. As if I was having a hard time holding on to the truth that I'd finally escaped the darkness of where I'd been. "I was skittish, nervous..."

"Naturally," Ellie said quietly.

"It wasn't only that I was suddenly free in the outside world again, it was that I was trying to come to terms with the death of my parents. I was grieving them. I was grappling with the fact that I'd taken someone's life." I glanced at her, but her expression didn't change. She'd known that. Everyone did. "I was struggling hard." I paused again. "One day George took Dominic and me to this fair. He thought, you know, that I could use some fun, to feel like a teenager. We got there and the lights, the people, it felt like everything was closing in on me and I sort of... went a little crazy. I freaked out and dropped to the ground as if I were in a war and being fired on. They had to carry me out of there."

"Oh, Gabe..."

"After that I didn't go out in public much anymore. I lost myself in stone carving, in the comfort of the people and the things I knew."

She was quiet as I thought about that time. "Once I did start going into town, people were wary of me. They didn't know how to react to me, if or how to approach me and so they just... didn't. I guess they wondered if I might just freak out again. Even now." I chuckled softly but there was no humor in the sound. It ended in a sigh.

Her brow furrowed prettily, and she nodded in understanding. "It's been so long, though. You were a teenager then. They should... try."

"Maybe I should try harder, too."

"Maybe," she said softly. The air was cool, and I pulled her close to make sure she was warm. She hooked a leg over mine.

"Do you still... struggle with having taken that man's life?" Her voice was soft, hesitant.

"No. I've found peace with that. I didn't enjoy it, but I'd do it again if I had to. In some ways that was the easiest thing to come to terms with. That was the thing everyone commended me for—finding the bravery to escape regardless of what I had to do. That was the topic no one was afraid to address. It's the things no one wants to talk about, the things everyone avoids, that you hold inside like a dirty secret that might somehow be your fault."

She looked up at me. "But you don't feel that way anymore."

I shook my head. "No, not anymore."

We were both quiet for long minutes, her head resting over my heart. I wondered if she was thinking about her own secrets, the things she had held inside for so long.

"Will you tell me about your parents?" she asked.

I smiled. "They were the best parents in the world. My dad was quiet, a thinker. And my mom was this Chatty Cathy. She couldn't go anywhere without stopping to have a conversation with about ten people."

"What else?" Her voice sounded wistful.

"She loved to read. She always had a paperback in her purse. Sometimes I'd look around at games when the other team was up, and she'd have her nose in a book." I smiled at the memory, at the knowledge I'd gotten my love of books from her.

She was quiet for a moment before she whispered, "It must have been such an awful, terrible shock to find out they'd passed away while you were gone." *Gone.*

"Yeah." It was half word, half breath, and I was silent for a minute at the memory of George breaking the news to me in that cold police station room, of the awful, aching grief that had followed. "But later…later I wondered if maybe having two extra angels on my side helped me escape that basement, you know?"

Her head tipped back, and the shocked look in her expression made me pause. Was she thinking of her own angels? Who had she lost? She looked down again, resting her cheek on my chest. "What are you thinking, Ellie?"

"I..." She shook her head slightly. "Nothing. That's just a...nice thought."

"What about you? Are your parents still alive?" I remembered what she'd said about how her dad had treated her, and stilled as I waited for her to answer. The moment had been so peaceful, and I didn't want to destroy that. But I yearned to know all about her, everything, the good and the bad, all the things that made her who she was.

"I guess my dad probably is," she said. "I wouldn't know. I left his home right after I graduated high school and haven't spoken to him since."

A lump formed in my throat. I'd noted she hadn't mentioned her mom at all. "I'm sorry."

"Don't be. I'm over it."

Are you, Ellie? I don't believe that and I don't think you do, either. My heart felt heavy, and we'd had a lot of heavy lately, and so I rolled her over, startling her and making her laugh. I smiled down at her before kissing her quickly, and the mood lightened.

I rolled off her again and we faced each other, our elbows on the blanket, our heads propped in our hands. I picked up a piece of her hair and rubbed it between my fingers, marveling at the silky texture. Lying here in the sunlight, it was a mixture of gold and red. "I'd want our children to have your hair," I murmured. "It's too beautiful not to be passed down."

She looked briefly startled as she blinked at me. "Me, a mother?" She shook her head gently, bringing more of that honey-hued hair over her shoulder as she laughed. But her laugh was shallow, no joy contained within it.

I regarded her. "Why not? Don't you want kids someday?"

"I...I don't know. I've never thought about it." She bit at her lip, looking off over my shoulder. The expression in her eyes was something close to fear. *But why?*

"I think you'd make a great mother," I said softly, leaning forward and kissing her again. I believed she had a heart full of love to give, whether *she* realized it yet or not. I'd seen the tenderness inside her, experienced her gentle nature. I was experiencing it now.

I leaned back, and the look in her eyes softened. After a moment, she asked, "How did your interview with Chloe go? Do you still feel good about it, now that you've actually experienced it?" I knew she was changing the subject, but I was okay with that. I'd learned that Ellie would confide in me when she was ready and not a moment sooner.

"Yeah. It did feel good." I considered her question a few seconds longer. "It felt good to be able to talk about what happened to me and feel the true sense of having moved past it. Some of the stuff we talked about brought up difficult memories, but I was okay an hour later, you know? In the beginning, it took such a long time to bounce back when some memory or another assaulted me. Now...I feel like I'm the one in control."

She nodded, and I couldn't dismiss the pride in her eyes. It warmed me, made me feel good, as if my survival was an accomplishment I could claim. She opened her mouth to say something but then closed it, obviously reconsidering whatever she'd been about to say. I watched as several expressions moved over her face. "Ellie, you can ask me anything. The things I told Chloe are yours, too, if you want them. There isn't anything I'd give to her that I wouldn't give to you."

She smiled a sad sort of smile. "I'm just not sure what to ask. I guess...I guess just how? *How* did you survive that kind of horror?"

I licked my lips, looking off into the field behind her, thinking how familiar this seemed to me in a strange, distorted sort of way. *Lying with Eloise in the daffodil fields.* "When I was first abducted, I was terrified of course. I was traumatized and confused and desperate to get out of there. But after a while, it was the boredom that started eating away at me. I knew that if I hoped to get out of there someday, I had to stay sane. I had to keep my mind occupied. I did math in my head a lot, but it didn't help the loneliness." I paused, thinking back to those days, remembering them as the most desolate of all the time I'd spent down there.

"One day I was scratching something into the wall with a penny I'd found on the floor, when a big chunk came loose."

"You started digging a tunnel?" she asked, her eyes wide.

I chuckled. "No. I was in a basement. I could have chipped through the entire wall over the course of fifty years and I'd still be underground."

Her face fell, the look in her eyes horror stricken, obviously imagining—maybe for the first time—the details of the situation I'd been in.

"I'd been carving with my dad since I was little. I had some skill for a kid, some promise anyway. I had the penny and I found a paperclip, and I used them to carve a figure, crude at first, but all I had was time and so I worked on it. I started over several times with smaller pieces I got from different places—behind the radiator, behind some boxes of old clothes he had down there, in dark corners—that wouldn't be noticed, and I made a set of figurines and named them for the things I loved. I was so afraid I'd forget what love felt like, and they helped me remember. They were a royal court of hope and they were my friends. My only friends. They were the reason I didn't break. They kept my mind and hands occupied and my hope alive. They reminded me that there are sparrows in the trees and fields of daffodils, and best friends, and even though I was in a cold dusty box, I might see those things again and that faith kept me alive until I did."

"Oh, Gabriel," she whispered, tears coming to her eyes. "They encouraged you when you had nothing else."

I smiled softly. "Yes." I tilted my head, thinking. "Maybe it was easier to accept the encouragement from characters, even characters I myself created, than for it to come straight from me. Funny, but it worked. It was like they embodied the people and things I loved and helped me remember their words of wisdom, the things they might have said to me if they could."

A tear slipped down her cheek, and I caught it on my thumb. "Please don't be sad. It's how I survived. It's how I saved myself. It's how I'm lying here with you now."

She leaned forward and kissed my lips, cupping my face in her hand. "Chloe called you extraordinary. And now I know exactly why."

I smiled at her, glad she didn't ask for more specifics at that moment. I'd tell her, but for some reason, I had a feeling now wasn't the time. She'd been trapped in a dark basement, too. Not by a tormentor, but by circumstances. Circumstances that had made me feel that she didn't belong in the Platinum Pearl when I first met her. Her circumstances had changed, but I sensed that in some ways she was still fighting for her escape.

CHAPTER NINETEEN

Beautiful things happen when you least expect them.

Lemon Fair, the Queen of Meringue

ELLIE

Chloe had stayed the weekend in Morlea so she had time to do some local sightseeing. She came over that night before dinner to say goodbye and thank Gabriel for the time he'd given her.

I left the room to give them a few minutes to talk, and when I came back into the living room, they were hugging, Chloe facing me so I could see the look of affection and sadness on her face. Her eyes were squeezed tight, and for a moment I just watched them, a streak of jealousy making me feel petty. I looked away as they let go of each other, and when Chloe spotted me, she rushed over and grabbed me in a hug, too.

"We didn't get to spend enough time together, Ellie. Next time?"

She stood back and took my hands in hers, squeezing them and smiling at me. "Will you be back?" I asked.

"Oh, definitely. I'm going to personally deliver a published copy of this paper when it's done." Her smile widened. "I'm going to make Gabriel proud with it."

I smiled back. "I'm sure you will."

She hesitated a moment, looking slightly unsure. "I talked to Dominic about what he did. I think he's really twisted up inside—"

"It's fine, Chloe, really."

"It's not fine. There's nothing fine about it. I just…I wish I could help."

I smiled at her. "You have helped by being a friend to me."

Her smile was big and it was contagious. "Call me if you ever want to talk, okay? If you just need a listening ear? Gabe has my number." *Gabe.*

"I will."

She smiled again. "Okay, good. You take care of yourself."

"You, too, Chloe."

She turned back to Gabriel and leaned up on her tiptoes and kissed his cheek. "Thank you again," she whispered. There was so much feeling in her tone it almost embarrassed me to be standing there.

He loves you, Ellie, I reminded myself.

Only because he didn't end up meeting Chloe first, that small mocking voice inside chided. I blocked it out as best as I could.

I didn't blame Chloe one bit for the affection she obviously felt for Gabriel, maybe even the love. She knew what I knew—that he had survived six years of hell by surrounding himself with love. With hope. How strong did your mind have to be—how beautiful your heart—to hold on in such a way? To *choose* love over fear again and again? Of course, he was lucky that he had so much love to draw upon. Not everyone was so blessed. Then again, I had a feeling Gabriel would have used any small glimmer of love—*of hope*—to stay strong. It was just who he was.

Gabriel, a boy who hadn't let himself forget what love felt like, and me, a girl who had made sure I did not remember.

We made dinner that night—a precooked lasagna that was really impossible to mess up, though if I'd been left alone, I probably could have managed it—and ate it on the patio. The evenings were getting chilly, so Gabriel turned on a heat lamp and we moved it next to the table.

Once the kitchen was clean, we curled up on the couch and watched a show, but I decided to turn in early since I was starting work at the quarry in the morning and wanted to be well rested. I was slightly nervous, too. What if I couldn't get the hang of the phone system and humiliated myself?

I had only held two jobs in my life. When I moved out of my dad's house, I'd worked in a movie theater for a little over a year, but couldn't afford anything more than to rent a small back room from a woman who'd advertised in the paper. When I'd gotten there I realized why it was still available. She had about twenty-five cats, and the whole place smelled like fish and dirty litter boxes. It was all I could afford, though, and it was better than my dad's house and so I'd taken it.

The next year, I'd met Kayla through some other people I knew, and she'd told me about the Platinum Pearl. I'd been loath to take my clothes off for anyone, but I'd been able to save up five hundred dollars for a car, a security deposit on my own apartment, and was able to get out of the cat house.

So now, my work experience included sweeping up popcorn and sliding down a pole in the nude.

I went to bed but couldn't sleep, and after twenty minutes of tossing and turning, I got up and opened the window, breathing in the freshness of the night air. I kneeled down and put my arms on the ledge, gazing upward for several moments at the clear, star-filled sky, trying to take the beauty inside me the way Gabriel seemed to be able to do so easily. Instead the beauty of the night seemed painful somehow and made me feel even more hollow inside.

Sighing, I closed the window and hobbled out of my room and into the garage as quietly as possible. William was there, smooth and white, his laughing face making my heart feel just a bit lighter.

I ran a finger over his head, marveling once again at what this had looked like only a month or so ago. How quickly Gabriel had brought forth life where there had seemingly been none at all. It almost felt like I knew this little guy, as if he might have a personality all his own. I sighed. "What if I don't do well tomorrow? What if I make a fool of myself?"

William continued only to smile and to stare at me with those encouraging eyes. I let out a breath. "Well, of course you'd say that."

I heard a small noise and turned around quickly, seeing Gabriel standing in the doorway in a T-shirt and loose sweatpants, leaning one hip on the frame and watching me curiously. I felt the heat rise in my neck and laughed, an embarrassed sound made mostly of breath. Gabriel smiled. I turned back around as the heat rose from my neck to my cheeks.

I felt Gabriel come up behind me, and he ran his hands down my arms, kissing the top of my head. "You're going to do just fine."

I turned my head to the side but didn't look back at him. "How do you know?"

"Because you're smart and you can learn anything."

You're smart and you can learn anything.

You're such a good, smart girl, Ellie. You don't forget that, okay? No matter what, you don't forget that.

I felt a sharp ache in my heart and pushed the words away, not willing to think about them—or who they'd come from— not when I already felt so vulnerable.

I moved my hand back over William's hard little head, felt Gabriel's solid strength at my back. The pain inside me rose up so suddenly, the honesty of it rolling off my tongue. "I've always pretended I was made of stone, but the truth is, I feel more like I was formed from sand, as if I might crumble at any second." I'd felt this way for so long, so long, and it *hurt*.

Gabriel wrapped his arms around me from behind as he'd done that day after I ruined dinner. He reached around me and laid his hand on top of mine on William's head. "But that's what solid stone is made from, Eloise. Sand and pressure"—he squeezed me lightly with the arm still holding me—"and time. That's all it is, my sweet love. Just sand and pressure and time."

I let the words roll through me, wanting so desperately for the pressure—the love—of his arms around me to help me achieve the confidence in myself that he seemed to have in me. It was the time part that worried me. How long? How *much* time until I felt solid and competent? How long until I wasn't pretending?

Gabriel had taught me so many lessons, and they were all important to me because he'd come by them honestly. The words he spoke weren't *just* words or platitudes—they were truths he'd *earned* through his own pain and suffering.

Just sand and pressure and time.

"I tried to look at the stars," I murmured after a moment, wanting him to know that I listened to every word he said to me. I wanted him to understand that I admired him above all others, even if I couldn't always manage to live his words the way he did. "I tried to appreciate the beauty around me, but I just don't think I did it right."

Gabriel blew out a breath that ended in a sigh. "Gratitude isn't a Band-Aid, Ellie. You still have to experience your feelings to work through them. Gratitude is meant to make it bearable. Sometimes gratitude gets you through the day, and sometimes it just gets you from one moment to the next. That's all."

"I was really looking more for a Band-Aid," I said, trying to infuse some humor into my tone.

He chuckled and it warmed me.

We were both quiet for a moment. "You probably think I'm crazy out here talking to a statue."

"No. They're good listeners. But so am I," he murmured against my hair, pulling me into him so my body was resting against his. "Why are you so hard on yourself? You don't have to be."

I didn't know how to answer that and so I just smiled, looking up at him. "Thank you."

He nodded, his eyes moving over my face as if he was trying to read my thoughts. Finally, he simply kissed me and then took my hand, leading me back into the house, where I went to bed and finally fell asleep.

* * *

I started work the next morning. George simply handed me the instruction book for the phone system before walking out the door toward the quarry, where I could already hear the machinery and trucks getting started doing whatever they did.

Gabriel chuckled softly at my look of surprise and said, "No one's answering the phones now. Even if you only pick up half of the calls that come in, we'll be better off." I knew he was only saying it to make me feel better, but it worked, and once he'd left for his workshop, I opened the instruction manual and began figuring things out.

Dominic came in around nine thirty, and my heart leapt with nervousness, but he simply smiled a tight smile at me and went to his office. No apology, nothing.

The day passed quickly as I taught myself the system, answered calls, only missing a few, and only hanging up on a couple, and before I knew it, Gabriel was walking back through the door, asking if I wanted to go to lunch with him, and then several hours later, picking me up to drive home.

He looked over at me in the cab of the truck, smiling broadly. "Did you like it okay?"

I nodded, a sense of accomplishment making me feel happy and at ease.

The week flew by, and although I got better at my job, teaching myself how to operate the fax and copy machines, and becoming adept at scheduling appointments using the online calendar, Dom's coldness affected my enjoyment of the job. In addition to not speaking to me, he would literally turn his back if I walked into the small break room to get coffee while he was in there, too, or pretend not to hear if I asked him a question. I tried to shrug off his immaturity, but I felt the utter disdain behind it, which made it difficult not to let it affect me. I refused to tell Gabriel, hoping Dominic would grow tired of his schoolyard antics and give it up.

But Gabriel walked the short distance to the office to pick me up every evening, and I escaped to his studio when I could, watching his beautiful hands work a piece of stone, knowing that though it had started out as nothing much, soon it would be something miraculous.

Watching his hands move over a piece of rock made me shiver now, wondering what they would feel like moving over every inch of me.

At night, after we'd eaten dinner, we would make out on the couch like teenagers, and I'd urge him in my mind to put his hand up my shirt, to undress me, to touch my skin, to release the pent-up desire that felt like a burning inferno inside me. But each night he'd pull himself away, and though his arousal was obvious, I told myself he just wasn't ready.

On Friday that week, Gabriel drove me to a doctor's appointment after work, where they checked my leg and determined my cast could come off. I laughed out loud when the heavy weight was peeled off me. "Freedom!" I said, and Gabriel grinned from across the room.

"Now you can literally get back on your own two feet," he said. I smiled, but inside, his words caused a spear of uncertainty and fear to slice through me.

We stopped on the way home and bought champagne to celebrate my reclaimed independence and made plans to order pizza for dinner.

I felt happy not to have to drag around a leg that felt twice as heavy as the other, but I also felt vaguely sad. He was right. I was literally back on my own two feet. There was no real reason for me to be at Gabriel's house anymore. I pushed the thought away for now. I wanted this weekend with him, even if it was the last one.

As soon as I walked in the door, I told Gabriel I was going to shave my leg. Seeing it in the bright light of the doctor's office had told me undoubtedly that I was long overdue. As a matter of fact, both legs could use some attention. I hadn't been overly concerned with my appearance in weeks. It had been a nice vacation from the constant grooming I'd needed to do as a stripper, but I didn't want to think about that right now, either. I wasn't shaving for aesthetics. I was shaving because, in all honesty, my legs just felt gross.

"Let me help," Gabriel said.

I laughed. "Shave my legs?"

He smiled a crooked smile. "Yes."

I shrugged. "If you want to."

We lingered over dinner and a couple of glasses of celebratory champagne, Gabriel laughing because I got up a couple of times and did a funny sort of jog/limp in place simply because I could, and because I needed to strengthen my muscles. I swore I was never going to take my body for granted again.

After cleaning the kitchen, he pulled me by my hand. "Come on." I followed him into his bedroom, glancing around at the simple furniture, the bookshelves overflowing with hardbacks and paperbacks, the small desk with a laptop sitting open on top, the bed made up with a navy comforter and a stack of pillows against the headboard.

Gabriel led me straight to the bathroom, where there was a large tub. He ran the water and I took a seat on the side, rolling up my yoga pants and swinging my legs over. I laughed. "This is definitely something I've never done."

Gabriel grinned as he rolled up his jeans and stepped into the tub, kneeling. I laughed again. "You're getting your jeans all wet."

"I don't care. Sit back. Let me pamper you."

I leaned against the wall, watching him as he took the cover off a new disposable razor and lathered his hands with soap. I sighed. Just the feel of soaking my feet in the warm water while I relaxed felt so good. He rubbed the soap gently on one leg, and I watched his hands slide over my skin. I couldn't help thinking of the work he did. This is what the puppies and rabbits and cherubs must feel like. Cared for. Cherished. Brought to life. This is what all those flowers and leaves and twining vines that used to be square lumps of rock must feel like. Set free. Renewed. Made beautiful beneath his capable hands.

I swallowed, the moment suddenly feeling so poignant, so intimate, so erotic as his hands glided down my legs, massaging gently until I moaned. I saw Gabriel's Adam's apple move as he, too, swallowed. His expression was so focused, so intent on what he was doing.

He glanced at me as he picked up the razor, and his pupils looked slightly dilated. It occurred to me that this wasn't only the first time he'd touched my skin with his hands. This was the first time he'd touched any woman. Tenderness exploded in my chest as I watched him drag the razor slowly up my leg. I felt breathless.

The razor moved gently up my skin, and his fingers followed behind it, ensuring he didn't miss any spots. The knees of his jeans were soaked now, but he didn't seem to notice. Steam rose in the air, and I realized I'd never been touched this way. Not once. Not ever. *Caressed. Loved.*

Gabriel rinsed the razor and turned the leg he'd shaved from side to side, assessing his work the way he did when he sculpted. His fingers moved to my anklebones and then down to my feet, where his hands massaged me lovingly. It felt so good I moaned again, longer this time. Gabriel's eyes shot to mine, looking slightly glassy. "You're so beautiful, Eloise. Every part of you." He ran his finger over my anklebone again and up the arch of my foot. "You're a work of art."

A work of art.

I'd been told I was beautiful before. I'd been told I was gorgeous, sexy, irresistible, but somehow I'd never allowed those words to penetrate. They'd just been...words. It was as if they'd sat there on the surface of my skin. But I felt Gabriel's words seep through my pores, into my blood, and deep to my bones. Right into my soul. I felt his words as if they were a benediction. And he'd only been talking about my ankle.

Butterflies fluttered in my tummy, and my clothes felt too tight, my skin too sensitive. With every movement, my T-shirt brushed over my nipples and made them feel tight and achy. A steady drumbeat of arousal was vibrating in my core, and my underwear was wet and too restricting.

"Gabriel," I whispered. I wanted him to kiss me. I wanted him to come up out of the shallow pool of water and lean over me and kiss me and then scoop me up and bring me to bed, but I didn't know how to ask.

It looked as if he was turned on, too, so why didn't he? He didn't have to wonder if I was on birth control. He knew everything about me in that regard after caring for me while I'd been too sick to care for myself. What was it? What was stopping him? Did he worry if I was clean? If I slept with the men from the club? That I was tainted? I had made lots of stupid choices in my life, but I'd never been unsafe. *Should I reassure him of that?*

Or did he hesitate because of his own inexperience? Was he worried I'd say no? That he wouldn't know what to do?

He ran his lathered hands up my other leg and then dragged the razor up it as well. I wanted to arch my back with the sensation, suddenly so overstimulated, I thought I might just slide down into the water and kiss him myself. Uncertainty assaulted me, though, and so I sat motionless as he finished the job and then rinsed my legs and my feet, standing and stepping out of the tub where his soaking wet pants dripped on the bathmat.

He grabbed a towel, and when I swung my legs out of the tub and over the side, he blotted them dry.

I watched his face as he did so, and he looked so intense, so focused. I thought for sure he was going to ask me to stay the night with him or that he would make a move of some sort. And so when he leaned up and kissed me on the cheek and whispered, "Good night," I froze and blinked.

Gabriel stood and walked stiffly out of the bathroom. I followed, whispering, "Good night, Gabriel," as I passed him at his bedroom door. I hesitated a couple of seconds too long, giving him a chance to ask me to stay, and we both stared at each other for several beats before I turned my head and walked out. I heard him release a shaky breath behind me.

I returned to my room and took a cool shower and then got in bed, still feeling frustrated and confused. As I lay there in the quiet, I realized that I didn't know what it was like to want like this. I'd never experienced it before. I'd never even known what wanting *was*, not really, and I was suddenly…amazed. And something warm and tender moved through me. *Oh God.* Gabriel had given this to me. And though it made me feel slightly crazed, it also made me feel powerful and alive.

I sat up in bed, a slow smile moving over my face as I gathered the sheet to my chest. Was he waiting for *me* to be ready? Was it another gift Gabriel was trying to give to me? The experience of knowing I wanted a man and offering myself to him, rather than only ever being taken? But wasn't it the same for him? I groaned. Of course it would be just like Gabriel to have been ready for weeks and to be waiting for me to know I was ready, too.

I got out of bed, nervous and unsure, and yet filled with a yearning so strong I was consumed with it.

I opened the door softly and stepped into the hallway, looking at his closed door. My nerves were like a buzzing in my veins, and I almost turned back, but I gathered my courage and walked quickly to his door, turning the knob and stepping inside.

His room was dim, the only light on next to his bed. He was lying under a sheet, his chest naked, with a book in his hand. When he saw me, a worried frown came over his face. He sat up on one elbow. "Ellie? Are you okay?"

I nodded jerkily, my heart beating so loudly, it seemed to echo in my ears. "You're reading—"

He laid the book aside. "No." He shook his head. "I've read the same sentence fifteen times now."

"Oh..." My voice came out in a croaky whisper, and I cleared my throat. Gabriel was so still, waiting. "I want you," I said in a whispered rush of words. "And I thought maybe you might...want...too." I swallowed, pressing my palms against the closed door at my back.

A look of such raw tenderness came over Gabriel's expression that I stopped breathing for a second before my breath resumed in a quick rush of air. I wanted to drink that look in, to make it part of me forever. "I do," he said. "I do want...too." His small, crooked smile, filled with love and a glint of teasing, made my shoulders relax.

He threw the sheet back and got out of bed. He was wearing boxers, and my heartbeat quickened when I saw the outline of his arousal through the thin material. I swallowed again, his beauty affecting me twice as much this time as it had the first time I saw him half-naked. This time...oh, *this time*, I was going to touch him and so much more.

If we see each other naked again, it won't be a job, or an accident. It will be because we both want it, and because it means something.

Yes.

Oh yes.

He pressed me gently against the door with his hips and brought his hands to my face, kissing me as I melted into him, my body softening everywhere to mold to his hardness.

"We fit so perfectly, don't we?" he murmured, and a rush of arousal raced through my blood at his words.

He kissed down my neck, feathering his lips over my skin, and I felt something in him that I hadn't felt before: He was holding nothing back this time. There was no reservation in his touch, no doubt in his kiss. I had offered myself to him, and he meant to give all of himself as well.

He led me to the bed and came over me as I lay back. "You might have to show me how to do this. I've never done it before," he whispered, a small smile on his lips and a hint of vulnerability in his eyes.

I brought a hand to his cheek. "I don't think I've done this before, either. Not like this. Let's just figure it out as we go."

He gazed at me so seriously before he kissed me again.

We undressed each other slowly in the soft glow of the reading lamp. I didn't feel a second of shame as his gaze moved over my naked body, and for a moment the lack of discomfort confused me. But then realization dawned: *this* was what it should feel like to be a woman. I'd never had any idea at all.

We touched and kissed with loving hands and open hearts, and I'd been right to think I'd never experienced anything like this before. It was tender and generous, and it was *everything*. Everything I'd never known.

I wanted to touch every part of him, to know his body the

way I'd come to know his heart. To willingly explore a man for the first time, to keep my eyes wide open and my mind focused on the moment because there was nowhere else I'd rather be. I wanted to actually feel pleasure, to know the thrill of giving over complete trust to the person I was with.

I started at his feet, and he laughed softly as I ran my hands over his toes and up his calves. I smiled, too, not just because he had, but because I'd never known laughter and joy could be part of sex. Everything was new and wondrous, and I felt a wild sort of reverence in the discovery of my own passion. I could feel this, too. I'd never known. Oh, I'd never known.

Gabriel's laughter turned into a moan as I continued up his thighs, kneading the muscles there, watching his face so I knew he was okay with my every touch, seeing him swell and harden and feeling the answering rush of wetness between my thighs.

I moved upward, running my hands over the warm hardness of his chest, across his broad shoulders, tracing a finger over the ridges of his stomach until he sucked in a breath and brought his lips to mine.

Gabriel turned me over and moved his hands over my skin as if I were a treasure he had just discovered—those beautiful artist's hands that held within them the power to bring forth beauty from within. And that's what I felt: beautiful, adored, *loved*.

He kissed and touched every part of me, and I had the faraway sense that he was mending me and I was mending him. We explored for what felt like hours, until I was slick and desperate, and the half-pained look on his face told me he felt the same.

When he pushed into my body, we both gasped, our eyes meeting in the dim light of the room, that same connection I'd first been so frightened of still there but now intensified a thousandfold.

I tried to focus only on his face, on the beautiful concentration in his expression, the way his eyes fell shut and his eyelashes formed dark crescents on his cheeks, the way his lips parted in pleasure. I tried to watch him as he rocked slowly at first, finding a rhythm and then increasing the pace, but my own swelling pleasure was so powerful, I was lost as it washed over me and through me, causing me to cry out Gabriel's name again and again. I fisted the sheets and pressed my head back into the pillow.

"Yes, Eloise," I heard him say. "Yes." Right before he groaned and then shuddered, collapsing on top of me, his breath shallow against my neck, a gentle throbbing where we were still connected.

Lying there afterward in his arms, his fingers running lazily down my arm, I wanted to laugh with joy. I'd been right: Every part of his body held a place that felt as if it had been made just for mine.

Later as I stared at the ceiling, listening to Gabriel's breathing grow deep and slow, I realized he had given me just what he said he would. His breath against my neck was a calming wind, his smile the sunshine, his touch was a thousand rainbows dancing on my skin, and I loved him so much I thought my heart would burst.

CHAPTER TWENTY

I will be a blanket of love warming you.

Lady Eloise of the Daffodil Fields

GABRIEL

I opened my eyes slowly, stretching my body as the night before came back to me in a sudden wave of sleepy elation; the way Ellie had come to me, the way my heart had soared to see her standing at my door, the words she'd spoken, the words I'd been waiting to hear. *I want you.*

Ellie was sitting on the side of the bed, staring at the light of dawn just peeking beneath the blinds. My eyes roamed the feminine lines of her smooth back, the way her waist dipped inward and flared out to the roundness of her hips, and I felt a soft throbbing again, despite having spent most of the night making love.

"Don't go," I said, my voice thick with sleep.

She turned, her eyes tender and vulnerable, her lips swollen with all the ways we'd used our mouths the night before. She looked soft; God, she looked so soft. And I'd been right—she was most beautiful in the first light of morning, and especially so after a night of being loved.

"The sun's starting to rise," she said quietly, bringing her hair back over her shoulder. "I don't want you to miss it just because I'm here."

I smiled. "Open the blinds. We can watch it from this bed as well as we can watch it from the patio."

She glanced at the window and back at me and then stood, opening the shades to the view of the sunrise just peeking above the forest behind my house. The room was washed in a pale golden glow, and her naked skin seemed iridescent. She returned to me and slipped under the sheets and smiled as she opened her thighs beneath me, creating a perfect cradle for my hips. And she accepted me into her body again as the sunrise welcomed us to a brand-new day.

And I finally knew what it was like to love a woman: body, heart, and soul.

* * *

That weekend was spent exploring each other's bodies and learning everything that brought pleasure to the other. I felt insatiable for her, both satisfied and yet constantly hungry. On Saturday, we didn't leave the bed much except to eat and bathe, but on Sunday, we took a walk so Ellie could exercise her leg and feel the freedom and pleasure of walking without crutches slowing her down. She had a slight limp, but the doctor had said that would lessen in time.

We held hands as we strolled under a different covered bridge than the one we'd gone to the weekend before, and I pulled her to me where I leaned against the ancient rough wood and kissed her. She laughed and kissed me back, and it felt as if the whole world had stopped and it was only us within it.

I was shaken from my reverie when we pulled up in my driveway and saw a car I didn't recognize parked there. We got out and two men in suits stepped out of the car, walking toward us. "Gabriel Dalton?" the blond man in the navy suit asked, extending his hand.

I shook it, nodding. "Yes."

"I'm Detective Cotterill."

I was slightly confused, but figured it was in reference to Ellie's case, so when she came up next to me, I introduced her, but he only gave her a fleeting glance. "I was hoping I could ask you a few questions."

The other man had walked around the car and introduced himself as Detective Barbosa, and we shook his hand as well before I answered Detective Cotterill. "Of course. Uh, come on in."

I led them to my front door and inside, where I gestured to the living room area. "Can I get you something to drink?"

They both declined and we sat down. I glanced at Ellie, and she looked slightly nervous. "I'm assuming this is about Ellie's case?"

Detective Cotterill shook his head. "No. This is about a boy who was abducted in town."

"Wyatt Geller?"

Detective Cotterill looked up from his notepad. "Do you know him?"

"I know *of* him. I've been following the case closely."

He looked at me strangely. "I see. Any particular reason for that?"

I frowned, looking back and forth between him and Detective Barbosa, who had leaned back on the couch with one arm resting on the back and an ankle on his knee. "If you don't know, I was abducted myself when I was—"

"Yes, we're aware of that."

What was going on here? "Okay, well, then you can understand why I'd be interested in what happened to Wyatt Geller."

Neither detective answered that, instead turning to Ellie. "You're Eloise Cates?"

"Yes," she murmured, scooting closer to me. I put my hand on her knee protectively, and Detective Cotterill looked at it there for a moment before turning his gaze back to my face. "And you work at the Platinum Pearl, er, gentleman's club?" He'd described it in polite terms though he looked at her distastefully, conveying exactly what he thought about her job. *Judgmental bastard.* Anger arced down my spine.

"I used to. I'm no longer employed there," Ellie answered.

"Is that where you met Mr. Dalton?"

"Yes."

"How often do you patronize the Platinum Pearl, Mr. Dalton?"

"I don't anymore."

"Hmm," he hummed shortly. "We spoke to the manager there." He flipped a page on his notepad. "Rodney Toller. He said you became pretty obsessed with Ms. Cates and made several of the other girls uncomfortable, almost had to be escorted out a couple of times."

Ellie shook her head. "No, that's not true."

"That's an inaccurate version of what happened. I'm sorry, Detective, what is this about?"

"The parallels in your case and the Wyatt Geller case are very similar. We're simply trying to figure out why. Do you know why that would be, Mr. Dalton?"

"In what way are our cases similar?"

"We're not able to share that information at this time. We were wondering if you might already be aware."

I paused. "If you're implying I know something about that little boy's disappearance that I haven't told the police—"

"We never said that, Mr. Dalton. After all, your abductor is dead. You stabbed him, correct?" By the look on his face, he knew very well I had. Condescending asshole. Next to him, Detective Barbosa picked at his teeth.

My heart had started beating rapidly, and I worked not to show that this was affecting me. I was confused and upset that I was being questioned in this case as if I were a suspect. "Do I need a lawyer?"

"Why would you think you need a lawyer?"

I let out a pent-up breath. "Listen, Detectives, I don't know a thing about the Wyatt Geller case that I haven't read in the news. And I can't speculate on why there might be parallels in our cases if you won't tell me what the similarities are."

Detective Cotterill closed his notepad and put it in the pocket on the inside of his suit coat, along with the pen he'd been holding. "We appreciate your time, Mr. Dalton, Ms. Cates," he said, standing.

That was it? I stood, too, rubbing my hands down my hips. Detective Cotterill followed my movement and then gave me a tight smile. "You think of anything we should know, you give us a call." Detective Barbosa pulled a business card out of his pocket and handed it to me.

I walked the detectives to the door and said a terse goodbye, shutting it behind them.

"What was that about?" Ellie asked, walking over to where I remained standing by the door.

"I have no idea." I looked at her and gave her an encouraging smile. "Just covering their bases, I guess." Still, a chill moved through my blood at the news that our cases were similar. How? And why? And what was that little boy enduring right this minute? God, I didn't want to think about it. But I couldn't help it.

I'd been there.

I already knew.

CHAPTER TWENTY-ONE

We're a team. If you hurt, I hurt.

Racer, the Knight of Sparrows

ELLIE

The weeks passed with no further communication from the police. I had to figure they'd just been doing their jobs by questioning Gabriel, although the way they'd done it, and the fact that they'd brought the Platinum Pearl into it, had shocked and shamed me.

They had looked at Gabriel as if he were some pervert when nothing could be further from the truth. Even I had recognized that he didn't belong in the club the very second I saw him there.

The detectives had twisted things in a way that made Gabriel unrecognizable, and it filled me with anger and a burning need to defend him. And yet, I had no way to do that.

He was everything to me. If I could have crawled under Gabriel's skin and lived there, I would have done it happily. I felt most complete when he was buried inside me, his eyes closed and his lips parted in pleasure. No other woman had ever put that look on his face. It was mine and mine alone. The sun rose and set in his eyes, and I was so deeply in love with him that I wanted nothing but to spend every waking second in his arms. It was only there I felt completely at peace.

Gabriel had all the things that brought him peace and joy. His work, his sunrise, his wind, and the raindrops on his window. But I didn't need any of that. To me *he* was all of those things— I *only* needed him and nothing more.

Gabriel asked me to stay with him at his house, and so I did. I guessed I'd have to go back to my own apartment at some point, but our relationship was so new and so wonderful that I didn't want to spend a second apart from him. Luckily for me, I didn't have to since we worked together, too.

I brought the phone headset with me as much as possible and answered calls in his studio, where I watched him work. If the noise and distraction disturbed his focus, he never said so. He was working on another piece of architectural carving for a library in Germany, a foliate band, he called it, that would go on the front of the structure. It was gorgeous with intricate vines, flowers, and butterflies. If I squinted, I swore those butterflies would start fluttering their wings and come to life. That's how real they looked.

At times I was in the office with Dominic, and although I avoided him as much as I could, his demeanor was still cold. Mostly he ignored me, but at times I felt so raw and defenseless. It seemed that my love for Gabriel had somehow revealed the most tender parts of me, and I felt exposed, bared in a way I hadn't anticipated. Or perhaps I had. Perhaps that's the reason I'd resisted it so fervently. But now...now I was like the works of art Gabriel created: Every sharp edge had been chipped away so that my insides, the parts that made me vulnerable and sensitive, were on the outside, whereas before they'd been encased in a hard coating of stone. It was an irony that I'd stripped for a living and yet I'd never felt more naked than I did now in a full set of clothes. I felt as if one sharp look would make me bleed.

I'd once been hardened against scorn, but suddenly Dominic's contempt somehow brought up every hurt I'd ever suffered, and I had no armor to protect myself from the memories. I was completely raw. When Dominic glared at me as if I were trash, the names I'd been called when I was a stripper repeated loudly in my mind—*trashy whore, cheap slut, piece of ass.* And it went deeper, too, to places my mind hadn't traveled in years—dark, painful places I didn't ever want to go again.

And yet, when Dominic turned away rather than look at me, I couldn't help recalling the way it'd hurt so deeply when I'd see girls at school hand out invitations to all the other girls in class except me, the way I'd tried so hard to brush it off, to pretend it didn't matter. How I'd secretly longed to be included, to be liked, how it was a deep ache in the pit of my stomach that never seemed to go away.

The memory itself made me feel self-conscious and ugly all over again. It made me remember how I'd wondered if it was my threadbare, too-small clothes that made them ignore me, or if it was the fact that I was self-conscious and shy, unwilling to approach them first. Or worst of all, could they see I was unloved and unwanted by the person who was supposed to love me unconditionally, and so were unwilling to take a chance on someone who couldn't even win a parent's approval?

I remembered dreaming that someday someone would invite me to a party, and I'd go and everyone would like me, and I'd suddenly have friends and life wouldn't feel so painful all the time.

I went through whole scenarios as I walked home from school, my imaginings my only company. And suddenly I worried—if I *was* ever invited to a party, how would I get the money to buy a gift? I couldn't show up empty-handed. And so one night when my father was passed out on the couch, I stole five dollars out of his wallet and used the money to buy a small makeup kit at CVS. I would take that makeup kit out and look at it sometimes, and it was like a small fire that I kept burning inside, the symbol of my girlish hope that one day I'd be included. That one day I'd be loved.

And then my father's friend Cory had done what he did. Afterward, I'd crawled out of bed in searing pain, still smelling like him—like sweat and beer—and I'd taken that makeup kit out of the drawer where I'd kept it. I'd sat down in front of my mirror and opened that kit and smeared the makeup across my face, caked it on my eyelids and cheeks and across my mouth so I looked like the ugly, garish, sorrowful clown I felt like inside. I'd stared at myself that way for a long, long time until I was too tired to stay awake anymore and then I'd gone back to bed, not caring in the least that there was blood smeared on my sheets and makeup smudged across my pillow. And, oh God, the memory tore through me like a red-hot knife. It made me want to scream and fall to my knees. I didn't want to remember those things. I wanted to push them away, forget all about them, but mostly I just didn't want to feel the emotions they invoked. I didn't feel strong enough.

I was tempted to stand slightly behind Gabriel as we walked through the world so he would shield me from the things I imagined might hurt me. My knight in shining armor. And, maybe, I thought, that was what love was *supposed* to do—peel your layers back and uncover all your tender spots so they, too, could be

healed. The problem was, I didn't know how to go about doing that. And so instead of healing, I remained peeled back and
bleeding.

I came into his studio one chilly afternoon, pulling my sweater
tight. A gust of wind followed me, and I pushed the door shut,
laughing as I turned to him. "God, it's cold out there all of a sudden."

Gabriel turned his head, his hands still moving over the piece
he was working on. "We'll have to light the fireplace tonight."

I nodded, taking a seat in the chair where I usually sat, and
watched him work for a few minutes, watched his gentle, skillful
hands move over the stone, hands that had now moved over me
in much the same way.

It was different watching his hands work now than when
I'd watched him reveal William. Then, I'd only wondered what
they might feel like. Now I knew and it filled me with a shivery
happiness to watch him work.

I glanced over to the shelf where William sat, and he wasn't
there. I frowned. "Gabriel, where's William?"

Gabriel stopped his work and looked at me. "Oh, he got
picked up by the shipping company this morning. They were
ready for him. I guess the museum exterior's almost complete."

A painful shock caused me to go rigid, and ice water poured
through my veins. "You didn't tell me."

Gabriel was looking at me strangely. "You were in town, picking up that stuff for George...Ellie, are you okay?" He started
walking toward me.

A loss so intense it scared me had settled in the pit of my
stomach. I wrapped my arms around myself, attempting to hold
the emotions at bay. Oh God, this was ridiculous. It was just a
statue...just...

"Hey," Gabriel said gently as he pulled me from my chair, wrapping his arms around me. "I'm sorry. I didn't think you'd take it like this. I'm sorry."

I melted into him, wrapping my arms around his neck and pressing my face into his chest, inhaling his scent—*comfort, calm*—and shaking my head. "No, I'm...I'm sorry," I mumbled. "I don't know why..."

He leaned back and held me away so he could look in my eyes, so much understanding in his, as if he knew just how I felt. He always did. "I should have let you say goodbye. I'm sorry."

I shook my head again, attempting a smile. "No, I'm being ridiculous. I guess...I just...I fell in love with you while William..." I didn't know how to finish that sentence. *Came to life? Was born?* Did I think of William as a child of some sort? The physical representation of my love for Gabriel? I took a deep breath. "I fell in love with you while you created William. He was special to me." I attempted another laugh, and this time it sounded more natural, though the lump in my throat was still there.

"You love me?" His voice was full of warm wonder.

I blinked. "God, you don't know?"

He smiled, so happily and just a little bit shyly, and my heart turned over. I felt ashamed as I realized I'd never said the words, even through all the nights he made love to me and held me in his arms as my heart burned with love for him. "I...hoped. But it's nice to hear the words."

I pulled him close. "Oh, Gabriel, I love you. I love you so much." It almost shocked me to know I hadn't said the words, but as I held him I realized that I'd held back not because I didn't know I loved him, but because the words didn't seem big enough for what I felt. *I worship you? I admire you? I need you?*

I depend on you? How did you mix all of that up and express it with only three small words? Wasn't love supposed to be peaceful and calming? And yet my love for Gabriel felt...desperate.

He kissed me, surrounded by all his beautiful things, the creations of his heart, and joy and loss and uncertainty mingled in mine. Love wasn't *supposed* to feel desperate. Was it? Was I so flawed that I couldn't even *love* right?

"I think we'll have to go visit William and tell him the big news," he said teasingly.

I sniffled and laughed, blinking so the tears gathered in my eyes wouldn't fall. "In France?"

"Why not?"

I shrugged. "I don't know. I mean, maybe someday." I just wanted William here. With me. Where I could look at him whenever I wanted. "Anyway, I think he knows. I think he was the first to know."

"Ah, Ellie," Gabriel breathed. "I love you."

We stood that way for a while until I felt better in the warm strength of his arms. "In the meantime, I'll have them send me a picture when he's mounted in his spot, okay?"

I nodded but inside, pain welled up in me again. I didn't want to picture William there. And though it was irrational, I couldn't help but wonder if he was lonely. "Okay."

"Okay," he whispered, leaning forward and kissing my eyelids, my nose, my lips until I breathed out a small laugh.

I collected myself, and when Gabriel returned to his work, he glanced up and said, "There's this fall festival in town every year. You know, bobbing for apples, hayrides, that kind of thing." He looked back down at his work for a moment. "It's this weekend. I was thinking you might want to go?" He paused and then said, "You know we talked about me working a little harder with the people in town. I was thinking this might be a start."

I tilted my head. "I think it's a good idea. I'd love to go."

His smile was slight. "Okay, good." He paused again and his brow creased. I waited for him to speak. "There was an article about Wyatt Geller in the paper this morning. My name was mentioned."

I blinked. "Mentioned how?"

He shook his head. "Just that I'd been questioned—that there were some similarities in my case and his."

He made it sound as if it was nothing, but I wondered again if the police would have been as hostile with him if he wasn't also connected to the Platinum Pearl. *To me.* I was silent as I considered that, my stomach sinking. I shook my head. God, some part of him must regret the day he ever stepped foot into the Platinum Pearl. Would my relationship with him cause him more problems? Would his already shaky standing in the community get worse, not better, because of his association with me? I picked at my fingernails, a frown creasing my forehead.

"Don't," Gabriel said.

I snapped my eyes to his. "Don't what?"

"Whatever you're thinking right now, stop it."

I blew out a breath, a piece of hair flying away from my face. I couldn't help the small smile that came to my lips. "How did you know—?"

He was smiling at me from where he sat on his work stool. "I know you, Eloise." There was so much love in his voice, it made my breath catch for a second, and warmth washed through me. Yes, he did know me, and he loved me anyway.

I dropped my hands and nodded in agreement.

He picked up a tool and then paused. "Oh, also, Chloe will be here for a couple of days. She wants to administer some test to me that she says will help support some part of her paper. She didn't think it was necessary at first, but now she does for whatever reason." He shrugged.

"Oh, okay. Does she need to travel all the way here to give it to you?"

"She says it has to be administered in person." He paused for a minute. "I think she likes it here, too. I think she's gotten attached to the area."

I wondered if it wasn't the people she was attached to, namely Gabriel, but I pushed the jealous thought aside. I liked Chloe, and I trusted her. "All right, then. Let's show those townspeople how amazing you are and how...your bobbing-for-apples skills know no bounds." I grinned. "If you can win over a hard case like me, you can win anyone over."

He laughed and my heart felt lighter. Though when I glanced to the spot where William had been just the day before, the sense of loss trickled back in, as if a part of me was gone, too, along with William.

CHAPTER TWENTY-TWO

Don't lose hope. You never know what tomorrow holds.

Shadow, the Baron of Wishbone

ELLIE

The morning of the Morlea Fall Festival dawned crisp and cold. I hadn't wanted to pull myself from the warm cocoon of Gabriel's bed, but I was a little anxious about going into town with him, so instead of lying there worrying about it, I pulled myself from beneath his arms and tiptoed to the shower.

I had just rinsed the shampoo out of my hair when Gabriel pulled the glass door open and joined me. I laughed and sputtered under the water in surprise. But soon my laughter turned to soft moans as he worshiped my body under the warm shower spray, waking me up completely in the most delicious way possible.

I dressed in a pair of jeans with strategically placed rips and pulled on a loose, wine-colored sweater that had a long band of lace at the hem. I took extra care with my hair, blow-drying and curling it in loose waves, the way Gabriel liked it best. "All this hair," he would whisper in the quiet of the bed we shared. "I could wrap myself in it." And the way he looked at me when it was left loose and falling over my breasts made me feel like the most beautiful woman on earth.

When I emerged from the bathroom, Gabriel's smile made me happy I'd put forth the extra effort with my appearance. I knew he thought I was just as beautiful with makeup on as without—and that he might even prefer me without.

"Ready?"

I nodded and took his hand and we left the house, driving the ten minutes into town and parking in the large grassy area that had been designated as a lot for the event.

Couples strolled toward the park where the festival was being held, wearing jeans and sweaters, scarves, and light jackets. The smell of popcorn and caramel wafted on the breeze, and I gripped Gabriel's hand, feeling a sense of excitement that seemed familiar in some distant way—as if I'd experienced it once upon a time and forgotten the sensation. *Happy anticipation*, that's what it was. Had it really been so long since I'd felt it?

I glanced over at Gabriel, who had been looking around at the people passing us. He caught my eye and smiled, though there was a nervous edge to his expression. I squeezed his hand, holding on to the hopefulness dancing through my veins. Maybe this was going to be okay. *Please let this be okay.*

I heard a female yell of excitement and looked up to see Chloe rushing toward us, a grin on her face, her arms open wide. I laughed out a startled sound as she clasped me in a hug and squealed again and then let go, crushing Gabriel as well as he grinned and hugged her back.

"God, could this day be any more gorgeous?" she asked as she stepped back, her cheeks flushed and her eyes sparkling, her

shiny curls bouncing around her face. She was wearing a pair
of dark jeans and a white sweater, with a pair of tall brown
boots and a scarf wrapped expertly around her neck in shades of
green, orange, and yellow. She looked classy and beautiful, like
the cover model on some fall fashion magazine.

I looked down at my own outfit, the one I'd felt good about
only half an hour before, and suddenly felt cheap and tacky. I
hadn't thought to buy any new clothes. I shifted on my feet,
wanting to step behind Gabriel but forcing myself not to.

"Thank you so much again, Gabriel, for making time for me
this weekend. I'll only take an hour of your time, I promise. I'm
just so glad I picked *this* weekend to be here. This is amazing."
She swept her arm around at all the stands, the laughing people,
the piles of pumpkins. "Fall is my very favorite season."

Gabriel chuckled. "It's no problem. I'm glad you're here.
Have you seen George yet?"

"Yes. He's over there with Dominic." Her eyes darted to me
for a beat, her expression concerned before she pointed behind
her and waved. Nerves punched at my belly at the mention of
Dominic's name. Gabriel hadn't said he'd be here. But by the
look on his face, he hadn't known, or he hadn't been sure.

"Will you tell them we're here?" he asked Chloe. "I'm going
to buy my girl a pumpkin-spice latte."

Chloe grinned. "Of course." She put a hand on my arm and
smiled encouragingly, and then she flitted away.

"Did you know Dominic would be here?"

Gabriel looked at me and shook his head. "He didn't say he
would be. But I thought things were better with you two. Has he
been bothering you?" His brow creased in a frown.

I shook my head. "No. He just doesn't like me."

He tipped my chin so I was looking up into his eyes. "Ellie, it's him, it's not you. He'll get over whatever he's got going on in his own head, okay? I promise. Please don't let him get to you."

"I know. I won't," I lied. I looked at the people milling around us and caught some of them staring. "I wish I had worn something nicer. I should have bought something."

He frowned again, looking down at my outfit. "You look beautiful."

I scoffed, picking at my fingernails. "You think I look beautiful in sweatpants."

"Hey," he said gently, wrapping his hands around mine so I was forced to quit picking. "What's this about? I would have bought you some new clothes if you wanted—"

My eyes shot to his. "I don't want you buying me clothes."

He paused. "Then you could have bought your own clothes. I just meant I would have taken you shopping."

I nodded, feeling small and petty, whiny and probably annoying. I forced a smile. "I'm sorry. I just want this day to go well for you. And here I am making it about me. I'm really okay. I think I just need some caffeine. That latte you mentioned sounds great."

He smiled, but his eyes still held a glint of worry. I smiled bigger to reassure him and he took my hand in his. "If my woman needs caffeine, my woman gets caffeine. Come on."

He bought me a pumpkin-spice latte that looked more like a dessert than coffee, and I noticed more stares as we stood in line. I tried my best to ignore them. Gabriel had reassured me they were just curious about him. But still, the attention—and the fear that they might be judging me—put a damper on my mood and made me feel more self-conscious.

We took our coffee-desserts and sat on a couple of bales of hay that had been placed here and there for decoration and for seating, and I felt better as we laughed and sipped our drinks.

A few minutes later, George, who we spotted standing with Chloe and several couples, gestured to us to join them. I recognized a few of the men from the quarry and figured they must be here with their families. "Want to go over and say hi?" Gabriel asked.

"You go." I nodded toward them. "I'm going to sit here and let the caffeine and sugar make it to my bloodstream." I smiled at him. In all honesty, I was enjoying sitting in this spot where I could just observe the event, and I wasn't up for chitchat at the moment.

"You sure?"

"Yeah." I nudged him. "Go. And when you get back, you can show me those bobbing-for-apples skills you've made so much of."

Gabriel laughed as he stood. "Deal." He shot a smile over his shoulder as he walked away, and my heart flipped. I watched him join the group and felt my lips tip up slightly. I loved seeing him interact with others, loved the way he paid such close attention when other people spoke, the way he smiled so sincerely. And I realized that despite what Dominic had said about my being bad for his brother, it appeared to me that Gabriel was even *more* at ease with himself since he and I had grown closer.

I could see who he'd once been—the quietly confident boy everyone had been so drawn to—and I knew he would have always been that way if his life hadn't been so horrifically interrupted when he was just a boy. He would have been "that guy," the one girls whispered about in the hallway, the one who didn't seem quite real, more like a hero on a movie screen, so effortlessly charming, so completely captivating, and yet still kind and genuine. Would he have been drawn to me if he had grown up as the person he was supposed to be? Would he have noticed me at all? I didn't think so, and it left an ache in my heart.

I watched as Chloe talked animatedly to him, and I smiled at her exuberance and the fact that I could feel it even from across a crowded gathering.

Gabriel bent his head close to hers, listening attentively, and then after a few minutes, he leaned back and laughed. She laughed, too, grabbing his shoulders and saying something else that caused them both to laugh harder. They were so beautiful together: joyful and carefree. It caused a stab of pain to slice through my belly.

"She's in love with him, you know."

I whipped my head to the left, where I saw Dominic standing, watching Gabriel and Chloe, too. His words caused my heart to catch, but there didn't appear to be any malice in his expression, instead almost…sadness. *Why?* I'd thought he wanted Gabriel and Chloe together. I swallowed, turning back to where Chloe and Gabriel were still leaned close together, their brown hair almost the same shade.

I saw the way Chloe took every opportunity to touch Gabriel, the way her gaze moved back to him even as someone else in the group joined in on the conversation. Of course she was in love with him. He was beautiful in a way that was almost difficult to explain unless you knew him. He was good and generous and smart and talented. God, who *wouldn't* be in love with him? "I know," I said softly.

I looked back up at Dominic, and he was regarding me thoughtfully, though not unkindly, and I was surprised at the lack of hostility in his gaze. It was the first time he'd looked at me with anything other than condemnation. He seemed to come back to himself and stood straight, looking around. "I'm starving. I'm going to go check out some of the booths. You want anything?"

"No, thank you," I said, surprised by the offer. He nodded and turned away, disappearing into the crowd. I looked back to where Gabriel, Chloe, and George were with the group of quarry families, and Gabriel caught my eye, smiling and giving me a small wave. I smiled back, holding up my coffee cup in cheers.

He looked back to the group as George said something, and I watched as a couple walked past, shooting Gabriel a curious glance and then the wife smiling slightly as Gabriel laughed at whatever was being said.

This was just what he needed—for the town to see him as his natural self, interacting with those he felt comfortable with. They just needed to see who he really was and they'd fall in love with him, too. How could they not?

When Gabriel had been sitting with me, we both received curious stares, the people of Morlea obviously being familiar with who he was. But now that I was sitting alone on the bale of hay sipping my coffee, I was mostly anonymous.

I took another minute to look around at the crowd, smiling at a toddler holding a pumpkin way too heavy for him. He weaved and almost toppled over before his dad took the pumpkin, chuckling as he steadied him. I laughed softly at the sweet display of parental affection.

A boisterous group was playing some sort of booth game a little ways from where I sat, and when they all let out a collective whoop, I turned my gaze on them. Whoever was playing had obviously won because they were all cheering. They parted as the winner turned, grinning a grin I'd seen before. My blood chilled, and the scene wavered before my eyes. One of the men who'd beaten me in the parking lot that night. Out on bail. *Oh no. Oh God.* I still didn't know his name, had never bothered to find out, in truth hadn't wanted to think about him in any personal terms.

I stood, stumbling forward and beginning to turn when we locked eyes. *Oh God, oh God,* I was going to be sick. The sweet coffee I'd just drunk came up my throat, and I put a hand over my mouth, afraid I'd throw up right there where I stood.

My instinct was to run away, to avoid him at all costs, but the man leaned down and whispered in the ear of the woman standing next to him, and she made a beeline straight for me. I blinked, frozen to the spot in confused horror. *Please don't let this be happening. Not here.*

"You stupid slut!" she yelled at me, stopping several feet from where I stood. It seemed to quiet all around me as people turned, looking from me to her. I glanced over at Gabriel, and he seemed to be listening to a story one of the men who worked at the quarry was telling.

I started to turn. Maybe if I just walked away, everyone would return to what they'd been doing.

"Don't walk away from me," she called. "You think you can lie about my boyfriend and get away with it? Just because he turned you down? You deserved what you got."

Is that what he'd told her? That I'd come on to him and he'd what...been forced to beat me unconscious? I almost laughed at the craziness of it, but my heart was beating so harshly, I couldn't muster even a small chuckle.

I crossed my arms over my breasts, hugging myself as the man who'd beaten me came up beside her. "Let's go. I'm not supposed to be anywhere near her."

Thank God. My eyes shot back to where Gabriel had been

standing, but I didn't see him there. A burst of anxiety shot down my spine just as I heard his voice. "Get out of here now." The words were spoken in a loud growl and I jolted, taken off guard by the cold command in his tone. He was standing just a short distance behind me and I turned, blinking as he stepped in front of me.

"Gabriel, it's okay," I mumbled. The girlfriend of the man was still calling obscenities at me, but I tuned her out as Gabriel walked forward, looking as if he was intending to engage physically with the man. *Oh God, oh no. What should I do?*

"Don't come near me, bro," the man said, backing away. The people in the crowd who were not already watching turned to see what was going on, and a hush fell over the gathering.

In an effort to move away, the man stumbled, but immediately righted himself and then stepped backward. He put his hands up in the air. "This was just a coincidence," he said. "We're leaving."

I couldn't see Gabriel's face, but I heard the rage in his tone as he said, "If it wouldn't end up hurting Ellie more, I'd do to you exactly what you did to her, you disgusting piece of human garbage."

I put my hands over my mouth, not realizing tears were streaking my face until I felt them on my fingers.

"Whoa, hey." George ran up with Dominic on his heels, and they each took one of Gabriel's arms and pulled him away from the man. Chloe was right behind them, and she looked stricken.

The man backed up, looking relieved to see Gabriel being forced to stand down. Despite what he'd done to me, he was a coward. If I hadn't known it before, I realized it then.

Even so, I was shaky with fear and shame. Someday soon I was going to have to face those men in court. How would I manage it? I didn't think I could. I wasn't strong enough. I'd *never* be strong enough.

That's when the whispers—the gossip—around me penetrated...

"...this happened before when he was a kid, you know. Do you remember that fair...?"

"...seems nice but then...violent..."

"...sometimes victims become perpetrators. There've been studies done..."

"Did you hear he was a suspect in that case...?"

"Who's the girl with him? Did you hear what that other girl was calling her?"

Slut.

Whore.

Trash.

I shook my head, trying to tune it out, sick with horror at what had just happened.

Gabriel shook George and Dominic off as the man, his girlfriend, and the others who'd been with him started to walk away, swearing and spitting on the ground. "If you ever come near her again, it'll be the last thing you ever do, you sick excuse for a man," Gabriel called after them.

The girlfriend turned and stuck her middle finger up, but the man pretended not to hear Gabriel, disappearing into the crowd. "Oh my God, what was that?" Chloe whispered. "Are you okay?" she asked me.

I nodded jerkily. For several heartbeats, Gabriel stood staring in the direction the group had gone and then turned to me, exhaling a large breath. "Ellie, Jesus, I'm sorry. Are you okay?"

I shook my head, my eyes darting around at all the stares, all the whispered words, all the judgment. "Can we go? Can we just leave?"

Dominic turned to Gabriel. "Who—?"

"One of the men who attacked her," Gabriel answered.

I felt the heat of shame moving up my neck, filling my cheeks and making me feel woozy. I turned my body slightly toward Gabriel, wanting to melt into him.

I didn't look at Dominic. I couldn't. I knew exactly what I'd see on his face if I did. The look that told me this was *my* fault, that my presence in Gabriel's life brought him nothing except hurt and further nonacceptance. "Can we just go?" I repeated. "Please."

"Ellie…," Gabriel murmured, moving closer, brushing a tear off my cheek. "I never would have left you alone if I had even considered—"

"You couldn't know. I never even once thought…" I shook my head again.

"Gabriel, why don't you call it a day?" George asked. "Get Ellie home, put her feet up, and let this roll off your backs, okay?" He was looking pointedly at me, as if I was the one who looked more traumatized. Maybe I did. I guess I was.

"Okay." Gabriel was still looking at me worriedly as he brushed a tendril of hair out of my face. "Let's go." He nodded to George, Dominic, and Chloe and took my arm in his, turning me toward the parking lot.

I hardly remembered the drive home, and so when we pulled into Gabriel's driveway, it surprised me—hadn't we just left the festival a couple of minutes before?

We went inside and Gabriel led me to the couch, where I curled up at one end. He sat right next to me and pulled me into his arms, kissing the top of my head. "I'm sorry that happened.

I'm sorry if I didn't handle it well." *He's sorry? I brought the negative attention on him and he's sorry?*

I shook my head. "You don't have to be sorry. Thank you for defending me." *Again.*

He let out a long breath. "I'd defend you to the death, Eloise."

I tipped my head to look up at him. "I think you would." I chewed at my lip for a moment. I was turned inside out. Guilt overwhelmed me, and I shut my eyes tightly. "I'm just so sorry."

"Ellie, don't blame yourself."

I looked down, recalling the hateful look in the woman's eyes as she'd called me vicious names. "Why are girls so mean to each other?" I whispered.

"They're not all that way. Look at Chloe."

Yes, look at Chloe. My heart dropped, and I didn't like that every mention of Chloe's name made me envious when she'd been nothing except good to me. It made me feel mean-spirited. "Yeah."

Gabriel pulled me closer, and we sat that way in silence for a while, me lost in my own thoughts, going over the events of the morning. I'd arrived with such tentative hope. Overwhelming sadness filled me as I looked up and into Gabriel's eyes. *I'll never be good enough for him.* "I wanted today to go well for you. I wanted—"

"Shh, that doesn't matter. I don't care about that. Those people...they can think what they want to think. *You're* the person who matters to me."

I gave him a tremulous smile, scooting closer and wrapping my arms around his waist. "I just...Dominic's right. You should have the life you were meant to have."

He frowned. "What does that mean?"

"Just that you should have the life you would have had if you hadn't been taken."

He was quiet for a good minute before he spoke. "I'm living the life I was meant to have, Eloise. My life—just the way it is, for good *or* for bad—is the life I was meant to have. I could walk around all day thinking about how I was cosmically robbed, but what good would that do me? I'm living my life—the one I was given. It's all any of us can do. To imagine otherwise is to deny that there's a purpose to the suffering we might endure. Yes, I experienced pain, but maybe...maybe the reason for it is that because of my actions, no one else will ever be harmed by the man who abducted me. I don't know. I don't try to figure it out. I just trust that this life, *my life*, is the life I was meant to have, and I find peace in that."

My love for him swelled in my chest so powerfully that, for a moment, I couldn't breathe. He was so good and so positive, but I had to wonder if Gabriel would accept nearly anything for himself because he was able to find peace in *any* outcome—it was his gift. It was in the gentleness of his soul, in his desire and ability to always choose happiness no matter what. To glimpse the small sliver of light when others could only see the darkness surrounding it. Maybe Dominic was right—maybe it was up to the people *around* him—those who loved him—to demand more for him than he would ever demand for himself.

CHAPTER TWENTY-THREE

It's okay to cry. It's how your heart speaks its pain.

Gambit, the Duke of Thieves

GABRIEL

Ellie seemed so vulnerable—even more than ever—and it didn't feel like I could do or say anything to reassure her.

Chloe came by the house to give me the test she needed me to take, and I hated that I rushed her, considering she'd driven all the way to Morlea, but the way Ellie watched the two of us together worried me. She observed us with this knowing sort of sadness, almost a sorrowful determination, and I wasn't sure exactly what it meant, but I didn't think it was good. Did she think I had feelings for Chloe? "I love you," I whispered to her what felt like a hundred times a day. "Only you." Couldn't she see it in my eyes? Couldn't she feel it with every beat of my heart?

"Hello?" George called as he entered my studio, carrying a box.

"Hey, George." I turned, sitting up straight and rotating my shoulders.

"Here's that piece of rock you wanted." He nodded to the box as he set it down on the table by the door.

"Thanks."

George came over and looked at the carving I was almost finished with. He ran a hand down the side. "It's beautiful. Those butterflies look real."

I smiled and shrugged. "I hope they like it."

"They're going to love it." He paused, leaning against the table behind him. "How's Ellie?"

I frowned slightly. "You mean after the festival?"

"Yeah, and just in general."

I pressed my lips together and then sighed. "I don't know, George, she seems so...breakable." I grimaced slightly. "I don't know exactly how to describe it."

"You changed her, Gabriel. She's having a hard time figuring out who she is now." He looked worried as he studied me. "I'm concerned she doesn't think she's anyone at all without you. You've become her entire world."

I took a deep breath, his words resonating. They hurt, and yet they felt true. Part of me *wanted* to be her whole world, but another more reasonable part knew it wasn't good for her. "What can I do?"

"I encouraged her to learn how to throw a punch. I thought it might empower her a little bit. She hasn't been back over, though I've asked her. I suppose she's been caught up."

Caught up. In me. I smiled, but it felt sad. I remembered George teaching me to throw a punch when I'd come home. I'd been fifteen and I spent hours in his garage, moving around the bag, lashing out at it instead of the world, instead of myself. And it helped. But it'd only been a small part of my recovery. "What else?"

He shook his head. "Ah, Gabriel, I'd tell you if I knew. Just...try to remember where you were in the years after you came home." He stood, smiling softly before turning and heading out the door.

"Thanks, George," I called. I sat there for a while thinking about that time, thinking about how I'd mostly stayed to myself, how I needed to learn how to trust myself again, how I had to rediscover my place in the world, how I doubted whether I had one at all. It'd been hard and it was lonely, but God, it was necessary. And I'd had to do the work to get through it. No one could have done it for me, even if they wanted to.

I sighed. No, I couldn't do the work Ellie might need to do for herself, but I could love her through it. And that's exactly what I *would* do. If she needed strength, I'd be her rock, if she needed comfort, I'd be her soft spot to land. I'd be anything she needed me to be. And yet something about that felt dangerous—I wanted Ellie to find her own worth, not to let my love determine that for her. She'd never be truly happy that way. I ran my fingers through my hair in frustration.

You can't fix me, you know, she'd said. *No,* I'd thought, *I can only love you.* And I'd been right. All I could do was love her.

The next day was gray and rainy, and as I sat in my studio working to finish the very final details on the foliate band for the German library, I paused now and again to glance outside at the watercolor scenery. The door opened and Ellie, smiling, ducked inside, closing an umbrella, a package under her arm.

"Hi," I said, smiling.

"Hey. Dominic went into town and picked up your order at the hardware store."

"Oh, thanks." I'd forgotten I even placed an order there. "Did he say how Sal was?"

She furrowed her brow. "Dominic?" She shook her head. "Dominic doesn't talk to me much." Her cheeks flushed slightly and I frowned. I'd asked her if Dominic was treating her poorly and she'd denied it, but I didn't quite believe her.

I pursed my lips, and she seemed to read my thoughts. "I told you it was fine between us. He's just...quiet around me."

Quiet? Dominic? That didn't sound right. I sighed. "Ellie, I can talk to him if you decide you need me to. You shouldn't feel uncomfortable at work."

She smiled, but it didn't quite meet her eyes. "I don't need you to talk to him. Everything's fine. Really." Her smile brightened. "Looks like you're almost finished." She nodded to the piece in front of me.

"Yeah. A couple of hours and it should be done." I focused on the carving as Ellie started unpacking the box. I got involved in the details, and when I glanced up a few minutes later, was surprised to see Ellie standing in front of an open cabinet.

I sat up straight just as she turned. Her expression was slightly stunned. She blinked at me. "Are those..."

My eyes moved behind her, and it dawned on me which cabinet she'd opened. I stood, walking to her. Slowly I took the figurines out, placing them on the table next to us one by one.

Her eyes met mine, wide and full of compassion. "They are," she breathed.

I looked at them for a moment, letting the feelings they brought forth wash over me. Picking up the first one, I said, "His name is Racer, Knight of Sparrows. Racer was my dad's nickname for me. He started calling me that after I won a race in first grade. He said I was the fastest kid he'd ever seen. It just sort of stuck."

She seemed to have stilled, her lips parted as she looked back and forth between the figure and me. "Knight of Sparrows…after the birds that sang outside your bedroom window."

I smiled a small smile. "Yes." I looked at the figure, the armor he was wearing, the tiny bird perched on his shoulder. "You can see he's the handsomest one, for obvious reasons." I shot her a bigger smile, and she blinked at me and then laughed softly.

"He…he represented you?"

I thought about that for a moment. "I think so, yes."

I placed Racer down and picked up the second figure, looking at his perpetually grinning face. "Shadow, the Baron of Wishbone. Shadow was our family dog."

I paused, pulling my bottom lip into my mouth for a moment. "I guess Wishbone was because of his love for burying bones, but also a memory of my mother drying one on the kitchen windowsill every Thanksgiving and my brother and me pulling it apart. I always considered that wish so important."

I smiled at the memory before placing the figure back on the table and picking up the next one, studying the way his lip curled up in a slightly mocking smile, the glint of devilishness in his eyes. "Gambit, the Duke of Thieves. My brother and I used to collect comic books. Gambit was one of my favorite characters from the X-Men. He was a former thief whose powers were charging objects with kinetic energy, enhanced agility, and hypnotic charm." I grinned, setting him down.

"There's a sticker of him on the dresser in the guest room."

"Yes. That was the dresser in my room when I was a kid."

I picked up the next figure, looking at her wise, motherly face. "Lemon Fair, the Queen of Meringue. Lemon Fair was a river my dad used to take us fishing at when we were kids. We'd camp...he called it 'guy time.'" I cleared my throat, the memory choking me up for a second.

Ellie was still, watching me so intently. "Lemon meringue is your favorite dessert."

"Yeah," I breathed. "My mom used to make it for me on special occasions."

I looked at the last doll, suddenly filled with nerves. I glanced up at the shelf that held the basket of small items I'd carved as I'd brought them to life—tiny loaves of bread, swords, combs, and books. I considered showing those to Ellie first, but knew they didn't really matter. It was the last doll that mattered, and the reason I was stalling.

I swallowed as I replaced Lemon Fair and picked up the last remaining figure. I met Ellie's eyes. "Lady Eloise," I said softly, "of the Daffodil Fields." Her forehead furrowed in confusion as she glanced from the stone girl to me and back again. "My mother collected children's books. She used to read a series to me about a girl named Eloise. My father would bring my mother daffodils in the spring. They were her favorite. She said they were the happiest of all flowers."

I looked down at the doll in my hands. "She, Lady Eloise, was the one who took my hand and led me away when *he* came downstairs." Ellie looked startled. She shook her head slightly as if she was both denying something and trying to work it out in her head. "I think...I think I loved her more than any of them because she was the one who saved me when I needed it the most."

I watched Ellie as her expression turned from shock and confusion to sorrow and pain. Her eyes moved to me, and I saw such deep hurt in them, I reached for her. "Is this why?" she asked on a broken whisper.

Confusion rolled through me. "Is this why what?"

"Why you love me? Is it because of...*her*?" She nodded down at the doll as a tear slipped from her eye. "Oh," she let out a shuddery breath, "it makes sense now."

"God, no, Eloise. I love you because of you. I loved you before I even knew your real name."

"But..." She looked so devastated, and it made my guts twist. God, I'd never imagined she'd react this way, that she would think I'd what...made her into some living, breathing version of the figure in my hand?

I held it out to her, stepping forward and placing it in her hands, wrapping my own around hers. "It's only a doll, Ellie. A piece of rock."

I let go of her hands and she held it up, studying the details of the small girl, the peaceful smile, the long, flowing hair, the flowers held in her tiny grasp. She'd been the last one I'd carved, and because my skill had grown with each figure I created, she was the most beautiful, the most detailed. I could see Ellie's hands shaking as she held her.

She sucked in a small sob and stepped back, losing her grip on the doll. It seemed to happen in slow motion. Ellie's eyes widened as she stepped forward and attempted to catch Lady Eloise. For a second I thought she had it, but her finger only grazed it, sending it farther from her hand, speeding to the floor where it hit with a smash and broke into a hundred pieces. I froze where I stood.

Ellie let out a keening cry as she fell to her knees in front of the shattered girl. "Oh my God. Oh no. Gabriel, I'm...I'm so sorry. I didn't mean to." She used her hands to sweep all the pieces together into one small pile. Her hands were shaking so badly now, I wondered how she even managed the chore.

I moved to go down to her, when she suddenly sprang up and ran to the table near the front door, where there was a plastic bag. She ran back and kneeled down again and scooped the pieces into the bag. "I'll fix it. I...I...I can fix it. If..." She let out another sob.

I came out of the strange trance I'd seemed to go into, the picture clearing as I fell to my knees in front of her. "Ellie, love, stop. Please. It doesn't matter. It's okay."

She shook her head sharply from side to side. "It does matter. She was—"

I pulled her into my arms, smoothing her hair. "Shh. It doesn't matter," I repeated.

"You always say that. You always just accept everything. But it does matter. It does." She sucked in a big, shaky breath and started to cry. "I'm sorry. I'm so sorry."

Anguish rose in my chest to witness the depth of her suffering. It seemed far too deep and boundless to really be all about a broken doll. God, what should I do? How could I ease her pain? I stroked her hair and kissed her tear-streaked cheeks. "Ellie, sweet love, you're breaking my heart."

She burrowed into me, crying harder, and all I could do was hold her in my arms until her tears finally abated. Finally, after what seemed like a long time, I helped her to her feet. She insisted on taking the plastic bag of broken parts with her, clutched to her chest. I called and told George she was sick and I was taking her home.

You can't fix me, you know.

No, I can only love you.

* * *

That night, I made love to her, attempting to show her with my body all the love I had in my heart. I held her in my arms and whispered words of love and devotion to her in the darkness, and she nestled into me, accepting the comfort I so badly wanted to offer her. But her silence told me she'd retreated into herself and I just had to hope she'd come back to me again by the time the morning came.

But when the sun dawned, I opened my eyes to see that she had pulled an upholstered chair up to the window. She was curled up in it, watching the small sliver of sun as it appeared. I sat up on one elbow. "Morning."

She sat up and turned, her expression soft and sad. "Good morning," she whispered.

"What are you doing over there?"

She bit at her lip and turned her face to the window for a second. She stood up and came back to the bed, sitting at the edge. The look on her face was so filled with sorrow, my heart started beating faster. "I think you know I have to go, Gabriel."

"Go? Go where?" Panic filled my chest and I sat up.

She took a deep breath as if she was attempting to calm herself. "I've been up all night, just thinking—"

"Ellie, if this is about that figure—"

She shook her head. "It's not, not really. I mean, I think I know your feelings for me don't exist because I happen to have the same name as the stone figure you carved." She sighed. "I just, I can't keep doing this to you, Gabriel. I can't keep doing this to *me*."

A lump formed in my throat, and I moved forward on my knees, taking her into my arms. She didn't resist; on the contrary, she melted into me as she always did. "I love you so much," she breathed. "And I know you love me, but I can't stop questioning why. I've tried so hard and everything inside me just…*hurts*. I'm so lost, and I don't think I can find myself here. And I need to, Gabriel. I need to find myself. I need to figure out who I am without you. I need to figure out what to hold on to and what to let go of."

"God, Ellie," I choked. "Please…" I pulled her against me tighter, panic and soul-deep pain warring within me. The agony of losing another person in my life slashed at my heart. *Stay. Let me help you through this. You don't have to do it alone.* I wanted to say those words to her, to *beg* her not to go, and yet something stopped me—perhaps the memory of the talk I'd had with George, maybe the recollection of what it'd felt like to be in the place she was in. Most likely both. There was truth in her words, and I knew instinctively that to stop her would be at least partly motivated by my own selfishness. But, God, it hurt. It hurt so damn badly.

"Where will you go?" I managed to choke out. *How will I be able to resist helping you? How will I survive wondering if you're okay?*

She shook her head slightly against me. I could feel the wetness of her tears on my bare chest. "Back to my apartment. From there…I don't know."

"You wouldn't—"

She pulled her head back to look up at me, her eyes full of tears and tenderness. "No. I'm not Crystal anymore. I can't ever be her again. I'll find another job."

I let out a loud whoosh of air and wiped a tear from her cheek. She paused before she asked quietly, "You paid my medical bills, didn't you?"

I opened my mouth and then closed it, not prepared for the question, unsure if she'd be angry about it or not. She placed two fingers over my lips and then moved them out of the way so she could kiss me. "Thank you."

I let out a relieved breath, understanding that her acceptance of my gift was a gift to me as well. My love for her was so intense in that moment, my whole body was shaking with it. "Will you come back?" My voice was a raw-sounding whisper, a broken plea.

Sorrow clouded her expression, and her lip trembled. "I need"—she clenched her eyes shut for a moment as if her words were physically hurting her—"I need you to go on as if I won't. I need that." She opened her eyes just as a tear slipped out and rolled down her cheek. *Crushed.* It felt as if my soul were being crushed.

I leaned down and pressed my forehead to hers, and for a moment we just breathed together. I wanted to beg. I wanted to scream at her and plead with her to stay. Beg her to want to come back to me. Not to leave me in the first place, but I couldn't. Would she understand that in not fighting for her to stay, I was fighting for her to heal? "Stay today. Will you just stay with me today?"

She stared into my eyes for a moment before answering, "Yes," so softly it was more breath than sound.

We lay back on the bed and I pulled the covers over us, determined to shut out the world this one last day.

We loved fiercely and sorrowfully, trying so hard to pack a lifetime of touches into a single morning. I felt desperate and heartbroken, but I knew in my heart that to stop her from going meant trapping her in its own way, and it was something I would never do. And so we took temporary refuge from the pain of goodbye and gloried in the moment: our heat and our bones and the tangling of our limbs. *Our love.*

We didn't talk. To do so would only hurt more, and I didn't think I could stand it, nor did I want that for her. When she finally pulled herself from my arms, I let her go. I lay there listening as she packed up her things in the other room, already missing the warmth of her skin and the smell of her hair and the way her smile felt like opening a window on a summer's day.

I heard the soft sounds of her crying, and I wanted to be the one to wipe away her tears. But I knew that would only make it worse. I also knew Ellie needed to find happiness, and if she thought she needed to do it alone, it would be wrong to stop her. I tried to find some comfort in knowing I was doing the right thing for her, but I couldn't manage it.

My stomach knotted as I rose from the bed we'd shared for the last couple of weeks, and I pulled on the jeans I'd thrown across a chair the night before. I used the bathroom and when I came out, Ellie was just exiting the guest room, carrying her bag. "I called George and asked for a ride," she said.

I was glad she had. I didn't think I could handle more than one goodbye. I smiled sadly at her and took the bag, walking toward the front door. It felt like the sadness of the moment was too much to bear, as if I might suffocate with it.

I pulled the door open. George's truck was already idling outside, although he was turned away, most likely to give us the privacy he must know we needed.

I leaned against the doorframe, putting my hands in my pockets to stop myself from grabbing her and begging her to stay. "I'll miss you." It seemed like the only thing to say, and by the look on her face, I could tell she'd heard my whole heart in the words.

She brushed the hair away from my eyes and then put her hand on my cheek and smiled so tenderly I almost grabbed her anyway, though I'd promised myself I wouldn't. "You will always be the great love of my life, Gabriel Dalton." And then she turned and she left.

I closed the door behind her and leaned back against it, sliding down until I was sitting on the floor. I put my head in my hands, and I let the agonizing pain envelop me.

CHAPTER TWENTY-FOUR

Whatever you do, do it with your whole heart.

Lemon Fair, the Queen of Meringue

ELLIE

I didn't do much other than cry those first few days. Entering my apartment had been surreal—as if the space had existed in another lifetime. In some respects, I supposed that was accurate.

The pain of leaving Gabriel was so acute it was a physical ache, and I felt as if my body and soul were being pinned under a heavy boulder. I hurt everywhere, my flesh and bones, and deep down to my very spirit. I knew in my heart what I'd done was right for both of us, but that didn't mean it wasn't agonizing.

I felt scared and so incredibly lonely, and I figured I'd flounder. But I'd known sitting by the window in the darkness of Gabriel's bedroom, listening to the soft sounds of his breathing: It was a floundering I had to do alone. I was lost and the only one who could save me was myself. It wasn't fair to either of us for me to hide behind Gabriel—both physically and emotionally— rather than facing the world.

And I had to set him free to choose Chloe if she was the
woman he was meant to be with if life's timing had been different. I pictured them together again like they were that day at the
Morlea Fall Festival—how happy and beautiful—and I knew in
my gut that to deny him the opportunity for a life like that would
be selfish. I loved him, his heart and his soul, and I cared for his
happiness above my own. I wanted the very best for him, even if
it wasn't me. Still, it was a sharp knife impaling my most tender
spots to picture him loving her, to imagine his hands moving on
her body the way they'd moved on mine, to see them married,
with sweet little brown-haired children. I clenched my eyes shut
against the vision, pushing it away. It would do me no good to
dwell on such things.

I'd called my landlady as soon as I'd arrived to thank her for
being so patient with me and to tell her I had my overdue rent
payment—dropping a check for two months' worth in the mail
to bring it up to date. I'd only earned three weeks of pay from
my work at the quarry office, and I needed to make sure I had
enough to get my car out of the garage and to buy groceries until
I could find another job. With the thought of bills and job hunt-
ing, a fresh wave of fear and loneliness swept over me, but I was
determined to figure something out. *I had to, God, I had to.* If
Gabriel had taught me anything, it was that life didn't have to
be filled with pain and doubt all the time. There was something
lovable about me; Gabriel had shown me that, too. I just needed
to figure out what it was and maybe, oh God, maybe find a way
to love *myself*.

My entire life had shifted under my feet, and I hadn't
known what to grasp on to, what to clutch so I didn't fall. I
had no idea how to get my bearings. And so I'd grabbed onto
the only thing solid in my life: Gabriel. I'd grown emotionally

dependent on him in a way I knew wasn't healthy for either of us. Every small thing caused me to doubt and to hurt, and to feel a thousand insecurities that might not even be real. I'd ceased being able to tell, and I knew in my heart that my desperate sort of clawing love would end up as a kind of prison for Gabriel. I loved him far too much to subject him to a second life sentence. He'd already experienced one. Leaving was the hardest thing I'd ever done, but it was right. I knew it was right.

And so after a couple of days of allowing myself to wallow in pain, I got up and cleaned my apartment, scrubbing every nook and cranny and opening the windows for a short time to air it out with the cold fall wind.

I called the garage where my car was being kept and told the guy who answered the phone I was coming by to pick it up. I put on my sneakers and jacket and made the two-mile journey. I had woken up with a crick in my neck, and it got worse as I walked. My leg pained me a little and my stride grew slower and slower, but despite my aches, it felt great to exercise, and the brisk air felt good in my lungs.

Ricky was at the front desk when I walked into the small front office of the garage, the smell of coffee and motor oil hitting my nose, the heat of the interior space warming me immediately. Ricky smiled warmly. "Well, look who it is. You look great."

I smiled back as Ricky came from behind the counter and gave me a quick hug. "Hi, Ricky. Thanks so much for keeping my car. Sorry it's taken me so long to get here."

He shook his head as he returned behind the desk, digging through a drawer and pulling out a key with my name scribbled on the large tag. He handed it across the counter. "When I told my dad you were coming in, he told me not to charge you. Said you'd been through enough."

I blinked in surprise. "Thank you. Oh, I...well, I couldn't—"

"You *can*. And seriously, get out of here before my tight-ass dad changes his mind." He laughed, and a burst of warmth filled my chest. I put my hand over my heart as if I'd be able to feel the heat emanating from the inside.

"Thank you, Ricky. I can't tell you how much this means to me. I...will you thank your dad for me, too?"

"Sure will. Your car's at the back left of the lot. You take care of yourself, okay?"

I nodded, trying my best to hold back the tears. "I will." And I meant it. Or at least I was going to give it my best damn try.

Once I'd let myself into my car, I turned the key in the ignition and listened as it came easily to life. I leaned my head back on the seat and felt thankful. The money Ricky and his dad had saved me meant so much to me right now.

As I passed through the downtown area on my ride home, I spotted a sign advertising ten dollars off pedicures at the nail shop I'd gone to once in a while when I had a little extra money. It was a small extravagance I'd afforded myself now and again. I certainly didn't have the extra cash now, yet I pulled my car over into an empty spot across the street, rolling my sore neck on my shoulders. God, sitting in the massage chair while soaking my feet in warm water sounded so wonderful; I stared at the shop window longingly as if I were walking through the desert and it was a lush, green oasis.

I shouldn't even spend twenty-five dollars on something that wasn't a necessity, and yet I'd anticipated having to part with two hundred and fifty dollars for my car that I now had in my pocket. Surely Ricky and his dad wouldn't mind my spending a small bit of it on a brief hour of pampering. Just this one thing, nothing more.

I crossed the street and walked into the busy shop. Lien Mai called a greeting from her spot at a pedicure table where she was using an electric file on an older woman's acrylic nails. "Long time no see, Crystal. You need pedicure?"

"Hi, Lien. Yes, but it looks like you're busy."

"Nah. Canceled appointment. You sit down." She nodded to the large black massage chair at the end of the row. *Ah, sweet heaven.* I walked to it, and a petite girl with long, pin-straight black hair smiled politely at me and started filling the basin with warm, soapy water. I sat down and turned on the rolling back massage and sighed as I sunk back into it, submersing my feet in the water.

"What color?" the girl asked, referring to polish.

I closed my eyes. "I don't care. You pick."

She giggled softly. "You need this, yeah?"

I smiled without opening my eyes. "Yes."

When she rubbed the grainy exfoliating cream into my feet and calves, an ache rose so strongly in my chest, I almost gasped. I pictured Gabriel's beautiful hands moving on my skin, and for a second, the pain of my yearning for him was so intense, I didn't know if I could make it to the next moment. I focused on my breathing, and after a few minutes, the worst of it passed, and it felt manageable again.

I listened to the chatter and the busyness of the shop as my muscles loosened beneath the chair's mechanical ministrations. The phone rang incessantly and sometimes it was answered, but mostly it seemed that it wasn't. "Don't you have someone to answer your phones?" I asked the girl sitting on a small stool at my feet.

She shook her head. "No. Lien want hire someone but too busy."

A flutter of excitement moved through me. "I have experience answering phones."

She looked up at me. "Oh yeah?" She turned toward Lien. "Lien, she want job answering phones."

Lien was just saying goodbye to the woman in front of her, and they both stood, Lien working to bring herself upright. Once her body wasn't being obscured by the table, I noticed she was about fourteen months pregnant. My eyes widened. "Oh yeah? You want job, Crystal?" She walked over to my chair and stood next to it, one hand on her lower back.

"Yes. I'd love a job. I have experience answering phones. I recently worked at the quarry over in Morlea. I can provide a reference."

"Hmm. Okay. You come back tomorrow and we try you out."

Worry settled in my gut, but I smiled and nodded. I could do this. I could try. It felt like the opportunity had fallen into my lap, almost as if it was meant to be.

When Lien had walked away again, I whispered to the girl, "How pregnant is she anyway?"

"She have eight week left."

I held my gasp inside. *Oh, dear Lord.* There was no way her tiny body could get any bigger than it was now.

The next day when I arrived back at the shop, I was nervous, but after an hour or so, I had a good handle on the phone system, and I was taking messages and scheduling appointments as if I'd been there for months. It was busy and the walk-ins were constant, but I handled it.

The longer the day went on, the more accomplished I felt, and when Lien came up to the desk at three, she told me to go into the back office and sign the new-hire paperwork. I felt giddy with happiness, and the first thought that came to my head was, *I have to call Gabriel and tell him!* But then reality came flowing back, causing me to stumble slightly and clench my eyes shut with sadness. I made a stop in the restroom to get my bearings before heading to the back room that served as Lien's office.

"Lien, I have to tell you something before I fill out this paperwork."

"What that?"

"Well, my name isn't really Crystal. It's Eloise. Ellie for short."

She regarded me for a moment and finally nodded. "That good. You better Ellie anyway."

A short laugh bubbled up in my throat. God, I hoped so. I really did.

CHAPTER TWENTY-FIVE

Something tells me I'm going to love you forever.

Lady Eloise of the Daffodil Fields

ELLIE

I settled into my job at Lien Mai's House of Nails and after a couple of weeks, I was practically running the place. Not just answering the phones, but ordering supplies, and keeping inventory. I loved the casual atmosphere of the salon, the chatter that rose and fell through the shop, both English and Vietnamese, the way the days whizzed by, and the way I was bone weary as I fell into bed.

I woke up one cold Friday night, gasping as I sat up in bed. I'd had the dream again, the one where my mother's voice called to me as I moved through the darkness. Only this time the walls of the space had been growing wider instead of narrower and she'd been urging me forward. *He's waiting for you*, she'd said again. He? The only he I wanted was Gabriel.

But maybe he *was* waiting. I'd had the dream when I'd been with him, though, too. Only...it seemed I'd traveled the wrong way toward him and ended up right in front of him with a barrier still between us. I'd had to turn away in order to travel the path that would bring me back to him, the path that ended with nothing separating us at all. I didn't know whether I should even dare to hope it, but in any case, the path I'd been on had been squeezing the life from me. I'd turned back not only for Gabriel, but for myself.

The feeling of the dream clung to me so that I couldn't fall back to sleep. I got out of bed, shivering, and turned up the heat slightly. It started to rain softly and I stood at the window for a few minutes, looking out into the darkness, the streetlights reflecting on the water puddles in the parking lot below.

Turning, I spotted the bag I still hadn't unpacked from Gabriel's and sighed. It seemed I could only let go in very small steps and this, too, I supposed was one of them.

As I emptied the contents, throwing the clothes into the hamper, my hand hit upon plastic and I startled, pulling out the plastic bag I'd completely forgotten about in all my misery. I lifted it out and held it to my chest. *Lady Eloise of the Daffodil Fields.* Seemingly broken beyond repair. But maybe…maybe…I set it down on the small desk I had by the window and switched on the light sitting on the corner. I grabbed a hand towel from the bathroom and then carefully, so carefully, I emptied the contents onto the towel, spreading the pieces out to determine if anything was recognizable. Yes, a small foot, and a bouquet of flowers, and two halves of her pretty face. *Hope.*

I sat down at the desk, rooting through the drawers until I located a tiny vial of superglue I'd bought for some reason I couldn't even remember now.

I felt completely overwhelmed, but I figured the best place to start was at the beginning, and so I picked up the little piece of foot and started from there. I couldn't help picturing that tiny shattered girl as a thousand pieces of me, and as I worked, fitting together small shards, I wondered if the work I was doing with my hands was a representation of the work I needed to do on myself. And so I hunched over that table until the light of dawn seeped through the curtains, and I thought about all the things in my life that had crushed and shattered me as well.

I thought about my mother, and that was the hardest of all. I thought about the day she'd left me with Brad—the hollow, aching grief that still clung to me like a second skin, the pain and the anger of being deserted, left scared and alone.

As my hands moved, finding pieces and trying to fit them, setting the ones back down that didn't work, and picking up a new one until the lines and ridges worked just right, my mind wandered. Something about the constant movement of my hands and the way my mind was half-focused on the task made me feel safe. I couldn't ignore thoughts of Gabriel, and wondered if he'd found a similar solace in his work when he'd first come home.

I didn't attempt to stop or control the wanderings of my mind. I didn't attempt to shut anything out. I thought about it all and I let it hurt. Tears rolled down my cheeks and into my ears, and I blotted them with my sleeve when my eyes grew too blurry to work, but I didn't move from my desk that night, not even once.

I thought about how my mother had looked that day, how ill—how *panicked*—and a lump formed in my throat so large I thought it might suffocate me. But it didn't. I continued to work and continued to hurt.

What had it felt like to be her? What desperation was she feeling to know she was dying and her last option was to drop her only child off with a stranger? She couldn't have known Brad would treat me the way he did. From what it sounded like, she'd barely known Brad at all. She'd taken a chance and I paid the price. But she hadn't known. She'd relied on hope alone. It was all she had.

Lord, please give me strength. I have no choice, I have no choice.

"Oh, Mama," I gasped, my voice small like the abandoned little girl I'd once been. "I forgive you. And I'm so sorry for what you suffered, too."

A week after I'd been left at Brad's house, he'd told me that they'd found my mama dead under someone's porch. She'd curled up there to die like a lost animal. He'd delivered the news in a monotone voice, and then he'd taken a sip of beer as if it hardly mattered at all. And inside, a whole section of my heart had come loose and crumbled.

I'd learned to encase myself in a seemingly hard exterior so no one could ever hurt me again the way my mother had by leaving me without saying goodbye. But the shell was so thin, so thin and so easily broken.

And then there was my father's friend Cory who had taken and used—*raped* me, though I'd never said the word before, not even to myself. I had thought I loved him because he was the first person in so long who had seemed to want me at all, who had even noticed me.

My feelings for Cory had been a different sort of desperate, clawing love, but I didn't want that to be the way I gave my heart. I wanted to offer something whole—pieced back together maybe, but whole nonetheless.

Just as dawn arrived, I surveyed my work and realized I had put back together two little bare feet. I laughed in wonder. There were still small slivers of missing pieces, parts that must have crumbled to dust, but each tiny toe was completely recognizable. Something in me loved those missing parts, too. To me they spoke of the things that were necessary to let go of—the pain I'd held on to for too long, the anger, the misery, the self-blame. And those empty spaces were just as important as the parts that made me whole. I smiled in triumph, wiping the remaining tears away and stretching my aching neck and back.

Opening the window shade, I took in the distant glow coming over the horizon. I thought back to Gabriel's story about seeing the tiny portion of light through the tinted window of that long-ago basement and remembered my own thought that sometimes that's all hope is—just a thin sliver of distant light. And for me that morning, that's exactly what it was.

* * *

My life became a steady schedule of work at the nail salon and work on the stone figurine. I spent most weekends up until dawn piecing the girl together, going over my life, my hurts, all the places my own heart had crumbled away to dust.

It was exhausting and it was hard, but I kept at it, buoyed by the representation of my work: the art that had been Gabriel's hope so many years ago. And in this way, it was as if he were there with me. I wasn't completely alone. In fact, despite how much it hurt, in some ways the nights I spent bent over my desk provided my greatest comfort.

You can't fix me, I'd told Gabriel once. And I'd been right. I needed to fix myself. And he had loved me enough to make me believe it was possible. *That I was worth fixing.*

Fall turned to winter and the days grew shorter; the trees outside my window, bare skeletons.

I celebrated Thanksgiving and Christmas with Lien Mai and her family, bringing Kayla as my date. The gatherings were filled with the same Vietnamese chatter that kept a smile on my face, and I felt both a pained yearning as I wondered what Gabriel was doing, and a warm togetherness and affection for my new friends.

A few days after Christmas, I checked my mailbox after having neglected doing so for about a week, and I was surprised to find what looked like a Christmas card with George's return address in the corner. With shaking fingers, I ripped it open and read the short note he'd included.

Dear Ellie,

I hope you're spending Christmas in a way that brings peace to your heart. We miss you around here. Chloe came for Christmas and is spending two weeks with us—she misses you, too. I think about you a lot, Ellie girl, and hope you're doing well.

Love, George

I'd read the card as I climbed my steps from the mailbox and grasped it to my chest, squeezing my eyes shut against the tears, then sitting down on the top step to catch my breath. God, I missed them all so much in that moment, I didn't know if I'd survive it. *Chloe came for Christmas.* A knife sliced through my heart. Surely she was there for Gabriel. Her work on the paper must be done, or if it wasn't, she wouldn't need two weeks of Gabriel providing more information. No, her visit must be of a personal nature.

I let the tears flow, hurting so badly inside it felt like a piercing of my soul. But I had to accept that Gabriel and Chloe might be together now. I'd wished it for him. I'd given him the room to explore his own heart.

Will you come back?

I need you to go on as if I won't.

I sat there for a moment as my tears dried in the frigid wind, looking down at the parking lot. There were still a few spots of snow that hadn't melted from the mild storm we'd had the week before. I caught sight of something purple and tilted my head in wonderment, squinting to try and make out what it was, but it was too far away.

I walked down the steps and squatted in the snow, sucking in a breath at what I saw. It was a purple flower growing through the frost. "How in the world?" I murmured, running a finger over one soft petal.

Gratitude isn't a Band-Aid, Ellie. You still have to experience your feelings to work through them. Gratitude is meant to make it bearable. Sometimes gratitude gets you through the day, and sometimes it just gets you from one moment to the next.

I heard his words as if they were being whispered in my mind and closed my eyes to stop more tears from coming. After a moment I looked back at the flower, taking comfort in the moment, finding thankfulness and *hope* in one delicate flower that had somehow found a way to bloom, even through the dark, icy cold.

On New Year's Eve, I drank too much champagne with Kayla as we watched the ball drop on TV. I almost called Gabriel, but forced myself not to. I pictured him kissing Chloe as the clock struck midnight and cried so hard Kayla asked me if she should call an ambulance. That made me laugh through my tears, and then I cried some more and laughed some more and fell into an exhausted sleep.

On January third, Lien Mai delivered a healthy baby boy, and I visited her at the hospital with a "bouquet" of blue balloons. I sat in a chair by her bed and took the small bundle into my arms and looked into the perfect round face of James Allen Nguyen and fell instantly and completely in love.

"You have own baby someday," Lien said. "You can no have mine." And then she laughed, a knowing gleam in her eyes as she grinned at me holding her baby boy.

I laughed, too, and then he grasped my finger and I sucked in a breath. "Oh, look, Lien, he disagrees."

Lien laughed. "Okay, we share him."

And in a way we did. After a two-week maternity leave, Lien brought James to the shop two days a week from nine until noon when her mother would pick him up. James slept in his car seat in the back office where it was well-ventilated, and if it was slow and Lien was busy, I'd sit back there and feed him his bottle, gazing down into his beautifully slanted eyes, and smoothing the inky black hair from his forehead. And I loved him so much it hurt.

I thought about a lot of things there, too, in the quiet as I provided sustenance to my friend's baby. It seemed love did that for me—brought everything inside me to the surface so I could examine it all slowly and carefully, casting out that which I was ready to, and saving the rest for those dark nights when I pieced together Lady Eloise.

I thought about whether I wanted to find out what had become of my father and decided that, no, I didn't need to know. He was a small missing part in the rebuilding of my heart, and I felt at peace that that was the way it should be. I'd hoped so hard for his love, longed for his acceptance, but he hadn't been able to give it. And I knew now, *believed*, that that was because of him, not because of me.

I also thought a lot about what I wanted to do with my life as I fed James.

You and your lifelong dreams, I had said disdainfully to Gabriel once upon a time.

I've got a few, he'd said as he'd smiled that beautiful smile of his. *I bet you do, too.*

The thing was, though, I never had. I'd never dared to dream because in my mind, dreams never came true. It was too *painful* to dream, to hope for what could never be and for what I didn't trust myself to obtain. Even the books I'd loved as a little girl, the stories I'd spent hours reading in the library after school as a teen, had inspired too many dreams and so I'd given them up. But now...now I found myself allowing my mind and my heart to join forces as they ventured out together into the misty land of hopes and dreams. *What would I do if I could do anything at all? What would that be?*

I thought about my mother, how I'd wished to heal her, how I would have done anything to provide her comfort. I thought about the sweet little man in my arms and how nurturing him brought me peace and happiness, and I wondered if I could be a nurse. Would I make a good one? Would I be able to pass the necessary classes? I'd always done well in school, despite my home life. I'd received good grades; I'd studied hard, and achieved my high school diploma. At least I had that.

Of course, going to nursing school would cost money. Money that I didn't have. I sighed, not dismissing my dream, but putting it into the category of future possibilities. Frankly, a miracle would have to arrive at my door if I was going to make that dream come true.

In February, that miracle arrived just as I was grabbing my purse to leave for the grocery store. I heard a knock at my door and frowned. *Who in the world could that be?* The only person who ever came to my apartment was Kayla, and she was working.

I pulled open the door to find an older woman with a strawberry-blonde bob haircut standing there, looking slightly nervous. I tilted my head, something about her looking familiar. "Can I help you?"

She cleared her throat. "Are you Eloise Cates?"

"Yes."

She released a breath. "Oh, good. I'm MaryBeth Hollyfield."

Hollyfield.

"Oh," I breathed. "Uh"—I stood back—"would you like to come in?"

MaryBeth shook her head. "No, I only have a minute." She looked back down the steps to where a white Honda Accord was idling in the parking lot. Opening her purse, she pulled out a check. "This is for you." She held it toward me.

I took it from her, frowning in confusion. Looking down, I saw it was made out to me for the amount of ten thousand dollars. I blinked. "This isn't mine," I said, attempting to hand it back.

She shook her head. "No, it is yours. It should have been yours. My mother left five thousand dollars to you. It was all the money she had to her name when she died. She'd spent almost all of her retirement savings, and in the last few years of her life she lived off the interest—mere pennies really—of the small amount of cash she had left and the social security she received." MaryBeth looked down, an expression of shame passing over her face. "We contested her will and won. I suppose you were never notified. There didn't seem to be a way to find you…"

I looked at her in shock. "No, I suppose there wouldn't be. My mother died…I went…" My words faded away as I shook my head.

"Well, anyway, I've always felt bad about that. My brother

and I didn't do right by our mother. I will always have that on my conscience. I can't do anything about that now. But I saw your name in the paper several months ago, and it's been sitting at the front of my mind ever since. I wasn't sure how to figure out interest, so I doubled it. I just hope somehow my mom knows that I made it right. I'm sorry it took me so long." She smiled a sad smile and turned to leave.

I looked down to the check and back up at MaryBeth. "Thank you," I called. I didn't know what else to say.

MaryBeth paused, turning back to me. "My mother loved you very much," she said. And with that she descended the steps, got in the car, and it pulled from the lot.

My legs felt like jelly as I shut my apartment door and sat down at my desk.

I didn't go to the grocery store that day. Instead I worked on Lady Eloise's hands, letting my mind wander to red Popsicles and rainbows that had formed on water, maybe not just *because* of the grime, but in *spite* of it. But mostly, I thought about a woman who had loved me, a woman who had been a sort of lifeline, not once, but twice. And I remembered Gabriel's words about having two extra angels on his side. Perhaps I did, too, and had just been too filled with pain to recognize their gentle, loving nudges.

* * *

A week or so after MaryBeth Hollyfield stopped by, I got another knock on my apartment door. And if I'd thought I was shocked by that visit, I was even more shocked by this one: Dominic.

I froze in surprise when I pulled the door open. He was bundled up in a winter coat and beanie, and for a second I didn't recognize him. His hands were in his pockets and the expression on his face was unsure, nervous. For a moment I just stared.

"Hi, Ellie," he finally said.

A spear of uncertainty stabbed at me, and I furrowed my brow. "Dominic? What are you doing here?"

He looked back over his shoulder as if stalling for a second, and when he looked back at me, he let out a breath. It plumed in the cold air and then disappeared into nothingness. "I was hoping we could talk."

"About what?"

"Will you come outside? I don't expect to be invited in, but if I could just have a few minutes...we could, uh...sit on the stairs."

I bit at my lip, almost tempted to tell him to go to hell, but he looked so sheepish, so different than I'd ever seen him before, and truth be told, I wanted to hear what he had to say. I was desperate for any news on Gabriel, but knew I wouldn't ask. I wanted it, and yet I also realized it would potentially set me back emotionally, and I couldn't risk it. I'd fought so hard for every step forward. "Hold on," I mumbled, turning away and grabbing my winter coat and pulling it on. I stuck my hands in the large pockets and closed the door behind me.

Dominic took a seat on a step below and turned as I took a seat on the top step. "I owe you an apology."

I tried not to show my surprise at his words, simply waited for him to continue.

He blew out another breath. "I treated you unfairly, Ellie, and I'm sorry."

"Where is this coming from? It's been months since I left. What made you realize this now?"

"Chloe. Chloe made me realize it."

I furrowed my brow. "Chloe?"

He nodded and smiled slightly. "Yeah, we've been, ah, spending a lot of time together. She came to stay with me over Christmas." He looked pleased and slightly bashful.

I blinked. Chloe had come for...Dominic? *Oh.* Is that why there had been sadness in his expression when he'd remarked on Chloe loving Gabriel? Because Dominic himself was falling in love with Chloe? Was Chloe's affection for Gabriel sisterly and the one she'd *actually* fallen for was Dominic? I couldn't help the relief I felt, though I didn't know if that was fair. Should I be relieved at Gabriel not finding love when I had taken mine away from him?

As if reading some of my thoughts, Dominic said, "Chloe does love Gabriel, but she's not in love with him. I shouldn't have said that to you. It wasn't only cruel, it was false."

I blinked at him for a moment, before I nodded my head. "It's...it's okay."

"No, it's not."

I smiled slightly. "Okay, it's not. How did things start between you and Chloe?"

"She came over with both guns blazing after that awful incident at my brother's house." He grimaced. "I was mad at her for a while, too." He shook his head. "But the only person who deserved contempt was me."

I studied him for a moment. He looked sincere, the expression on his face was humble, a touch embarrassed. For a moment he reminded me of Gabriel, of the first time I'd met him when he'd asked me to help him endure the closeness of another person, and I felt a sharp pinching in my chest. "I...well, thank you for the apology. I forgive you, Dominic. You can officially remove me from your guilty conscience."

He paused, his eyes roaming over my face for a second. Uncomfortable, I looked away. "Can I explain why I did what I did? Why I treated you so terribly?"

I moved my gaze back to his, noting the hope in his eyes. "Sure."

He nodded slowly, looking forward so I was facing his profile. From this angle, he looked more like Gabriel. They had the same nose, the same high cheekbones, the same ears. For a moment it hurt to look at him. But then he faced me again, and I saw the obvious differences in their faces, the ways in which they were unique.

"I was with Gabe the day he was abducted. You might know that, but what you probably don't know is that Gabriel came to that vacant lot because I had gone there even though my mom told me I couldn't. I was being a bratty little kid and I'd disobeyed my mom, and she'd sent Gabriel to go find me." He inhaled a deep breath and let it out through his nose. "It was because of me that he was even there that day. If I had just listened to my mom, if I hadn't been a stubborn little asshole, my brother never would have been taken."

I studied him for a moment, the tight way he was holding his mouth, the heartache in his eyes as he recalled that day. I didn't want to let him off the hook so easily, and yet I understood how the things a person held on to could eat them away from the inside, causing them to lash out at those who didn't deserve it.

Choice *is such a loaded word, isn't it?*

And, yes, that's what Chloe had meant. Choices, though our own, were so weighted down with all the things that had come before, so stained with the messes of our past. Who knew that better than me?

"There was no way you could have known that," I said softly. "It was just a matter of terrible circumstance. You were only a kid. You didn't mean for him to be hurt."

He looked at me for several long moments. I saw the gratitude in his eyes a second before he glanced away. "Yeah, that's
what Chloe says. I know it in my head, but I've just carried
around this awful guilt. It feels like I've been carrying it all
my life." He paused again before continuing. "After he was
taken, it was almost like he was a celebrity." He shook his head
and grimaced. "An awful sort of celebrity, but…" He paused
again, squinting into the distance. "My parents were so grief
stricken and everyone talked of nothing but Gabe and I just sort
of…faded into the background."

"You were jealous," I murmured, feeling sympathy for the
eight-year-old boy he'd been, the child who must have been so
scared and confused when his whole world turned upside down.
I could relate to that.

He nodded. "Yes. Jealous and heartbroken and guilt ridden."
He let out a long breath. "I guess because I blamed myself for
him being abducted, hated myself for the envy I felt over the attention he received, and the way I became invisible; later, I made
myself responsible for him getting his life back. I felt like maybe
it would right the wrongs I'd committed against him. Through
the years I've done everything I could to try to encourage him to
live the life he should have lived—the life I felt I was responsible
for stealing from him. But it turned into a twisted sort of control.
When you came along…well, you know what I thought. I made
it clear."

He shook his head and frowned. "I didn't give you a chance. I
judged you without getting to know you at all. I hurt you when
you'd already been hurt. I tried to drive you away and it worked,
and I'm so damn sorry for that."

"You didn't drive me away, Dom. You didn't make it easy to
stay, I'll admit that. But I left for my own reasons." I remem-

bered, too, that Dominic had been drunk that awful night he kissed me, but he hadn't tried to use that as an excuse, and I appreciated his apology all the more for it.

He pressed his lips together. "What can I say to make you come back?"

I blew out a heavy breath and shook my head. "Nothing. Not now. I appreciate you coming here." I smiled. "It was courageous, and I really do forgive you. But I have some things to work on, and I'm trying my best to do that."

He nodded. "I get that. God, if anyone gets that, I do. I'm working on myself, too. I want you to know that."

"Thanks, Dominic."

He smiled at me. "You take care of yourself, okay?" He stood and I followed suit.

"Yeah, you, too. Hey, Dom?"

"Yeah?"

I tilted my head. "Gabriel said something to me once. He told me that the life he *has* is the life he was meant to live. He doesn't feel robbed or cheated—he's grateful for the life he's living despite the pain he endured. He meant it, Dom, and he's found peace in that. And I think the people who love him have to as well. And not just for him but for ourselves."

He considered me for a moment as if he was turning the words over in his mind. Then he smiled. "I think you're right. Goodbye, Ellie."

"Goodbye, Dominic."

That night I dreamed I was in the dark alley again, only this time my arms were stretched out to my sides, and when I squinted my eyes, I could see a bare sliver of light in the distance. *Keep going, my love. You're almost there*, I heard whispered, and so I did.

* * *

A hush descended over the crowded courtroom as my name was called, and I made my way to the front. My hands were shaking slightly as I laid the piece of paper on the podium in front of me, smoothing out the wrinkles. I took a deep breath, giving myself a moment to prepare before I looked up at the men sitting at the table with their lawyers. I forced myself to make eye contact with each man, but the only one who met my gaze was the one with the black hair, the one I knew had turned both himself and his friends in. His expression was inscrutable, but that was okay. I wasn't looking for anything from them. I wasn't even really looking to influence their sentences—I'd leave that to the court. I was here for more important reasons.

I cleared my throat, glancing down at the words I'd written on the paper the night before as I'd sat at my desk, the half-finished stone girl resting on the folded towel on the corner. "Several months ago the men being sentenced today beat me so severely that I didn't know if I'd survive. They battered and bloodied my face so I was no longer recognizable to myself. They broke my ribs and my leg and my spirit. They did all this behind a Dumpster. I mention this because it's relevant—you see, they thought of me as trash, and truth be told, I thought of myself the same way."

I took a deep breath, glancing up to find all three pairs of eyes on me. I moved my gaze from one man to the next, to the next, and then looked away.

"I want them to get the punishment they deserve, but when it comes down to it, I'm not here today for them. I'm here for me. I'm here because it took almost dying for me to realize that I'm not a piece of garbage. I'm a woman, with a heart and a soul, and with pain and regrets. I've made mistakes and poor choices, but I don't deserve to be hit. I don't deserve to be used. And I don't deserve to be left to die in a pool of blood in an empty parking lot. It took almost dying to realize that the words you used against me only hurt because I agreed with them. But I don't agree with them anymore. I don't know what brought you to the point where you felt justified in beating a woman unconscious, and I hope you figure that out. But that's not my concern. I'll say it again: I'm not here for you. I'm here for me."

I folded up the piece of paper and nodded to the judge, who nodded back. Turning, I made my way back down the courtroom aisle. Once outside, I let out a huge breath, leaning against the wall, a feeling of accomplishment and pride swelling my chest. I'd done it. It was over.

The sound of a door to my right caught my attention, and I saw a man with a head full of gray hair just exiting. Something about his stride looked familiar, and I wondered for a moment if it was George. But I decided not to follow him. I decided this day was about me, and no one else.

CHAPTER TWENTY-SIX

You know what you have to do, right? You must. It's your only choice.

Racer, the Knight of Sparrows

GABRIEL

Spring came early, bringing buds to the trees and flowers sprouting from the softened soil. I was thankful the quarry was open for the season again, and most days I worked myself so hard, I hardly had the energy to think. Then I'd go to my workshop and lose myself in whatever piece I was currently carving.

I missed Ellie so damn badly it was a constant hollow ache inside me. The holidays came and went, and I wondered if she was lonely, if she'd celebrated at all, and I felt so sad I didn't think I could bear it.

Was she hiding herself away from the world in a self-protecting bubble, allowing no one in? Or even worse, was she allowing people in who might hurt her? Did she have a job? Was she eating? I wanted so desperately to check on her in some way, in any way. I even considered driving by her apartment just to see the lights in her window, but I didn't. I knew if I went there, I wouldn't be able to drive away, knew I'd find myself at her door, and she didn't want that. So I stopped myself.

But, ah hell, I wanted to. I wanted to so much it gnawed at my insides as if I were being slowly eaten away. Those were the days I went moment to moment, finding something to be grateful for, some beauty to make me believe the pain wouldn't always be so bad.

I went into town more often, and though the whispers were worse after what had happened in the fall, and because of the newspaper articles that continued to mention my name, I found I cared less, and that made it easier to endure the gossip.

On a mild day in late March, I pulled into the parking lot of the hardware store. The air held the scent of damp earth and the tang of ozone. It was going to rain, although the thunderclouds looked to be a ways in the distance.

The bell over the door jingled and I entered the store, the familiar smell of dust and oil hitting my nose. It was Saturday and the place was busy, customers ready to get started on all their spring home and garden projects.

I was just picking up an order, so I stood in the line of people waiting for Sal at the cash register. As I waited, my mind wandered to the projects I needed to do around my house. I planned to exert myself cleaning up my yard and getting it ready for the trimming and mulching that would need to be done as the weather warmed.

A man at the register laughed at something Sal said, and I froze, my whole body going rigid. As if I were moving through a black tunnel, I was suddenly *back there* in the damp basement, listening to the sound of footsteps above me and that same distinct laugh full of wet-sounding congestion.

I blinked, pulling myself from the memory as if I were swim-ming to the top of a pool of water I'd just been plunged into.

I knew that laugh.

I leaned around the customer in front of me and took in the man being helped at the register. He was in his sixties and was tall, wearing a cowboy hat and a pair of cowboy boots with spurs on the backs. My brow furrowed underneath the baseball cap I was wearing. Who wore cowboy boots in Vermont?

You're gonna ding up my baseboards with those. Quit walkin' near my walls.

The memory of the words slammed into me as if I'd been hit on the head with a two-by-four, and I jerked backward. It had been such a strange thing to say, and I'd thought about it later, wondered what it meant. *Could it be...*

The man waiting in line directly in front of me glanced back and frowned and then looked forward again. Ah, Jesus. It couldn't be...could it? My captor, Gary Lee Dewey, had had a visitor—just once—and I remembered that phlegmy cough, re-membered the strange click-clack of his shoes, what Gary had said to him. The kitchen had been right over my head, and I'd listened as water ran and bits and pieces of conversation drifted to me through the heating ducts. I'd been stunned to hear voices, and it'd taken me a moment to decide what to do before I started yelling, "Help! Help!" A door had slammed and the voices were gone. I'd assumed whoever had been there hadn't heard me. But maybe he *had* heard me. Maybe he'd *known* I was there and didn't care because he was the same as Gary Lee Dewey. Or wanted to be.

God, but it was just the shadow of a memory. Nothing really. *Only...*

The man in the boots thanked Sal and turned from the register, heading for the door. As he passed by me, I smelled the overpowering scent of cigarette smoke—most likely the cause of that awful, loose cough.

Without letting myself consider it too much, I turned and followed him out, lagging behind so he didn't notice. He got in a nondescript black pickup, and I followed as he turned out of the parking lot.

I stayed a few cars back, and continued driving as he pulled into the driveway of a home about ten blocks from the house where I'd spent six miserable years of my life.

Pulling to the curb a few streets over, I considered what to do. Should I call the police? Were a laugh and the sound of some shoes, a few remembered words, enough to get the authorities to check it out? I thought back to the way the two detectives had questioned me, and felt even more uncertain. If this turned out to be nothing, as it likely would, I'd appear even crazier.

But I'd dismissed my instinct before in favor of my own pride, and because of it, Ellie had ended up bloody and beaten behind a Dumpster. I let out a loud whoosh of breath, turning my truck around and heading back toward the house where the man presumably lived. This time, there was no truck in the driveway. I thought maybe he'd pulled it into the garage, but I'd seen him exiting his truck as I'd driven by. Had he returned home momentarily and left, or was it not his house? "Jesus," I muttered. "Help me out here if you have some spare time."

I drove past the house and parked a block up the street, walking back and trying to look as normal as possible. There was a woman in a track suit power walking on the other side of the street. I slowed down so she passed me, and I turned into the driveway of the house the man had gone into. Removing my baseball cap and tucking it into my back pocket, I peeked into the window of the garage. The garage was dark and the window tinted, but I couldn't see a vehicle parked inside. I let out a relieved breath.

There was a row of junipers between that house and the one next door, and I circled around, concealed completely by the closely spaced trees. The last thing I needed was the police showing up while I cased the house. If I wasn't considered a person of interest in the Wyatt Geller case now, I'd most likely be one after something like that.

There were small, tinted basement windows below the line of the yard with curved, tin window wells. Bars covered them. My heart started beating more harshly. I supposed it wasn't unheard of to have bars over basement windows, but at the sight of them, in conjunction with the tint on the glass, my blood ran cold.

I looked down into the small gravel area and eyeballed whether I'd fit or not. I just needed to get a peek into the basement. If I didn't see anything, I'd leave and determine whether I should call the police. I'd prefer to do it with a little more information than a long-ago memory and a gut feeling. I didn't know if the police were overly responsive to such things.

Looking around to make sure I was completely out of view from the street and from neighbors, I maneuvered myself into one of the wells and squatted down to look into the window, shielding my eyes against the light. It was so dark inside, I had to press my forehead directly against the bars.

There was movement on the other side of the window. I pressed my face harder against the unforgiving metal. The tinted glass looked like the same type of glass that had been on Gary Lee's windows—soundproof, unbreakable. *Oh, Jesus. Jesus.* A shadow moved behind the glass, small and childlike.

I heard a sound behind me and jerked just as something hard came crashing down on my head. Everything went dark.

* * *

The world swam around me, colors and light breaking through the fog in tiny pinpricks of pain. I moaned and tried to grip my head, but my hands were bound. I fought for consciousness, a burst of adrenaline bringing me from the depths of the blackout I'd been in.

I cracked my eyes open and looked around, immediately spotting a scared boy sitting at the end of the couch I was on. He was gaunt and terrified. I widened my eyes. "Wyatt Geller?" My voice croaked.

His eyes were wide, too, as he nodded his head.

Up above I heard a voice. "Goddammit, get over here and help me figure this shit out. There's enough on my computer to have the police at your door in fifteen minutes." He paused as if he was listening to someone on the other end of the phone. "I know what you told me. I'll get rid of it, just help me out here." He was quiet again, and then he mumbled some sort of good-bye and hung up. For a moment all was silent, and then I heard him pacing, recognized the click-clack of what I now knew to be cowboy boots.

I pulled at the bindings on my hands, feeling more alert. My head was pounding with pain. My feet were tied, too, and I'd been shoved on the sofa in a strange position that made my back ache. I straightened myself as much as possible and started frantically working my bindings. "I need help," I told Wyatt.

"He said he'd only be upstairs for a second. He'll kill me if I help you. He'll kill my parents, too."

I glanced at the stairs, fear licking at my spine. I'd been here before. Oh God, *I'd been here before*. I worked to control my racing heart, the frantic need to free myself. I knew from experience that the longer we were here, the less chance we had to escape.

The man upstairs had been taken off guard by my presence, and I had to use that advantage if we were going to get free. If not, he'd come up with a plan, he'd calm his own nerves, his reinforcements would arrive—maybe all of those things—and we'd stand no chance. *I knew.* I knew better than anyone. It was now or six years from now. More likely never.

I turned my eyes back to Wyatt. "He'll kill both of us if you don't. Help me out of these and I'll help you get out of here."

He was shaking so hard, his lips were quivering. "I just want to go home."

"I know, Wyatt. God, believe me, I know. Your parents are waiting for you—Brent and Robin, they want you home so badly. Help me, please."

Hearing the names of his parents caused his lip to start trembling and his eyes to fill with tears. "They want you back," I repeated. "Help me so I can bring you home. It's now or never, Wyatt. This is our best chance. Please."

He paused another moment as I held my breath, and then he slid toward me, glancing back once at the stairwell. I let out a burst of relieved, pent-up air and turned and held my hands in his direction so he could work at the knots. "I...I was a Boy Scout. I kn-know how to work on knots."

"That's good, Wyatt. That's perfect. Just do it quickly, please."

He'd only been working at the bindings for about thirty seconds when the footsteps suddenly started getting louder and the door at the top of the stairs banged open. Wyatt jumped away from me, back to where he'd been cowering, and I turned quickly, laying my head back and moaning as if I was just regaining consciousness.

The man in the cowboy boots appeared in front of us. He'd removed his hat. "You're awake," he noted. His face was flushed, and there were dark rings of perspiration staining the armpits of his light blue shirt.

"Who are you?"

"Won't matter to you." He paused. "I'm gonna have to put you in the ground. Damn sorry about that. You shouldn't have come nosing around. Goddamn it to hell." He turned, running his hand through his thin, blondish-gray hair, pacing for a few minutes. I worked frantically to remove the loosened rope around my hands. "Fuck, fuck, fuck," he murmured. I glanced at Wyatt, and his face was white with fear as he pressed himself into the couch as if trying to disappear inside the cushions. His eyes moved back and forth between the man and me.

The ropes loosened and I slipped one hand free, halting all movement the second he turned back toward me. "You're going to kill me?" I stalled. I already knew the answer.

"What fuckin' other choice do I have?"

The sound of my own heartbeat thrashed in my ears. I had to do something now before the other person he'd called got here. I might have a chance of taking on one man with my feet tied together, but I'd never take on two. They'd knock me out again, and I knew that time I wouldn't wake up. I had to do it now because, as God is my witness, I'd rather die than let the opportunity to give Wyatt a chance slip by.

Working to gain control of my heart rate, I pictured Eloise, pictured that smile that had been on her face when the prism cast rainbows around the room, the way she'd grasped one in her hands. *If I don't make it out of this room, if I never know whether you would have come back, keep grasping rainbows, Ellie. Hold them in your hands and know I loved you until my dying breath.* I whispered it in my mind, hoping the feeling behind my words would carry—*somehow, someway*—straight to her heart.

Thunder suddenly cracked loudly, shaking the house, and we all startled, the man looking back toward the window. My opportunity. I gripped the rope in my hand as I lunged with every ounce of strength in my body.

Taken by surprise, the man yelled as all my weight crashed into him. We both went down hard, but he took the brunt of the fall, breaking mine with his body. A loud grunt came from his chest as I scrambled up on my knees next to him as fast as I could with my feet bound together, grasping the rope between my hands and wrapping it around his neck.

"Run!" I bellowed at Wyatt as I used all my strength to strangle the man. I thought I caught movement in my peripheral vision—Wyatt running past me and up the stairs. *God, please let him be running.* But I couldn't check. I was in the fight of my life with the man beneath me. He tore at the rope at his throat as I pushed it down with all my might, hoping desperately to cut off his air. He was big, and he was strong, but I used the strength in my arms and my thighs—the strength that had been gained lifting rocks and walking up and down a canyon as if in preparation for just this moment.

We struggled and fought for what felt like forever as I prayed that I could hold him down at least long enough for Wyatt to get out of here. My arms were straining so hard, they were shaking with fatigue. At one point, with a sudden burst of renewed energy, he surged upward and I was knocked backward. He came over me, now having the upper hand. I allowed my gaze to move to the couch. Wyatt was gone. *Thank God, thank God.* Had he been able to escape the house? Had he made it to a neighbor's home?

With the knowledge that Wyatt was gone, my body and my will strengthened once more, and I let out a guttural yell, pulling my bound legs upward and slamming my knees into his soft gut. He let out an ugly gurgling sound of pain and reared back slightly. But when I tried to get out from under him, he pulled his fist back and slammed it into my face. Stars exploded all around me, and my head hit the hard concrete floor. For a minute, I thought I'd pass out again, but I didn't. I gave it my last bit of strength and grabbed onto his shirt, pulling him toward me and pushing him to the side so I could swing at him. The punch I landed was sloppy and ineffective since we were in motion, but I swung again and connected to his face in a sickening sound of cracking bone and splattering blood. He screamed and suddenly there were footsteps and a door slamming open and loud shouts from above.

Two young black men were suddenly right on us, yelling and pulling the man off me, holding him down as I fell back on the floor, gasping for breath.

"The boy's okay," one of them said, directing his statement at me as the older man struggled fruitlessly. His energy was used up, and his will was obviously gone as well. There was a bright red mark across his neck where I'd attempted to strangle him, and his expression was dazed. "The police are on their way." With those words the man gave one last attempt at escape, but it was a wasted effort. The two men holding him looked like linebackers. In the distance, I could hear the wail of sirens, and outside the small window, the soft pitter-patter of rain.

I could feel blood running down my cheek, knew one eye was

swelling shut, but I didn't care. Help was here. "The little boy's safe," one of them repeated. "He's with my girlfriend."

I offered a weak smile and held my thumb up in the air. It was all I could manage.

* * *

Rain pounded on the hospital room window, the noise drowning out the hustle and bustle of the corridor outside my door. I lay back on my pillow, enjoying the first moment I'd had with my own thoughts since the EMTs had carried me up the stairs of the basement I'd later learned belonged to Neil Hardigan, now in the custody of local police.

My head swam with everything that had happened since I'd walked into Sal's hardware store the afternoon before. I was still having trouble believing it hadn't all been a strange, fuzzy, half-formed dream. And yet, the joy that moved through me at the thought of Wyatt Geller at home with his parents right this very minute felt overwhelmingly real. They'd come into my room that morning and had barely been able to form words. His mother had hugged me so long and hard, it'd hurt my battered body, but that didn't matter. *They had their son back.* I hadn't been so lucky to be reunited with my parents the day I'd shown up in the hospital after facing the same trauma Wyatt had faced. But he had. He had, and I'd taken a part in it, and I took deep comfort in that.

We'd both arrived at the hospital together, and I'd later learned that after Wyatt had run up the basement stairs, he unbolted the front door and raced out into the street, waving his arms frantically, too terrified to yell at all.

It just so happened that three college kids on their way home from playing hoops in the neighborhood had been walking by on the other side of the street at that exact moment. They'd stopped when they saw Wyatt, and the one girl in the group stayed with him and called the police, while the other two ran into the house to help me. Wyatt had found his voice once the three of them rushed to meet him, and he told them where to find me. "The good guy has his feet tied together," he kept repeating over and over like a mantra.

There had been a car pulling into the driveway at the same moment Wyatt came running out—most likely the man Neil Hardigan had called—and when the college kids came running toward him, the car backed out quickly and raced away. The police, with information retrieved from Neil Hardigan's computer, had later arrested that man as he was packing up his car to make a getaway.

The police also hinted to me that the information they were currently confiscating from the hard drive of Neil Hardigan's house would not only put him away for a very, very long time, but had revealed a ring of pedophiles in the area, including information on Gary Lee Dewey. Gary hadn't kept such information at his home, but Neil had, and with his arrest, authorities had hit the jackpot. Men linked to them both were being rounded up all over the East Coast right this very moment.

The police had questioned me extensively the day before, and I was told the news media had been camped out at the hospital's entrance through the night. It was surreal. It was familiar.

The door opened and George came in, holding a package in his hands. He set it down on the table next to my bed and put a hand on my shoulder, squeezing it very gently. I'd only seen him and Dominic briefly the night before. They'd been stunned, quiet, George had tears in his eyes as he said, "This is the second time you've escaped from a basement and landed yourself in the hospital. Let's not do this again, what do you say?" I'd laughed and heartily agreed.

"How are you feeling this morning?"

I grimaced a little as I stretched my neck. "Like I want to get out of here."

George smiled. "The nurse outside said the doctor would be in with your release papers in a few minutes."

I nodded, looking over to where George had placed the package. "What's that?"

"I'm not sure. The woman at the nurse's station said it was dropped off for you."

I raised my eyebrows. "Huh." Picking it up, I noticed that only my name was written on the front. It felt so light, I wondered if anything was even in it.

Setting it on my lap, I untied the string and took off the brown wrapping. There was a plain white box inside, and I removed the lid carefully. Sitting on top of the white tissue paper inside was a folded piece of paper. I opened it, reading the line once and then again.

To Gabriel, finder of beauty, rescuer of souls.

My heart started beating faster as I put the note aside and pulled out the extra tissue paper to finally reveal what had been placed carefully inside a nest of cotton.

I let out a strangled gasp as I lifted out Lady Eloise of the Daffodil Fields, marveling as I turned her in my hands, studying every side. She had been painstakingly put back together, piece by piece, sliver by sliver, so that she was now whole again, though not perfect. Tiny cracks and small missing pieces appeared everywhere from her toes to her hair, but somehow, *ah, somehow*, she was even more beautiful.

Ellie. God, Ellie.

I set the doll back down in the soft nest and picked the note back up, my eyes moving over every loop and curve of the handwriting. Ellie's handwriting. I'd never seen it before, but now I knew what it looked like, and I studied it greedily, desperate for another small piece of her I hadn't had until now.

"Ellie?" George asked quietly.

I only nodded. After a minute I looked up at him. "What if she doesn't come back, George?"

George's eyes were filled with a pained sympathy. He paused for so long, I wasn't sure if he would answer my question. But finally he said, "Then I guess you have to find meaning in the ones who stayed."

A gut-wrenching sadness overwhelmed me, the overpowering love I still had for Ellie rushing forward to mix with the myriad of emotions from the last twenty-four hours. I wanted more than just the doll. I wanted her. I missed her smiles, her kindness, her inner beauty, her intelligent mind, her soft skin, her body molded to my body each night. Having gone without it for so long, and then to have had it back so briefly, I missed being touched. Her touch. And in that moment, not having her right there with me felt too painful to endure.

I put my head in my hands as George gripped my shoulder and his comforting presence steadied my heart. And I cried.

CHAPTER TWENTY-SEVEN

It's now or never. Aim for the heart.

Shadow, the Baron of Wishbone

Plunge it deep.

Gambit, the Duke of Thieves

With all your strength, my love.

Lemon Fair, the Queen of Meringue

I believe in you. Be brave. For me. For *us*.

Lady Eloise of the Daffodil Fields

GABRIEL

April was a whirlwind of interviews and ceremonies. I only did one major TV network interview, and that was with Wyatt and his parents. The fear in Wyatt's eyes had disappeared, and he looked like a different kid than the one I'd first seen in that basement what now seemed like a million years ago. He had a strong will. He'd be okay. And if he needed someone to talk to, I'd always be available.

There were a few dinners held in town for me, and I looked at them as opportunities to make a new start with the people of

Morlea. I was embarrassed to be regaled as a hero, but I went anyway and after they were over, I was glad I had.

Still, it was nice when things quieted down and I was able to get back to the simple life I enjoyed.

Dominic surprised me one day with a small black puppy he said he'd found wandering around the quarry, obviously abandoned by someone. I didn't believe his story—he thought I was lonely and was trying to provide me some companionship. "You don't have to take him," he said. "I just thought I'd offer. It's your choice."

I smiled at his need to be overly cautious when it came to trying to guide me or my life in any capacity. I appreciated that he recognized how overbearing he'd been in the past and the problems it'd caused in our relationship, but I also knew he had brought the puppy over because he cared about me. "Hey Dom, you don't have to walk on eggshells around me. I'll let you know if you need to back off, okay?"

He nodded, huffing out a thin laugh. "Yeah, okay."

I gave my attention back to the puppy, who was looking between Dom and me, waiting to find out if he had a new home. I supposed I could use a friend. So I took the small, sad-eyed dog and named him Dusty.

I was out back repairing a break in my fence one blue-skied spring day when Dusty started barking his high-pitched puppy bark. I stood up slowly, taking my baseball cap off and smoothing my sweaty hair back before replacing my cap.

Dusty was chasing a butterfly nearby, romping and jumping through the daffodils that grew in the field behind my yard. For a minute, I let the moment soak into my skin—the strange mixture of loss I carried inside and the peacefulness of a puppy scampering in a field of yellow. How extraordinary life could be:

so filled with glorious beauty and heartrending despair. And so often swirled together so that you couldn't separate the two.

Dusty suddenly lost interest in the butterfly and started running in the other direction.

I turned to see Eloise walking toward me from the front of the house.

My heart skipped a beat and my breath stuttered as I froze, unblinking, as if she might be a vision, a dream that would disappear into a wisp of smoke and drift away if I closed my eyes for even a moment.

But no, she was real, and she was smiling as she came closer, holding a bag of some sort on one arm, and a small box tied with string in the other, wearing a flowered sundress that swayed around her calves as she walked. Her hair—all that beautiful, chameleon hair—was down and curling in front of her breasts and down her back. The sun was shining on it, and I had a brief flash of the very first time I'd seen her under the stage lights. The color of her hair had reminded me of a bottle of honey sitting on a windowsill, and I thought the same thing now. Only this time there was something in her eyes that I'd never seen there before—a sort of calm steadiness in her gaze.

"Hi," I breathed when she stopped in front of me. I took off my cap and, without looking, tossed it in the general direction of where my toolbox sat on the ground. My eyes roamed Ellie's face, drinking her in, my heart racing at the unexpectedness of this, of her.

"Hi," she said. She smiled nervously, sweetly as she held up what I now saw was a vinyl cooler and a pie box. "I made you dinner. Pesto pasta with chicken. And I baked you a pie—lemon meringue." Her smile grew. "It only took me two tries before I got it perfect. You were right, I can do lots of things if I try hard enough." She bit at her lip. "Sometimes it's the second try that really sticks."

Hopeful joy rose up in my chest, and I let out a small laugh, nodding. "Yeah."

Dusty came charging up to her, wagging his tail and barking happily at her feet. She set the cooler on a patch of grass, putting the pie box on top of it. She laughed and bent down, taking Dusty's face in her hands and scratching his chin. "Well, hi there. Who are you?"

I cleared my throat. "His name's Dusty. Dominic got him for me."

"Dusty," she murmured, running her hand over his black coat. "It's a good name." He rolled onto the ground and presented his belly, and she laughed and rubbed him there for a moment before standing again. I swallowed.

"I've read every article about you. I . . ." She paused and shook her head, looking off in the distance for a moment as tears filled her eyes, "I saved every one of them. I watched the show with you and Wyatt's family and I . . . God, I was so scared when I learned what you'd done. Scared but mostly proud. So proud . . ." Her words dropped away as she licked her lips, stepping closer.

"Thank you." I felt frozen with nerves, as if I were standing on a precipice, waiting for Ellie to tell me if I was going to fly or if I was going to fall. I didn't know if she was here to say she was going to stay, and the fear of her leaving again bubbled inside of me. My chest felt tight with desperation and longing. *Tell me I'm going to soar, Ellie. Please.*

She nodded. "I have so much to tell you. I want to tell you about my mother." She smiled so slightly, a sad sort of tilting of her lips. "I want to tell you about how much I was loved, and how it caused me to crumble into a thousand tiny pieces to lose that love the way I did."

She paused, tilting her head, her hair sliding over one shoulder. "I want to tell you all of it, but mostly, I want to tell you how I've realized that I spent so much time trying to hold myself together when what I really needed was to break apart. You made it so I was brave enough to do that. And I'm so sorry I had to do it alone, I'm so sorry I caused you pain."

She took a shaky breath, glancing down for just a moment. "I wanted to come to you in the hospital, so much. But I wasn't ready then, and I couldn't see you and then go away again. I couldn't do that to you, or to me."

"Eloise," I said, my voice sounding strangled, filled with all the emotions coursing through my body. "Are you back?"

She blinked, seeming startled. "If you still want me."

I let out a sound that was part breath but mostly groan and pulled her into my arms, relief and gratitude spilling through every part of my body like warm sunlight. I felt weak with it. "Want you? God, I've been waiting for you. I would have waited forever."

She let out a small sob as she pulled me even closer, burying her face in my neck. "I never stopped loving you, not for one minute, not even for a second. Not ever. I want to love you if you'll let me, Gabriel. I want to love you with the kind of love you deserve."

"Let you? Oh God, Eloise. I love you, too. I loved you then, I love you now. I'll love you forever."

She gave me a soggy smile, a slight awe-filled laugh before she shook her head slightly. "I'm still a work in progress. I suppose I always will be."

"We all are, sweetheart. All of us."

She tilted her head back, and I brought my lips to hers and kissed her as if it were the very first time, taking my time to reacquaint myself with the taste of her—that same sweetness I'd never know how to name even if I tried.

"You've been with me all this time," she whispered between kisses. "Your love, your words, the way you make me feel." I smiled, kissing her cheeks, her eyelids, her smooth forehead. "I had to…" She whimpered softly as I brought my lips back to hers, her tongue meeting mine for long minutes before she pulled back slightly. "I want you to understand so you'll forgive me."

"There's nothing to forgive." I kissed her neck as she let out a shuddery breath.

"It's just…I had to…oh…" She laughed breathlessly. "Oh God, Gabriel, take me inside."

I laughed, too, swinging her up into my arms. Dusty started yapping at my heels, running ahead as if to show us the way to the house.

"Wait, the food." She laughed again.

I bent to it and picked up the string on the pie box and the strap of the cooler with the hand under her knees. Then I stepped carefully through the daffodils, trying not to crush them.

I placed the two items in my hand on the kitchen counter and carried Ellie into the bedroom and set her down, closing the door against Dusty, saying, "Sorry, bud, you're not allowed to see what's going to happen in here." He moaned and I heard the click of his nails on my floors, moving away from my room. Off to destroy one of my shoes most likely, and I couldn't have cared any less.

Afterward, when Eloise and I finally pulled apart, our limbs languid, our heartbeats calming and our breath returning to normal, I smoothed her hair back and whispered all the words of love I had saved in my heart. I told her how much I'd missed her, and she told me the same.

She spoke of the hurts of her past, the shattering of her heart, but mostly she spoke of healing and how she'd learned that damage is a slow piecing back together.

"Once," she said, using a finger to trace my cheekbone, "you told me that solid stone is nothing more than sand and pressure and time." Her hand dropped from my face to lie flat against my chest. "I was the sand, so easy to crumble. You provided the pressure, Gabriel, the holding together, the love. All the confidence you had in me was what I needed in order to take a chance on myself. And then you gave me the most selfless gift of all: time, so I could finally break apart and put myself back together."

Lying there in the quiet of my room, our naked bodies pressed tightly, I looked into her unguarded eyes and saw the steady strength that had only flickered there before. And, impossibly, I fell even more deeply in love with her. I heard the same whisper in my soul that I'd heard the first time we'd met: *She's mine.*

Mine to care for. Mine to love.

Later, when we emerged from the bedroom, we walked into the kitchen to find the lemon meringue pie splattered on the floor, a torn-open pie box, and one unremorseful-looking puppy. I froze, turning to Ellie, who gripped the sheet to her chest and bent forward in laughter. "I can make another one," she said.

I pulled her into my arms and we danced for a moment, me in my boxers and her wrapped in a sheet, the floor smeared with pie, and I loved her to the depths of my soul. "Be my wife," I murmured in her ear.

She pulled back to look at me, her eyes soft, the glimmer of a smile on her lips. "Because I can make lemon meringue pie?"

I laughed. "Well, no, but it doesn't hurt."

She laughed, too, wrapping her arms around my neck and pulling me close. "I'm in nursing school."

I tilted my head, surprised but happy. "Then be a nurse and my wife."

She smiled. "Shouldn't we wait just a little while? Shouldn't we give it more time?"

"I don't need more time. Do you?"

She tilted her head, her eyes filled with love and honesty, and she shook her head, the expression on her face happy and perhaps a little bit amazed.

"No," she said. "No." She brought her hand to my face, her smile tender. "You've always been so sure about me. Thank you for that gift. Thank you for waiting for me to be sure about myself."

I kissed her, my heart feeling so full. Outside the window, the daffodils were a carpet of yellow, and this time, Eloise was in my arms, and it was as if my arms had been made for her and her alone. I no longer regretted the years I'd felt too terrified to be close to someone. In my solitude, in my fear, I'd somehow saved myself for Eloise. She was my one and only. Together we would carve our future. And for the first time in so very long, I was truly home.

EPILOGUE

ELLIE

"Hey," Gabriel whispered, bending to kiss me, "is she giving you trouble sleeping?" He smoothed the back of his finger over our daughter Mila's silken cheek. Though she was asleep, the contact caused her to begin instinctively nursing again where she lay at my breast. After a couple of small sucks, her tiny rosebud mouth went lax.

"No." I smiled down at her, loving her with every beat of my heart. "I just wasn't ready to put her back in her cradle yet. And the sun was rising." I would go back to work part-time in a couple of days, and I wanted to enjoy every waking second of the time I had at home with my family. Though I loved being a nurse and it fulfilled me in a way nothing had before, the last couple of months at home with my newborn daughter had been the sweetest days in all my life.

Gabriel had brought his work home and did his sculpting in the garage just like he had when I first came to stay with him. Then, I'd sat with him, small pieces of my body and my heart healing as I watched his beautiful, loving hands move over the seemingly unchangeable stone. But now, I held our daughter in my arms as I watched him work, and we spoke of our plans and dreams for the future.

We took long walks under covered bridges, pushing the stroller slowly along dirt roads. We napped while the baby was sleeping, and ate picnic lunches in the backyard, our daughter between us on the blanket as we gazed down at the miracle we'd created together.

Gabriel sat down in the chair next to me and stared out at the small sliver of daylight just emerging over the trees.

Light. Hope.

"Maybe we'll go into town for dinner tonight?" he asked.

I smiled and nodded. "That sounds nice."

"Want me to take her?"

I would have held Mila all day, but I loved to see Gabriel holding her, too, so I nodded and handed her over. He cradled her gently, gazing down into her sleeping face, and I drank in the look of loving reverence in his eyes. Sometimes watching them together filled my heart so full so suddenly, I had to suck in a breath or it felt like my lungs might collapse beneath the pressure. *The overwhelming love.*

He ran a hand over the small amount of peach fuzz on her head and smiled over at me. "I still think it's yours," he said, referring to the color of her hair.

I laughed softly. "We'll have to wait for a few more strands to grow in before we can tell." I loved him just for his wishful thinking, for making me feel so beautiful, not just my body, or my face, or my hair, but my heart and soul.

The man who had loved me unwaveringly.

So unfailingly.

The man who'd loved me enough to wait for me to love myself.

The man who'd helped me become solid again, whole. And just as importantly, the man who'd helped me see that there was even beauty in the missing places.

The sun continued to rise, casting its light over the earth, brightening the darkness and chasing away the shadows of what had been. And every single day, it reminded me that though life could be lonely and painful, it was also filled with rainbows on water, with fields of daffodils, and angels that emerged from rock. It was filled with delicate flowers that, against all odds, found the strength to turn their faces to the sunshine and thrive. It was filled with miracles that arrived when you least expected them and the hard-won knowledge that healing, like stone, is just sand and pressure and time.

Acknowledgments

So many people helped me bring this story to life. I couldn't have done it without you.

First and foremost, to Angela Smith who read the first three chapters of this story and gave me direction and confidence. I will never forget the image in my mind of you reading on your Kindle in a hospital room chair. Thank you for always making time for me.

To Marion Archer whose guidance and support is invaluable. And who always pushes me to make people cry just a little bit more.

Thank you to Karen Lawson who gifted me with Karen's-Book-of-Knowledge yet again. I will never be able to do without it.

Gratitude to my beta readers, Elena Eckmeyer, Cat Bracht, and Michelle Finkle. I value your input so very much.

Special thanks to Amy Pierpont for your care and great attention to detail. The focus and thought you put in to editing this story will forever be appreciated. Your feedback helped make me a better storyteller and a better writer and that is a true gift.

Thank you to Madeleine Colavita for your expertise and for making this story shine.

The entire Forever team has been wonderful to work with. Thank you for making my first traditional publishing experience such a good one.

Immense gratitude to Kimberly Brower, the best agent in the universe. Thank you for being my champion and always having all the answers.

To you, the reader, thank you for choosing to spend your time with my story when there are so many others out there. Thank you for recommending my books to others, for your unending support, and the lovely messages I treasure.

Thank you to Mia's Mafia. You all mean the world to me. And! It's where the Platinum Pearl was born! (Thank you, Nelle Obrien).

To all the bloggers, tweeters, Instagrammers, and book groups, thank you for spreading the love for my books with your reviews, your messages, your tweets, the beautiful teasers, and amazing staged photos. I couldn't be more thankful.

And to my husband, you. Most of all, you.